EMBER'S BLOOD

Nichole M. Bridges

Copyright © 2021 Nichole M. Bridges

All rights reserved.

No part of this book may be reproduced by any means without the expressed written consent of the author. This is a work of fiction. Any names, places, businesses, or events are from the author's imagination or used in a fictitious manner. Any resemblance to persons alive or dead, events, or other circumstances are coincidental.

ISBN-13: 978-1-7343416-2-1

To all the bands that were my soundtrack while writing this book, thank you for kick-starting my imagination.

Seether
Three Days Grace
Shinedown
Papa Roach
Theory of a Deadman
Badflower
Saint Asonia
Asking Alexandria
Breaking Benjamin

1

My body slammed into a wall, and I saw stars before I could blink away the haze. The blow cost me crucial seconds, but as my head cleared, I noticed a fist headed toward my face. I ducked fast enough to avoid it then swept my legs out, knocking down my assailant.

He hit the ground with a grunt, but I didn't wait for him to come at me again. Using my kinetic power, I held him down on the ground, effectively immobilizing him for while I planned my next move.

"What's the matter, James? Something got you down?" I snickered.

"Not for long," He replied from under me.

James brushed off my hold with whatever magic he had that allowed him to counter my powers. It was humbling to know that I wasn't able to hold him for long. He had proven it enough times today that I had learned to anticipate how long it would take him to free himself. My time had just run out.

I sprung forward before he could get off the floor and tackled him. After a second of struggle, I had him pinned in what I was calling my signature pretzel maneuver. It was a wrestling move James had taught me that we modified to work for my smaller build. It was magic against a larger opponent like James.

"Looks like you are still flat on your back," I said proudly.

"I've got you right where I want you, Em." He said eyes sparkling.

James hadn't been able to get out of this hold before, so I was doubtful until he flipped me over and pinned me a second later. I lay there shocked until I heard clapping from the peanut gallery.

My vampire boyfriend walked out to where I struggled to break James' hold on me and leaned down so I could see him.

"You pinned him faster this time and you moved as fast as a vampire to avoid that last punch," Marek said then backed away so James could let me up.

That was the signal that the training session was over. I was relieved in a way but hated that it ended with James winning.

"If I had a few more minutes, I could have won." I pouted.

"If it was anyone but me, you would have won. I've gotten to know you too well." James said, assuring me, but it didn't make me feel any better. I wanted to win every fight.

"Kicking your ass is high on my list of things to do, James," I said, smiling.

He smirked and helped me to my feet. He pulled so hard I stumbled into him. My hands landed on his chest. Before I let myself enjoy the feeling, I took a step back and wiped at the sweat that had gathered on my brow. James had worked me hard and my body was feeling it.

James smiled at me, then excused himself to meet his next student. He walked toward the locker room but instead of going in, he met someone that was coming out. I knew the man by silhouette alone. I should. He and I have known each other for over fifteen years. It was Nikko Manetti, my ex-boyfriend.

I let my eyes linger on Nikko's narrow waist and wide shoulders. He is Italian with golden bronzed skin and dark hair that falls just below his ears. He looks equally good in a three-piece suit as he does in sweats and a t-shirt. He wore the latter now and I had to tear my eyes away from him.

"You will win the next, I have no doubt," Marek said, pulling me toward him and out of my thoughts.

Marek took inventory of every bruise and cut on my body as he spoke. For as much as he wanted my training to be realistic, he was an overprotective vampire who could hardly bear a scratch upon my skin. I was surprised his words hadn't been an offer to take his blood to heal.

"Why is Nikko here?" I asked, trying not to watch Nikko walk toward me.

Trying to ignore Nikko looking sexy is like trying not to breathe. It works for a second and then your body forces you to do it anyway.

"He took us up on our offer to train him. His body is strong from his workout routine, but he does not know how to fight. I believe the beating he received from The Egyptian illustrated that point well enough for him to seek help." Marek said.

The Egyptian, aka Asher Sanz, was a formidable opponent who was hired to kidnap me and when he made his attempt, he and I fought. Thankfully Nikko was nearby and jumped in so I could make my getaway. Unfortunately, Nikko ended up in the hospital from his injuries. I could understand how that would prompt him to train.

"It's my fault he got hurt. I should've been able to take care of Asher on my own." I said, feeling bad about what had happened.

"He knew the consequences. Besides, you nearly killed Asher the next time you saw him. I think you proved your capabilities." Marek said.

"Maybe," I said softly watching Nikko as he drew closer.

Marek noticed me looking and he moved slightly in front of me. His eyes bore into mine as if challenging me to look around him. I rolled my eyes and stepped around him. He caught my arm before I passed him and the hurt in his eyes stung. I hadn't considered him a jealous man, but at that moment, he was feeling it keenly.

"You have been rolling around on the ground with James and now you stare at Nikko as if you want to take him to your bed. I am not a saint Ember." Marek said softly.

His accent became thicker and the Russian almost overtook his English. I took pity on him.

"The last time I saw him, he had barely recovered from his hospital stay. I'm just glad to see him healthy again." I said, trying to sound certain.

It was mostly true. I was glad to see Nikko recovered and looking like himself again. Although I've always been drawn to his rugged good looks, the image was tainted now by the fact that he had cheated on me. That was why he was my ex and not my current boyfriend.

Marek gave me a look that was both indulgence and disappointment. I ignored him and smiled at James and Nikko as they approached. At least one of us could be polite.

The two men were laughing when they got close to us. James slapped Nikko on the back and looked at me like I would have enjoyed the joke with them. I had a distinct feeling that I was the subject matter.

I raised an eyebrow and watched as they tried to calm their faces in light of Marek's presence. Seeing Marek dash the humor of people I enjoyed spending time with was disheartening.

"Hey Em, I heard you kicked James' ass in your workout today," Nikko said, his eyes sparkling with humor.

I looked at James and the smirk on his face told me he hadn't been entirely truthful with Nikko.

"I put him down, but he got me in the end," I said.

"If only...maybe you can join us Ember. I think it would be good for you to have a new partner to work with and Nikko could benefit from a strong opponent like you." James added.

I narrowed my eyes at him then looked at Marek to see if he noticed the first comment. It wasn't like James to poke the bear and the comment about him not getting me "in the end" was controversial at best. My working out with my ex was even more of an issue for me, not just for Marek.

"I need Ember to look into a few things for me today but maybe another time," Marek said smoothly and pulled me toward the locker room.

I waived at the boys then yanked my arm out of Marek's grip. His fingers were bruising, and I didn't want him to be so possessive.

"Did you and James get in a fight I don't know about?" I asked as we walked.

"No, why?" Marek replied coolly.

"Because his comments could only have been meant to piss one of us off and I know he isn't mad at me," I said.

"James is a good Guardian, the best actually. As a Guardian, he does his work without comment, and he does it better than anyone else. His personal life is different." Marek said.

"How so?" I asked.

Marek paused and turned to me, "He has only been in love once, and he is not handling it well that you do not love him back."

My jaw dropped. Marek had told me that James was in love with me before, but I had not noticed any change in his behavior. As Marek said, he is the best at his job.

"Then why on earth are you making him train me every day? There are other Guardians that can do the job." I said incredulously.

"Like I said. He is the best at his job and he can match you better in a fight than anyone else on the team. He is the ideal sparring partner for you. He also has a vested interest in making sure you are trained well. He would not have it any other way, nor would I." Marek said, clearly comfortable putting James in that position.

I looked over at James and watched as he spoke to Nikko. I assumed he was explaining how the workout was going to go. They stood opposite each other and contrasted nicely. James, with his tall blonde surfer-boy good looks and Nikko, with his muscular dark appearance, made a striking pair. Ignoring the fact they each had a personal stake in me, it was a lovely view.

I sighed and started walking to the locker room again. Was there ever going to be a time when some man wasn't secretly harboring feelings for me or out to get me in some way?

As if on cue, Viktor tugged on our mental bond and I opened it up to hear him. Viktor Ivanov is a master vampire I had to form a blood bond with to save my life. It was his scheming that facilitated my life being in danger in the first place so I wasn't happy about it. Since he and I now share a bond that isn't going away anytime soon, I had promised to let him through more often and to visit him, but I had kept him shut out until now.

"What is it, Viktor?" I asked him mentally.

"Master," He replied.

My shock must have shown because Marek grabbed my arm. I shook my head and held up a hand to let him know I needed a minute. He could feel the connection open with Viktor and he knew to wait.

"Viktor," I said, humoring him for the moment.

"Sweet Natalie was just here for a visit. She said I have you to thank for it." Viktor said.

"I merely suggested it would be best for her to spend time with her maker," I said.

Viktor was in custody for attempting to kill me and for various other crimes he committed. The Council of Guardians was the authority over supernatural matters in Colorado so they had him locked up in this building while he waited for his trial to begin. My sister Natalie was made a vampire by him in what he says was an effort to save her life. The fact he had kidnapped her and abused her prior to that didn't cross his mind as an issue.

"Thank you. When will you be here? I heard the Guardians talking about you." He said.

"I thought of coming down today. Why did you reach out? Was it because the Guardians were talking about me?" I asked.

"Your business is not theirs for discussion. They should be more discrete." He said in his usual haughty tone.

"That they should. Thank you, Viktor." I said and shut off the link.

Marek stared at me expectantly.

"I need to go down to see him," I said.

"I was going to ask you to do the same. We need more information about his run-in with Magdalena. What does he want?" Marek asked, knowing I had been speaking with Viktor.

"He said your Guardians were discussing me and he didn't like it. I don't like it either. They shouldn't be gossiping about me within earshot of Viktor or anyone else for that matter." I said.

Marek's eyebrow ticked in irritation when he said, "Consider it taken care of."

I nodded then left him to hit the showers. Viktor's communication was troubling in two ways. First, the Guardians knew he could hear them, and they talked about me anyway. Second, I agreed with Viktor. Since when did I start agreeing with my mortal enemy?

After getting cleaned up, I went down to the detention center. I was greeted by stoic Guardians, who appeared ambivalent to my arrival. Technically, I was now their superior since Marek hired me to be the Head of Research and Asset Development for The Council of Guardians. It was time that I showed it.

I walked into Viktor's cell and ordered the team to leave.

"That is against protocol Madame Summers," a Guardian named Murphy informed me.

None of the Guardians moved. I met each of their eyes to be sure I had their attention.

"I told you to leave us," I said with steel in my voice.

"Yes, ma'am," Murphy said and led the others out of the room.

Viktor was smiling at me when I looked back at him.

"It suits you to be in charge even if this is an insolent group of misfits unworthy of your presence." He said.

"Thank you, I guess." I tried to keep the smile off my face.

Since a blood bond formed between us I've felt a certain pull toward Viktor that has softened my heart ever so slightly to him. His superiority complex has become somewhat amusing instead of solely maddening.

"They do not see your value as I do. Even my son, Julien sees you as I do." He said, beaming with pride.

Julien was made a vampire by Viktor and he and I had met at a party he threw to introduce the community to his newest vampire, Sasha. She was a sweet young thing with an excellent sense of humor. Julien had taken a quick liking to me and the feeling was mutual.

"Julien offered me his friendship the other night," I said taking a seat in front of Viktor.

"He may have been swayed by the way you looked in that blue gown I sent you to wear for dear Sasha's unveiling." He said.

"You sent the dress?" I asked, confused.

The party invite had come with a gorgeous gown that showed off my curves and complimented my skin tone perfectly. I had thought the dress came from Julien.

"I knew you would be stunning in blue satin." He said, smiling.

I let out a sigh and tried to gather my thoughts. He was always trying to sway me to think of him romantically.

"Somehow that doesn't surprise me but I'm not here for a social call." I began.

"Ember my darling, we are well beyond pretense," Viktor said.

"If that were true, you would see that I have no interest in you romantically and that this mission of yours to possess me is hopeless," I said leaning forward.

"That is where you are wrong. I am not merely interested in you romantically. I wish to worship you like the goddess that you are." Viktor said in a serious tone.

I laughed then realized he really meant it. "What are you talking about Viktor?"

"In vampire society, a mate is someone you commit to loving for the rest of your long life and a wife is someone you align with to increase your power and fortune. There may be sentiment paired with a wife, but it isn't required. I want you to be my wife." He said.

I was stunned into silence. Viktor wasn't talking about being obsessed with me, he was talking about me taking a position of power in his coven and his life. Vampires don't do marriage like humans, they combine empires, or they mate for life. I didn't have anything to offer Viktor, so his admission didn't make sense.

"You cannot be serious Viktor," I said sure he was trying to manipulate me.

"Do you recall how you were treated by vampire society at Julien's party? Do you think anyone could direct all vampires to give respect to someone that didn't deserve it? You earned that on your own." He said smugly.

At the party, I was greeted by every vampire in the room as "Madame Summers" giving me the rank of a master vampire. It wasn't something I asked for or thought would happen. Vampires are ranked by power level and my power was higher than most. According to Marek, my power was even greater than his although I could argue the point. I've seen his power and he and I are very closely matched.

"Reverence is one thing, but I know what you are saying you want and it doesn't make sense," I said, shaking my head.

"You are the most powerful woman on this planet. I cannot live without you." Viktor said with complete seriousness and conviction.

"You want to possess me because I'm valuable. I don't want any part of that." I stated.

His brow wrinkled as if he didn't understand what I said. Not only could I see the wheels turning in his head, but I could feel his confusion through our bond.

"I have much to offer you Ember," He said.

"So I am told but I am interested in love, not power Viktor," I said.

"Said by someone who has yet to wield the power I am offering." He said smirking.

I rolled my eyes and got to the point of my visit.

"That isn't why I'm here, Viktor. I have to ask you something and I'd rather you told me directly so I don't have to command you to answer." I said.

"What do you want to know?" Viktor asked.

"What do you know about the vampire Magdalena and her plans?" I asked.

He sat back in his chair giving the appearance of being relaxed. I knew he was anything but relaxed. His unease was pulsing through our bond like a strobe light.

Magdalena is an ancient vampire who was out to get me for being romantically involved with Marek. The reason for which I had yet to get out of Marek.

"She is a manipulative and powerful vampire who is extremely angry at the fact Marek Volkov tried to kill her forty years ago. She is capable of anything and her resources are extensive. You need to walk away and leave her alone. It isn't your fight, but she will make it about you if you pursue her." Viktor said.

"She threatened my sister and you know first hand how I react when someone tries to hurt my sister," I said.

"How do you know about that?" Viktor asked confused.

"I'm a Seer Viktor, I saw her threaten you and then you told her where to find Marek. What I don't understand is why she didn't show up at Sasha's party." I said.

Viktor had told Magdalena that Marek would be at the Le Veneur mansion on the night of Sasha's unveiling. She should have been there but I didn't notice her. With all the chaos happening that night, it could have been the perfect backdrop for someone to sneak in and out without being recognized.

"I am afraid that if she was there, she saw you defeat Asher Sanz and captivate the vampire community with merely your presence. She will not be pleased." Viktor said.

"But what will she *do* Viktor?" I asked.

"She will eliminate the competition and take Marek for herself. How she does it is not important. What is important is that I cannot remain here while you are being threatened by her." He said with such conviction that I almost agreed with him. Almost.

"Why are you suddenly set to protect me? You did anything but that up to now." I said.

"I have been in your head and I like it. I don't want to lose the connection I worked so hard to obtain." He said looking confused.

And that made the most sense of anything he had mentioned so far. For Viktor, it was all about control and possession.

"Your trial is next week but I don't think you are getting out of here anytime soon Viktor. You kidnapped my sister and almost killed me. I believe the Council will hold you accountable for your actions." I said.

"They will see reason. I just need to speak with Julien. Will you permit me a phone call?" He asked.

"I don't think that is up to me Viktor," I said.

"You ordered a team of Guardians to ignore commands from their superiors and listen to you instead. I think you have a lot more power than you are willing to admit." He said reverently.

"I'll see what I can do but I'm not making any promises," I said reluctantly.

If I could get him what he wanted he might give me what I want.

"Thank you," He replied.

"Now tell me what you are hiding about Magdalena. You know more than you are letting on." I said.

Viktor stared back at me and I could feel his unease again through the bond.

"What is your relationship with Marek?" He asked.

"I think that should be clear based on what you know," I said referring to the fact Viktor knew full well Marek and I had been sleeping together.

"I know you are fucking him Ember but what I need to know is if your relationship is anything more than sexual." He asked.

"Of all the people I would have this conversation with Viktor, you are not one of them," I said rubbing my hands over my face.

Viktor smiled and leaned forward. He seemed amused but there was something else going on with him. I knew he didn't want to tell me, and he was dancing around trying to keep me from ordering it of him. Since I am his master, I could do it.

"Marek isn't who you think he is and you should be careful before getting deeper than allowing him to warm your bed." He said.

"That may be too late," I admitted.

"A power merge is temporary at best. At least you haven't agreed to be his mate. You should know who he is before making a lifelong commitment to a vampire such as him." Viktor said.

I let him think I was only referring to the power merge, something Marek and I had done when our emotions were running too high to stop it. We did not need to discuss the fact that Marek and I had already exchanged the "L" word.

"Tell me who you think he is," I insisted.

I wasn't sure I could believe a word he said but there was something about what I was feeling from Viktor that made me want to hear what he had to say anyway.

"Is this room being monitored?" He asked looking up at a camera in the corner.

I stepped out of the room and talked to Murphy. “Is this room being monitored?”

“Yes, all cells have basic monitoring.” She said.

“Please turn it off. Now,” I said.

She looked at me and I could see the wheels turning in her head wondering if she should contact Marek to confirm the order. I tilted my head daring her to question me.

She nodded sharply and pulled out her phone to relay orders to the control room. I waited until she confirmed it before returning to the room.

Viktor had moved to his bed and was laying down when I re-entered the room. He glanced over at me and rolled over, propping his head upon his arm. He looked like he was posing for a photoshoot.

“No one can hear us now,” I said.

“Good, then I can tell you the truth.” He said, but he didn’t look happy about it.

2

An hour later I was done speaking with Viktor and had no plans to visit him again anytime soon. What he said to me didn't just shock me, it sickened me to the core. If Viktor was to be believed, Marek was not the person I thought he was.

I found myself sitting in the living room of my sub-penthouse apartment without remembering how I got there. My bond with Marek was shut down tight and I kept it that way. Feeling anything from him right now would have tipped me over into a state of panic.

Someone pounded on the front door and I almost jumped out of my skin. I should have been scanning the perimeter, but I had other things on my mind. I reached out with my senses and found it was someone friendly.

I opened the door and walked away, letting him follow me if he chose.

"Are you hiding from anyone in particular?" James asked following me in.

"I'm clearly not doing a good job of it if you were able to find me so easily," I said dropping down onto the couch.

"What happened Ember? You ordered surveillance off in Viktor's cell. Then Marek blows a fuse, and no one can find you." James said sitting down next to me.

"I wasn't lost. You found me." I said looking into his eyes.

It was a soft place to land after the chaos I had been feeling. James has always had that effect on me. He can buffer the hardest of blows.

"What did he tell you Em? You know you can't trust Viktor." He said, sounding as if he thought I lost my mind.

"You warned me off Marek many times. What do you know about him?" I asked, changing direction.

"I know he loves you and would do anything to protect you. Anything." He said, his tone was resolved as if he had learned to think that way.

"Your loyalty is clear," I said, thinking that talking to James wasn't going to get me what I needed.

He was Marek's right-hand man and if I talked to someone it would have to be someone who had no loyalty to the Guardians or to Marek.

"Ember, what is wrong?" James asked, sounding truly concerned this time.

"Nothing, I just needed some time alone after listening to Viktor's bullshit," I said and smiled at him.

I was sure the sentiment didn't reach my eyes, but I tried to pull it off anyway.

"He knows where you are," James said, referring to Marek.

"I don't want to talk about it," I said.

James pulled me into his arms and said, "Please tell me what's wrong, Em."

It felt so good to have him hold me. He has been my rock since all this paranormal business landed in my life. He wasn't just my Guardian. He had become my best friend somewhere along the way.

"What have I done James?" I said breaking down.

He squeezed me closer and I sunk into his embrace. He smelled good, like cedar and citrus. It was masculine and comforting. It was James.

He let me cry. It wasn't a hard cry but more of an I'm an idiot why didn't I see it cry. It held anger mixed with disappointment.

"I'm sorry, James. I shouldn't be crying on your shoulder." I said pulling back.

He didn't let me get far.

"Get back here." He said pulling me back into his arms, "Tell me what's upsetting you."

I looked up at him and saw the sincerity in his eyes. He truly cared about me.

"Thank you, James. I don't mean to push you away but sometimes I think I'm taking advantage of you." I said.

He smiled then kissed my forehead. It was as if he thought I was cute.

"Ember, you could never take advantage of me. I care about you deeply and any time you need me, you have to know that I will be here for you not just as a Guardian but as your friend." He said.

The last part sounded painful for him to admit. I thought back to what Marek had said about James struggling with his feelings for me. I could confront that now and take the focus off of me but I needed him right now. I'd talk to him later about his feelings.

"Do we ever really know the people we care about do you think? Or will it always be a surprise to find things out about them?" I asked.

"What do you mean?" James asked.

"Vampires live a long time usually and I know people change over time. How can you ever trust a vampire?" I asked.

"In my experience, you can't at least not fully." He said.

"What about your peers on the Guardian team? You trust them." I said.

"I trust them to have my back and to do their duty. They can be friendly and we spend so much time together that we need to get along. I wouldn't say that I trust any of them completely." He admitted.

"What about Marek?" I asked, trying not to sound anxious about his answer.

"Marek is a different beast entirely. He is the boss." He said.

"It's just you and I James friends chatting on a couch." I prompted.

He looked down at me and how his arms surrounded me.

"If a stranger walked in right now, would they see friends on a couch?" He asked softly.

His voice was husky and it sent a shiver of excitement down my body. It had been a while since James elicited that sort of response from me. I had been so wrapped up in the sexual pull Marek had on me over the past weeks, I had pushed all romantic thoughts of James away.

"I suppose not," I said, dropping my head onto his chest. "Then what are we James if we aren't friends?"

"Somewhere between being friends and wanting more," He said softly.

I let the statement hang out there. I wasn't sure I wanted more but I couldn't deny having that feeling too. Neither of us spoke for a while. He continued to hold me and I snuggled into him, taking all the comfort I needed.

I pondered my life choices then and the result was that I acted too rashly with Marek. I should have considered the fact he was a vampire before getting involved with him but that was also part of the draw.

I loved the way my heart sped up when I was with Marek. He could give me a look that sent my libido on fire or chill me to the bone at the same time. It was a fine line but I liked it. That was probably what was bothering me the most. I knew what I was getting into but I ignored it. I read enough about vampires to know they were cold and uncaring creatures who sought power and influence more than love.

Marek wasn't like the vampires I had read about. At least, I didn't think he was. Sure he could be cold and ruthless but that was his job to be that way. He had to lead a team of vampires, werewolves, and humans and somehow get them to work together to protect those who couldn't protect themselves. It was almost altruistic.

When we spoke earlier, Viktor painted a picture for me of a vampire who was not only just like the textbook version I had read but was also sadistic and incapable of love. Somehow the sadistic part wasn't what bothered me the most. Love was the foundation of every relationship I had in my life. It was the degrees of love I had for people that kept them close to me. If there wasn't love, there was no foundation to be with someone.

"I think I need to spend some time with my friends, my human friends." I said.

James flinched slightly at my words and I felt sorry for saying it the way I did. He is only half-human and is shunned by the vampire community because of it.

"What I meant is that I need to get away from the vampire for a while," I clarified.

"He won't like that," James said.

"It won't be for long. He'll survive." I said sounding more confident than I felt.

James raised an eyebrow and I could imagine he was questioning my sanity. To say that vampires are possessive is a major understatement of the facts. Marek hasn't acted as possessive as I had expected him to but I knew it was there. He just needed the right push to let it all show.

I sat up, giving up the warm body next to me for what I was sure to be a cold and angry encounter with my vampire. I could feel him approaching the apartment and he wasn't happy. Although I had our bond mostly shut down, he knew something was wrong.

"What is it?" James asked.

"Marek is on his way up. You might want to clear out before he gets here." I said.

"Not possible, I'm your guard." He said.

He leaned over to kiss my cheek then he stood up. Marek flung open the door a moment later. I was relieved he hadn't been a few seconds earlier.

"James," Marek said and nodded sharply at James.

It was his signal that James was being dismissed. James turned to me for confirmation and I nodded it was okay for him to go. He was my guard and I was of equal rank to Marek. It was an odd tightrope of protocol that I was learning and with which I was not yet comfortable.

James gave Marek a look then walked slowly to the door.

"I'll be right outside," James said to me.

I smiled at him and nodded. He was making sure that I knew he was here for me and not the grumpy vampire.

As soon as James left, Marek turned to me with fire in his eyes. It was a look he had never given me before and I was suddenly glad to have James on the other side of the door.

"You broke protocol with Viktor and then disappeared for hours leaving me to explain what happened. Sebastian will want to have words with you when he finds out. What happened?" Marek said with his lips tight and his teeth clenched.

I took a deep breath and let it out with a sigh. I looked up at him and didn't see a shred of my vampire. He looked like a crazed lunatic.

"I had a conversation with Viktor that required privacy. I could have done it through our bond but connecting with him like that feels greasy and gross." I said in explanation.

"What possible topic required that kind of privacy?" He asked crossing his arms.

"You," I said angrily.

He didn't have the only right to be pissed about what happened. He failed, as he often did, to tell me what I needed to know.

"What did he say?" Marek asked so calmly I had to do a double-take to be sure it was the same person standing there.

I wasn't going to just spill it. He held information back from me that was vital to my understanding of the situation with him and Magdalena. The ancient vampire who was after me because of him. It was an old habit of his that angered me more than anything else he has done to date.

"Magdalena for starters," I said.

He took a step back and looked shocked for a second before his blank vampire face was back in place.

"He hardly knows the whole story," Marek said.

"He knew more than I did, which by the way is nothing thanks to you. You have avoided all my questions about her and I've given you space so you could tell me when you were comfortable. You haven't made any effort to tell me why she would be obsessed with you. She has threatened my life and that of my sister but again, you haven't told me anything." I said feeling my anger rise all the way up.

Marek took another step back, realized it then walked over to the couch to sit down next to me. I stopped myself from moving further away from him. It was hard but I managed it.

"While I should have been the one to tell you, I did not anticipate you pulling surveillance on Viktor. It was a dangerous move Ember. The safety protocols we have in place are there to protect anyone that goes into a cell. You were alone in a room with a master vampire who may use that fact in a less than honorable way." He said and his voice was a little snide at the end.

"What exactly are you implying?" I asked confused.

"Viktor could say that you had sex in that room and no one could dispute it." He said.

I laughed. I couldn't help it. I couldn't care less if Viktor told lies about me and him in a room together. If that was all Marek feared that would have been the end of it.

"Is that really all you're worried about?" I asked.

"No," He said then shut down.

His face fell and I could tell that he was not only upset but scared. Seeing him sit in front of me looking vulnerable thawed some of the ice that had encased my heart. I reached out and grabbed his hand. He wasn't much of a hand holder but he instantly moved my hand to his mouth, turned it palm up, and kissed it softly.

He held my hand in his and said, "I am sorry."

"For what Marek? For doing the things you did in your life or for me finding out about them?" I asked.

"Both," He said.

I took my hand back from him. Touching him was clouding my ability to be mad at him and frankly after what Viktor said I wasn't sure I was comfortable being in the same room with Marek.

"You need to tell me your version of the story or I'll be left with only Viktor's," I said.

"I cannot possibly tell you my entire life story." He said, clearly stalling.

"Neither did Viktor. Start with how you know Magdalena and why she would be obsessed with you," I said.

"That is also a very long story." He said.

"Then I'll make myself comfortable while you talk," I said and motioned for him to start.

He looked uncomfortable and I was afraid he was going to refuse to tell me anything. Then he started talking.

Marek started at the beginning with how he met Magdalena. She was a descendant of Queen Isabella of Spain, a Habsburg, and quite possibly insane. Her mother had been committed to an asylum shortly after she was born in 1603. I tried not to faint at how old that made Magdalena.

They first met in Moscow in 1924 when Marek's sire invited her to stay with them. She was already ancient by then and she wanted to visit the city, having never seen it before. Marek was appointed as her guide during her stay so they spent a great deal of time together. She became enamored of him and asked his sire to release him into her care.

It wasn't something Marek wanted at the time so his sire refused her. Marek found out after spending several months with her, it was clear that she wasn't completely sane. His sire was aware and had approached the vampire council to entice her away from Moscow, leaving Marek behind. He said that no one wanted a mentally unstable vampire in the city so they made it happen.

He ran into Magdalena again years later in Paris. He noticed that she seemed different. She had moved her coven to France and they had a tight-knit group that took care of her. Ancients are mentally fragile creatures and they need a lot of support to survive over the centuries. He said by then she was almost 400 years old but still looked twenty-three and her personality had lost some of the mania he had seen in her before.

He looked wistful as he spoke as if it was a happy time for him. I couldn't imagine what it was like to have lived so long. He and I have never discussed his age before but based on this story I would put him at just over a hundred. He wasn't ancient yet but he was old enough to be a master. Any vampire that passed the century mark was likely to become a master. Marek hit master status long before he hit the number of years it would require most other vampires to get that kind of power surge.

Marek continued his story by saying that he spent a number of years with Magdalena and her coven in France. He became a trusted member of their community and she began to depend on him to take care of problems for her. It allowed him to build a reputation of being a fixer who worked with ruthless efficiency. The vampire community started reaching out to borrow him for their own special projects including the vampire council in France.

Marek made a lot of connections in the council there and across the world. It was how he ended up being assigned to assassinate Magdalena. The council recruited him to betray her and he found a way to kill her.

"Only, I was not successful," Marek said.

He looked upset but there was something else there that I couldn't put my finger on. The story lacked any hint of emotion and that seemed very important.

"Why does she want you so bad?" I asked, thinking about the parts of the story he left out.

"She has always wanted me with her." He said.

"There has to be a reason why. What aren't you telling me, Marek?" I asked.

"I told you what you need to know. She is insane and extremely dangerous." He said.

"Why would you stay with someone you thought to be insane? Did you love her?" I asked.

"I was fond of her," He said flatly as if he couldn't bring himself to show any more emotion than that.

"According to Viktor you two appeared to be madly in love yet you betrayed her for money and power," I said hoping to have him defend himself.

He looked at me like I had insulted him in the worst way. His usually ice blue eyes were filled with fire and it scared me. It was the first time since I had gotten to know Marek that I was truly afraid of him.

"Is that why you shut me out after talking with Viktor?" Marek said.

"Yes," I answered honestly.

"You were angry," He guessed.

"I wasn't angry exactly. I was scared." I admitted.

"Of me?" He asked.

His body went stiff and his face went blank. It hurt him to think I was scared of him. I didn't want to hurt him but I also didn't want to lie to him.

"Yes," I confirmed.

His pain spiked at my acknowledgment and I wished I hadn't gone down to talk to Viktor. I wished I had taken Marek with me so Viktor couldn't lie to me and poison my thoughts against him. He leaned back, putting some distance between us.

"What did he say that made you feel that way?" He asked carefully.

"I don't believe everything he told me," I said.

"What was it Ember?" He said.

I hesitated thinking if I really wanted to tell him. I wasn't sure if it was true and I wasn't sure if he would deny it.

I reluctantly told him, "He said you are a killer who is incapable of love. That you proved it when you thought you killed Magdalena."

"And you believe him," He said. It wasn't a question, it was a statement as if it were fact.

"I don't know what to believe, Marek. You are holding so much back. We hardly know each other and my experience with vampires has been filled with fear and fighting. It isn't a far leap." I said.

"I see," he said.

Marek stood up and walked toward the door. I tried to grab him but he is a vampire so I couldn't move as fast as him.

"Marek!" I yelled.

He turned around and looked at me. “You made your feelings clear. I will not stay where I am not wanted. I have an insane ancient vampire on the loose to capture. I do not know what else Viktor told you but I can imagine what it might have been. Right now I need to find Magdalena and you need to decide if you can trust me.”

He walked out the door. I heard him talk to James and then he was gone. I tried to track him with the bond and although I knew his general direction, I didn’t have a single emotion or thought that I could discern.

I could understand why he was upset, I was upset too. What I could not understand is how he could just walk away from me. It was like he didn’t care about me at all. Finding Magdalena was more important than our relationship and that hurt, deeply.

3

I wiped the tears from my eyes and pulled myself together. Crying over it wouldn't change a thing and I didn't really know what this meant for us anyway. Marek was a duty first kind of person, I clung to that thought as best I could.

The front door opened, and James walked into the apartment. The look on his face told me his thoughts.

"He isn't used to having someone to care about. He doesn't know how to act." James said sitting down next to me.

"He just walked away, like I don't mean anything to him," I said.

James pulled me into a hug and assured me it would be okay. How could it be okay when the man I loved walked away like he didn't feel a thing? My thoughts instantly flashed to what Viktor said about him. I didn't want to believe Marek wasn't capable of love.

"Marek said he had something to take care of and that until he came back I was in charge. I assume you know what he was talking about." James said.

"He was upset but he also said he needed to find Magdalena," I said.

"Did you two fight?" He asked.

"He was upset that I talked to Viktor, even though he asked me to do it. Then he was angry after what Viktor told me. I don't know if I can trust him. He told me about his connection to Magdalena which is good but he left out all the parts that Viktor told me. He isn't being forthright and you know how much I hate being left in the dark." I said.

My chest hurt and felt heavy. My love was being squashed by doubt.

"What did Viktor say?" He said, looking confused.

I told him the gist of it and his eyebrows rose.

"Can vampires love? Can Marek?" I asked.

"Ember, I don't know Marek's heart as you do but he certainly acts like a man in love. He is not the man I would have picked for you but I don't think he would tell you he loved you if he really didn't." He said, it hurt him to say it but he believed it.

"Viktor said he pretended to love Magdalena so he could kill her. If that is true, then Marek is capable of anything. How do I know if he really loves me or if what Viktor said is true when Marek won't even talk to me?" I asked.

"You are a Seer Ember. Read him." James said as if it was obvious.

"That feels like invading his privacy. I rather he told me directly." I said, not feeling good about it.

"He walked away. It's your only option if you want to confirm or disprove what Viktor told you. Would you believe him if Marek told you himself?" James asked.

"Based on his behavior today no," I said reluctantly.

"Then reach out and see what you can see," James said.

"Alright," I said and sat down on the couch.

James sat next to me and pulled my hand into his. He held it and smiled at me reassuringly. I wasn't sure if he was confident because my fears would be confirmed or because they would be proven wrong.

I shook off the doubt and took a deep breath. Then I grabbed my bond with Marek. Although it was mostly closed off, I could feel his anguish pouring through. Our conversation had put him in a tailspin and he was reacting instead of thinking. It was a good sign that he cared about me but I had to know for sure.

I thought about Magdalena and Marek and tried to see them together. Marek's story of them together in France is what I focused on. I imagined them walking along the street together and an image started to flicker in my mind.

I saw Marek holding Magdalena's hand with her looking up at him adoringly. He smiled down at her then he pulled her hand up to his lips and kissed her palm. My breath caught and a searing pain instantly filled my head. It felt like my skull was cracking and my vision went blank.

"Ouch," I moaned and grabbed my head.

"What's wrong?" James asked urgently.

I couldn't speak, I could hardly breathe. Tears poured down my face while my head felt like it was literally splitting open. All I could hear was the rush of blood through my veins. When I opened my eyes it looked dark and a wave of nausea hit me like I was in a stormy sea.

I ran to the bathroom, making it just in time to empty my guts into the toilet. A washcloth appeared before me and I used it to wipe my mouth. James' arm moved in front of me and the toilet flushed. Nausea bubbled up again at the smell but I held it back.

The floor felt like it was moving even though I was sitting on the floor. Strong arms wrapped around me, keeping me from tipping over. The pain in my head leveled out slightly but I couldn't open my eyes because the light hurt too much.

"Are you okay?" James whispered.

"I don't know," I said turning into him to bury my face into his chest.

He stroked my back while holding me. It was soothing but the pain in my head was not subsiding. I had never had a headache like this before and didn't know what was happening.

"Is it your head?" James asked.

I nodded yes and he pulled out his phone. He spoke to someone asking them to send a doctor up to us. He set his phone on the floor and tilted my head up to look at him.

"Can you open your eyes?" He asked softly.

I squinted them a bit and looked up at him. The light made stabbing pains occur in my head so I closed them again.

"It hurts to open them. The light is too bright." I said.

"How is your stomach? Are you okay to move yet? I can make the bedroom dark so you could lay down in there." He said in a soft caring voice.

I told him I was okay to move. He helped me off the floor and into the bedroom. He drew the curtains in the bedroom to block out as much light as possible for me. It helped but the pain in my head persisted. My equilibrium was all messed up and I felt like I was going to fall even though I was laying down.

James told me to try to relax while he met the doctor at the door. Every sound was amplified and the front door closing sent pain zinging through my head. The voices of the doctor and James hurt too.

I pulled a pillow over my head to block the noise. When the doctor came into the room she had to push the pillow aside to get a look at me.

"Ember, it's Dr. Wallace. Can I take this pillow off of you?" She said softly.

"Yes," I mumbled.

"Can you tell me what happened?" She asked after lifting the pillow.

I told her as best as I could what had happened and then she let me put the pillow back over my head. I heard her talking to James and then he must have walked her out because it got really quiet.

Between the pain and nausea and vertigo, I must have passed out or fallen asleep. I woke up sometime later in James' arms. I was snuggled up to him on the bed and my head felt a little better.

"How long was I out?" I asked groggily.

"Just over two hours," James said.

"What did the doctor say?" I asked.

"She thinks it's most likely a migraine headache," He said. "How are you feeling now?"

"Better, my head isn't splitting anymore. Still hurts but it's more of a dull ache now." I said.

"I'm glad," he said then kissed me on the top of my head.

"I thought we were going to have better boundaries, James." I said looking up at him.

"Mmmm, we did say that but for some reason, we keep ending up in bed together." He said smiling.

"Fully clothed, unfortunately," I joked.

"Don't tease me Em," He said, and he looked hurt.

"I'm sorry," I said and sat up.

I dropped my feet to the floor and waited for my head to stop throbbing.

"What happened before the headache, Em? Did you see anything when you tried to look back at Marek?" James asked getting up and heading toward the door.

I thought back to when I was trying to see Marek and Magdalena together and cringed when I flashed back to him kissing her hand. I didn't like it. He did that with me and it was something special that was now ruined knowing he had done it with someone else.

"I didn't see much. Just the two of them walking together before the headache hit." I said trying to forget the pain.

"The doctor said you can take something over the counter for the pain but if it gets to be too much she can prescribe something. Do you want me to get you something?" James asked.

I tried to get up but lost my balance. James was able to catch me. My breath whooshed out of me when he grabbed me and it took a moment for me to get my air back.

James was looking at me with such concern on his face like he was so worried about me. It made me feel bad.

"I just keep making it worse for you don't I?" I said.

"It's okay," He said brushing the hair out of my face.

"James," I started.

He looked like he was either going to kiss me or run. Then he shook his head as if he were trying to clear his thoughts and looked serious.

"He called me while you were sleeping. He felt your pain." James said.

"Who?" I asked unsure if it was Marek or Viktor.

"Marek. He said he was worried about you," James said, looking at me like I was thick in the head.

"Oh, that's good. I thought I was blocking him but it must have slipped when the headache hit," I said, feeling a little sick at the thought of Marek possibly knowing I was trying to see his past.

"You seem to be standing on your own now but should you get out of bed?" James asked.

"My head still hurts but it's manageable. I don't have time to be laid up in bed. My parents are expecting me for dinner and I promised Sam I'd stop by after that." I said walking past James and out to the living room.

"I can drive you wherever you need to go. I just need to check in with the team before we leave." James said.

He pulled out his phone and went to work doing Marek's job. He did it with smooth efficiency and it sounded like the team didn't question his authority at all. That was most likely due to James leading the team anytime Marek was out in the field.

I turned my thoughts to Sunday dinner with my parents and tried to think of what I could bring as a side dish. Unlike past weeks, I actually had access to a trained chef to pull something together for me so I called down and ordered something to go.

Going head to head with my mother while fighting a headache was not going to be fun. I checked the time and hoped that if I took some over the counter meds it would help my head before I had to leave. I checked the bathroom cabinet and found some ibuprofen. I swallowed two pills and drank a glass of water.

James found me staring at myself in the bathroom mirror. I'm not sure what I was doing exactly but the look of pity on his face made a sharp pain hit my chest. It was hard to take. I didn't want to be that woman that fell apart the second her man said something harsh. I had shit to do that had nothing to do with Marek.

"I'm fine James," I said, partially for his benefit and partly for mine.

"Are you sure you want to go to your parents' house? Your mom is not going to take it easy on you." He said.

He was right but I had been absent from the weekly family dinner for too many weeks in a row. My mother liked to have her daughters present so she could keep up on the gossip and make sure we knew what she wanted us to do with our lives.

My sister Natalie couldn't make it to dinner this week because she was a newly made vampire. She also couldn't tell my parents that. Her idea was to delay seeing them long enough that when she did finally make an appearance they wouldn't notice anything different about her.

"I'll survive it," I said trying to put a smile on my face that would sell the lie.

He didn't look convinced and said, "I'm driving you and I can come in with you. With me there, your mom will be distracted and maybe it will draw her attention to me instead."

"You'd do that?" I asked thinking he was crazy for putting himself into the line of fire.

"Would it help you?" He asked.

"Yes, my mother loves to entertain my friends. I think she loves them more than me." I said cringing.

"Then I'll join you for dinner," He said smiling.

His face lit up when he smiled and it made me happy to see it. Over the past month, I had seen him frown more often than I had seen him smile. It was a shame because his smile made me happy.

An hour later we were in the car headed to my parent's house. I had called ahead and my mother was thrilled that James would be joining us. It almost distracted her from asking about Natalie.

"What do I need to know before we get there?" James asked.

"Are you implying that you need to get on the same page with me on whatever lies I've been feeding my parents?" I asked.

"Yes, yes I am." He grinned.

"The only lies are regarding Natalie for the obvious reason that she is a vampire but you know my parents can't know that. They think she is on an extended trip traveling with Viktor for his work before they set a date for the wedding. That should give her enough time to gain control and figure out what she is really going to tell them. On some level, I think she still believes that she and Viktor will be married. I haven't got the heart to tell her otherwise yet. I'm hoping he will soon." I said.

"Do they know about Marek?" James asked cautiously.

"No, they just found out that Nikko and I aren't seeing each other. I don't think they need to know about Marek yet." I said.

"Okay, I'll keep him out of the conversation." He said.

James pulled up in front of my parents' house a few minutes later. I sat a little too long in the seat unwilling to get out. James opened my door and offered me his hand. I took it graciously and held tight while we walked to the door.

"Just friends?" James said looking down at our hands.

"Right," I said and let go before my mom saw us.

My dad would just laugh it off but if my mom saw it, she would drill into me until I admitted something I didn't want to admit. She was good like that.

I rang the doorbell and held my breath while we waited for the door to open. James put his hand on my back and it was enough to make me feel better. I took a deep breath just as the door opened.

My father's face lit up when he saw me and he pulled me into his arms for a big hug. It was the kind of hug that makes everything feel better. I needed it like I needed the air I was breathing and somehow he knew it.

My dad has always been intuitive. It's made me think that maybe I got my clairvoyance from him.

"Thanks, Dad," I said when I pulled away from him.

"I've got you, baby girl," He said.

I pulled out of the hug and gave him a big smile.

"Dad, this is my friend James. James, this is my dad Michael." I said introducing the two men.

They shook hands and smiled at each other. Then my dad led us into the house and I made my way to the kitchen to drop off the food I brought. My dad led James to the living room where I was sure he was going to grill him a little bit about why he joined me. He wasn't nearly as bad as my mom but he would find out quickly how James felt about me. He was a feelings magician.

I found my mom with her head in the oven poking a thermometer into a roast. It looked like she had quite the spread going for our dinner. She didn't usually go to this much trouble which meant she had expected Natalie and Viktor to be here as well. At that moment I was glad I brought James along.

"Hi mom," I said, setting the fancy baked brie I brought on the counter.

My mother turned around and smiled then looked at the platter confused. Given my normal contribution to the meal was something she rather I did not bring, this one gave her pause. It was fancy and up to her standards.

"Where did you get that?" She barked.

"I thought I would pick something up instead of making something myself. Do you like it?" I asked.

"Yes, it will do." She said.

"You seem disappointed," I said with humor.

"Your usual effort doesn't match this Ember," she said and turned away to fuss with something else in the kitchen.

"Is there anything I can help you with?" I asked.

"No, go save your friend from your father." She said distractedly.

I paused wondering where the usual tongue lashing was but gave up quickly to go to the living room. I found James seated on the couch with my father in his leather recliner chair. They weren't speaking but they were staring at each other in an odd way.

James looked up at me and looked almost relieved to see me. I looked at my dad and he had a smirk on his face that told me he was enjoying himself.

"Are you two getting along or should I not have left you alone?" I asked, sitting down beside James.

"I managed to get a little information out of James and frankly Ember I'm disappointed in you. Why are you stringing this poor fellow along if you have eyes for another man?" He said looking pleased with himself.

"Dad!" I said shocked.

"What? He seems like a genuinely nice man and it's clear he likes you." My dad said.

James looked pained and a little shocked that my dad got the information out of him.

"I didn't say anything, he just figured it out," James said mystified by my dad's charms.

"Is it Nikko or someone else?" My dad asked.

"Dad, I don't want to talk about it," I said.

My mother walked into the room at that moment and her eyes sharpened at my comment.

"What don't you want to talk about?" She asked.

"My love life," I replied.

"Oh well, I don't blame you. Leaving Nikko was the worst thing you could have done. That man is husband material. You probably dumped him because we approved of him." She said casually while sitting down in the other leather recliner.

My jaw dropped and I couldn't think of what to say to shut her down. I think it was because I agreed with her. He was husband material.

"Nikko is a good guy if you overlook the fact he cheated on Ember," James said.

My mother's eyes went wide and I smacked my palm into my forehead. I did not want that information coming out to my parents.

"What? Ember, you didn't tell us anything about that." My mother said.

"And for good reason," I said shooting daggers with my eyes at James.

"I'm sorry. You said they knew you two broke up." James said innocently.

I narrowed my eyes at him but to be fair, he wouldn't know I never told them. He was capable of more discretion than that but I think he was acting as himself instead of as my guard. He had feelings for me and hearing my mother sing Nikko's praises had to chafe.

"You should have told us Ember," My mother chastised.

"I'm sure she had her reasons, Nancy," My father defended me.

"I didn't tell you because we are working on remaining friends and so far it is going well. I know how much you like him." I said feeling uncomfortable saying those things in front of James.

"I like him less now," My mother proclaimed.

"How is work Ember?" My dad said making an attempt to change the subject.

"Um...work has changed," I said.

"Because of Nikko? Was he giving you a hard time in the office?" My mother asked.

"It has nothing to do with Nikko. I received an offer from a security firm to head up their research division and I accepted." I said.

"What firm?" My mother asked.

I looked at James. I wasn't sure what to call The Council of Guardians to someone outside of the supernatural world.

"I work for the same firm. TCG has been around for a long time providing security and data mining for elite clientele around the globe. It's a prestigious company to work for and the firm is lucky to have her." James said beaming.

I rolled my eyes at him but watched as my mother changed her posture. She leaned back as if deflated. She was ready to tell me I made a terrible choice but what James said stopped her in her tracks.

"I haven't heard of them. Where are they located?" My dad asked.

"They're downtown. In fact, they gave me an apartment to live in so I'll be moving in over the next week or so. The residential building is right next to the office." I said.

"They gave you an apartment?" My mother asked skeptically.

"It's a penthouse suite actually." James offered.

Both of my parents raised eyebrows at that.

"I'll be on call 24/7 so they want me close by," I said, trying to downplay the apartment given I probably only got it because of my vampire boyfriend who happens to run the organization.

Was he still my boyfriend? I wasn't sure if he walked away entirely or if he just needed space.

Our bond made its presence known at that moment and I caught a glimpse of Marek talking to a woman I didn't know. The image was followed by a sharp pain in my head and the vision went dark.

"Em, are you okay?" James said.

When the pain died down I realized I had buried my face in his chest and he was holding me. My parents probably questioned the "friend" description after that little show.

“It’s my headache. It spiked again but I’m okay.” I said sitting up straight.

“What’s wrong?” My dad asked.

“She had a migraine earlier but after she rested she felt good enough to come to dinner,” James said.

“I’m fine. It was just a little pain. It’s gone now.” I said trying not to squint at the bright light.

The room wasn’t particularly bright but for some reason, my headache hated what little light there was with a passion.

A ding from the kitchen signaled that the food was ready so my mother asked us all to gather in the dining room. My father dug into the baked brie and passed it over to James while my mother brought out the rest of the food.

We ate family style passing each dish around the table. James kept his eyes on me throughout the entire meal. I tried to pay attention but my headache kept me distracted enough to miss most of the conversation. It was probably a blessing in disguise.

4

After dinner with my parents, James drove me over to my friends' place. Sam and Todd have been my closest friends for more years than I can remember. James worked with Todd for a short time as a way to weasel his way into my life. Therefore, he was acquainted with Todd and Sam already.

"Do you want to come in with me?" I asked when we pulled into the parking lot.

An alert on his phone had him ignoring me to read the message. He gave me a look that I could only interpret as his discomfort with whatever information he had just received. I could guess who it was that messaged him. It had to be Marek for him to be this squirmy.

"I will pass this time. Something came up and I need to meet someone." He said.

"What's going on?" I asked, pointing at his phone.

"Nothing you need to worry about, Ember. I'll be around if you need me." He said, forcing a smile.

I rolled my eyes at him. Then I got out of the car and walked to Sam's door.

When I knocked, I heard Sam yell, "Ember's here!"

A moment later, Todd pulled open the door and practically tackled me with a bear hug. When I finally untangled myself, Sam was there to hug me too.

"I missed your ass!" She exclaimed, throwing her arms around me.

"Apparently you both did. It hasn't been that long since I saw you last." I insisted.

"I'm spoiled from getting to see you every day at lunch. I haven't seen you since you quit your job." She said.

I expected her to be more upset about me leaving my job at the law firm. She worked in the same building and we did spend a lot of time together because of it. My reasons were completely selfish. I couldn't work full-time and chase my sister to Arizona where Viktor had taken her after kidnapping her.

Sam knew I was going after my sister but she didn't know about the vampire situation. She just thought Natalie was in an abusive relationship, which was true but in a different way.

"I know you're spoiled," I said to Sam.

She narrowed her eyes at me but when I looked at Todd, he laughed. Sam gave him a hard look

"What? It's true." He said to her.

"Whatever. Get your ass in her Ember and spill it. What's going on with you?" Sam asked.

I turned to sit down on the couch, but I froze when I saw a familiar muscle car enter the parking lot. The deep blue '69 Chevelle pulled into the parking space next to James and my heart skipped a beat. Until I saw his car, I didn't realize Marek would show up. What was he doing here?

I must have said it out loud because Sam asked, "Who is here?"

"It's Marek," I said walking toward the window.

"Who is Marek?" She and Todd asked at the same time.

I turned to them and said, "He's kind of my boyfriend."

"What? When did that happen?" Sam asked indignantly.

She was the first person I told everything to but I had kept this from her. It was an accident that I let it slip just now. I hadn't meant for her to find out this way.

"Hang on," I told her. "I'll be right back. Then I'll explain."

I walked out the door and practically ran to the car. When Marek stepped out of the car he looked at me but didn't say a word. Instead, he turned to James and spoke to him.

"I need to speak with you alone," Marek said glancing in my direction.

"Why are you ignoring me?" I asked Marek.

He was holding himself so still, I could have mistaken him for a statue. I pulled on our bond but it was shut tight. Marek wasn't going to let me in and I couldn't tear the connection open in front of witnesses.

"Go inside," Marek said to me.

It was said like a command as if I was just someone on his payroll. Is that what I have become?

"Who's the asshole?" Todd asked from behind me.

I looked back at Todd and he stepped forward, pressing his body into mine. It was a sign of support but it raised the hackles of my vampire. Marek visibly changed his posture from a neutral stance to one that said he was pissed off.

"Step away from her," Marek said to Todd.

His voice was calm but it was clear he would tear Todd's head off if he didn't do what was asked.

"It's fine Todd," I said pushing him back slightly.

"You can really pick them Em," Todd said and the insult hit me hard.

"What is that supposed to mean Todd?" I said raising my voice with anger.

"Nothing," He said then realized how mad I was and said, "I'm sorry Em. It just slipped out. This guy isn't worth your time. Come back inside."

"He's right Ember. Please go back inside. It will be fine." James added more compassionately.

Marek stiffened at James' words but nodded his agreement. I looked Marek in the eye and pushed words through our bond.

"You are going to explain this to me soon or I will force my way in using my vision to see what you are hiding." I said.

"Maybe you should force it," Marek said in my mind then turned back to James.

I raised my eyebrows at him. Was he inviting me to spy on his past?

Todd tugged me away from the angry vampire and I let him pull me back to the apartment. Sam was standing in the doorway with her mouth hanging open.

When I got closer she said, "He's sexy in an angry villain sort of way. You don't normally go for the bad boy."

I felt a sliver of amusement come through my bond with Marek before he shut it down. I rolled my eyes and pushed Sam back into the apartment.

"Why is James here?" Todd asked after he closed the door.

"He gave me a ride. I had a headache earlier so he offered to bring me over." I said.

"Sounds like you two have gotten close," Sam said with a little eyebrow wiggle that made me laugh.

"Stop it Sam. He and I are friends and as of tomorrow we will be co-workers too." I said.

"Wait, where does he work?" Sam asked.

"Some security firm," Todd added helpfully.

I smiled at Todd because he was partially right. "I'm going to head up the research division of TCG. It's a security and data mining company based in Denver. I have a leadership role but I'll also have a chance to do a lot of travel and fieldwork." I said.

"That sounds amazing but how does the asshole fit in?" Sam asked plopping down on the couch.

I sat down beside her.

"He has a name Sam. Marek is the head of operations for the same company," I said.

"Hold on. You are dating the head of the company you start working for tomorrow?" Todd asked sitting down on the other side of me.

"Yes, which sounds bad out of context," I said.

Sam laughed, "Did you get the job before or after you slept with him?"

"Sam!" I exclaimed.

"What? You had the same issue at your last job and it bothered you that people might think you only had your job because you were sleeping with the boss' son." Sam said.

"I didn't think about that before I accepted the position. I just saw a great opportunity." I said.

I could feel my cheeks grow warm with a blush.

"I'm sure it will be fine," Todd assured me.

"Thanks, Todd," I said feeling better at his confidence.

He wrapped an arm around my shoulders and Sam cuddled up on the other side of me. I was in the middle of a "friend sandwich" and it felt really good. I missed this. I missed them more than I realized and I was on the verge of tears at the emotion of it all.

"What's wrong?" Sam said, wiping a tear from my cheek.

"I've missed you both," I said.

"That reminds me. I have something for you," Sam said with mischief in her eyes.

She jumped up and headed for the kitchen.

"What is she doing?" I asked Todd.

"She's probably going to prepare something alcoholic," Todd said. Then squeezed me tighter and whispered. "I missed you too."

He kissed me on the top of my head and I could feel the warmth spread through my body. Todd was the brother I never had. His love seeped in through his hug. I smiled up at him.

"Don't worry," He said. "I won't let you get too drunk."

He tucked my hair back behind my ear and smiled. I gave him a look of uncertainty. The last time I had been drinking with him didn't end well.

"I'm calling it a Denver Iced Tea," Sam said dropping a giant glass filled with brown liquid in front of me.

"Does it actually contain any iced tea?" I asked, looking at Sam.

"Nope," She said smiling.

"I'm a lightweight. This looks like a serious drink." I said picking it up to try to figure out what was in it.

"You look like you need it." She said seriously.

Sam was right. I needed a drink after seeing Marek and after all the crap I had been dealing with for the past few months. I needed a night with my friends.

"I hope it tastes good because I may need more than one," I said, feeling adventurous.

"While you drink, tell me how you got mixed up with the asshole?" Sam asked. "The last I heard, James was the most likely candidate to find a spot in your bed."

"Sam!" Todd exclaimed.

"What? You were thinking it too." Sam whined.

I tried not to laugh. Sam could state anything bluntly and it was okay because it came from her. I had to leave out all the supernatural parts but filled her in on the story.

"I met him through James which I guess is a bit of a sore spot now for James," I said, realizing the statement was truer than I intended.

Sam snorted, "Smooth, Em."

I took a taste of her cocktail and almost choked. It was strong but had a nice tea-like flavor. I took a few more sips and could feel it kicking in already.

"Take it slow, Em. You know Sam has a heavy pour." Todd warned.

"Noted," I said, taking another big swig.

The alcohol burned as it went down and it temporarily made me feel better. Sam smiled at me and raised her glass in solidarity. We clinked our cups together and I liked the sound the glass made. Sam smiled wickedly then Todd groaned.

Todd knew all too well how the two of us could get when we had been drinking. The last time we all had a drink together I had said or done something inappropriate because Todd hadn't treated me the same since. That was also when Viktor had slipped me his blood for the first time so it could have been his influence instead of the alcohol.

Vampires have been messing with my life for some time now. They don't care about the consequences of their actions. They only care that you do as they command.

"Don't worry Todd. I'm not driving myself tonight. James is on call as my chauffeur in case I need him." I said.

"Is that his new job?" Sam asked, snickering.

"No," I said, thinking up a lie that was also true. "He is working in the area and offered to pick me up if I needed him."

"How sweet of him," Sam said. "Too bad you already have your heart set on the asshole."

"He isn't an asshole to me," I said defensively.

"He sure fooled me earlier. I thought for sure he didn't care for you at all." Todd said.

He looked concerned and I had to admit that my interaction with Marek tonight had not been favorable when seen from Todd's perspective. I decided not to try to convince them.

"He and I had a disagreement and we haven't worked it out yet. He was being an asshole." I admitted.

"Sam, does your drink include a truth serum? I've never seen Ember back down so easily." Todd said.

"I'm not in the mood to argue," I said. "You don't know Marek. I don't blame you for thinking he is an asshole. I thought the same thing when I first met him."

Sam and Todd's eyes got big and they gave each other a look.

I took a giant gulp of my glass of alcohol and felt even better. "Don't worry. I'll be back to normal in no time."

"You'll pass out before then," Todd said taking my glass away.

"Hey! Give that back." I insisted.

"Take a break. This is mostly alcohol." Todd said, looking concerned.

"Yes father," I said, slumping down into the couch.

"Todd, let her cut loose. She isn't driving." Sam said, batting her eyelashes at Todd.

He smiled and handed the cup back to me. I slammed the rest and handed it off to Sam for a refill. Todd looked pained but he didn't say a word.

"Don't worry Todd. Once I'm numb to the world I'll stop drinking." I promised.

"That's what I'm afraid of," He said.

"After dealing with Nikko's betrayal and my sister's domestic issues, I need an escape. I've been running myself ragged," I admitted.

"You don't need alcohol for that," Todd said, looking saddened by my words.

"I have more burdens than one person can reasonably bare Todd. I can only hang on for so long." I said.

"Then talk to us about it. We can help." Todd insisted.

"I rather bury it all under copious amounts of alcohol," I said.

"Copious amounts of alcohol is something I can provide," Sam said dropping another glass in front of me.

"This one looks different," I said, looking at the color of the liquid.

"That looks like my root beer," Todd said.

"I thought you wouldn't mind donating to the cause," Sam said to Todd.

"What's she talking about?" I asked Todd.

"It's my home-brewed hard root beer," Todd said.

Sam just smiled at me and motioned for me to drink up. I obliged by slowly taking a sip so I could savor the flavor of it. A warm spicy sarsaparilla with a hint of vanilla was my reward. I felt a slight burn of alcohol in the background that didn't detract at all from the experience. It was delicious.

"That is amazing," I said to Todd while taking another sip.

"I knew you'd like it," He said looking proud.

"I don't like it. I love it," I said taking a deeper drink of the yummy concoction.

"Stop it Ember. You're going to inflate his ego bigger than I can handle." She said wryly.

Todd had a big grin on his face and I realized that Sam was a genius. She had successfully taken the spotlight off us getting drunk and put it on his master brew making.

She leaned in and kissed him on the lips then patted him on the head like he was a good boy. Actions that were contrary but spoke volumes about their relationship. Todd preened at the attention.

"I'm thinking of doing a ginger beer next," Todd said.

"Oh, that sounds yummy too," I said taking a long drink of my root beer.

We talked about nothing and everything for hours. By the end of the night, I was drunk enough to no longer care what Marek did or if I saw him again. Okay, so I cared if I saw him again but I had made my mind up that I wouldn't let his temper tantrums bother me again. I would use my gifts to find out what he was up to and enlist James to help me.

I must have fallen asleep because I woke up to pounding on the front door and an overwhelming sense of dread. Familiar voices filled the room and I opened my eyes to see what was happening. Todd was talking to James and they were looking at me like I was a fragile thing they were afraid to break.

"What is it? What's happened?" I asked, dazed.

"Welcome back," Sam said leaning over to me. "James is here to take you home."

"You passed out and since we knew you planned on having James pick you up, I took the liberty of calling him for you," Todd said.

I looked at James and knew he would have arrived had he been called or not. Something had happened but he couldn't tell me about it here.

"Thanks," I struggled to say.

I was clearly still very drunk but I tried to clear my head and stood up. Sam saved me from falling back toward the couch. She held me until my balance returned.

James rushed over to me and slid his arm around my waist. It boosted my balance substantially and I was grateful for it. I was grateful for James. He consistently had my back. Whether it was his duty or not didn't matter.

"Let's get you to the car," James said.

He turned and thanked Todd for calling him. While James was talking. Sam mouthed "he likes you" and wagged her eyebrows. I just laughed and shook my head. She was right but I wasn't going there.

I waved goodbye to my friends and let James lead me outside. When we got to the bottom of the stairs he lifted me and carried me the rest of the way.

"Always there to save me," I said drowsily.

"You need to sober up, Em," James said.

I shook myself awake and looked up at James remembering the feeling of dread I felt before. His face was strained and it wasn't because of carrying me.

"What happened?" I asked.

"Get in the car," James said, putting me down and opening the door for me.

I didn't waste any time and did as he said. I looked up and noticed Todd watching us from the front window. After what he just saw, I would have some explaining to do. Carrying someone to the car isn't a normal thing a friend would do.

When James got in the car, I turned to him. "Tell me," I insisted.

"I need you to track Marek," He said.

"Why?" I asked.

"He was supposed to check in with me hours ago and he isn't answering his phone." He said.

"Where was he going?" I asked.

He hesitated and I knew what he had done instantly. The bastard had gone after Magdalena alone.

"He knows her better than any of us and had the best chance of getting in and out unseen," James said.

"Don't make excuses for him James. He likes to rush into danger and forget all about the rest of us." I said.

"Can you try, please?" He asked.

I nodded yes. Then I tried to find my connection with Marek only to find myself swimming in a numbed pool of inebriation. Sharp pain in my head told me continuing to try would only lead to another migraine.

"I may have had too much to drink to do much of anything," I said, feeling sweaty.

James drove out of the parking lot and onto the street. His jaw ticked but otherwise he held it together. I'd never seen him so concerned.

"You can try again after you've sobered up a bit. The alcohol may be what's hindering you." James said.

I watched him as he drove and hoped he was right.

5

James got me home safely to the penthouse and he was now pacing back and forth in my living room. He had made me coffee and was checking occasionally that I was drinking it. My protests that coffee wasn't able to sober anyone, scientifically speaking, caused him too much pain. Therefore, I was drinking it dutifully along with a large bottle of water which had more hope of flushing the alcohol out of my system.

"You are scaring me, James. I've never seen you worried about Marek before." I said, the fear of what might be happening bubbling up in my stomach.

"An ancient vampire is not someone to trifle with and this one has a particular reason to wish him harm. I do not believe he is acting in his right mind after his argument with you. I cannot let the team know or risk them thinking he has lost control." He said the last in a whisper so that no one but I would hear.

I closed my eyes and tried my hardest to reach Marek. Warm electricity spread through my body as we finally connected. I was so relieved that I almost missed the fact that he was in pain.

"Marek, are you alright?" I said through our connection.

"Milaya Moya," He said, saying his nickname for me but it was weak.

"Tell me where you are. Are you hurt?" I urged him to answer.

"I will be fine. You need not worry." He assured me.

"Marek, where are you?" I demanded.

"Only James can know. Promise me only you and James." He said.

"I promise," I said anxiously to hear where he was.

"Tell him he can find me at the location we discussed this evening. He will know it." Marek said.

"I'll tell him," I said.

"Good, good." He trailed off.

I told James what Marek said and he moved to the door without looking back.

"Hold on!" I yelled, and James came to a halt where he was.

"What is it?" He asked.

"I'm coming with you," I said grabbing my coat and hurrying after him.

"I don't think that is a good idea," James said in protest.

"Duly noted, but I'm coming along anyway," I said and pushed past him to the door.

James gave me a look that said I was crazy. I ignored him and pushed the button for the elevator to take us down to the parking garage. James sent a few text messages while we waited and darted concerned glances at me during the process.

"What?" I asked.

"I have to order your team to stay here." He said in a low whisper.

It took me a minute to figure out why I had a team trailing me. Then another minute to realize why he would have to pull them off me for the night. Getting this drunk had seemed like a good idea until this moment.

I was about to say something to that effect to James but he put his finger to my lips to stop me. He mouthed "not here" as the elevator doors opened.

We got in and rode in silence all the way down. He kept his hand on my back from the time we stepped out of the elevator until he had me seated in the car. He engaged the door locks before he even started the vehicle. Paranoid much? I tried not to giggle and failed.

"Of course you find this funny," He said, sounding exasperated.

"When I'm drunk I either laugh or get horny. Which do you prefer right now?" I said, perfectly serious.

"I uh," James fumbled to find the words he wanted to use. "Are those my only options?"

I laughed at his awkward response. "I'll try to be serious but I have to warn you that I'll either laugh or get horny whether I want to or not. Until I'm sober, anything can set me off."

"You are going to get us killed." He said under his breath.

"I'll sober up the second we are in danger. I know that for a fact." I said.

He looked at me warily, "I should have locked you in a room so you couldn't come after me."

"I have to be with you tonight. I can feel it," I said, giving him a look that I was serious.

I'd felt it since I woke up earlier. I needed to be with Marek when he was found. It wasn't just a selfish wish to make sure he was okay.

James knew me well enough that if I said I felt something, he honored it. I'm sure that is part of the reason why he didn't protest bringing me along in the first place. I was also good in a fight and given Marek's mission, we would most likely run into trouble.

"So, now that we are alone in the car away from prying ears, where are we going?" I asked.

James had maneuvered us out of downtown and onto I-25 heading north.

"He's near a farm in Firestone. It's close to where Magdalena's base of operations is but removed enough that she shouldn't take too much notice if we show up." James said. "Are you sure you'll be okay?"

I felt a blast of pain from Marek right then and it was with shortened breath that I answered.

"I'm feeling soberer by the minute. Drive faster. He needs us," I said.

James increased his speed to just beyond reasonable which wasn't fast enough for me. Traffic wasn't too bad since it was a Sunday night. He was able to weave in and out of cars and make progress toward speeding in the open stretches.

His Mustang GT was up for the task and for the first time, I was impressed with his car. If you're going to drive a Mustang it should be a cool color. Jame's car is white...white! The color gave the impression of being wimpy but I realized that it had all we needed under the hood when we hit a long stretch of empty pavement and James floored it.

Before I knew it we were exiting the highway and heading east toward the farm. Now on deserted roads, James sped like Marek's life depended on it.

"Given your intake of alcohol this evening, I think it would be best if you help Marek to the car while I watch your back. When we get there, go straight to him and let me deal with any threats. If he's hidden you will be able to find him faster than me anyway." James said.

"Agreed," I said.

I held on as James turned onto a dirt road. He didn't slow down and I was feeling anxious about what we would find. A large farmhouse was off to our left and a few outbuildings dotted the landscape. James headed toward the furthest outbuilding.

"We are almost there. Hang on," I said to Marek through our bond.

He didn't answer but I could feel his relief. I could also tell that he wasn't in one of the buildings. He was out in the field.

"Park behind the outbuilding. He's out in the field behind it." I said.

James nodded and shifted at the last moment to swing behind the building. Just when I thought we were going to crash, he came to a stop perfectly in line with the back wall. I caught my breath and jumped out of the car. I took off running toward Marek.

I felt James on my heels and was thankful for the backup. We were literally running blindly into an unknown situation. I couldn't see anyone around but could feel a few vampires and humans too close for comfort. I imagined the humans were the farm owners but they could just as easily be bad guys.

As I got closer to Marek, I felt the vampires moving toward me.

"Shit, we are about to have company, James," I said.

"I see them," James said and stopped running.

I kept going and almost stepped on Marek. Instead, I dropped to my knees and rolled him over. His face and chest were covered in blood. I couldn't tell if it was his blood or someone else's but it was clear he was in bad shape.

"Ember?" Marek moaned.

"I'm here. Can you stand up? We need to get you to the car before all hell breaks loose." I said pulling him up.

He moved slowly but was able to get on his feet. I swung his right arm over my shoulders and used my kinetic power to help keep him upright. We fast-walked to the car but we had a long way to go and nothing but open field between us and the approaching vampires.

"Why do I smell alcohol?" Marek asked.

"Because I've been drinking but all this running and adrenaline has me feeling completely sober," I said.

"Why were you drinking?" Marek asked.

I couldn't believe he was making small talk while we ran for our lives. I made a mental note to check him for a head injury later.

"More running, less talking." I insisted.

I could hear grunting coming from behind me and could only imagine what James was doing. There were a good thirty yards between us and the car when a vampire jumped out of nowhere and tackled us. Marek went down hard because I dropped him to focus on our attacker. The impact of the hit only knocked me for a moment. I jumped to my feet and reached out with my power to slam the vampire to the ground.

All the training I had been through with James lately helped me know what to do next. Instead of following through with the one on the ground, I looked around to see if there were any others. Two vampires approached from my left so I kept hold of the one I had beside me and used my pyrotechnic power on the other two. When they started to burn I refocused on the one on the ground. Marek was moving toward him and within seconds had snapped his neck.

The two burning vamps went down and I added a little extra flame now that I wasn't dividing my attention. They fell to the ground. A quick sweep of the area showed no other vampires near us. James was engaged with two of his own but I left him to it. My job was to get Marek to the car.

I lifted Marek back to his feet and helped him the remaining distance. We didn't see any other vampires but a new obstacle presented itself. James' car was a two-door and I needed to get a tall vampire into the back seat.

I propped Marek up against the car while I opened the door and threw the front seat forward. He started sliding down to the ground before I could get back to him. I grabbed him with my power and maneuvered him so I could dump him in the back. It wasn't going to be gentle but it was all I could do.

When I pulled Marek off the car, I noticed large streaks of blood on the white vehicle. That was going to be a problem.

After pushing Marek's legs inside the car I turned around to check on James and sweep the area for any other baddies. There were a few vampires headed this way but they were almost a mile out.

"James! Time to go," I yelled.

I immobilized the vampire he was fighting and he made short work of breaking her neck. While he ran to the car I looked around for a way to get rid of the blood on the car. There was nothing but dirt. No handy bucket with soapy water sitting around for me to use. Dirt!

Cars in Colorado have a few stages of cleanliness. There is an "I've been to the mountains and my car is covered in mud" look. There is "it's been snowing and the splash-back is clearly evident" look. There is also a fresh from the car wash or recently washed look. Basically, dirt doesn't stand out as blood would.

I grabbed dirt from the ground and threw it at the shiny blood. It stuck easily and was an effective camouflage.

"What are you doing?" James said as he ran to the driver's door.

"Covering all the blood," I said.

Satisfied it no longer looked like blood, I got into the passenger seat and shut the door. James took off just as my door closed. We rounded the outbuilding just as the vampires I had sensed appeared in the field behind us.

"James," I started to say.

"I see them," James said and proceeded to stomp on the gas peddle.

We left in a huge plume of kicked up dirt. I hoped it helped obscure our escape. If not, we would be in a car chase.

"Why were you drinking?" Marek said from the back seat.

He sounded weak and it tore at my heart to hear it. He was beaten and bleeding but more concerned about why I had been drinking.

"Because you're an asshole and I missed my friends," I said catching his eyes.

He looked confused and I could feel him trying to figure out why I said it.

"How badly are you hurt?" I asked trying to distract him.

"Bad," He said.

"Shit," I said under my breath as I felt him lose consciousness.

I tried to climb into the backseat but James stopped me.

"Please fasten your seatbelt and wait until I am sure we aren't being followed. I can't drive and worry about you at the same time." James said.

I reached back to Marek and was satisfied that I could touch his hand. I did as James said and immediately afterward James did some driving that made Steven McQueen's car chase in the movie Bullitt look like nothing.

We cut through yards and flew down side streets only to run red lights and at one point we were on the wrong side of the road. I didn't think it was possible anyone could follow except for the police. Someone had to have called them and reported a crazy driver.

James drove us across town and into a Boulder neighborhood near the college campus. It looked like frat house row but these were private homes. James pulled into a driveway and jumped out of the car. He opened a keypad on the garage and entered the code. The garage door lifted.

He pulled the car in and told me to wait until the door went back down to get out of the car. I was holding Marek's hand and hoping he wasn't hurt worse than James could heal.

It felt like five minutes before the garage door was down and I could get out of the car. I was leaning into the back seat within seconds.

"If you can line him up, I can pull him out," James said.

Getting a six-foot-tall vampire out of the back of a tiny backseat was not easy. While I pushed, James pulled and we got him out. I followed after him and grabbed the door.

James carried Marek straight ahead into a bedroom. I tried to ignore the dripping blood as he went. If Marek wasn't already healing, something really bad had happened.

James laid Marek down and told me to remove his clothing so we could see what we were dealing with. James left the room and returned with a bunch of towels and bandages.

I peeled off Marek's coat and found a few places he had been stabbed. One wound was gaping so badly I could see his insides. James handed me the kind of scissors you see on TV emergency shows. They are blunt on the end so you can cut off clothing without hurting the patient. I used them to cut Marek's shirt away first and pointed out the obvious wound in his abdomen.

James went to work stitching it up while I cut off Marek's pants and took off his shoes. Marek's left leg had been slashed by what I could only imagine had been a sword. His knee was out of joint and I couldn't believe he had actually walked on it.

James handed me a wet washcloth and motioned for me to clean Marek's face. I found many small wounds and a large one where most of the blood was coming from. Head wounds were big bleeders because the blood vessels were nearer to the surface of the skin than on other parts of the body. This one was slow to drip but I figured it was because Marek had already lost a lot of blood if the wet trail down his body was any indication. There wasn't much left to bleed.

"He's going to need blood and a lot of it," I said.

"We have some on hand," James assured me.

I went back to cleaning Marek's body and found a few more wounds that require stitches. Whatever had happened to him, he got his ass kicked. I didn't know how he made it to the field on his own and why he didn't reach out to me for help. I'd yell at him after he was out of danger.

Once Marek had been stitched up and James performed a few healing treatments, James left the room to get an IV of blood ready. He didn't have to tell me to be careful but he did anyway. A vampire hurt that badly could lose control and attack one of us.

I pulled a blanket over Marek and laid down next to him watching for any sign of his regaining consciousness. I grabbed his hand and squeezed and he squeezed back.

"How are you doing?" I asked softly.

"My body hurts," he said so softly I almost couldn't hear him.

The link between us flared and I could feel his pain. There was also a hunger for blood that was overwhelming.

"James is getting an IV ready for you," I assured him.

"Good," He said, then seemed to pass out again.

I moved to check on James but Marek's fingers tightened around mine and

I could feel him willing me to stay. I pressed my body into his and felt him respond. He wanted me near him.

I heard James wheeling a squeaky IV pole down the hall. He entered the room with several bags of blood and tubing to get Marek hooked up. He raised his eyebrows at my clearly not staying away from the vampire when he said Marek could be dangerous but didn't say anything.

"He woke up briefly then passed out again," I said watching James attach the IV.

James moved like a medical professional with swift efficiency. He had a full bag of blood in Marek within an hour and set up a second. I stayed next to Marek the entire time. He wouldn't let go of my hand.

"I'd like him to have all three bags before we try to move him. He should be able to heal most of the remaining injuries himself once he has enough blood. He may not want to though so anything you can do to help would be appreciated. I'm going to do a sweep to be sure we don't have any visitors. Call me if anything happens." James said then left the bedroom.

I heard a door open and close and then felt James move out toward the back of the house.

"He's like a hovering nanny," Marek said.

"He can probably still hear you," I said smiling.

Marek opened his eyes and looked at me. "Why did you come?"

His words stung and I felt myself pulling back from him. He noticed something was wrong.

"You were drunk. You could have been killed." He said.

"Because you were hurt and there was nothing that could keep me away," I said.

He smiled and moved to wrap his arms around me.

"Wait, you'll hurt yourself." I protested.

"I am hard to kill," He said while pulling me into his arms. "The pain means I am still alive."

He pressed his lips into mine and I forgot briefly why I was protesting. Marek's skin was cold against my lips. He needed more blood.

"Take my blood," I said stroking his cheek. "You feel cold."

"Cold is my natural state," Marek said.

"But you usually feel warm," I asked, confused.

"It is easier to regulate my temperature to a more human level when I am not trying to heal multiple injuries," Marek said.

"Then why are you refusing my blood?" I asked.

"I did not refuse," Marek said. "It will hurt this time."

"I don't care. You need it." I said.

He leaned closer and hesitated. He didn't want to hurt me. I encouraged him by pulling him closer. His teeth grazed my skin and my body shivered in response. Marek's teeth pierced my skin and he was right, it hurt. A lot.

At first, it was just a pinch but as he latched on and the tugging started I had to hold back my natural reaction. My subconscious was telling me to blast

Marek across the room. I held out and focused on how my blood would heal him instead.

Marek drank greedily from my neck. If it hadn't been him, I would have been disgusted. It made me think about why I liked him biting me in the first place. That's when I felt it. A trickle of pleasure coming through our bond. It was a hint of what I normally felt when he bit me but it was exactly what I craved.

A golden warmth fell over me. Then the full pleasure of his bite hit me and I relaxed into the sensation. I could feel his pain lessening with each swallow of my blood and was happy he would survive. I was so overcome with the feeling that I didn't hear James come into the room.

"Let her go, Marek. You're going to drain her." James said with venom in his voice.

Marek stiffened but didn't release me. That's when I realized that I was getting dizzy. When I looked up at James, black spots appeared in my vision.

"Ember's skin is pale. You've taken too much." James said moving next to the bed and putting a hand on Marek.

Marek stopped drinking but his reaction wasn't good. "Mine!" he said then bit me again.

A wave of bliss hit me and I had trouble breathing. This wasn't right.

"Marek, that's enough," I said finally finding my voice.

He slowed as if thinking it over. James didn't give him time to decide. He pulled a gun and put it against Marek's head.

"Release her now," James said.

That escalated quickly.

Marek stopped drinking and pulled away. His eyes were unfocused and he was looking at me strangely.

"Get off the bed Marek and go into the other room," James ordered.

Marek moved slowly but he did as he was told. James didn't move the gun from Marek's head the entire time. Marek ripped the IV from his hand and walked out the door. James stayed in the room with me, making sure Marek did as he was told.

When James was satisfied with where Marek was, he closed the bedroom door. He tucked the handgun into his waistband and hurried over to me.

"Can you sit up?" He asked.

I stared at James in amazement, unable to find words. He had just forced a master vampire to stop feeding and leave the room with nothing but a gun. That didn't seem possible.

"Ember, can you hear me?" James asked growing frantic.

"Yes, I'm okay," I said but couldn't sit up.

"Yeah, you're ready for a marathon," James said sarcastically.

He felt my forehead then grabbed my chin and turned my head to the side so he could get a look at my neck. I rolled my eyes at him. He stood up and walked to the door.

"I'll be right back. You are going to need blood and a bandage for your neck." James said then left.

I scanned the house to feel where he was and where Marek had gone. James was in the hall and Marek must have been in another bedroom. The feelings I was getting through our bond didn't make sense. It felt like he was drunk.

James returned to the room and quickly went to work cleaning my neck. It stung but I tried to hold still so he could bandage me up. I wondered why he wasn't using his healing ability but figured he might have used up all his energy on Marek already.

"Thank you, James," I said and smiled at him.

"You should have pushed him off of you before it got to that point. He could have killed you." James said upset.

"You're right. I should have," I said.

"If I can't trust you to take care of yourself, I won't be able to leave you two alone. Do you understand what I'm saying?" James asked and he sounded both scared and upset about it.

"What's wrong with him?" I asked feeling stupid for not understanding.

"He's blood drunk. Draining a powerful Seer will do that to a vampire." James said it like I should have known that would happen.

"Blood drunk?" I said not expecting a response.

"He locked himself in a bedroom on the other side of the house. It won't keep him in if he really wants to get out but I think he knows what he did." James said.

James set out supplies to start an IV but I didn't see a blood bag.

"What are you doing?" I asked.

"I'm going to start an IV then have the vampire donate his blood for you." He said.

"I could just drink it." I offered.

"I'm not willing to allow him to get that close to you. He will sit in that chair and not touch you." James said in a tone that made it clear there was no room for negotiation.

When he had everything ready, he left the room to fetch Marek.

6

James sat on the bed next to me making sure the blood was flowing properly. Marek sat in the chair like he was told and avoided my eyes. It was beyond awkward.

"Okay, that should do it. You should feel better within a few minutes." James proclaimed.

He took my blood pressure and looked concerned. He checked the IV again and it must have passed his inspection because he set his supplies aside then returned to sit next to me.

We sat in silence so long I felt like screaming. I decided that a conversation would be better.

"I'm feeling much better by the way," I said to no one in particular.

Marek met my eyes briefly then looked away. James raised his eyebrows but didn't say anything.

"I could have killed you," Marek said.

"But you didn't and I wouldn't have let you no matter what James thinks," I insisted.

Marek gave me a look that said he didn't believe me. Regardless of who was right, he was looking much better.

"Fine, changing topics. Now that you aren't bleeding out in a field. What's the story? How did you end up there?" I asked Marek.

James turned to look at Marek and if I didn't know better, I would have said Marek squirmed under his gaze.

After a long pause, Marek spoke. "Our intel said that Magdalena's coven was small and lacked leadership. I entered the compound to investigate and confirm the security. I did not anticipate finding several master vampires who were competent fighters. Masters rarely stay in a coven given they have the power to control one of their own. It put me at a disadvantage I was unable to overcome."

"I managed to retreat just at the right time and made it halfway to the farm before collapsing. I crawled the rest of the way." Marek said.

"You crawled? How far?" I asked horrified.

"Not far," Marek said.

"Marek..." I started but couldn't find the words when I saw the look on his face.

James looked at me and made a slight side to side movement of his head indicating I should drop it.

"We'll send in a team next time," James said and I was certain it was what he had suggested in the first place.

Marek nodded in agreement. He looked distracted and was scratching his stomach where his stitches sat. I could feel his discomfort and unease through our bond.

"If we hadn't come for you, what would have happened?" I asked not sure I wanted to hear the answer.

Both men stared back at me as if they were afraid to answer. That worried me even more than if they had immediately replied. It told me the consequences would have been dire.

Marek was the one that broke the silence, "What matters is that you showed up right before the coven found me."

Our bond snapped to attention and Marek's pain throbbed in my mind. He was trying not to answer the question but his unease told me enough.

"The fact they sent eight vampires out to find him shows they expected to find him alive," James said to me.

"Maybe," I said not believing it based on what I was getting from Marek.

"What do you want us to say Ember?" Marek asked.

"When you needed help, why didn't you reach out to me? I know you were mad at me but were you that mad?" I asked.

James stood up and moved to the door. He leaned against the wall with his arms crossed. It gave me a clear view of Marek so I could look him in the eye while giving him a good view of the scene.

"I did try to reach you," Marek responded.

Marek's face took on the stoic blank he used when he didn't want anyone to know what he was feeling.

"What do you mean? I didn't feel anything from you." I said.

"I thought you were shutting me out. When I tried, I hit a brick wall." Marek said.

"I wasn't blocking you," I said confused.

"You drank so much you passed out. That could have been the problem." James said offering his two cents.

"You never fully explained why you got drunk," Marek said.

"No, I didn't," I said.

I refused to look Marek in the eyes when I answered. The anger at how he treated me flooded my mind again.

"How about you do that now?" Marek asked.

"There is nothing wrong with a lady getting her drink on," I said tightly.

Marek studied me then asked, "Why are you avoiding the question?"

"Because it's your fault!" I yelled, losing the little control I had.

I ripped the IV out of my hand and moved to leave the room. Marek jumped out in front of me and stopped me from going out the door.

"What is my fault?" Marek asked.

Marek held me in front of him. He searched my eyes and our bond for answers. I could feel him doing it.

"Let go," I said.

"Tell me," Marek demanded.

"Dammit, Marek! You walked away. You said you couldn't be with me and left. Then you shut down the bond which you agreed never to do." I said with tears in my eyes.

"So you drowned your sorrows in alcohol dulling your senses? If you were attacked, you could have been killed." Marek said.

My anger rose at his words.

"Let me get this straight. You only care about the fact I got drunk?" I asked.

"Yes," He said, then he saw my face and said, "No."

"Well, which is it? Either you care about me or you want nothing to do with me." I said.

Marek stepped into me and I was surrounded by his presence. It reminded me of what drew me to him when I first met him. No matter how often I had been scared or wary of him there was always something drawing us closer.

"I do not care about you," Marek said.

I took a step back. My disbelief overwhelming my ability to comprehend what he had just said.

"No," Marek said closing the distance between us.

He pulled me into his arms and I saw James move closer as if to pull us apart.

"I do not *just* care about you, Ember. I love you so much it hurts. When I could not reach you as I laid in that field, I thought I may never get the chance to tell you." Marek said.

I stared at him unable to process what he just said. Then it hit me.

"Is there something wrong with your head?" I asked running my fingers through his hair searching his scalp for a bump.

"It is muddled by the blood loss making it hard to get the words out, but the sentiment is true," Marek said.

"Okay then," I said leaning into him.

He pulled me into his arms and held me tight. I breathed in the scent of him and felt the beat of his heart through his chest. It was a cocoon of warmth and love. It was what I had been longing for since this morning.

James broke the silence and spoke to Marek, "Can I trust you?"

Marek replied, "On my honor."

James nodded his head. Then he ducked out of the room, closing the door behind him.

I looked up at Marek and said, "You had me fooled into thinking you were walking away from me."

"Never," Marek assured me.

He dipped his head down and placed a gentle kiss on my lips. I got swept away in a vanilla woodsy haze of yummy man. How he could smell that good after laying in a field covered in blood was beyond my understanding.

I pulled back from him and asked, "How are you feeling now?"

"I need a shower but I feel much better. I also need to get these stitches out." Marek said, pulling his shirt up to look at his stomach.

The wound that was previously a giant hole in his middle was now nothing but a line of thread. There wasn't another mark left on his skin from the battle he had been in. I guess taking most of my blood paid off for him.

"I'll get James so he can cut them out," I said stepping out of Marek's arms.

"No, it can wait," Marek said stopping me.

"But it's bothering you," I said.

"All I need right now is you," Marek said leaning in for a kiss.

I kissed him back. Then I held on to him as if he might blow away. I didn't believe what he and James told me. I knew Marek was close to real death before I found him in that field. What I didn't understand, was why he was lying to me about it.

Marek stayed quiet while he held me. I had a feeling that he had as many thoughts running through his head as I did. We were destined for another fight and I was afraid this one would be about Magdalena. Marek still hadn't told me the full story about their relationship.

"Let's get your stitches out then get you in the shower so we can head back home," I said.

"You need to clean up too," Marek said pulling my t-shirt up over my head.

As he pulled it off, I saw how it had been stained with his blood. I hadn't even realized it until then. The image of Marek bleeding to death in my arms flickered in my vision. I started to shake and my legs went weak. Marek caught me before I fell.

"What is wrong?" He asked concern etched on his face.

"You would have died. If James hadn't come for me and woke me up, you would be dead right now." I said tears stinging my eyes.

"I am hard to kill," Marek said.

"I should have been there sooner. I should have been with you. I drank myself into a stupor so I couldn't feel you anymore and look at what happened." I said pulling up his shirt and pointing at his stitches.

"Ember," Marek said holding my face in his hands so I couldn't look away. "None of this was your fault."

"Then how did it happen? I've seen you take on an entire compound of vampires single-handed and you took them all out." I said.

"I had help that day if you remember." He said stroking my cheek.

"You are deflecting. What happened Marek? You're a badass. I don't get it." I said completely confused.

He sighed and sat down on the edge of the bed. He ran his hands through his hair and wouldn't look at me.

"I let my head get in the way. Instead of thinking, I reacted." He said.

I grabbed his hand and asked, "Were you mad?"

"That and other things. I never should have gone in by myself. Do not tell James I said that," He said giving me a warning look.

"You're secret is safe with me," I said leaning in to kiss his cheek.

He met my eyes and smiled.

"We should get moving. It's late and your first official day at work for the Council is tomorrow." Marek said.

He told me where to find a spare t-shirt and I left him so he could remove his stitches and shower. I was digging through the hall closet for a shirt when James came back inside the house. He stopped short and stared at me.

"You've seen me in my bra before," I said pulling out a shirt that looked like it would fit.

I slipped the shirt over my head and pulled it down to my hips. James' eyes followed the motion. He was going to get himself beaten or worse if Marek saw him looking at me that way. I raised an eyebrow at him.

"The car is clean. Did you help Marek with his stitches?" James asked.

"No, he said he would do it himself," I said.

James nodded and he went to check on Marek. He must not have thought it was a good idea to let Marek handle the stitches himself. I'm not sure it was a good idea to point that out to Marek.

I made myself comfortable in the living room while James pulled nurse duty. I hoped he didn't get his head bitten off for helping when Marek wanted to be alone.

While I waited I did a sweep of the neighborhood trying to feel who was nearby. There were mostly humans but then I found them. A group of vampires was making their way toward the house.

I jumped off the couch and ran to the bathroom. James was removing the last of the stitches.

"Time to go, now!" I whisper yelled.

"What is it?" Marek said softly following me out of the room.

"Vampires. Headed this way fast," I said.

I ran to the garage and the guys fell in close on my heels.

"James, in the back," Marek said taking the keys to the car.

Marek started up the car and we all strapped in. Before the garage door was even up, Marek gunned it and shot down the driveway. There wasn't any movement on the street but I could feel the same vampires we had outrun before closing in.

"They're two blocks away," I told Marek.

He nodded and gunned it. We hit a bump and caught some serious air before hitting the ground again. Marek pushed us as fast as he could go on the small side streets. He was trying to make it to a major street so we could get lost in the traffic.

Marek fishtailed around a corner and came within inches of hitting the cars parked on the side of the road. My heart was in my throat from the speed but I tried to keep tabs on the enemy anyway. They were farther away now and fading.

"I think they stopped at the safe house," I said feeling slight relief but not giving up my sweeps of the area.

"We will be at Foothills Parkway in a moment. We can hit the Boulder Turnpike from there and head back downtown." Marek said.

"That was close," I said feeling the hard beat of my heart.

"We are not clear yet," Marek said.

We hit the main road at speed and then Marek dialed it back to draw less attention.

"I can call in a team to divert our tail from following us." James offered.

"Do it," Marek said.

James made a call and gave the order.

"How did they find us?" I asked.

"I do not know," Marek said.

We hit the highway a minute later and I relaxed back into my seat. I hadn't realized I was doing it but I had been sitting on the edge of the seat holding the dashboard.

"You use that house often. They probably picked up your scent when they got close enough." James offered.

"A mistake I will not make again," Marek said.

"I should have thought about that before I brought you there," James admitted.

"In this case, keeping Marek alive was the most important outcome. You can pick apart your perceived mistakes later." I said making sure both of them knew I didn't want to hear it.

If anyone was culpable, it was me and Marek. We shouldn't have let our argument go on the way it had. If we had listened to each other and talked things out, we could have avoided the entire situation. Although, he probably would have gone into that compound regardless. He just would have done it with backup nearby.

"I do not see anyone following us. Ember, do you sense them?" Marek asked.

I expanded my awareness and found a few vampires here and there while we whizzed by on the highway but none that were pursuing us or felt like the group we had left behind. I told Marek and he visibly relaxed.

"They are serious about getting to you Marek. Losing you tonight won't stop them from continuing their search. Have you thought about what you want to do next?" James asked from the backseat.

James was scrunched up with no headroom and very little legroom. It would be hilarious if we weren't running from crazy vampires.

"We need to review all our safe houses to see if any of them had unwanted visitors recently. Let the team know not to trust any property until the sweep is complete." Marek said.

James made some calls and relayed the information Marek wanted to be broadcast to the team. No one questioned his orders or asked for more information. He was smooth and confident, a leader.

James saw me watching him and he preened from the attention. A spark of a vision teased at my consciousness. I reached out for it and was greeted by a searing pain in my head. I cried out, grabbing my forehead.

"What is it?" Marek asked reaching for me.

"A headache," I said confused by why I got a headache instead of the vision.

"Is it like before?" James asked.

I tried to respond but the pain was too much. I slid down in the seat to block the lights from shining in my face. It helped a little but I was so lost to the pain that I couldn't understand what was being said in the car.

Marek spoke urgently to James and I felt the car speed up. Hands touched me and I felt warmth spreading through my body. It would have been nice if my skull wasn't trying to turn itself inside out. At some point, I blacked out.

I came to in Marek's arms. He was carrying me into the hospital wing at Council headquarters.

"I don't want to be here," I said trying to push out of his arms.

Marek kept me in his arms without much effort on his part. It was hard to argue the point with him given my lack of strength. I didn't want to risk more pain by using my powers so I huffed out my disapproval and literally rode it out.

"The doctor wants to examine you," Marek said.

His voice was gentle and soothing but it was a deception. I could feel his unease and anxiety through the bond. My headache wasn't normal.

We ended up in a familiar room that might as well have my name on the door due to my frequent visits. Marek laid me down on the bed. I cringed away from the bright lights and he quickly turned them off.

My head had its own heartbeat and nausea was overtaking my waking thoughts. I searched the room to see if there was a trash can or something I could hold in case I had to vomit. James noticed and brought over a small bucket that must have been made to do the job. I tried to smile at him but probably failed.

"We have to stop meeting like this," A soft voice said.

I looked over and saw the doctor I had talked to during my last headache, Dr. Wallace. She took my pulse and listened to my heart with a cold stethoscope. After taking my blood pressure, she started in on questions.

"How does this episode compare to the last one you had?" She asked.

"They were both out of the blue. Although, I was under stress both times." I said.

"What were you doing minutes before this one started?" She asked.

"I was using my power to search the area for vampires. Then I sensed a vision coming and I guess you could say I grabbed onto it. That's when the pain hit." I said.

"And the last headache? What were you doing moments before it hit?" She asked.

I had to think for a minute before I could answer. The headache was taking my ability to process information too.

"I was using my power to see a vision. I wasn't able to see the whole thing because the headache interrupted," I said leaving out that the vision had upset me.

"Was the vision upsetting or were you upset prior to the vision last time?" She asked.

"Both. I was very upset before and during the vision." I said.

"Okay. Thank you, Ember. I'm going to give you something to help with the pain and nausea you are feeling. I'll be back to do some tests a little later. I've called in a member of the staff who can scan your brain for any abnormalities. It will be much less invasive or painful than doing a CT scan." She said.

She smiled at me and moved to leave the room. She motioned for James to follow her into the hall. He looked at me then followed her out.

Marek moved closer and stroked my forehead. It brought a shiver through my body and helped ease the pain slightly. It must have been the reaction he was hoping for because he took it as an invitation to curl up in the bed with me.

He pulled me snug into his chest, curling his body up behind mine like the perfect big spoon. It made me feel loved which brought me comfort. Having him there helped me push away the fear that was threatening to invade my mind over this headache. The connection between the pain and using my seer ability couldn't be a coincidence. I clung to Marek hoping I was wrong.

7

A few hours of cuddling with Marek didn't prepare me for the "testing" I would undergo for my headaches. The doctor decided that she needed to do a full work up to understand what was happening. Testing included both traditional medicine and the woo woo stuff I was growing used to with exposure.

Dr. Wallace was sitting across from me in a room that looked like it belonged in an insane asylum. The walls were white and padded, and the ceiling covered with what looked like gray foam egg cartons. All the padding created a muffling effect on any sounds that felt oddly serene.

The room had two brown padded chairs bolted to the floor. I sat in the one facing the door and the doctor sat across from me. When the door closed, the room became so quiet that I could hear my own breathing. It felt like being locked in a closet.

I started to panic, and the doctor noticed.

"You are safe. The door is unlocked, and you can leave at any time. Marek is right outside the door to make sure you can get out and that no one but he can come in." She said in a soothing voice.

The doctor said Marek would be a distraction if he came in the room with us. He didn't react well to that, but after I asked him to stay in the hall, he consented. I was glad he did because knowing he was guarding that door made me able to relax.

"I take it you've had a few runners," I said.

"I have," She laughed softly. "This room can unsettle some while soothing others."

"I think I can understand why," I said, taking a deep breath.

"Ember, as I told you before we came in here, this room will eliminate any outside influences on your powers. That will allow me to evaluate what is happening to you in a more controlled environment. Do you understand?" She explained.

"Yes," I replied.

"Good. Now sit back and relax," The doctor said, standing up and approaching me. "Lean your head back and clear your mind of thoughts."

The doctor moved behind me and placed her fingers at my temples. At her touch, I felt a tingling sensation spread across my scalp. Then I felt a humming sensation vibrating my skull gently. It was weird but not unpleasant.

"Try to access a vision, Ember. It can be anything, but if you can try to see the one that started the first headache, that would be ideal." The doctor said.

I took a deep breath and pulled at the vision I had of Marek with Magdalena in Paris. It made my stomach hurt to even think about it, but I dove right in disregarding the pain. The image flickered to life in my mind. I watched as Marek grabbed Magdalena's hand and turned it palm up to place his lips on the tender flesh. Her face filled with love as Marek pulled her into his body for a hug. The look on his face didn't match hers.

Marek's face was neutral but not quite his signature bland look. There was a hint of disgust before he managed it. It was clear he didn't want the crazy ancient vampire in his arms to know how he really felt. That was the part of the vision I was unable to see before. It changed how I felt about Marek's former relationship with Magdalena.

I let the images fade from my conscious mind feeling my headache ease. It was as if a knot untangled and allowed me to see again.

The doctor stepped away and sat back in her chair. She looked at me with empathy. I wondered if she was able to see the vision.

"No pain," I stated the obvious.

"Have you been under a lot of stress lately?" Dr. Wallace asked.

I laughed at the absurdity of the question. I'd been in the hospital wing more than I'd been home in the last two weeks.

"You have read my file, right? I'm sure it tells you how often I've been hurt." I said.

"I'm not talking about physical injury. That's well documented. What I'm more concerned about is how you are handling this life." She said.

Her voice held notes of concern and a hint of reproach.

"I haven't had a chance to contemplate it. I've been busy trying not to die and chasing crazy kidnapping vampires. The emergencies are never-ending. There isn't time to deal with it. I can only react." I said.

"That could explain why you have these headaches. Based on what you say, it sounds like you don't rest your powers." She said.

"I didn't know that was a thing," I said, confused.

"That is why we used this room. If you recall, this room blocks all types of energies and can even dampen a vampire's bond. You have too many layers of power turned on all the time. This room allowed you to sort of power down and relax your subconscious use of power." She said.

The doctor continued, "During our test, I did not sense any outside influence or blocks on your power. Therefore, the headaches may be a result of your overuse of power."

"How do we fix that? I don't know how not to use my power." I said.

"It's imperative that you learn, but in the meantime, this room can be helpful. The headaches are just the first symptom, Ember. The situation will get much worse if you don't rest your power and learn to take care of yourself. It won't just be your gifts that suffer but everyone around you too." She said ominously.

"I don't have to be a seer to know that a certain vampire lurking in the hallway is likely to lock me in here and not let me out when you tell him what is going on," I said.

"This isn't the first time he has dealt with a diagnosis like this for someone in his care. However, given the nature of your relationship with Master Volkov, I will be recommending that Guardian Leigh handle your medical concerns. He is already familiar with your symptoms and can be more objective." She said.

I inwardly rolled my eyes, thinking about how Marek was going to have a fit over James being in charge of my health concerns. James wasn't exactly an objective party either, but I didn't bring that up to the doctor. Of the two, he was the lesser of two evils.

"Okay," I agreed and tried to calm my panic.

If I wasn't allowed to use my powers, I wasn't sure how safe I would be.

"Hang tight in here for a while. I'll arrange for the next steps in your treatment plan and tell the vampire to stay in the hall. It's important for you to know that your bond with him is a direct agitator on your power. Just being near him can trigger an unconscious use of your gifts and heightened emotions between you should be avoided until you have more control." She said.

"Doctor, that sounds an awful lot like you telling me not to fight with or get intimate with my boyfriend," I said cringing.

"Take it to mean whatever you like. Avoid the spike of emotions and heal." She said.

I nodded and tried to relax as she opened the door to talk to Marek. He popped his head into the room and a tiny spike of pain needled into my forehead. It was like I was allergic to him.

The doctor pulled Marek back into the hall and closed the door. It was like turning off a switch in my headache. My anxiety spiked at the thought that I couldn't spend time with him without triggering a pull on my power.

We hadn't even really talked about our fight which would definitely heighten my emotions when we went there. I tried to clear those thoughts from my brain and relax.

This room made me feel fantastic. It was like I felt before I knew all about this crazy world of supernatural creatures and paranormal powers. I didn't regret my entry into this world but having a break from the chaos felt wonderful.

Muffled voices in the hall reminded me of my reality. Mark was most certainly pissed off. Although I couldn't feel his emotions, the bond was still there buzzing in the background of my mind.

I closed my eyes and relaxed further into the chair. My breathing evened out and sleep teased me until it took me away into a dream.

James walked in a room with nothing but a towel wrapped around his waist. His blonde hair was wet and dripping down the smooth planes of his chest. The ink of his tattoos stood out in contrast to the perfect lines of muscle. He was a sight to be seen.

He moved to his bedroom and pulled out some clothes. Before I could prepare myself, James pulled the towel off his hips. My brain froze and all I could do was watch as he used the towel to dry his hair and then his body.

James dropped the towel then got dressed. I found out he wore briefs and that he looked delicious walking around in them. It was a shame when he pulled on a pair of jeans.

His phone rang and he answered it, “Ember, what’s wrong?”

James paced back and forth as he listened. He looked upset.

“Stay there. I’m on my way.” He said and hung up.

James finished dressing with speed. Then without warning, he punched a hole in the wall.

“Damn you, Marek! I will kill you if you hurt her again.” James said while running out the door.

He jumped in his car and tore down the driveway as if my life depended on him. Given his reaction, it probably did.

James pulled out his phone and made a call to his team. He told them to move in and to take Marek down as soon as they had him in sight. James told them the order came from me and my chest exploded with hurt and betrayal.

The shock of the dream woke me up. If I couldn’t trust James, my world would come crashing down. He was the one person that remained a constant source of support for me. It was James that protected me the first time I was attacked. A bond had formed between us that until now, I had thought was unbreakable.

I pushed the hurt away and thought about the dream. I was missing vital information that would answer the question of James’ loyalty. If this was a vision, it was one that punched me in the gut. I needed to know more before I jumped to conclusions. I learned my lesson the hard way with Marek, I wouldn’t let this make me doubt James until there was a solid reason to doubt him.

The door to the quiet room opened and James walked in. I rubbed the sleep from my eyes and tried to smile at him.

“Did I wake you?” James asked.

“No. I woke up a few minutes ago. How long have I been in here?” I asked.

“A few hours. I thought for sure you would have come out before now. Are you okay?” He asked.

“I’m feeling much better. This room helped.” I said.

“The doctor doesn’t want you to spend too much time here. It’s an artificial crutch that can lead to dependency.” James said.

“Well, where to then?” I asked standing up from the chair.

“Home. It’s the middle of the night. I’m guessing your bed would be more comfortable for sleeping." James said.

"That is very true. Where's Marek? I would have expected him to barge in here." I said.

"Dr. Wallace encouraged him to create some distance from you to help you rest." He said.

I tried not to let that bother me. The doctor said Marek could trigger me but I wanted nothing more than to cuddle up with him the remainder of the night.

Without saying a word to James, I reached out with my senses to find Marek. As soon as he showed up on my radar I felt him moving closer. It made me smile to think that feeling me cause him to move toward me.

"I hope the doctor won't be too upset," I said feeling Marek's magnetic pull and moving to meet it.

"About what?" James said following me out the door.

I didn't answer him. I just moved in Marek's direction with speed. The hallways were long and mostly empty. The people I did see ducked out of the way quickly. I must have been running because I heard James' feet pounding behind me. I didn't ponder it too long because Marek was close.

I turned a corner and found Marek at the end of the hallway near the residential elevators. The sight of him made my heart speed up and my breathing become labored. It was like he was the drug I needed to survive.

A smile grew on his lips as he realized the effect he had on me. I could feel the physical pull his body had on mine. It was easier to recognize after spending time in the quiet room and disconnected from him for hours. I wondered if what I felt for him was entirely related to sharing blood and power with him or if I really did love the man.

My steps faltered and I had to put my hand on the wall to keep from falling down. James was there within a second wrapping his arm around my waist. My mind flashed to the images of him from my dream and I pushed his arm away.

"I'm fine, just overwhelmed." I lied, trying to hide the heat crawling up my cheeks.

James let go and took a step back. I looked up at Marek then. He was right in front of me now but he didn't reach for me. His stoic blank face was in place but I could feel the rush of emotion coming from him.

I closed the distance between us and pulled him down for a kiss. The movement must have knocked some sense into him because he wrapped his arms around me and kissed me back. It didn't have the passion I had hoped for but we did have a babysitter.

"Ember, we should get you to bed," James said, interrupting a perfectly good kiss.

"The nanny has spoken," Marek said dryly stepping away.

"Not going to happen. You are coming with me." I said pulling Marek to the elevator.

"That isn't a good idea, Ember," James said following us.

"I don't care. If you would like to avoid my temper, Marek and I are sleeping together tonight." I said with steel in my voice.

James raised his arms in surrender. He didn't back down completely. He got in the elevator with us.

Marek was smiling as if he would laugh at any moment.

"What?" I asked him.

"You just publicly declared that you were taking me to your bed," He said.

His eyes were sparkling with delight and my cheeks burned hot.

"Oh," I said feeling stupid.

The supernatural hearing in this building probably picked up on what I said. The majority of the staff had enhanced senses which is why we were supposed to keep statements like that to ourselves.

Marek gathered me into his arms and tucked my head under his chin.

"I liked hearing you claim me," He said softly.

His voice was seductive. It felt like soft fur running down my body. It made me want to get him upstairs faster than the elevator was moving.

"I hate my job," James mumbled.

I turned to look at him and saw the pain in his face.

"You love your job. You hate this." I said gesturing at the three of us.

James cringed at my bluntness. He couldn't be coddled no matter his feelings for me. He needed to step up or step down.

"Are you able to perform your duties?" Marek asked, knowing where I was going with my comments.

"Yes, sir," James replied.

"Then do it," Marek said.

James gave him a sharp nod and stood at attention facing the door. I hadn't realized how relaxed he usually was until he moved into a formal guard stance. It was the difference between having my friend James in the elevator with us to having a bodyguard in here. The personal touch was suddenly void.

Seeing James like this hurt. I knew it was to spare his feelings but I wanted my friend.

"He will be fine," Marek said into my mind.

"No, he won't. This is bigger than either of us thought." I replied.

"Why do you say that?" Marek asked tilting my head up so I would look him in the eyes.

"Because I had a vision of him ordering a team to take you down. He did it because of me," I said.

"Was he protecting you?" Marek asked.

"Yes," I said.

"Then there is no concern," Marek said and dropped a kiss on my lips.

"But he gave an order to take you down. Doesn't that worry you?" I asked.

"His duty is to protect you at all costs. He is your Guardian. Although he has to be reminded you are not his romantically sometimes." Marek said with a small smile.

"So I shouldn't be worried?" I asked.

"Not at all. You can trust James more than you can trust me. After all, he

*does not crave your blood, just your company."*Marek said.

I thought about it as the elevator opened at the penthouse level. I have not been thinking of Marek as a vampire. Since attending a party at the Le Veneur mansion, I had been thinking of vampires differently. They could seem so normal that I had been letting my guard down with the ones I know. That was a dangerous practice I needed to end.

James checked the hall before motioning us forward. He had us wait while he inspected the apartment. Watching James move reminded me of the dream and his lack of clothing. James turned to me at that moment and I felt the heat rise in my cheeks. He looked confused but decided to ignore it.

"All clear. I'll be at the door if you need me." James said looking pointedly at me.

"Thank you, James," I said.

As he left, he gave Marek a hard look. It was Marek's turn to raise his hands in surrender.

After the door closed, I asked. "What was that about?"

"A reminder for me to behave," Marek said.

I raised an eyebrow at him.

"I am a bloodthirsty vampire if you recall," He said.

I walked over to him and clasped my hands behind his neck.

"I recall hearing something like that a few times today," I said.

"It is true. Vampires are monsters regardless of the pretty packaging you see on the outside." Marek said sounding serious.

"Are you trying to get me to stay away from you?" I asked.

"I am trying to get you to take this seriously. The only difference between me and Viktor is self-control. As you saw today, when my control slips, I am a danger to you." He said looking into my eyes.

He believed every word he was saying and I would be an idiot to disregard his message.

"I hear you. I'll remember you are a vampire." I said.

"Good," he said and I felt the satisfaction through our bond.

"Now that we are clear on that point, will you please take me to bed? I need a few hours of sleep before I start my new job this morning. I don't want my new boss to think I don't take the job seriously." I said winking at him.

"I think your new boss will not mind if you are a little late or tired." He said wagging his eyebrows as if mischief was on his mind.

Since Marek is technically my new boss, he would know.

"The doctor said to avoid heightened emotions. Are you trying to get me in trouble?" I asked with a smirk.

He smiled in response then lifted me into his arms. I kept my arms around his neck and pulled him in for a kiss while he walked to the bedroom. His arousal was easily felt through our bond and it was infectious.

Marek stepped into his dark gray bedroom and laid me down on the soft white coverlet of his low king-sized bed. His body followed mine as if we were magnetically attached to each other. Our lips never broke apart and when

Marek's body pressed into mine, I let out a huge sigh of relief.

The feel of him in my arms with my legs entwined in his made perfect sense. We were connected psychically so when we connected in body, it was an overwhelming feeling of rightness. It was as if we were made to fit together.

My fingers found the edge of his t-shirt and I pulled it up until he caught it himself. Marek pulled the fabric over his head then sent the shirt flying across the room. I watched his muscles ripple and pull as he moved. When he turned his head back to me, my eyes must have shown the intensity of my desire because he smiled down at me knowingly.

Marek pressed his hips into mine sending a zing of pleasure throughout my body. My fingernails dug into the flesh of his back involuntarily in response. A growling sound came from the back of his throat and he captured my lips, kissing me senseless.

When I was good and kissed, Marek started pulling my clothes off one piece at a time. By the time he got to my bra and panties, my breath was coming in pants and gasps. Marek had that effect on me. The anticipation of sex with him was almost enough to send me over the edge.

Marek ran his hand down the length of me from chin to hip, stopping only when he reached the apex of my thighs. He pushed the fabric of my underwear to the side and slid his hand over the sensitive flesh. My body reacted immediately, sending heat blooming throughout my core.

I was done waiting. I pulled at his sweats and he helped me by taking them off. The smile on his face told me he liked that I wanted him naked. I removed the remaining fabric from my body then pulled him to me. I wrapped my arms and legs around him and enjoyed the weight of his body pressed into mine.

The heat of his skin felt good against my own. I smiled up at him and the desire in his eyes melted me in ways I couldn't describe. This man, this vampire was my undoing.

I was the moth and Marek was the flame. I was drawn to him in ways that were set within my DNA. It was impossible to resist, not that I wanted to.

Marek shifted above me and I felt him push into me. Our bond flared to life as our bodies connected. I put the breaks on allowing it to run open and free. I didn't want a repeat of our power flaring through the building besides Dr. Wallace's warning that I needed to learn better control.

Any thought I had ceased when Marek began rocking his hips into mine, his length sliding in and out of me in delicious ways. I wrapped my legs tighter around him and met him thrust for thrust. We were both panting and clinging to each other as if we needed the other to breathe.

He kissed a trail along my jaw bone, finding his way to my neck. I wanted him to bite me so badly a whimpering sound came out of me. He laughed softly at my need but I could feel how much he wanted the same thing. We were both on the verge of an orgasm and the bite would push us both over the edge.

I saw the decision in his eyes when he made it. He rolled onto his back and pulled me on top of him without losing the rhythm of our movement. My disappointment fled as soon as I felt him slide deeper into my body. I couldn't stop myself from immediately riding him hard and fast.

Marek's eyes never left mine until we both exploded into a mind-blowing orgasm. I collapsed on top of him and he gathered me into his arms. He kissed my sweaty forehead as if it didn't bother him at all.

8

We must have fallen asleep shortly after having sex because I woke later with Marek still holding me while he slept. He had pulled a blanket over us, tucking us together nice and cozy. I wondered what time it was but didn't have to ponder it too long.

"It is too early to be awake," Marek mumbled.

I laughed softly and asked, "Did I wear you out?"

"I am ready for another round," He said nuzzling into my neck.

I shivered at his touch and said, "Sounds good to me."

My voice came out breathless betraying my need for him to bite me. Our blood exchanges were as important to me as sex. It was a connection that I couldn't have with anyone else and probably wouldn't have with anyone else.

Marek truly has ruined me for other men. Only another vampire would be able to match him and that was a sobering thought. Was I really only attracted to vampires now? My mind brought up the image of James naked in my vision of him and I realized attraction wasn't the problem.

It must have shown on my face because Marek's mood changed.

"What is wrong?" Marek asked.

"Umm," I hesitated. "I'm not exactly sure."

He gave me a look that said trying to bullshit him was pointless. He could read my emotions through our bond.

"Try to explain," He insisted.

"I'm freaking myself out about how much I love it when you bite me. The level of disappointment I felt last night when you chose not to and how much I need you to do it right now scares me." I said.

Marek relaxed and a soft smile lifted his lips. He must have been anticipating something direr.

"Do I have to remind you again that I am not a man? Feeling the pull of a blood exchange with me means you wish to renew our bond. It is acceptance of me as a vampire and an expression of your desire to deepen our relationship." He said.

"Huh, I hadn't thought of it like that at all." I said, marveling at how his thinking was so different from mine.

"So, should we continue to discuss it or do it?" Marek asked lifting an eyebrow.

"Do it," I said pulling him to my neck.

Marek kissed the sensitive skin there. Then sucked on my pulse before finally sinking his fangs into my neck. The familiar rush of pleasure hit me as he began to feed. I let myself fall into it and felt the bond between us blow open completely. The raw emotions and thoughts we both had mingled together into a sweet feeling of love.

We lingered in that feeling for a bit before Marek pulled back licking his lips clean. He smiled at me as he leaned over to open his side table. He pulled out a pocket knife and used it to cut a small slit in his neck for me. Marek smiled at me as I leaned into him to close my lips over the wound.

I pulled the sweet nectar of his blood into my mouth and let the flavor of warm caramel coat my tongue. The power within his blood exploded out into every cell of my body as Marek let his hands rove over my skin. Swallowing his blood while cradled in his arms healed something in me that had been broken when I saw him hurt last night.

I took a few more sips of his blood before pulling away. My body had a nice gentle hum going on combined with the warmth of Marek's body next to mine. I didn't want to move.

"Can we just stay in this bed all day?" I asked feeling perfectly content.

"Someone will interrupt us. It is a wonder no one has come in yet," Marek said.

"You just jinxed it," I said frowning at him.

He laughed, "Welcome to The Council of Guardians. Your hours of work will no longer follow a human schedule."

Marek leaned over and kissed me then got out of bed. I groaned at his loss and pulled the blanket up over my face.

"If you move now, we can share a shower." Marek teased.

I peaked my eyes out from the blanket and watched his naked butt disappear into the master bathroom. At the same moment, I heard a knock at the bedroom door. I could feel it was James. I made sure the blanket was covering me and called for him to come in.

"Sorry to bother you," James said.

His eyes landed on my neck and a flare of anger flashed behind his eyes. Clearly, he wasn't happy that Marek had bitten me.

"What's up, James?" I asked.

"The team reported back in on all the safe houses and we have a few problems." He said still standing in the doorway.

Marek walked out of the bathroom in a towel to answer James.

"Have the team assemble in the war room. We will join them shortly." Marek said.

James nodded then looked at me as if waiting for me to say something. I realized after he raised his eyebrows at me that he was waiting for me.

"Thanks. I'll be down after a quick shower." I said.

The slightest hint of a smile flitted across his lips before it disappeared. He ducked out of the room, closing the door behind him.

I sat up to go to the shower and noticed Marek watching me.

"What?" I asked.

"Did you have to give him the mental image of you in the shower?" Marek asked smirking.

"Shut up," I said throwing off the blanket and walking toward the bathroom.

He just smiled and watched me walk toward him. I pushed him back when I got to the door.

"Move it, mister. We have a team of people waiting for us." I said.

"Yes, ma'am," Marek said smirking as he moved out of my way.

I got the shower going and successfully avoided any shenanigans with Marek to complete our shower quickly.

While I dried my hair, Marek made a few phone calls. One was to have my work clothes brought up so I had appropriate attire for the day. I didn't think a t-shirt and jeans would do it considering Marek wore stylish suits when he was in the office.

I walked out of the bathroom to find Marek dressed to kill and barking orders into his cell phone. I picked my jaw off the floor and wiped the drool off my chin. He had on a navy suit that was clearly a designer brand and a creamy white shirt with a navy tie. He looked like he belonged on the runway at a fashion show.

An assortment of my clothes was laying on the bed. I didn't have anything as flashy as Marek's outfit but I did have a nice sheath dress that was professional but could cross over into sexy if I let it.

I pulled out the undergarments I needed and put them on. Then I pulled the dress up over my hips and put my arms through the holes. I smoothed my hands down the front and was happy with how the creamy white looked.

Marek made a noise and I looked over to find him staring at me with hooded eyes. I hadn't realized that he had been watching me.

"Will you zip me up?" I asked turning my back to him.

He walked over and placed his hands on my hips. He leaned in and kissed my neck giving me shivers. Then he moved his hand to the zipper. He kept a finger inside the dress while he zipped it so that it dragged up my back the whole way. I had to close my eyes and take a deep breath to shake the urge to turn around and push him down on the bed.

"Shall we go?" Marek asked softly.

I nodded unable to speak. Marek leaned in and gave me a quick kiss on the lips. He grabbed my hand then pulled me out of the room. I followed him and tried not to stumble following his fine ass.

We stepped out of the apartment where James was waiting for us. He took point as we moved to the elevators. We all filed into the elevator car and

James pressed the button for the ground floor. He kept his back to us as we descended.

"What did the team find?" Marek asked the back of James' head.

James turned around and looked at Marek. I wasn't sure he would answer the question based on the look on his face.

"Most of the safe houses reported back clean. The Aurora house and downtown Denver house, however, were found to have similar activity as the Boulder safe house. They have been systematically tested for weaknesses and have been deemed unsafe." James said.

"Were the same vampires involved?" I asked.

"Yes," James confirmed.

"Then they are testing all of our operations not just what is near their base," Marek stated.

"It looks that way," James replied.

"What do we do next?" I asked, unsure what my role would be, let alone what the Council should do.

We exited the elevator and a man dressed in a black business suit approached before James or Marek could answer me.

"Excuse me," the man bowed then asked, "Madame Summers?"

"Yes," I asked wondering who the man was.

He bowed so deeply that I was worried he might topple over before he righted himself.

"The Grand Master has requested your presence. He would see you now." The man said it as if I had no choice but to go immediately.

I looked to James and Marek and they both nodded their heads that this was on the up and up.

"I will coordinate with you after your audience with Sebastian," Marek assured me.

James motioned me forward and as soon as I took a step, the errand boy (for lack of a better term) turned on his heel and led the way. While I followed him I couldn't help the feeling of being summoned to the principal's office like a teenager who had done something naughty. Having James following behind me made me feel better.

I tried to hang back and walk next to James so I could talk to him but he put his hand on my lower back pressing me forward. I took the hint and walked ahead of him. The little I knew of vampire etiquette stated that he, my guard, did not have the same rank and therefore had to remain behind me.

I used the walk to the Grand Master's office to shake off my insecurities. Navigating the politics in the office was something I had not thought about before accepting a job in the organization. It was something I needed to keep in mind when I walked through the office doors.

We passed through two security doors before arriving in the reception area outside Sebastian's office. The security was solely for entry to the Grand Master's office. It was an impressive amount of security for one man or vampire rather.

The errand boy that brought me here ducked back out the door we had come through, leaving me to approach the large oak door without him. A familiar person, Caden Thorn aka Guardian Thorn, stood at attention. His eyes lit up upon seeing me and he bowed appropriately to acknowledge my rank.

"Good morning, Madame Summers," Caden said.

He rapped his knuckles on the door without turning around in two quick hits. Then paused and struck once more. It must have been code for "your next appointment is here".

Caden flashed me a warm smile before turning to open the door. He must have heard a response that I couldn't pick up.

"This way Madame. Your Guardian can wait here while you meet with The Grand Master." Caden said.

While he was looking at me, he was clearly letting James know he wasn't welcome to enter the office with me. I could only imagine the conversations that occurred in that office. The Grand Master probably had more secrets than anyone else in the organization except for maybe Marek.

I walked into Sebastian's office and found myself in a large room filled with plants and art. It was tastefully done and just edgy enough to be cool. He had a seating area with a couch and two chairs off to the side and a large mahogany desk with two chairs opposite.

Sebastian had another guest sitting across from him. When he turned around I almost gasped but held it together. Why was Nikko Manetti talking with the Grand Master?

"Madam Summers, welcome," Sebastian said standing up then bowing to me.

I returned the bow feeling thankful for all the research I had done on what was expected of me.

"Madam Summers," Nikko said bowing to me.

"Come, my dear. Let's sit over here. I had a small amount of food delivered in case you were hungry." Sebastian said leading me to the seating area.

He settled into one of the chairs and I sat on the couch near him. Nikko sat in the chair across from Sebastian.

I grabbed a mug and poured myself some coffee while eyeing a few pastries that looked delicious.

"You are probably wondering why I asked you in today?" Sebastian said.

"I admit I'm curious," I said watching his face for any clues of what might be going on.

I hoped he wasn't going to yell at me for ordering surveillance off when I met with Viktor yesterday.

"Most importantly, welcome to the team. I look forward to what you will accomplish and how you will compliment Master Volkov." Sebastian said.

"Thank you. I am honored for the offer and the opportunity." I said.

"I do have a matter of some delicacy to discuss with you. I've asked Mr. Manetti to join us to lend his expertise to the conversation. I asked to meet you here so that our conversation could not be overheard." He said.

"Okay, what is going on?" I asked growing concerned.

"Viktor Ivanov has made a claim of negligence against you and is petitioning the Council to release him into the custody of his eldest son. His lawyer filed the motion this morning and a hearing has been scheduled for this afternoon to determine the validity of his allegations." Sebastian said.

"Negligent how? I don't understand." I said confusion making a fog out of my thoughts.

"Viktor states that you are his master but you have done nothing but torment him since forming the bond. He says you have withheld your blood and not allowed him to connect with you in a meaningful way." Sebastian said.

"With all due respect, the bond was never meant to be permanent. It was a means to remove the curse he put on me to prevent my death. My intention from the very beginning was to let the bond fade or to break it if that was possible." I said feeling my heart beat faster in my chest.

"We have Master Volkov's account of the events and I do believe that no ill intent was premeditated on your part. What we are challenged with now is disproving his allegation of neglect after the fact. Fortunately, since you are now an employee, the Council has been put in the position of defending you. For that, we have retained Mr. Manetti to represent you and protect the Council's reputation." Sebastian gestured to Nikko.

Nikko flashed me one of his thousand-watt smiles. Nikko was wearing a charcoal gray suit paired with a blue button-up shirt and black tie. He looked delicious and I tried not to let it distract me.

"You couldn't have chosen a better attorney. Nikko is the best." I said.

My comment pleased Nikko and even made Sebastian grin in approval.

"I have been studying the allegations and the first-hand accounts of your interactions with Master Ivanov since the bond formed. Do you mind if I ask you a few questions?" Nikko asked.

"Not at all. I understand the process." I said feeling nervous.

"Some of these questions may be difficult to answer or cause you distress. Please know I do not ask them lightly." Nikko said.

"I trust you," I said and felt the shock of actually believing what I just said.

Nikko smiled and went on, "Since creating the bond with Viktor, have you shared blood with him?"

"No, I haven't," I answered.

"Why not?" Nikko asked.

"Several reasons I suppose but mostly because I never wanted the bond in the first place. I want it to fade." I said.

"Again, I apologize for having to ask these questions but what are your other reasons?" He asked.

I thought about it before answering, "I can't stand the thought of anyone but Marek having my blood. I also can't stand the thought of anyone but Marek giving me blood. Besides that Viktor kidnapped my sister and tortured her before finally turning her into a vampire. He and I don't get along."

"Are you bonded with Marek? I didn't think it was possible to be bonded with more than one vampire." Nikko said scribbling some notes on his pad.

"From what I understand it shouldn't be possible. In fact, I thought my bond with Marek shattered when Viktor forced me to bond with him. Sometime later I felt pieces of the bond between Marek and me. I don't know how, but I pulled our bond back together without breaking the bond with Viktor." I said.

Nikko looked at Sebastian as if sharing a private thought. Sebastian nodded his approval and Nikko proceeded.

"Tell me what happened when you met privately with Master Ivanov after asking the guardians to leave the room and for surveillance to be turned off?" Nikko asked.

"I was asking him about what he knew about an ancient vampire we are tracking named Magdalena. He said he would talk to me but only if we were alone. We needed the intel so I met his request." I said.

"Did anything happen during that conversation? Did Viktor express any concerns with you or make any requests?" Nikko asked.

"He was very helpful and told me a great deal. I thanked him but he did ask for me to visit him regularly." I said.

"Have you seen him since?" He asked.

"No," I said.

"Did you grab his hand or give him a hug? Any physical contact what so ever?" He asked.

"I grabbed his hand when I thanked him. I didn't like the look in his eyes when I did it and let go immediately." I said.

"He states that he is pining for you Ember. He cannot stand to be without you for this long of a stretch. This is why he filed the motion." Nikko said.

"I don't have time to hold his hand while I'm searching for a crazy vampire. He is a master and can take care of himself. He forced me into the bond. The only reason I'm his master at all is that I was more powerful than him." I said.

"That may be so but you are required to tend to your thralls or they wither. If he wasn't in custody, he could come to you when he needed you but that isn't the case. He has no way to get what he needs physically and emotionally." Nikko said.

"Wait a minute. You are saying that Viktor is my thrall? That can't be true. He's a master vampire." I said.

My heart was racing and my head felt light. I didn't think it was possible to harm Viktor.

"Tell me why you negotiated with Viktor to answer your questions instead of compelling him to answer?" Sebastian said.

"Because ordering him to do it felt wrong," I admitted.

"You have compassion for him that is good. I met with Viktor and his guards earlier this morning. I found that he is unable to resist your commands and often craves your touch. He cannot help the way he feels even though he has tried. The guards confirmed his behavior is like other thralls they have held in the past. I do not think any of us realized it before now because he has been trying to hide the effects." Sebastian said.

"So I *am* neglecting him. I never thought I would feel bad for Viktor." I said feeling sick to my stomach.

"I think it best we offer a compromise to Viktor that will make this complaint of his go away and solve the problems he is having. Going to live with his son's coven would only temporarily relieve his distress. Given his past service to the Council, I think it would be best for us all to agree to move Viktor into your care, Ember." Sebastian said.

"What does that mean exactly?" I asked, not liking the sounds of it.

"Viktor will be your responsibility until next week when a more permanent solution can be found. He will live with you in your assigned residence. It will be up to you to keep him in line as well as to ease his symptoms." Sebastian said.

"There has to be another option." I insisted.

"I've spoken with his lawyer and this is an arrangement Master Ivanov finds agreeable. It is what's best for your thrall and the Council. It will also save you from facing a charge of neglect which would cost you your job and possible imprisonment." Nikko said.

"Well, I believe that concludes our business," Sebastian said. "It was good to see you Ember. Please coordinate with Guardian Leigh to process Viktor's release. Do take a pastry with you."

Sebastian shook my hand and motioned for the door. I looked back before leaving and caught Nikko's eye. He gave me a look of pity which didn't reassure me at all. I walked out of the office in a daze wondering how I was going to tell Marek.

9

My eyes landed on James when I walked out of Sebastian's office. I couldn't keep the truth of what just happened from my face. He was looking at me like he could see the pain.

"What's wrong?" James asked.

"We need to find Marek. Now." I said stomping out of the waiting area.

"He should be in his office if he's done meeting with the team. We should find him there." He said.

"Show me the way," I said.

James took me down the hall to Marek's office where he was dismissing the team. As they filed out the door I pushed my way past them unable to wait a moment longer than necessary.

Marek met me and held up his hand for me to wait for the others to leave. He closed the door behind the last person and turned to me expectantly.

"What is wrong?" He asked.

"Viktor is claiming I am neglecting him as his master. His lawyer filed a motion formally accusing me of neglect. Moving him to my custody is Sebastian's solution to the problem. He says Viktor is my thrall and that I need to fix the problem I created." I said.

"Your thrall?" James and Marek said together.

"I know. I'm not a vampire so it shouldn't be possible. But, Sebastian tested Viktor himself and he says it's true. Viktor's been hiding it from your Guardians." I said feeling my knees getting weak from the stress.

Marek looked mad enough to pull the arms off whoever missed the signs. From what I understood about thralls, they would die if they didn't have regular blood exchanges with their master. Physical touch was another big part of the equation but the facts about how much was needed could vary from person to person.

"James, pull the logs on which Guardians have been on Viktor's rotation then arrange for him to be transferred into Ember's custody. I want any Guardian that failed to report symptoms put on immediate disciplinary review." Marek said.

"Yes, sir. Do you assume primary guard for Madame Summers?" James asked.

"Yes, of course. I will not let her out of my sight until you return." Marek said.

Marek's face was blank but the emotional turmoil coming through our bond felt like a tsunami. I expected him to be upset but the depth of what I felt was overwhelming.

I fell back onto the couch in his office after James left.

"Talk to me," I said to Marek.

Marek kept the stoic blank face in place as if it were a shield against the news. I could imagine what was going through his mind. The same thoughts were probably running through mine too.

"If Viktor is your thrall, that explains how we were able to keep our bond after you formed one with him," Marek said running his hands through his hair.

He looked like he might start pulling the hair out.

"This is bad right? How did this happen?" I asked needing him to reassure me.

"It is neither bad nor good. We have established your power does not work as anyone else's might. It would be best if you refrain from taking or sharing blood with anyone but Viktor until we know more." Marek said.

"I am not sharing blood with Viktor!" I said.

Just thinking about exchanging blood with Viktor made me angry.

"You must. He is your thrall and cannot function without a blood exchange. This is not like our bond. We can go without but he will wither and die if you do not nourish him." Marek said.

"I know but this is Viktor we are talking about not a stray cat. I don't want to take him in. Why didn't he say something?" I said feeling overwhelmed.

"Would you have believed him if he told you?" Marek said.

"No," I said feeling sick to my stomach.

He sat down on the couch next to me and pulled me into his arms.

"You can do this," He said with more certainty than I thought possible.

"From what I already know about thralls, I want nothing to do with this," I said.

"You have to admit what you feel for Viktor has changed since before the bond. I have seen you with him. You care for him." Marek said softly.

I pulled back out of his embrace to look him in the eyes.

"There have been moments that I can't explain and feelings I don't want to have when I'm near him. It's better when I don't see him. I'm scared to have him near me all the time." I admitted.

"He has to obey any order you give him and you will order him not to harm you. That will help." Marek offered.

"Sure, I can do that," I said but didn't admit what I was truly worried about.

Getting close to Viktor on a personal level was going to blur the line I had drawn of him being the bad guy. Sharing blood was going to hit me hard emotionally. I don't want to like him and I already have feelings I don't want.

"You could invite Natalie to stay with you. She could be a buffer between you." Marek suggested.

"No, I can't use her to shield me. She can visit. That will make them both happy but I can't have her there for when we..." I couldn't even say exchange blood.

Marek didn't say anything which I appreciated. I couldn't handle him telling me not to do it or to get jealous.

The office door opened then and James walked in. He noticed that he walked in on something.

"What happened?" James asked.

"It is good you are back. We were just about to talk about the safe houses." Marek said.

I gave him a look of gratitude. A change in subject was very welcome.

Marek proceeded to catch us up on what happened while I was meeting with the Grand Master. He ordered the Guardians to avoid all safe houses and doubled protection on new assets. That left less manpower to go after Magdalena's coven. Marek suggested we use outside resources to hunt them down.

"The Le Veneur coven has helped us in the past to hunt rogues. They could handle the bulk of the leg work and bring in all the vampires they find." James suggested.

"Julien's coven?" I asked.

"He did name you a friend of the coven, Ember. Maybe you can sweet-talk him into a good deal?" James said.

The grin on James' face didn't give me the warm and fuzzies. It actually made my stomach hurt again.

"It could be your first official act in your new role. You could bring Viktor with you to help negotiate." Marek suggested.

"You have got to be kidding. Bring Viktor with me?" I asked incredulously.

"You need to keep him with you to nourish the bond. He is Julien's sire. It cannot hurt to bring him." Marek said.

"Fine. A field trip it is then." I said. "James, when can I pick Viktor up?"

"Nikko was filing the paperwork when I went downstairs so he should be ready now," James said.

"Manetti is working the case?" Marek asked.

"Sebastian hired Nikko to advise on the case and act as my lawyer. He would have defended me had they not come up with a compromise Viktor would accept." I said.

"I see," Marek said but his teeth were so firmly clenched it was almost too difficult to make out what he said.

"So how do I do this? Do I call Julien and set up a time to meet or is there a protocol I'm not aware of?" I asked.

"Your assistant can take care of it," Marek said.

"I have an assistant?" I asked.

"We share one. All you need to do is let him know what you want and he will make it happen," Marek said.

"Good. I guess I'll get on that then." I said.

I stood to go but Marek grabbed me first.

"Hey," Marek said taking my face in his hands. "Be careful with Julien and with Viktor. Do not forget they are vampires."

"I'll be fine," I said.

He kissed me softly on the lips then let me go.

"James knows your job better than anyone. He can teach you what you need to learn. The rest Benjamin will take care of for you. Check-in with me later." Marek said.

"I will," I said then followed James out of Marek's office.

James walked a step behind me until we left the offices. As soon as we stepped into the common area James slid his hand into mine. I clutched it tight and tried to keep the tears away.

"I can always count on you to know what I need. What would I do without you?" I said looking up at James.

"You never have to worry about that. I'm yours. Forever and always," He said then brought my hand up to his lips.

He kissed my hand and I felt a sort of tingle travel from his lips through my arm. It didn't stop until it hit my heart.

"What was that?" I asked turning to face James.

"I made you a solemn vow, Ember. I will always be true to you and you can always count on me to be what you need." James said.

"James, it felt like magic," I said confused.

"There is nothing to worry about," James smiled. "Now. Let's go get your vamp and take him to his son. If we are lucky, he may even help."

"I don't think help is possible with Viktor," I said.

"As usual, you underestimate your influence," James said.

I gave him a doubtful look. He had more confidence in me than I had in myself. It was a trait I liked about him but when it came to Viktor, I didn't desire a pep talk.

I knew my way to the holding cells but needed James to help me get Viktor out. My only experience had been visiting prisoners, not taking them home.

We met with Guardian Murphy who accompanied us to Viktor's cell. She had been his guard every time I visited him.

"You may not recognize him when you see him. Master Ivanov has been fighting it but he needs a blood exchange ASAP. I recommend you do that before you leave the cell." She said to me.

"How bad is it?" I asked shocked.

"Bad," She said looking concerned.

Murphy opened the cell door to let me in. Viktor was huddled on his bed in the corner. He was shaking but when he heard the door he immediately straightened and tried to hold himself up. He ended up in a sort of half upright half slumped position that was pitiful.

"Viktor," I said in a soft voice.

"Master, you have come for a visit?" He said it like a question.

Viktor's eyes were cloudy and his skin dull. His hair hung limp. He looked like he belonged in a hospital.

"Damn it Viktor! Why didn't you tell me what was going on?" I said rushing to his side.

I wrapped my arms around him and he collapsed into my embrace. His hands searched until they found the bare skin on my arms. The moment he touched skin, his shaking stopped. It was like a switch had been flipped making him better.

The bond between us snapped into place and I could feel his hunger for me. What surprised me was that I felt a spike of hunger for him. It was different from my craving for Marek.

"Are you really here? Or am I dreaming again?" Viktor said in a weak voice.

"I'm really here," I said stroking his back.

Viktor pulled back to look at me. His eyes had cleared slightly but they were still cloudy.

"This can't be real," He said then looked away.

He seemed to be searching for something to ground him. It was shocking. It hadn't been that long since I saw him last and he was perfectly fine then. He had no symptoms of whatever this was.

"Hey," I said turning his face back to mine. "You're sick. You need to take some of my blood to make you better."

Those were words I never thought I would speak. I pushed down nausea threatening to rise at the thought of allowing Viktor to bite me. He needed this and it was my punishment for not taking care of this before now.

"You would let me drink from you?" Viktor asked and light sparkled in his eyes.

"Yes, take my wrist and drink," I said clenching my teeth in anticipation.

Viktor didn't wait. He bit into my wrist as soon as he could get it to his mouth.

The pain of his teeth entering my flesh made me flinch but it quickly turned into something pleasant. As he swallowed my blood, a light floating feeling overcame me followed by a pleasurable tingling sensation that settled into my chest.

I found myself petting Viktor while he drank. With each touch, he made a slight purring sound that made me happy. After a few seconds, his skin regained a healthy look and his hair became soft and shiny.

James made a noise and I looked over to see a pained look on his face.

"What?" I asked.

"I think he's had enough," He said.

I looked back at Viktor, realizing James was right.

"That's enough, Viktor. Stop drinking." I said.

He stopped mid swallow and the blood that hadn't made it down his throat ran out his mouth and onto my lap. I was about to yell at him when it hit me that he did exactly what I said. He literally stopped drinking, leaving what was left in his mouth to run out.

Viktor looked at me with clear eyes and smiled. Even with the blood dripping from his chin and staining his teeth he looked good.

"Time to go," I said standing up.

Viktor looked at me confused.

"Well don't just sit there. You are coming with me." I said and turned to walk out of the cell.

"I don't understand," Viktor said scrunching up his face.

I took his hand and pulled him toward the door, "I'm springing you from this joint. You're going to stay with me instead of rotting in this cell."

All he could say was, "Thank you, master."

We walked out of the detention center with all eyes turned our way. I had blood on my clothes but their eyes were on Viktor. James stayed behind Viktor and Viktor walked just behind me.

When we reached the elevators for the residences I realized I had been holding Viktor's hand the entire time. I let go and tried to hide the awkwardness by pressing the elevator button a few times.

"Where are we going?" Viktor asked.

"I need to change since you got blood on my white dress and so do you," I said.

Viktor looked remorseful and I almost laughed.

"James, can someone bring Viktor something to wear? I imagine he will want to look good when he sees Julien." I said.

Viktor perked up and took inventory of his attire. He must have found it lacking because he frowned down at himself.

"I'll make a call and have something brought up," James said.

"A suit in my style if you please. I don't want to look like I've been in jail for a month." Viktor said.

I smiled at his rude behavior. He was back to the Viktor I knew.

James rolled his eyes and stepped away while he made his call.

"Why are we going to see Julien? Not that I am complaining, my dear." Viktor said.

"It's official business of the Council. We need to hire his team." I said.

"Why are you going and not one of the Council errand boys?" Viktor looked confused.

"I work for the Council now and Julien made me a friend to the coven. Marek thought I would be the best person for the job." I said just as the elevator dinged.

We stepped into the elevator car and James hurried in behind us. He put his phone in his pocket and gave me a sharp nod. He must have arranged for

Viktor's clothes.

"What's the job?" Viktor asked.

I looked at James and he didn't warn me against telling Viktor so I caught him up on the situation. Considering he was going to be living with me for the next week, he was bound to hear about it anyway.

"The information is confidential Viktor. You may not share it with anyone unless I give you the okay to do so." I said.

"Yes, master." He said dutifully.

"Do you have to call me master?" I asked.

"You gave an order and I acknowledged it," Viktor said.

"Very well but I prefer you to use my name when we are in private, understood?" I said.

"Yes, master. I will call you Ember when we are alone." He said with mischief in his eyes.

"You are impossible. How can you make that sound sexual?" I said exasperated.

"What male wouldn't want you alone?" Viktor asked perfectly serious.

I squirmed under his gaze but didn't find any relief when I met James' eyes. They seemed to burn with desire too.

I was saved by the elevator reaching our floor and I bolted from the confined space. If the guys noticed, they didn't say anything. I practically ran to the door of my apartment and let myself in. James made some grumbles about checking the place that I ignored.

I went straight for the master bedroom and tried to unzip my dress. After the third combination of bending my arms didn't work, I felt hands on me. I whirled around to find Viktor standing too close.

"What are you doing?" I asked.

"Helping you to unzip your dress," He said looking innocent.

"I can get it myself," I said.

"Uh-huh. How were you doing that exactly?" He asked and stepped closer again.

"Viktor I don't trust you and I certainly don't want you undressing me," I said stepping away from him.

"That zipper was not designed for self-service. Did you zip it up yourself this morning?" He asked.

"No," I said.

"I promise to only undo the zipper then let you be," He said.

I heard voices from the front room. Viktor's clothing must have arrived.

"Fine. Help with the zipper then leave." I said.

Viktor walked forward slowly as if he was scared I would run away. It was a smart move. Running felt like a good option.

When he was next to me, I turned around and lifted my hair out of the way. Viktor pulled the zipper down to my waist then stopped. I heard him take a deep breath and when I turned around he was walking out of the room. He left the door open when he exited so I followed him to close it. When I reached the door, he turned around and gave me a small smile.

I slammed the door in his face and locked it. I ignored the thumping of my heart while I picked out a new outfit. I opted for a skirt and blouse to avoid any zipper situations that I couldn't handle myself. Not that I had much of a choice. Most of my clothes had already been moved to Marek's penthouse.

I made a mental note to have some of my clothes brought back down. There was no way the three of us were going to share an apartment. I would stay here with Viktor and go to Marek's place when I needed an escape. Alone time on a separate floor would be better than behind a door especially with vampire hearing.

I finished tucking my blouse in then went out to the living room. James was sitting on the sofa. He looked relaxed until I realized he was staring at one of the bedroom doors. I walked in front of the door and knocked.

The door opened to Viktor in his underwear.

"Put some clothes on!" I yelled.

"I was doing that when you knocked," Viktor said.

"Hurry up. I'm ready to go." I said and walked away.

"Yes, Ember," He said and I swear he purposely made it sound sexual again.

I gritted my teeth and ignored it. I also tried to scrub the image of the salt and pepper haired man naked down to his undies. For an older man, he sure had a lot of muscle tone.

"You stepped into that one," James said smiling.

"I'm aware," I said and plopped down next to him on the sofa.

I leaned my head against his shoulder and breathed him in. It had a calming effect on me. The reality of having Viktor in my home was liable to cause me to panic more often than normal. I was glad to have James here.

"I won't be able to come in with you to the meeting. Dhampirs aren't allowed in a vampire's den." James said.

"Crap James. I forgot about that. So I'm going in alone with Viktor as my backup?" I asked.

"Yep," He said.

"Here's hoping Julien really is a friend," I said.

10

Viktor walked out of the bedroom and he finally looked like the vampire I knew. There was no trace of the sickness that had crippled him earlier. His eyes were bright and even twinkling with a hint of mischief.

"I leave the room for five minutes and you cuddle up to the dhampir?" Viktor said.

"Shut it, vampire. He's my friend." I said standing up.

"Yes, master," Viktor said bowing.

"Viktor, that wasn't an order," I said watching him struggle.

I walked over to him and took his hands. He was reacting with extremes and I didn't like it.

"I hate to interrupt but we're going to be late if we don't leave now," James said.

I dropped Viktor's hands but he immediately placed his hand on my back as I started to walk away as if he had to touch me. He probably did and that made me uneasy. I had to figure this out or he was going to be attached to my hip, literally.

We made our way downstairs and into the garage. James had called down ahead to have a car brought around. I shouldn't have been shocked when I saw the car but I didn't anticipate a luxury ride.

A blood-red Maserati Quattroporte with heavily tinted windows pulled up in front of us and my knees got weak. I love cars and this car is one of the sexiest luxury vehicles on the planet. Marek has a black one and if I knew the Guardians had access to vehicles like this I would have borrowed one for a joy ride weeks ago.

James stepped forward and opened the back door for me, motioning for me to get in. Viktor walked to the other side and sat behind the driver. James closed my door then moved to the front seat.

"Where to?" The driver asked.

"Murphy?" I asked seeing the driver for the first time.

"The one and only," She said turning to look at me.

"The Le Veneur mansion," Viktor said in a crisp tone that showed he didn't think much of Murphy or that I was speaking with her in a familiar tone.

I gave him a look and he just shrugged his shoulders like he was asking what the big deal was. He looked more relaxed wearing a suit and seated in a luxury car but I didn't let that fool me. He wasn't okay.

I used my connection to Viktor to speak privately with him, mind to mind, *"Tell me how to fix this. You feel broken."*

Viktor cringed at the word broken. He looked at me and his eyes traveled to my neck where I knew my pulse was beating away at a higher rate than normal. As much as I didn't want to admit it, I wanted him to bite me again. In fact, I had a sudden urge to bite him back.

"Tasting your blood took the edge off my dear but without a full blood exchange, I will remain 'broken' as you say," Viktor said using our mind link.

"You need me to take your blood too?" I asked knowing it was right without even saying it.

If my instincts were correct, and I thought they were, Viktor would need both my blood and me taking his blood to achieve balance. Once he was balanced, he would be himself again.

"Now would be a good time before Julien sees me like this. He knows an allegation was made but he thinks it was a trick to get me out. I don't want him to know how bad it really is," Viktor said.

Viktor's eyes were pleading for me to give him what he needed. The problem was I agreed with him and agreeing with Viktor always upset me.

"Fine," I said aloud.

Viktor smiled and it made me happy. I couldn't keep the scowl off my face in response.

"What's that?" James asked turning around.

"Eyes forward Guardians," I snapped.

"Yes, ma'am." James and Murphy said together.

I shocked myself at how quickly I ordered my guards. Viktor pulled my attention back to him. He removed his suit jacket and rolled up the sleeve of his shirt. As soon as his skin was exposed enough to keep from getting blood on his sleeve, he bit into his own wrist then he offered it to me.

I pounced on it like I was starving and his blood was the first food I had seen in weeks. The flavor exploded on my tongue and something within me clicked into place. I heard a growl and couldn't tell if it came from me or Viktor. Maybe it was both. Whatever it was, I liked it.

Viktor's evergreen scent engulfed me while the sharp fresh flavor of his blood filled my mouth. I pulled on his arm and sucked harder but the flow was slowing. Damn vampires and their healing speed. I bit down encouraging the flow and was rewarded with a fresh gush of the delicious nectar.

The world shifted and I got a little dizzy. I forced myself to release Viktor's wrist and realized I was now on his lap with him cradling me from behind. His face was pressed into my neck and I could feel his fangs scraping the delicate skin. My body shivered as thoughts of him biting me overtook my consciousness.

"Yes," I said into his mind.

Viktor bit me a second later and my entire body thrummed with rightness. We completed the blood exchange cycle. I could feel Viktor fully again and knew he was back to himself.

"That's enough Viktor," I said out loud.

He removed his fangs then licked my neck clean. I tried not to enjoy the feeling but couldn't help myself. The neck is a sensitive area to begin with then add in a vampire who knows what he is doing and you have a recipe for heaven.

Viktor whispered into my ear, "Thank you, Master."

I ignored the goosebumps that popped up on my arms and scooted off his lap. He followed me, keeping an arm around my shoulders.

"Please return to your side of the car, Viktor," I said gently. "And pull yourself together."

I pointed at his disheveled clothing and he immediately rolled down his sleeve. While he fastened his cuff and pulled his blazer back on I checked my own clothing. I made a point to avoid the eyes of the Guardians in the front seat. I was not looking forward to seeing the censure in James' eyes.

Just as I finished my self-inventory, we pulled onto the Le Veneur property. Viktor turned me to face him. He ran his eyes over me, checking for anything amiss.

"You have a drop of blood on your bottom lip," He said.

Without thinking I swept my tongue over my lips and was rewarded with a tiny spark of bliss at finding the blood. I ignored the look in Viktor's eyes. I didn't need to see what I could feel so acutely between us. Seeing me ingest his blood filled the need he had been denied before.

The car stopped moving and Viktor jumped out. He moved so fast, I thought he was getting away. I was about to yell for my team to recapture him when my door opened. Viktor stood there looking smug and holding out his hand to me.

I rolled my eyes at him then indulged him by taking his hand. He helped me out of the car then he stepped up behind me. His hand went to the small of my back and he waited for me to take the lead.

I snuck a glance at the Guardians. They stayed in the car, letting me run point and acknowledging Viktor's right to be by my side. Taking that as permission, I moved to the front door with as much swagger as I dared.

Viktor's fingers stayed on my back as the front door opened without a knock. Someone had clearly been watching our approach. The vampire who came into view looked between Viktor and me, looking confused.

"Madame Summers to see Master Le Veneur," Viktor announced from behind me.

The greeter immediately bowed low to me and motioned for us to enter. I walked forward pretending to ignore the guy that opened the door. Truth was, I didn't trust any of them including Viktor. When the door closed behind me I tried very hard not to flinch. I spared a thought for James wishing he was the one walking in with me but let it go so I didn't get distracted.

The house was familiar but the vampires milling around were not. A woman dressed in a mini skirt and tight blazer stepped into my field of vision. She wasn't wearing a shirt under the jacket and I hid my smile instead of laughing out loud. Viktor made a noise behind me and the woman nodded sharply.

She bowed low to me and I marveled at how her boobs stayed inside the blazer. Her bleach blonde locks and mask of makeup hid whatever there was of her natural beauty. She was human and I assumed the outfit and makeup were to hide whatever flaws she had so she could stand out next to the vampires in the coven.

"This way please madame," She said then turned on her heel and walked down the hall.

I followed her and hoped she didn't fall off her five-inch stilettos. She wiggled her way around a corner then motioned for us to go through the door beside her. We went in and settled in on a couch that faced two chairs. I wanted to have Viktor right next to me in case I needed him for something.

"May I get you anything while you wait?" She said, leaning her head to one side and baring her neck by pulling her hair to one side.

"No," I said a little too sharply.

Viktor grabbed my hand.

"That will be all, Misty," Viktor said.

"Master Le Veneur will join you momentarily," Misty said, seeming not to notice my rude remark.

She bowed then left the room.

"It is customary to offer a master the blood of a human to show hospitality," Viktor said softly.

"I know. I've just never seen it happen." I said.

"Get used to it my dear. You are a master and will be offered blood any time you visit a nest." He said eyes sparkling.

"Then they need to offer me vampire blood," I said and then kicked myself for admitting it.

Viktor smiled like he was proud of me, then entwined his fingers with mine. He lifted my hand, placing a kiss on the back of my hand. He kept eye contact with me while he did it and I felt my breath hitch.

"That's enough," I said gritting my teeth.

Having Viktor as my thrall was one thing but this dance of seduction he was playing pushed me too far.

"My apologies, Master," Viktor said letting my hand go.

A noise at the door had me turning to see what it was. Julien stood there in amazement looking between me and Viktor. He looked like he didn't know quite what to say.

"It's true," Julien said stepping into the room.

Viktor and I stood and I was ready to bow when Viktor said in my mind,

"You do not bow to him. You are the master of his sire."

Viktor cocked his head to the side as if chiding Julien for not dropping at my feet. He noticed and immediately bowed. Then he walked forward and took my hand.

"It is lovely to see you Madame Summers or should I call you Master?" He said kissing my hand.

I smiled at him and said, "Since you are my friend, you know you can call me Ember."

I knew enough about vampire politics to never turn down a title. I also reminded him of the friendship we formed not so long ago.

"As the master of my sire, I find it difficult to depart from ceremony where you are concerned," Julien admitted.

"Julien," Viktor said with impatience.

"Yes, Sire," Julien said never letting his eyes leave mine. "Ember, you look ravishing as always. To what do I owe the pleasure of your visit?"

Julien motioned for us to sit. He took the chair directly across from me and crossed his legs in a relaxed pose. He looked anything but relaxed.

"It's good to see you too," I said smiling. "I wish I could say it's purely a social call."

"Business then. I have to say I am pleased to see my Sire out and about. When he called me, he was rotting in a jail cell." Julien commented.

"I do enjoy her company infinitely more than that of the Council Guardians," Viktor said with a smile.

I tried to keep the blush off my cheeks but let's face it, you can't hide blood from a vampire. Julien's lips curled up on one side as he thought of what my reaction meant. He probably thought Viktor and I were having sex which made me blush again.

Viktor took my hand and it grounded me. Julien's eyes caught the movement.

"I had hoped to woo you myself but the line of interested parties keeps getting longer and longer. My heart doesn't heal well from rejection," Julien said leaning forward.

"I can't imagine anyone rejecting you if your intentions were true," I said smiling.

He was a smooth-talking French-speaking gorgeous man. What wasn't there to like?

"Mmmm," Julien purred. "If you open yourself to suiters, please do consider me one of them."

"Julien is considered one of the most sought after mates in the vampire community. It would honor me if you chose him." Viktor said.

I could feel his unease at the prospect of his child mating with me. While I knew it would be an honor for someone in his line to mate with someone powerful, Viktor wanted the honor to be his.

"I have not declared an interest in taking suiters. However, if that happens to change, I will remember you offered." I said smiling at Julien.

"Good. Now, what can I do for you Ember? My coven and I are at your disposal." Julien said.

I laid out the Council's needs and negotiated a price. Julien's hunters would track down and deliver as many of Magdalena's vampires as they could. They would avoid her nest so as to not poke the monster directly.

Viktor had a few provisions added on my behalf that I wouldn't have thought to ask for and I was grateful. Marek had been right that he would be an asset. Julien didn't fight too hard against them. I wondered if he didn't actually enjoy the process.

We completed our business and headed back to the Council compound. Viktor was quiet on the ride back and I was thankful to have some time to think. What we did in this car on the way to Julien's place was bothering me.

James had yet to make eye contact with me. I figured he either already reported the blood exchange to Marek or he would as soon as he checked in. I didn't want it to come from him. I needed to get him alone before I saw Marek.

When we pulled into the garage complex I asked Murphy and Viktor to step out of the car. James sat staring straight ahead until I said his name. Then he turned around and met my eyes for the first time in hours.

"We need to talk," I said.

"I know what you are worried about but you don't need to be. I swore a vow to you Ember. That supersedes any oath I have to the Council." James said.

"What did you do, James?" I asked scared.

"What I had to do to satisfy the ache in my soul. I am yours. I may work for the Council but you are my master." He said.

I felt a chill roll through my body. If what he said was true, I now had two people with which I was responsible for their care.

"This isn't the time to discuss this but we will discuss it," I promised him.

"Yes, ma'am," James said then stepped out of the car.

James opened my door and bowed while I exited. Both Murphy and Viktor looked at each other as if to check if they both saw the same thing. I ignored it and hoped it didn't mean something bad for James. I didn't want him hurt.

I checked for Marek's location using our blood bond. He was in his office so I headed there. Viktor and James fell in step behind me while Murphy jumped back in the car and drove away. The three of us walked together and if the looks we were getting from the people we passed were any indication, my little party made a statement.

We arrived at Marek's office and I walked in through the open door. I found him sitting behind his desk pouring through what looked like an endless pile of paperwork. It was an image I never expected to see from my warrior-like vampire.

Marek looked up at me and smiled.

"How did it go?" He asked.

"She was magnificent," Viktor said unhelpfully.

I rolled my eyes at him and plopped down into a chair in front of Marek's desk.

"The deal is struck. Julien's hunters will bring in all the vampires they can find and share any intel they pick up." I said.

Marek narrowed his eyes at Viktor as he took a deep breath. It was like I wasn't even in the room.

"Did you hear me?" I asked sharply.

Marek shook his head as if to clear his thoughts. His eyes met mine and the icy blue depths appeared to be on fire. That couldn't be good.

"Good work," He said to me then turned his eyes to James.

Whatever he saw seemed to disappoint him.

"Report," Marek said to James.

"Madam Summers was transported without incident," James said.

"And?" Marek prompted.

James said nothing which seemed to anger Marek.

"Will the two of you please wait outside while I speak to Marek?" I asked watching a vein throb in Marek's temple.

"Anything for you, my darling," Viktor said.

He and James stepped out of the room and closed the door behind them. I waited a moment before saying anything. I didn't want to piss off Marek more than he already was but I feared that was inevitable.

"Do I want to know why you are so angry?" I asked.

"I expected your scent to change because of Viktor. I was prepared for that." Marek said.

He stood and started pacing the room. He ran his hands through his hair and loosened his tie before sitting on the edge of the desk facing me.

"What did you do to James?" Marek asked.

"I didn't do anything to James," I said defensively.

"Why is he no longer deferring to me as his superior?" Marek asked.

"I'm not entirely sure I know. He said he made a vow. Then he said he was mine forever and always." I said.

Marek looked shocked. I didn't think it was possible to shock him.

"It appears your status as a master has been solidified," Marek said.

"What are you talking about?" I asked.

"James making you a vow of loyalty and you taking Viktor as a thrall means you are now a master just like a master vampire. Your power level was already there. Taking thralls, willing or otherwise is the switch that flips your status." He said.

"Wait, James is a thrall too? That can't be right." I said.

"He appears to be a willing servant which is different. James will be susceptible to your orders but is capable of making his own decisions. It is very similar to the oath of a Guardian however his vow to you trumps the one he made to the Council." Marek said.

"Will that jeopardize his work with the Council?" I asked concerned.

"Yes, the only thing he is good for now is guarding you," Marek said.

"Not to sound flippant but that's most of what he's done since I met him. Guarding me is what he does best." I said feeling protective of James.

Marek raised his arms in surrender.

"I have lost my best Guardian. Forgive me for being upset." Marek said turning around and returning to his seat behind the desk.

He sounded sullen and resentful.

"You didn't lose him and I did not ask him to do this, Marek. I didn't even realize James had done it until a few minutes before we walked into this room. Even then I didn't know what it meant." I said.

"I am not blaming you," Marek said.

He met my eyes and I saw the sorrow there. I could feel it coming through our bond too. He was mourning the loss of his best Guardian.

"I'll talk to him. Get him to take it back." I offered.

"That isn't possible. The magic behind the vow makes it impossible to break. James has committed his life to you Ember." Marek said.

"Forever and always..." I repeated James' words.

Marek's face was blank but the turmoil within the bond was clear.

"We are likely to have a long night. Take some time away from the office to spend with Viktor. It will help him recover and allow him to be more self-sufficient later on. I will let you know as soon as the hunters start reporting in." He said.

"About that. The hunters will be reporting to me. It was a stipulation of our deal." I said.

The desk cracked under Marek's hands. I jumped out of my seat and moved to the door so fast I didn't realize I was doing it until my shoulder hit the wood. Marek's desk was missing a big chunk about the size of his two palms. He was looking down as if he didn't know how it happened.

"Forgive me," Marek said looking at the hole he made in the desk.

The office door flew open and Viktor and James ran in.

"Are you okay?" James asked stepping in front of me, his back to Marek.

Viktor approached Marek but I couldn't see past the mountain of James to know what he was doing.

"I'm fine. The only casualty was the desk." I said.

James ran his hands over me to be sure. I slapped his hands away and stepped around him.

"Are you okay?" I asked Marek.

He looked up and I saw the pain behind his eyes. After everything that had been said in this room, I wasn't sure which part was hurting him the most.

I pushed Viktor to the side and stepped around him to Marek. Marek took a step back.

"I think it would be best if you took your retinue somewhere else for a while," Marek said.

"Retinue?" I said trying to figure out what he was talking about.

"He means me and Viktor," James said helpfully.

"Oh, did the dhampir sign up for the entourage when I wasn't looking?"

Viktor asked.

"Shut up Viktor," I said.

"Ember," Marek said and it sounded like a plea.

"We'll be upstairs. I'll call you if I hear anything." I said and turned to leave.

Marek grabbed my hand. My guys bristled but I turned back to him.

"I am sorry for scaring you," Marek said.

He sounded sincere. I nodded then pulled away. James and Viktor fell in behind me as I left the office. I kept walking until we reached the elevator.

"What..." Viktor starting to ask something but I interrupted.

"Not here," I said.

I kept them quiet until we were in my apartment behind the closed door. My retinue as Marek referred to it sat on the sofa while I paced the room. We needed to have a come to Jesus meeting about what we were and how we were going to function going forward.

11

Viktor and James both raised their eyebrows at me when I stopped pacing and stood in front of them. I had a dialog running in my head of what I was going to say up until I looked in their faces.

"What's happening?" I asked instead.

"To what are you referring? Your boyfriend tearing a hole in a solid mahogany desk or the dhampir declaring his life to you?" Viktor asked.

My brain froze. I blinked a few times before it thawed.

"Both, neither, I don't know," I said confused.

James stood and walked over to me. He pulled me into his arms and held me, stroking my back.

"Talk to me, Em. What's wrong?" James asked.

"Within a few hour's time, I acquired a thrall, and whatever it is you are to me now. Marek can't handle it so how can I be expected to?" I asked, voice rising at the end with a crack.

I would have cried had I been able to make enough sense of what was happening enough to be sad.

"You are the most powerful Seer to have appeared in centuries who is able to bind master vampires to you on a whim and inspire Guardians of the Council to ignore their oaths and make a life bond with you. What you are is magnificent. Volkov should be bowing at your feet." Viktor said haughtily.

The look on his face showed his seriousness.

"I can't believe I'm about to say this, but I agree with Viktor," James said.

"I have to be dreaming. It's some kind of nightmare. It has to be." I said.

Viktor walked up behind me and laid his hands on my shoulders. I was sandwiched between the two men and I couldn't decide if I was upset about it or not. Viktor pressed himself further into my back and spoke into my ear.

"Ignore Volkov. He is clearly jealous and threatened by your power." Viktor said.

I moved a hand to rest on Viktor's hand and kept while keeping hold on James. Having the two of them touching me gave me a sense of well-being that shocked me. It was like the completion of a circuit allowing the energy to flow through us freely.

"Why aren't the two of you fighting?" I asked realizing both of them were holding me harmoniously.

They looked at each other over me and looked uncomfortable for the first time since we made this little sandwich together.

"Allow me," Viktor said turning me to face him.

James smiled at me and let him do it. Color me curious.

Viktor grabbed my hands and smiled down at me.

"When you bind more than one person to you the people you bind are also connected. It allows a master to form as large a coven as they see fit. The magic of the bonds creates a kind of synergy between all of them they can all feel. As the master, you are able to turn that up or down at will. Right now, you have it dialed up to the maximum setting if you will." Viktor said.

I looked into his eyes and saw he was speaking the truth. I felt it in the bond.

"I didn't bind James. How is he able to feel it?" I asked turning back to face him.

"I bound myself to you but you had to accept the vow for this to work," James said.

"I understand all that but I don't understand why Marek is upset. I've never seen him like this." I said.

"He doesn't want to be on the team. He thinks it should be just him." Viktor said from behind me.

"What?" I asked feeling stupid for not understanding.

I turned back to Viktor and his look of pleasure had me concerned.

"Marek was the first one you bound. That means he's part of the entourage." Viktor said smirking.

My brain must have short-circuited when he spoke. I couldn't grasp what he was saying.

"How is that?" I asked.

"You bound him first. Then you proved you were a master by binding me next. I could tell he wasn't your master the first time I was in a room with the two of you. Why do you think I've been so interested in you? Besides your obvious charms and looks, your power is irresistible." Viktor said.

"I was the one that bound us. I didn't know what I was doing at the time but I know I did it." I said.

"You knew what you were doing with me," Viktor cut in with a snarky tone.

"I knew I was binding you but I didn't know I was making you a thrall. I never would have done that had I known it was possible." I assured him.

"My darling, you will hear no complaints from me. Although I do question your decision to accept a dhampir into our little group," Viktor said looking contrite.

I looked uncomfortably over at James reminded of the vow he made.

"Viktor, do you think you can check in with Julien for me? See if he has any updates for us? You can connect with him without a phone right?" I asked.

"I can. And you can tell me to leave the room, my dear. I won't be hurt." Viktor said kissing my cheek.

I could have resisted the urge to roll my eyes but I didn't. He left the room and closed himself in the bedroom without another word. He would have been able to hear everything I said but I appreciated the semblance of privacy.

"Marek says you can't take back your vow to me. Is that true?" I asked James.

"It is," He said.

His stance stiffened and I found it strange to be in a position of having to interrogate my good friend.

"Then why did you make it?" I asked.

"I have struggled to find a way to deal with my feelings for you while performing my duties as a Guardian. I may have had a chance to get over you but Marek refused to reassign me. The more time I spent with you the more I realized that I could never leave your side. If Marek changed his mind and reassigned me, it would shatter me. Therefore I made the vow." James said.

His emotions were plain on his face. I finally saw how much he loved me.

"How could you be sure I would accept it? I didn't even know I had myself." I said.

"It doesn't require words to solidify when freely given especially not after a heartfelt declaration. I knew you would accept because you care for me too." James said.

"Oh James, you've given away your life," I said with a tear in my eye.

"Don't, I'm here for you because I want to be." James said pulling me toward him.

He pulled me into his arms and I relaxed into him, letting his warmth envelop me. I nuzzled my face into his chest and tried to empty my thoughts of all the chaos swarming me. The magic of James' arms fought away my fears and helped me accept that this man pledged himself to me.

Viktor was happy about his fate but I knew there was more to it than that. He was sure to sneak and connive his way into exactly the right position he wanted. I was glad to have James watching my back with Viktor around. I was starting to have a blind spot when it came to Viktor and I needed James to be the one to open my eyes.

"You will likely be up all night once the hunters start bringing in suspects. You should try to take a nap." James said.

"It's the middle of the day. I'm not going to be able to sleep. How about we watch a movie? The thought of waiting here doing nothing is going to drive me insane." I said.

"A movie sounds good. It's been a while since we've hung out together." James said.

"Well, grab the remote my friend and I'll pop some popcorn," I said smiling.

James sat on the couch and searched for a movie while I went to the kitchen. A normal afternoon would be nice after all the running around and fighting we've done. I could ignore the greater world for a few hours.

As I popped the popcorn in the microwave, I heard the front door open. I knew who it was instantly and could feel his pain bubbling up through our bond. I hoped he wasn't here to fight. Our last encounter was less than friendly.

Marek walked into the kitchen and leaned against the counter. He looked like a runway model on a break between trips showing off the latest fashions. I loved him in a suit. It made my heart flutter.

The popcorn beeped so I pulled it out to dump in a big bowl. Before I could finish, Marek moved behind me and pulled me back into his chest.

"Hi," Marek whispered in my ear.

"Hey," I said breathlessly.

Marek kissed my neck and ran his hands down my arms stopping on my hips. He pulled me closer until I could feel how happy he was to have me against him. Heat pooled in my belly as I imagined pulling off his fancy suit piece by pretty piece.

Marek turned me around to drop a kiss on my lips then deepening it until I was breathless and dizzy. As kisses went, it was fantastic.

"Keep that up and your beautiful suit will end up in a heap on the floor," I said running my hands over his chest then smoothing his tie.

"At least I know you still want me," Marek said grinning.

Self-deprecating humor wasn't his style so it fell flat.

"What's wrong? You never fish for compliments." I said searching his eyes for a clue.

"I can feel your bond with Viktor and it is...distracting." He said grinding his teeth together.

"You can feel it?" I asked. "I didn't believe Viktor but I guess it's possible."

Marek's eyes narrowed and he said, "What has the vampire been saying?"

I looked at James sitting quietly in the living room and got no help from him.

"I'm not stepping in that unless you command me to do it," James said waving his hands as if that would clear my thought.

"Fine," I said.

Turning back to Marek I said, "Viktor seems to think you are like him."

A twitch in Marek's left eye preceded his next words, "A thrall..."

I let the statement hang in the air as if that would make the blow fall softer. The flow of emotions from Marek ping-ponged all over the place. I couldn't keep up with the flow.

"He is wrong," Marek announced.

"How do you know?" I asked.

"Because we are equals. I feel the balance between us. You can make me bow to you with great effort but you cannot command me like a thrall." He said.

His words were sure and confident. I thought about every interaction we ever had, searching for any sign of him being a thrall. I couldn't find it.

"Good," I said closing my eyes with relief.

"What else has he been telling you? He may be your thrall but he is still a cunning master vampire perfectly capable of subterfuge and lies." Marek warned.

I nodded my agreement and Marek pulled me back into his arms.

"If anyone can keep that vampire in line, it is you." He said softly.

"Well, it's not a job I want," I said. "Did you come up here to talk about Viktor or was there something else?"

Marek put his blank face back on before asking, "Speaking of Viktor. Where is your phone?"

"I don't know," I said checking my pockets.

I checked the couch and coffee table but didn't find it. The bedroom was a bust as well so there was only one place left to search.

"Viktor!" I yelled.

He could hear me without yelling but somehow yelling made me feel better. It was Viktor. Annoying him was much more fun than feeding his bond.

"What is it, my dear? Are you being attacked or do you need me to perform a more salacious duty?" Viktor said walking into the living room.

Viktor's dress shirt was rolled up to each elbow exposing his muscular forearms. He looked like he had been hard at work doing something. What, I didn't know.

"Do you have my phone?" I asked.

"Did you misplace it, my dear?" Viktor asked.

"Don't 'my dear' me. Where is my phone?" I insisted.

Viktor pulled it out of his pocket and offered it to me. I grabbed it and checked the history. The call log had been cleared and all text messages were gone. I never cleaned anything so that was suspicious at best.

"Who did you contact?" I asked. "The text and call history is empty."

"We can trace any calls or texts. I can get the team on it right now." James offered.

"Do it," Marek said.

I ignored them in favor of watching Viktor. The smug look on his face told me he was enjoying our anxiety. I also noticed he hadn't answered the question yet.

"Answer me, Viktor," I said putting power into my words.

He flinched and took a step toward me. He realized it and his eyes widened. I knew then that he had been faking most of his reactions to me.

"My coven has been without me for some time. Julien has been bearing the burden of their care on my behalf but they needed to hear from me." He said.

As answers went, it was weak. I looked at Marek knowing there was a reason he had come up here. It had to do with whomever Viktor had contacted.

"It was more than a check-in, Viktor. You tipped off Magdalena." Marek said.

"What? I told you that you couldn't share any information without my direct consent." I said.

"Yes, darling, but it wasn't an order. You really are so naive," Viktor said smiling.

My anger took over and before I knew it I had slammed Viktor to the ground pressing him flat with my power. I was ready to separate his head from his body but Marek stopped me.

"You cannot kill him," Marek said.

"Oh, I can and will." I insisted.

"The Council wants you to care for him not to kill him. He is a political ally and we do not know yet what he told her." Marek said.

Viktor laughed until I pressed him down harder. I realized he wasn't laughing at me.

"You make so much effort to avoid her pet name, Volkov. Haven't you always called her Lena? She would be upset if she could hear you now." Viktor said.

Marek's face stilled and his mask of no emotion slid into place.

"Stop poking the bear Viktor and tell us exactly what you said and to whom," I said then put power into my voice.

"I told my people to reach out to Magdalena and tell her the Council had a bounty out on all of her coven," Viktor said.

"And?" I prompted.

That couldn't be all.

"And that's all," Viktor said.

"That can't be all. How long did you have the phone?" I asked.

"An hour," Viktor said.

I sat down on the floor next to Viktor and put my hand on his cheek. His eyes rolled up to meet mine.

"Tell me everything or I'll burn it out of you," I said.

"Ember!" James snapped at me.

James looked shocked that I would consider burning Viktor but when I turned to Marek, he looked pleased. I'm not sure what that says about me and my taste in men.

"She burned you once before. How did that feel?" Marek asked practically grinning.

Viktor gave Marek a hard look. I hadn't just burnt Viktor in the past, I had almost killed him. He shook his head like it was stupid to say.

"I called her myself. I couldn't risk having someone else do it. She needed to know I was cooperating with her," Viktor said. "I did it to protect you and Natalie."

"Protect us how?" I asked and I released my power.

He sat up as soon as he felt me let go.

"She knows about you and Natalie, what you mean to me," Viktor said.

A lightbulb went off in my head.

"I know," I said frowning. "The night you were in the hospital recovering after her vampires broke in to kidnap Nat. You were dreaming about it and I fell into it when I grabbed your hand."

In the vision, Magdalena had thrown Viktor through a wall to get information. When he didn't talk, she threatened me and Natalie. He gave her what she wanted immediately.

"You were holding my hand when I woke up. I wondered why you left so quickly," Viktor said looking confused.

I stood up and moved away from him. I couldn't stand to touch him and remember how I felt that night. I had cared for him as if he was one of my loved ones. It's obvious now looking back that the bond between us made me feel something for Viktor. I couldn't reconcile his past behavior with the emotions crashing through our bond.

Viktor stood up beside me and grabbed my hand. I was ready to hit him until I saw his face. It forced me to open the bond between us.

"I can't help but protect you in any way possible including working with the enemy," Viktor said in my mind.

"Why?" I asked.

"I don't want to have feelings for you, but I do." He said.

"It would be so much easier if you went back to trying to kill me again," I said.

"I've never wanted you dead. Turned? Yes. You would make a fantastic vampire," Viktor said smirking.

I rolled my eyes at him but he wasn't phased by it.

"What are we missing?" James said.

"Nothing," I said.

"Everything," Viktor said at the same time as me.

I gave Viktor my best shut it or die facial expression and his eyes went soft like a puppy. Innocent, he was not but at least he was being honest.

My phone chose that moment to ring. It was Julien.

"Hey, what's up?" I said.

Marek cringed at my casual greeting.

"We have a development in the search but it's out of scope for my team to handle by themselves. Can you meet them?" Julien asked.

"Yes, text me the location. Who will I be meeting?" I asked.

"Someone you know. I'll send over the details." Julien said then hung up.

"I'm going to need a babysitter for Viktor," I said to Marek.

Viktor had the nerve to look offended.

"Done. Fill me in later," Marek said.

I gave him a look wondering why he wasn't coming along then realized he was the babysitter. Vampires didn't burst into flame in the sun but that didn't mean they were comfortable in it. If it was night, he would have made more of an effort to come along.

After a quick change into field appropriate attire, James and I headed down to the garage to grab a car. I asked James if we had access to an SUV in case we had cargo on the way back and he walked us over to a dark blue Ford Explorer. It was equipped with tie-downs for prisoners and lots of room for other passengers.

James drove us to the location in Julien's text. It was an address in Boulder not far from Chautauqua Park which was an area overrun with hikers and mountain bikers on most days. Our meeting point was a few blocks away near a home Julien's team had staked out.

We pulled up behind a windowless white van. It would have looked out of place in the neighborhood had it not been disguised as a city utility vehicle. A bright orange cone sat behind it as if someone were hard at work.

I hopped out of the car and walked up to the van's back doors. My instructions were to knock so I did. The door opened and a familiar face peeked out.

"Madame Summers, come in," Sasha said motioning for us to climb into the van.

The last time I had seen Sasha was at her vampire coming out party. The night had ended with a battle in the backyard of her sire's mansion. She is one of Julien's vampires and from what I can tell a favorite of his.

"Please, call me Ember," I said stepping in behind her.

James followed and I was surprised we all fit. Sasha introduced us to her two teammates Nick and Kaleb then sat down in front of a video screen.

My eyes were immediately drawn to Kaleb. He was a vampire with bright blue eyes and white blonde hair. It was long enough on top to stand up and yet still flop a bit to the side in a sexy model look that you would usually find in an underwear advertisement. He had the body to match.

"It's good to see you again," Sasha said smiling.

Her words drew me back to her but based on the look on her face she understood the effect Kaleb had on me. He must get that all the time.

"You too. Sorry about your party. I didn't intend to make a scene." I said trying to ignore the piercing stare of the blonde.

"It wouldn't be a vampire party if someone didn't throw down before the night was over." She said smiling.

"Good to know. So what do you have for us?" I asked.

"We've got some video for you to watch. Tell us if you recognize anyone." Sasha said.

She sat down next to the dark haired vampire, Nick. He cued up the video and let it run. They had hours of footage but with Nick's help, we sped through it, pausing when faces came into view. By the time we got through it all, we had identified several vampires.

Kaleb held himself back from the other two while they worked. He seemed to be the one keeping an eye on the area while the rest of us were distracted by the video. He looked as young as Sasha. Early to mid-twenties before he was turned but had been a vampire long enough for his power to warm my arms.

I rubbed the feeling away while trying to pay attention to the conversation in the room.

"How did you find this place?" James asked.

Nick eyed him like answering him might be a security risk.

"We can't give away all our secrets but we got a tip there was vampire action in the area which led us here. I tapped into the security feeds and we tucked in to watch. When we reported what we found, the master told us to expect a visit from you." Nick said.

"Is this the only location you've found?" I asked.

"We have another team checking out a few other places but this one had the most activity," Sasha said.

"What's next?" I asked eager to do something.

"We wait for dark then we move in. The master figured you would want in on the action." Nick said.

"Kaleb will lead the operation," Sasha added.

From there, we listened as Kaleb outlined the plan. It wouldn't be easy. There were too many vampires in that house for us to go in by ourselves. Our only option was to call in backup. Kaleb said they had another team nearby that could be here by nightfall. When they arrived, we would take the house by force.

James pulled out his phone. I could guess what he was about to do. He looked at me and my expression must have said it all because he put his phone back in his pocket without sending a message. We both knew that if Marek was aware of the plan, he would try to keep me from taking part or insist on going in with us.

I moved to the end of the van and sat next to James. I bumped my shoulder against him to make him look at me. When our eyes met I smiled.

"You really are the best you know that?" I said.

"He is going to kill me. You're going to have to find someone else to corrupt." James said.

"He won't kill you. I'm pretty sure I've corrupted Marek too," I said smiling.

James looked at me like that wouldn't save him. He might be right.

We waited in silence for night to fall, the backup team to arrive, and the show to begin. The plan was risky but I had to trust Julien's team knew what they were doing. James and I were along for the ride whatever the outcome.

12

The hunter team prepared for the raid by splitting into two and four-man teams. They paired James and me with Kaleb because he wasn't willing to let us go off on our own and Kaleb's own team had an odd number. Their fourth was usually the one that stayed in the van as backup but he was off on a solo mission of another kind tonight.

"I've seen what you can do, Ember. I was there when you took down The Egyptian at the mansion. With that kind of power, you should be able to incapacitate a group of these guys all at once. If so, we can avoid some bloodshed." Kaleb said.

"I'll do what I can," I said trying to forget how I ended up in the hospital after that night.

"Unleash your inner badass to take these guys out and you'll have me in your fan club forever," Kaleb said seriously.

A thrill ran through me at his words.

"Her fan club is full," James mumbled.

Kaleb cut his eyes to James and smiled a knowing grin. He looked amused but may have seen the posturing from James as a friendly competition. I didn't get an amorous vibe from Kaleb so he probably just wanted to rile James up a bit.

I shook my head at James. It wasn't like him to be sulky or possessive.

"How many do you sense?" James asked me getting his head back in the game.

I mentally did a sweep of the building and the surrounding area. We had ten vampires inside with three humans who didn't have any power. I assumed they weren't there to fight, but I didn't rule it out completely. There were more vampires nearby but there was no way to know if they were part of our team or Magdalena's.

"A lot. I'll hold down as many as I can while your teams round them up. I've never held down a sizable group before so be on your toes in case anyone slips through." I warned.

Kaleb nodded then led us to the front of the house. The plan was to knock on the door and force our way in if necessary. The other teams would file in as soon as Kaleb gave the signal. It would then turn into chaos and I hoped I could tell all the bad guys from the good ones.

James held himself back in the shadows while Kaleb and I rang the doorbell. We weren't sure they would be dumb enough to open the door for us but it was worth a try. As a human, I wouldn't spark as much distrust standing on the doorstep so I stood front and center. Or as James described it, on the front line right in the line of fire.

I heard movement behind the door and felt Kaleb tense up behind me. The door swung open to reveal a woman holding a handgun pointed at my head. It wasn't what I was expecting.

"What do you want?" She asked.

"For you to get that gun out of my face," I said.

Her face showed her anger and annoyance. I scanned her for power and didn't find much. That probably explained the gun.

"Leave and your problem solves itself," She suggested while waving the gun past me and in front of Kaleb.

Kaleb watched the barrel of the gun. When it leveled on his chest, he grabbed it and pushed the woman back inside the house. I followed on his heels using him as a shield in case there were other vampires with guns. His body blocked me from seeing too far into the room but that also meant it hid me.

"Where are all your buddies?" Kaleb asked while jerking the woman's arms behind her and subduing her with armbands made for restraining vampires.

I felt them before I saw them. Vampires ran up from the lower level of the home out into the living room. Just before they reached us, I slammed my power into them and froze them. Kaleb looked at me with a smile.

"I could get used to working with you," He said smiling.

"Don't get cocky. There are too many of them to hold for long." I said straining.

My control was already thready and I hadn't been holding them for more than a few seconds. Each vampire tugged on my power as if they were attached to me by strings. While I held them, the strings wavered as if blown by a breeze.

A crash behind me signaled our fight was just ramping up. I spun around to see James take out one of three vampires that came in through the front door. Unfortunately, I released half the vamps I was holding while my attention was on James.

By then my head was pounding and another headache was rearing its ugly head. All hell broke loose then as I lost my hold on the remaining vampires in the room. I was suddenly thankful for all the training I did with James to prepare for the field.

I ducked to avoid a fist to my face only to run right into a broad chest that felt like a brick wall. Dazed, I stepped back only to remember who I was dealing with. This wasn't a human and I couldn't afford mistakes headache or not.

A hand gripped my throat when I stepped back into the brick wall vampire. His face contorted with rage. I guess invading his little clubhouse would do that to some people. I didn't let it distract me. Instead, I pushed my hand into his chest and let loose a pulse of power. The vampire flew backward into the wall behind him and a stab of searing pain shot through my temple.

He looked shocked. While he hesitated, I punched him in the throat. I put power into the punch which resulted in a broken neck for him and a queasy stomach for me. I shook off the feeling as I scanned the room for other threats. The room was in chaos with vampires flying every which way.

Nick's team ran in through the back door just as more vampires come up from the basement. There had to be at least twenty enemy vampires plus our teams. My initial count of ten was way off. It was a good thing the house was big because there were fights happening all over the first floor of this home.

Another vampire came at me moments after I subdued the first one. Her approach was fast but messy. I knew she didn't have much experience fighting because she looked like she was falling when she hit me. I took her weight and rolled to the floor twisting her into my signature pretzel maneuver.

The smile on my face must have made her angry because she broke my hold and hit me hard on the jaw. Having my clock rung slowed me down so much that the vampire got her hands around my neck. I don't know what their fascination was with my neck but I didn't like it.

I wanted to burn her but with so many of my team sensitive to flame and my head threatening to explode in pain; I took another approach. As she squeezed my throat, I grabbed her face and pushed heat into her skin until it crackled and smoked. She let go of me and scrambled backward.

I pushed off the floor following her and delivering a kick to her chin. Her head snapped back, and the ashes of her face crumbled. It was completely disgusting but it seemed to incapacitate her.

James yelled from behind me and I turned in time to block a knife headed for my throat. Unfortunately, my forearm took the brunt of the attack with the tip of the blade hitting bone then glancing off through the flesh. When the vampire pulled back for another strike, I held him back with my power then heated up his blade until he dropped it.

Now that he was less stabby, I punched him in the nose. The bone broke with a snap. Using the heel of my hand, I rammed the broken bone into his skull and dropped him. He crumpled to the ground. I didn't think he was dead. Vampires are harder to kill than that but it would slow him down for a while.

James came up behind me and spoke into my ear, "You are bleeding profusely. Come with me."

He tried to push me toward the door, but I didn't let him. The fight was still going strong, and I wasn't about to leave a fight unfinished. Besides, leaving now would look bad in front of the Le Veneur coven. I wasn't willing to compromise my alliance.

"I'm fine," I said breathlessly heading the opposite way James wanted me to go.

He rolled his eyes and followed me. I picked the knife up off the floor sparing a glance for the vampire who used it against me. He wasn't moving, so I stepped away to find another target.

By then, I was more than a little dizzy and my head hurt so badly I wasn't sure if I could walk in a straight line let alone continue to stand. The fight wasn't over so I pulled all the strength I could muster together.

A group of three vampires had Sasha pinned in a corner of the living room. I froze them and met her eyes. She smiled at me then dispatched the vamps with precision. I made a mental note that sparring with her would up my skills considerably. I joined her and looked for any remaining vampires.

"You're bleeding," Sasha said pulling my arm up while blocking another vamp that came at us.

I froze him too, and James stepped in to take him down.

While he did his thing, Sasha ripped a strip of fabric off a nearby curtain to tie around my forearm. James gave me a look like he didn't understand why it was okay for Sasha to help me but not for him to do the same thing. I wasn't sure why that was the case either but I just stood there while she fixed me up.

The tide had turned in the fight and our team now had control of the room. Kaleb strode toward me with purpose. He eyed my arm then took in the three of us. Whatever he saw must have satisfied him because he didn't comment on it when he stepped up next to me.

"We have two captives that are conscious and half a dozen still alive but incapacitated. We can take them to our holding cells or to the Council detention center. Which do you prefer?" Kaleb asked.

"Take them to the Council," I said.

Kaleb nodded then walked away to arrange transport for the prisoners. Sasha smiled and gave me a wink before following Kaleb. Before I could process what her meaning was, James pulled me toward him so he could look at my arm.

"Interesting choice of bandage," James said peaking under the curtain fabric.

"It did the trick," I said watching his face.

He met my eyes but didn't respond. I could imagine what he would have said. Holding his tongue was an excellent idea.

"Kaleb's team has cleanup covered. Let's head to the car." James said.

He must have known how I was feeling because he slipped an arm around my waist pulling me in tight against his side. It gave me support without looking like he was holding me up. No one seemed to notice, and I was glad for it.

By the time we got to the SUV, I was dry heaving and my vision was blacking out. James settled me into the back seat so I could lie down then pulled out his phone.

"The prisoners will start arriving soon. I'll bring Ember to her apartment and have the doctor meet us there. Her headache is back. She may need to spend more time in the deprivation chamber but I'll let Dr. Wallace determine what to do next." James said.

I assumed he was talking to Marek. I felt a tug on our bond and I didn't fight it. Marek needed to know what was happening so he could help.

To my surprise, I felt both Marek and Viktor connect with me. It felt good at first then my headache intensified causing me to cry out. James cursed and dropped his phone. He climbed into the backseat and put his hands at my temples. The warmth of his healing power spread into me and the worst of the pain subsided.

"Thank you," I said breathlessly.

"I'll get you home and into the doctor's care. Can you hold on long enough to make it there?" He asked.

"I'll make it," I said hoping I didn't have to puke in the car.

James buckled me in then slid back into the front seat. He retrieved his phone and redialed. James drove away from the scene and caught the person up on what was happening.

"Tell the doctor to be ready. The headache got worse after I put her in the car. I gave her a healing treatment, but she isn't doing well." James said looking nervously into the rearview mirror at me.

He was silent for a few moments as the person on the phone spoke to him.

"If it was anyone but me, I would agree. As it is, I need to pay attention to driving. You can yell at me when we get there." James said with obvious notes of anger in his voice.

James dropped his phone into the center console.

"Who was yelling at you?" I asked.

"You know the answer to that question. How are you doing?" James asked.

Marek's yelling aside, I was feeling stable.

"I'll live but I'll feel better when I'm in a bed instead of a moving car," I said.

A flash of headlights from another car made me wince. I threw my arm across my eyes to block out the light.

"I'll have you there in twenty minutes, Em," James promised.

It was more than a twenty-minute drive which meant he would haul ass. I braced myself for the ride by keeping all light blocked with my arm over my eyes. It was surprising how much that helped. Now I just had to make it back to home base without vomiting.

James stayed true to his word and made it to the parking garage in twenty minutes. He left the car at the curb and helped me inside. A Guardian who I didn't know, took the keys from James and whisked the car away.

A wheelchair was waiting just inside the door but I refused it. I didn't need help walking and couldn't afford to be seen that weak. James put a hand to my back and fell into step behind me.

"*Milaya moya*, you need not prove anything by walking," Marek said stepping out from around a corner.

"I have a headache, not broken legs." I snapped.

Marek's lips fell into a tight line on his face. He jerked his chin down as a quick affirmative then led the way to the residential elevators.

"Now I know why all the men are falling at your feet," Viktor smirked.

He was leaning against the wall a few feet ahead of Marek. He looked like one of those metal silhouettes of a cowboy with his hat tipped back and one knee bent. Although Viktor wouldn't be caught dead in cowboy attire. It would offend his vampire sense of fashion.

"If this is the welcoming committee it leaves much to be desired," I said.

Marek ignored me then walked right past Viktor without saying a word. Viktor smiled and fell into step beside me.

"He's been brooding the whole time you've been gone. I think he may be jealous that you had a mission and he was stuck babysitting me." Viktor said conspiratorially.

I felt Marek's annoyance through our bond but I didn't comment. Until he said something, I wasn't going to push. He had every right to be worried. If it was me in his place, I would be.

"Stop poking the bear, Viktor," I said.

He managed to look innocent and I sighed. Viktor was never innocent.

Marek held the elevator doors open for us. He made sure to end up next to me after hitting the button for the sub-penthouse.

Marek slid his arm around my waist and pulled me in close. I leaned into him and let my head fall against his chest. Holding myself up was getting harder as the exhaustion from the fight made itself known. Combined with my headache it was a wonder I was still upright. Although I wouldn't admit it.

By the time I made it to my bed, I was ready to pass out. Unfortunately, we weren't alone. Dr. Wallace was seated in a wingback chair in the living room. She spoke to James before coming in to see me.

"Madame Summers, we have to stop meeting like this." She said sitting on the edge of the bed.

Dr. Wallace had a small smile on her face full of compassion and ready to hear about my pain. How doctors could have a seemingly unlimited supply of empathy baffled me.

"As much as I enjoy your company doctor, I'd prefer to stop needing your help," I said trying to prop myself up so I could see her better.

"Here," She said putting another pillow behind me.

"Is this where you tell me I didn't follow the doctor's orders and I've gotten myself into a mess?" I asked.

She looked at me kindly and said, "Why tell you something you already know?"

I sighed heavily and said, "I didn't have a vision this time. It happened during the fight."

I assumed she knew the scenario having talked to James already. So I didn't waste time explaining how I ended up in the field.

"From what Guardian Leigh says, you use your clairvoyance when you fight. It helps you anticipate your opponent's moves." She said.

"Yes, it's how I can fight a vampire and stay alive," I said.

"He also said you had a bit of a revelation after I saw you last. You've formed a retinue." She said.

I instantly felt uncomfortable. It was something I hadn't really accepted yet myself so talking with her about it caused me anxiety.

"I suppose I have," I said.

"I'm going to recommend a different treatment and some training. As a new master, you need to know how to care for your little group and how to feed on them." She said.

"Feed on them?" I asked partly disgusted and partly confused.

"Masters form covens for many reasons but the most basic is to share power. It's how master vampires boost their power level. The feedback loop created within the coven feeds them power that they consume and store for later. In theory, it should work the same for you." She said.

"In theory maybe, by my power doesn't work like everyone else's," I said feeling concerned.

"I understand that and I think I may know why. Your blood tests have shown biochemical properties consistent with that of the Fae. It is common to find Fae markers in humans as they have interbred with humans for millennia but you are different. Do you know who your parents are?" She asked.

"Of course I know my parents and neither one of them is Fae." I insisted.

"The Fae are adept at hiding in plain sight and based on your test results you most definitely have at least a one Fae parent which makes you at least half Fae." Dr. Wallace said.

I thought about it but I couldn't imagine either of my parents as anything other than human. Not that I would know a Fae if I saw one. All my information comes from fictional tales, not supernatural history books.

"Regardless of my parentage, you were going to tell me how to treat my headaches," I said deflecting that landmine.

"Yes, you need to feed on your retinue." She said.

I started to protest but she held up a hand.

"It will not harm them. In fact, they get something out of it too or vampires would not do it. Your headache may be a symptom of an imbalance and a strain on your power. Forming a power loop with your retinue should heal your thrall and your power issue." She said.

"I think we did it briefly earlier today," I said thinking when Viktor and James held me earlier.

Dr. Wallace nodded, "You need to do it daily in addition to regular blood exchanges with your thrall. Right now the blood exchanges may need to be more frequent but once he has been fortified you can get on a weekly routine with him instead. I recommend sleeping with them both next to you the more skin touching the better."

My eyes got wide and she smiled.

"It does not need to be sexual unless you want it to be," She said.

I looked at the door and could feel James, Marek, and Viktor trying to hear every word the doctor said. I could only imagine how this was going to affect my relationship with Marek. He has been more than understanding to this point but he is a master vampire. They don't share well with others.

"If you don't have any other questions, I'll let them know they can see you now. And Ember?" She asked.

"Yes?" I said.

"They each need physical contact with you. Think puppy pile and go with it." She winked then left the room.

I closed my eyes and cringed only to suddenly feel intrigued. It had felt wonderful to have James and Viktor connect to me earlier today. What would happen if we added Marek into the mix?

13

My harem fantasy was short-lived. After I explained to the guys what we needed to do, Marek just stood there with his arms crossed looking severe. Viktor on the other hand jumped onto the bed and made himself comfortable at my side. James looked torn between laying next to me and obeying whatever order Marek might issue.

With the other two occupied, Viktor took the opportunity to pull me into his arms and spoon me from behind. My headache lessened a fraction and the sound I made must have persuaded the others to do as they were told. There was some jostling for position before Marek pulled me over to lay on his chest while Viktor and James placed themselves to either side of us.

As soon as they were all touching me, my headache changed from a sharp pain to a dull ache. But it wasn't enough so I shifted my right leg to entwine with James' leg. Then moved my left foot so it was touching Viktor. My left hand reached back and Viktor entwined his fingers with mine. As soon as he did my headache was gone.

I let out a sigh that might have also been a moan. The guys all scooted in closer and then I felt the loop come alive. Their power merged with mine and we all moaned together as it slithered between us. It was like a warm silk sheet sliding between us and cocooning us in its power. I grabbed the loop realizing it was like the bond I had with Marek and pulled it to me.

The guys all reacted by rubbing against me as if trying to get more. I pulled on the power some more and then pushed some of it back into them.

Marek tilted my head up so he could look into my eyes. His expression was that of wonder and amazement. He pulled me up until his lips could reach mine. Then he kissed me as if he needed me to breathe. Our power pulsed together, and I could feel the other men respond in kind.

"No," I said pulling back. "This is not going to turn into a group sex situation."

Marek smiled. He actually smiled! As if I was being silly or cute. Did he want that?

"If we were alone, you would already be naked," Marek said still grinning.

"I wouldn't mind playing along," Viktor said sounding breathless.

I looked over at James, and then I had to look away. He was clearly feeling it too. What is wrong with me?

"There is nothing wrong with you *Milaya moya*," Marek whispered.

"I can't do this if all of you are going to...to," But I couldn't say it.

"Express ourselves sexually?" Viktor said.

"Damn it Viktor!" I yelled and started to move away from them.

"No!" James called out, and I looked at him again.

I realized it would hurt them if I broke contact while the loop was open. I took a deep breath then settled back into Marek's arms. Everyone shifted until somehow I was perfectly comfortable again.

"How is this possible?" I said referring to the four of us cuddling together peacefully.

"We explained it before," James said.

"You are worth it, my dear," Viktor said surprising me.

"Speaking of that, we need to determine a schedule of who connects with Ember and when. Having all of us together at the same time is not practical long term," Marek said.

"I'm surprised you're willing to share," I said looking into his eyes.

I knew him well enough to see the struggle and to feel it through our bond. A bond that now included two more men.

"I am if you are willing to make me your second in this retinue," He said.

I knew enough about vampire covens to know there was a pecking order that maintained discipline within the family and settled disputes. What I wasn't willing to do was to make Marek seem like my underling.

"Not possible," I said and felt him tense. "You can't be my second and be my boyfriend. It doesn't work."

"I am older than him and more capable with a coven of my own. I would make you a marvelous second," Viktor said.

"No, Viktor. I can't trust you enough to make you my second." I said.

Marek was looking ill which was saying a lot since he typically didn't show any emotion at all.

"James is the obvious choice," I said and saw James look shocked.

"You can't mean that," James said.

"I do. You are the best choice and have been doing the job long before you declared yourself to me." I said.

"Ember," Marek started, but I cut him off.

"You don't need to be my second. You are my boyfriend which makes you my equal." I said.

He smiled slowly finally understanding what I was saying.

"Hold on," Viktor said. "That makes me what? Third? Unacceptable."

"There are ways to remove you from the retinue if your rank displeases you," Marek said.

"All of them resulting in the final death? No thank you!" Viktor yelled.

"Then I suggest you learn to like your place," Marek said flatly.

"Please stop fighting," I said feeling my headache creep back in.

They all fell silent.

"Who is interviewing the vampires we captured tonight?" I asked.

"Caden," Marek answered.

"I'd feel better if it was you or James," I said.

"My place is here right now and James doesn't leave your side," Marek said.

"Then I'll go," I said trying to get up but being stopped by six hands.

"If you will stay here, I will go," Marek said.

"Thank you," I said and kissed him.

"Get some rest and draw strength. I will return with any news I discover." Marek promised.

He waited for me to drop the loop before leaving the warm nest of bodies surrounding me. As soon as he was off the bed, the loop opened again and Viktor and James pressed closer into my body. Viktor spooned me from behind again while James pulled me into his chest.

James dropped a hand to my hip and pushed a leg between my knees being careful not to push too high up and risk stoking more intimate areas. I let my hands rest against his chest feeling the muscle definition and power of his body.

Viktor moved my hair away from my neck and nuzzled into the sensitive flesh. Goosebumps flowed down my body ending in a zing of excitement in my stomach. Vampire bites were addictive, and I had experienced enough of them to know that even Viktor's bite would be enjoyable.

"May I?" Viktor whispered then laved his tongue over my pulse.

I shivered and looked into James' eyes for permission. I didn't need it. He wanted to feel what I felt when I was bitten. It was clear within our bond since we were all connected.

"Yes," I answered Viktor and cried out when his fangs pierced my skin.

Viktor wrapped his arm around my stomach and pulled me in tight to his body. He isn't my favorite person on most days but Viktor gave good vampire.

James touched his forehead to mine. His breathing became ragged as he felt the power pool between us. I had to admit that it felt fantastic amplified within us. With the loop open, we could all feel what Viktor and I were feeling. It was surreal.

Viktor didn't show any signs of slowing down so I stopped him myself.

"That's enough Viktor," I said.

He took one last pull of my blood then licked the wound clean. Vampire saliva could heal so the tiny wounds closed up at his command. While he did that, I pulled his wrist up to my mouth only to have him pull it away.

"A moment, my dear," Viktor said.

He bit into his wrist then put it in front of me. My mouth locked over the wound. It was a reflex. Vampire blood is full of power and tastes different depending on the vampire. I would have preferred to drink from Marek but completing the blood exchange with Viktor would be equally satisfying.

Vampire blood was like drinking power from a firehose. It was wonderful but if you weren't careful, you could take too much. Then you would bond with the vampire. That ship had sailed for me so I just laid back and enjoyed it.

Each swallow filled me with a surge of power unique to Viktor yet still clearly vampiric. As the flow tapered off, I pulled back and released Viktor's wrist. He kept his body snug up against mine creating a cocoon of sorts between him and James. It was surprisingly cozy.

James pushed my hair away from my face and asked, "How is your head doing?"

"It's much better," I said.

"She just needed a little of my blood," Viktor added.

"Viktor, why is it you can ruin any moment just by opening your mouth?" I asked.

"It's a talent, my dear." He said smugly.

I rolled my eyes, and James smiled. He was the only one that could see my face.

"Perhaps we should let Ember get cleaned up so she can get more comfortable?" James suggested to Viktor.

A bath sounded divine. My clothes were bloody and covered with other things that I couldn't identify. I could guess I didn't smell great either.

"I should clean up too. Viktor, keep an eye on Ember until I get out of the shower." James said.

Viktor nodded in agreement, and I hid a laugh. Viktor was not anyone's choice for a guard and having him with me while I took a bath was unacceptable. I assumed James was trying to keep Viktor busy.

James left, and I headed into my bathroom. Viktor stayed in the bedroom which allowed me to prepare for my bath alone.

I turned the water as hot as I could stand it then dumped some vanilla bubble bath in. After undressing, I slipped into the sudsy goodness and let my body go limp. I expected to feel a sting on my arm from the knife wound I suffered during the fight but when I looked down; it had completely healed.

I guess there were major perks to having James lend me power given his healing power. I could recall the familiar feeling of warmth from his power when we merged all of our power together. Combine that with the vampire blood I drank and it was no wonder the wound was already healed.

Viktor knocked on the bathroom door.

"Come in," I said.

Viktor entered looking better than I'd seen him in weeks. His hair was shiny, and his skin looked alive. His cheeks were almost rosy from the glow. If I didn't know about his cantankerous personality, I would have called him handsome.

He sat down on the edge of the tub and leaned back against the wall. It didn't look comfortable, but it showed off his lean body. His long legs crossed at the ankle and he looked at me like I was a goddess.

I ignored him and instead focused on how good the water felt on my skin. The bubbles were thick enough to keep my modesty intact.

"I could wash your hair for you," Viktor offered.

"I hadn't planned to wash it," I said.

"It smells of blood and ash." He replied.

"Then I suppose I must wash it," I said taking it down from the bun and letting it fan out into the water.

"Did you want something, Viktor?" I asked.

"I very well can't monitor you from behind the door," He said.

"You know James wasn't being literal when he said to keep an eye on me. What's really going on?" I asked while dipping my head back into the water.

He stayed silent for a beat before speaking.

"You chose the dhampir over me without hesitation. Why?" Viktor asked.

"Viktor, you and I have a complicated relationship. Our bond has changed it but I cannot forget the things you did to me and my sister. I can't fully trust you." I said.

Viktor stood up and started pacing back and forth in the bathroom. He appeared agitated and possibly hurt given the way he had his lips mashed together.

He stopped and looked down at me. His expression was angry.

"I have devoted myself to you at great personal detriment. Becoming your thrall will damage my reputation and put my coven at risk. This is not a game for me. You must understand!" Viktor said.

"I will try," I said reaching out to hold his hand.

He came closer and grasped my hand. I pulled him down so he was at my level. He kneeled next to the tub.

"May I?" He said looking at my hair.

"Fine, go ahead," I said giving in.

He rolled up his sleeves and grabbed the shampoo. I sat stiffly until Viktor started massaging the shampoo into my scalp. His long fingers stroked the sensitive flesh of my skull, and I groaned in satisfaction.

"It would be better if I was in the tub with you," Viktor said.

"Boundaries, Viktor, boundaries," I said.

"There is no harm in asking for what I want," He said.

"I have a boyfriend," I said in response.

"Until you take a mate, you are available for courting," Viktor said.

"Not the point, Viktor," I said.

He continued to wash my hair, rinsing it, then putting conditioner on. He piled my hair back on top of my head and clipped it in place. I leaned back into the water. I felt much more relaxed after having a scalp massage.

"I hear James. I'll leave you to his tender care," Viktor said walking away.

"Wait a minute," I called after him.

He turned around, and the look on his face surprised me.

"Either you've forgotten everything I told you about Marek or he's convinced you it isn't true. He has built a career on lying. Why do you think he didn't react to hearing you have Fae blood?" Viktor asked.

"I don't know," I said, suddenly realizing Viktor had a point.

The guys were all in the next room when Dr. Wallace told me what she found in my blood. A vampire wouldn't have any trouble hearing what she said. Marek should have made a big deal about it or asked the doctor to check her test to make sure it was accurate.

"He already knew about your lineage. Why do you think he took such a personal interest in you? It wasn't because James couldn't handle the assignment. James is his best Guardian. Marek didn't need to go out in the field, he wanted to," He said then left the room.

He slammed the door behind him, and it made me jump. Sometimes I could look at Viktor and think of him as an unfeeling, uncaring ass. I forgot he had emotions that were just as valid as my own. Seeing him hurt broke something inside me. I had never been so callous in my life but I frequently exhibited the trait with Viktor.

My gut said he was sincere which made my stomach churn. If Viktor was being honest, then Marek was lying to me. I had never questioned Marek's sincerity and I should have. I hardly knew him even if he was the capable, powerful leader of the Guardians who passionately protected me at a significant cost to himself. Or so I thought.

Marek and I had made up, but I wasn't sure it was because we settled anything or if it was because I let it go. My stomach hurt.

I rinsed my hair and got out of the tub. Instead of relaxing, I should interrogate the prisoners. It was my operation and my responsibility to finish. Marek snuck out while I was vulnerable.

Viktor was standing at the bedroom window with his back to me. I secured my towel and started pulling clothes from the closet. I could have asked him to step outside but somehow I knew he didn't intend to turn around. I dressed then pulled my wet hair into a tight bun securing it with a hair tie and a few bobby pins.

I took a few minutes to swipe a line of eyeliner and some mascara on my eyes. Then added deodorant and called it done.

"I'm headed down to the detention center," I said.

Viktor turned around and smiled, "I would love to watch you work."

"I'd rather you stayed here. I don't need an entourage when I'm in the building." I said and walked toward the door.

Viktor moved with vampire speed to block the doorway. I stopped just short of smacking right into him.

"Please, Ember." He said placing a hand on my arm. "I will be an asset."

There was no sign of his usual mirth or snark. This was a serious Viktor trying to prove himself. I wondered how long it had been since he had to do that.

"Fine, but don't make me regret it," I said.

He moved aside and motioned for me to pass. I collected James on the way out and the three of us took the elevator down to what the Guardians affectionately called the bunker, an underground detention center that was more secure than any other facility in the state.

We arrived just as Marek walked out of an interrogation room. The look on his face told me he was greatly distressed which concerned me. It was rare for him to show any emotion. Our eyes locked, and a new emotion showed on his face. He was angry.

Marek looked at James and said, "You were to keep her upstairs. What are you doing here?"

"Addressing James instead of me will get you nowhere fast," I said incredulously.

Marek looked startled then his face went blank. He stepped forward then reached for my hand.

"Forgive me Madame Summers, it will not happen again." He said bowing low and placing a kiss on the back of my hand.

I nodded to accept his apology and tried not to let my shock show on my face. I expected more of a fight. Then I realized that we were in public and his acknowledgment of my rank solidified my standing within the team and the vampire community. If he hadn't, the entire team would not recognize my authority.

"What have you learned so far?" I asked Marek.

"The prisoners have not said a word." He replied.

"Then it's good the Master is here to step in," Viktor said.

The Guardians in the room looked confused. Their eyes darted around as if trying to figure out who Viktor was talking about. Some even looked at him as if he was speaking about himself. Not one of them looked at me.

"She does have a unique way of persuading others," Marek said although he didn't sound happy about it.

The room went silent. All eyes landed on me the moment they realized Marek confirmed that Viktor was referring to me as the master. I pasted on a smile and walked forward with purpose. If I was going to take over, I was going to have to act as if I deserved it.

James moved to the door we saw Marek exit from and motioned for me to enter.

"Viktor, with me," I said then entered the room.

Viktor walked in behind me as I motioned for James to stay by the door. Marek joined me as I walked up to the prisoners. There were two of them chained to the wall. They looked like they had been through a battle even after the original fight we went through to capture them.

"Since you did not give me what I asked for, you now have Madame Summers to deal with," Marek told them.

His words made me shiver. It sounded like I was the monster that would torture them. Marek stepped back to let me take over just as Viktor walked up beside me.

Now that I was there, I had no idea what to say. I didn't have any experience questioning suspects. My strengths were in finding patterns and making connections. Marek was the interrogator between us.

As the seconds ticked by, I thought using my clairvoyant power could help but I didn't have a connection with these vampires. There wasn't the slightest blip of a hint of a vision in the air either. What I needed was a way in.

A thought occurred to me. I opened the bond between Viktor and me, "*I have an idea.*"

I pushed my thoughts at Viktor and he smiled a wicked grin. Apparently, he was on board.

"We know you have the information we want. The question is how far are you willing to go to keep those secrets?" I asked the vampires.

They both smirked as if a mere human threatening them was funny.

"Viktor dear, would you mind?" I asked.

He struck so quickly neither the prisoners nor the Guardians had time to react. By the time he stood next to me again, he had already bitten both prisoners. He placed his hand on my shoulder then opened the connection between us.

"What the hell was that?" A guardian yelled.

"Enhanced interrogation technique," Viktor answered licking his lips.

"That is a violation..." The same guardian started to say.

"Your protest is noted. Now be quiet or be removed." I said.

James took a step toward the guardian. The guy must have realized he was outnumbered and shut up.

Through our bond, Viktor offered me the threads of the tentative bonds he had just formed with the prisoners. Taking their blood gave Viktor and by default me access to their minds. Having a vampire of questionable moral character was handy sometimes. Like the guardian, Marek would have protested the action I had Viktor take. Lucky for me, I hadn't asked him first.

"Tell me what you know of the vampire known as Magdalena," I said to the prisoners.

I didn't wait for them to speak. I could feel their thoughts flickering in my mind. Images of Magdalena flipped on and off but I couldn't make sense of them. The vampires were fighting me.

Instead of asking more questions, I pulled at the images Viktor was feeding me. I held onto one of them that kept repeating. It was of a house surrounded by farmland with several outbuildings situated around the property. It was the same location Marek had infiltrated when he went in alone and almost got himself killed.

I held onto the image and pulled harder. The vampires grunted and I felt the Guardians in the room tense up. Ignoring the people in the room, I focused on extracting more information. The more I pushed the less I got from them. It was like the image was nothing but a photograph.

What was the point of having Viktor bite these vampires if this was all I could get from them?

14

Viktor moved closer resting his hand on my back. His fingers found the hem of my t-shirt then wiggled their way beneath the cloth. As soon as his fingers touched my skin, the images coming from the prisoners tripled. I sorted through them until I found the vampire for which we were searching.

Among them was a scene of Magdalena standing in a large living room looking down at a man on the floor. The man looked vaguely familiar. He was covered in blood, having survived some kind of fight or torture. He was in bad shape.

Magdalena looked elegant standing above him in a spaghetti strap red dress and bare feet. She walked a path around the man like she was trying to find the right spot. She must have found it because she stopped suddenly then kicked him so hard that he slid across the room. His body crashed into a wall and his face came into view. My gut twisted.

While this vision was relevant, I wasn't sure it was what I needed to get more intel on Magdalena's organization. It was clear that Marek had left important information out of his story given he was the person on the floor getting his ass kicked.

Magdalena chased after Marek picking up a small knife on the way. She stabbed him in the stomach with a slashing motion. He cried out and tried to defend himself. She said something that made him stop moving. Then she proceeded to stab him a few more times for good measure.

Magdalena dropped the bloody knife on the floor then knelt down next to Marek. She stroked his hair and cooed something I couldn't understand. It was like she was comforting a child who had skinned his knee. If I hadn't already known she was crazy it would have told me she was insane by the way she was smearing his blood down his face.

I shuddered at the insanity. The look on Marek's face didn't help either. He seemed resigned to die at her hands. It was so contrary to everything I knew of his character that it shook me more than anything else I had seen.

I felt Viktor wrap his arms around me and pull me tightly into his chest. I must have been shaking harder than I thought. He was the last person I would normally take comfort in but given we were already connected in this vision, I didn't fight him. I also sensed that he was concerned about what I was seeing. Marek should be the one concerned.

A disturbance of some kind distracted Magdalena from Marek. She looked up to see several vampires run into the room.

"Master, she has left the compound. Now is the time if you want to capture her." A skinny blonde woman said.

"Follow her. If an opportunity presents itself take her." Magdalena said.

She motioned for the group to leave and they dutifully ran back out of the room.

"Please Lena," Marek gasped from the floor. "I will do anything. Do not hurt her."

"Mi Corazon, what does it matter now that you are mine again?" She asked kneeling beside him.

"She is important," He said struggling to breathe.

"To whom Carino?" Magdalena asked stroking his cheek.

"The world," He said.

"Liar!" She said grabbing him by the throat.

She pulled him off the floor and pressed him upright against the wall in one liquid-smooth movement. Blood dribbled out of his mouth but he didn't move an inch. He let her hold him there.

"She is your lover! I will kill her for thinking she can have you. With her gone, you will be free to love me again." She said.

Marek closed his eyes as if he was going to pass out. Instead, he spoke.

"As you wish," He managed to say.

She dropped him immediately upon hearing the words. He hit the ground and appeared to be unconscious. She regarded him for a moment before walking out of the room. Her guards went with her, leaving Marek alone in the room.

After a moment, Marek moved. He struggled a great deal but managed to stand. Using the walls as support, he walked slowly out of the room. He moved slowly for a vampire but faster than a human. I watched as he found his way out of the house leaving a trail of blood the whole way.

I knew the rest of his journey and I couldn't believe he made it as far as he had on foot. I tried to pick up a vision of Magdalena but I wasn't the one with a deep connection to her. Viktor couldn't help me either.

I let the vision go and opened my eyes to the two vampire prisoners. They squirmed at my gaze. I stepped out of the comfort of Viktor's arms, the irony wasn't lost on me.

"Now that she lost her big prize, what is Magdalena up to?" I asked them.

"The Master will kill you," the skinny blonde from my vision said.

"I'm certain she will try. That's where you come in." I said stepping toward her.

Her eyes got big and she leaned back as if she could melt into the wall behind her. I could feel her fear through the tentative bond that Viktor formed and I used it to my advantage.

"I won't tell you anything," She said.

"You won't have to," I assured her.

I touched her arm and she relaxed. Moving my fingers so I touched her skin, I pulled at her connection to Magdalena. According to my previous vision, she was an important member of the organization. If one of these two knew anything, it would be her.

Marek cleared his throat. It must have been to get my attention. When I looked at him, his eyes bore into mine. I opened our bond enough to feel he didn't want me questioning this vampire. He knew her. The problem was I wasn't sure I could trust him anymore.

"It's okay," I told the vampire. "This won't hurt a bit."

I held my hand out to Viktor. He moved to me immediately and grasped my hand. The instant he touched me the link between him and the vampire strengthened. Now that I was also touching her, I could feel her connection to Magdalena.

"Clear the room," Marek said.

Everyone turned to him and froze. It wasn't like him to break protocol.

"Sir," Guardian Johnson started to protest.

"Now!" Marek yelled.

Everyone scrambled out the door with the exception of Viktor, James, and me. I was suddenly proud of the way James and Viktor looked at me for approval. Unfortunately, Marek wasn't happy with that turn of events.

"You too," Marek said looking at my guys.

"They get to stay," I said.

Marek narrowed his eyes at me.

"May I speak with you before you proceed?" He asked.

"No. Why are you interrupting?" I asked suddenly furious.

"Damn it Ember, I need to speak with you immediately." He said.

He was unraveled. It was so unusual for him that I granted his request.

"James, take over for now," I said.

James agreed although I could tell he wasn't happy about Marek's behavior either. I followed Marek out of the room where he showed me into another smaller room. He closed the door behind us.

"You need to be careful. That vampire is Magdalena's most trusted spy." He said.

"How do you know that?" I asked.

"She's been with Magdalena for a long time and she is credited for training some of the most successful female spies in history." He said.

"What does that have to do with me interrogating her?" I asked.

"She was captured for a reason. Whatever you get from her will most likely lead you to be captured." Marek said.

"You could have warned me before I went in there. Why drag me out in the middle of finding things out?" I asked.

"I was surprised by your arrival. I left you upstairs tucked into bed where I thought you would stay. Why did you come down?" He asked.

"You were the reason. I found it strange that you left me behind after I had been hurt. It was uncharacteristic of you." I said.

"I see," He said pacing the small room.

"I know you too well, Marek. My only question is why did you want to speak to the prisoners without me?" I asked.

"I hoped you would rest and recuperate. I was clearly wrong." Marek said.

"What about my previous behavior told you that would work?" I asked.

"You had two handsome men encircling you in your bed. Viktor was barely holding back his urge to bite you. I thought if I left he would give in and you would enjoy the attention." He said.

I didn't tell him how much I enjoyed the attention. What was missing from the enjoyment was Marek.

"Manipulating me is a new low for you, Marek. If I didn't know better I would think you are trying to get me to stop trusting you. Viktor feels strongly enough on the topic that it has me questioning your motives." I said.

Marek stopped pacing and walked over to me. He pulled me into his arms until his lips were almost touching mine.

"My only motivation is keeping you safe. If you doubt that, you haven't been paying attention." He said then kissed me.

It was the kind of kiss that takes your breath away. When he let me come up for air, the intensity in his eyes told me everything. He loved me more than life itself.

"Her name is Violetta and I know her from the years I spent with Magdalena. She isn't the helpless thing she looks like. She is a viper hidden as a puppy. Promise me you will be careful." Marek said.

"I'll be as careful as you would be," I said and walked out of the room.

I ignored his angry stomp behind me. Vampires don't normally make noise when they walk so I knew he was truly upset.

When I walked back into the room with the prisoners, James was shaking his head and Viktor was smiling. Viktor happy was never a good sign.

"What did I miss?" I asked walking over to my guys.

They parted and moved to either side of me. It was like having armor that fell in place on its own. It was more than cozy. It felt right.

"Master," Viktor said bowing to me. "The prisoners were resistant while you were away."

"Thank you, Viktor," I said trying to hide my smile.

I don't know what it was with him lately but his snide remarks delighted me. It had to have something to do with sharing blood with him because I used to only find him annoying. To be fair, he was still super annoying.

"I wish to speak with Violetta alone. James, please remove the other prisoner." I said.

"Yes, ma'am," He said.

James called in a few Guardians to assist him. They removed the male vampire from the wall and escorted him out. He went quietly which was surprising.

I looked at Violetta and saw her smirking back at me.

"Viktor, please wait outside," I said.

He was about to protest but I raised an eyebrow at him and he seemed to remember I was his master. Viktor bowed and left the room which left Marek and me alone with Violetta.

"May I stay?" Marek asked.

I nodded a yes at him then turned back to our vampire prisoner. Her level of amusement raised a few points. She must have wanted the two of us together.

"You seem to be in good spirits," I said to her.

"My old friend and a new enemy together. It's enough to put my heart aflutter." She said.

She spoke with a slight French accent as if it had been a long time since she had lived in France.

"What does your master want you to do here? You allowed yourself to be captured so that we could speak. Now's your chance." I said.

Her posture suddenly improved. Instead of looking like a beaten foot soldier, she became a regal master before our eyes. Her blonde hair became a bouncy shiny mane and her skin obtained a rosy hue. She was beautiful even if slightly more plain than I would have expected.

"Mongrel, you will die by my hand. I'll make sure Marek watches so he remembers his place." She said to me then turned to Marek. "This streak of independence has been amusing but the fun is over, brother. It is time you return to where you belong."

"My place is by Ember's side," Marek responded.

"Oh Marek, your loyalty has always been misplaced but this time could be the death of you. That little prank you pulled on Lena should have been enough to shake her devotion to you but somehow she still pines for you. You are lucky she is willing to give you another chance." Violetta said.

"What does she have planned?" Marek asked.

Violetta just smiled in response. Marek smiled back and her smile faltered.

Marek's hand went to her throat so fast I didn't see it happen. He pinned her against the wall so hard I could see her neck compress under his hand. A wave of nausea hit me but I fought through it.

"Please don't remove her head before I'm done getting answers from her," I said softly.

Marek released her after pressing harder for a split second. Violetta's face turned a shade of red before returning to a more vampire appropriate pale shade.

Instead of asking her a question expecting her to respond with a crushed larynx, I moved forward and grabbed her arm. There was no way she was going to voluntarily tell us anything, so I took it from her mind.

"Since my partner so helpfully shut you up, I'll take a different approach,"

I said glaring at Marek.

Violetta couldn't swallow so the saliva in her mouth dribbled down her chin. It was pathetic but I didn't get caught up in sympathy. She was the enemy and I needed to find out what she knew.

She flinched back from me but I kept hold of her.

"What is your boss up to, Violetta?" I asked then let my clairvoyance take me into her thoughts.

I couldn't read minds but I could get flashes of events when I concentrated on someone. Having Violetta in front of me should help the process along as it had before when I saw Marek beaten by Magdalena. The trick was finding the right thread to pull.

I concentrated on her, searching for an image to lock onto and read. A twinge in my head distracted me. I pushed harder for what I needed only to find pain.

"Ember," Marek said grabbing me.

I tried not to lose the images that started flickering through my mind. Pushing harder caused the pain to intensify. Mashing my lips together didn't do much to hold back the cry that escaped my mouth.

"I'm fine," I said unconvincingly.

"James!" Marek yelled.

"What's the matter, Marek? Is your pet broken? I wonder what could possibly be wrong with her." Violetta said sarcastically, her voice healed enough to speak again.

Marek glared at her then turned to James when he entered the room. He took one look at me and rushed to my side.

"Let's go," James said.

The look on his face told me he wouldn't accept any argument from me. As my second, he had to take orders from me but as my friend, he didn't need them.

"You take all the fun out of the interrogation," I said.

"Is she seriously that breakable?" Violetta said.

Marek turned and punch her in the face so hard she lost consciousness.

"Marek!" I yelled shocked that he lost control.

"I will do this my way from here. Take her to the doctor and Ember?" He said.

"Yes?" I replied wincing.

I shouldn't have yelled.

"Please do what the doctor says. If you are not okay..." He let the statement hang in the air.

"I'm fine," I said trying to reassure him.

"Make sure that statement is true," Marek said, then kissed me gently on the forehead.

James walked me out of the room. Viktor joined us and I could feel his anger simmering. The two of them escorted me directly to the doctor. When I got there, I collapsed into an all-consuming pain.

James held me close and Viktor stayed near while we waited for the doctor. Finding myself in this situation time and time again was frustrating. We needed to find the cause.

"Hang on, Em. Dr. Wallace is on her way." James said.

"The doctor is incompetent. We need Julien," Viktor said.

"Why? How can Julien help?" I asked cringing at the light when I tried to look at Viktor.

"He can do things no doctor can do. Trust me on this, he can help." Viktor assured me.

I looked at Viktor and opened our bond. He was distressed and desperate for me to be okay. It took my breath away to feel that from him. Viktor caring for me was, strange.

"Call him," I said.

"Ember, you can't be serious," James protested.

"James, I need this illness to go away. What happens when I go down during a fight? It almost happened earlier tonight. You know we need to do this. I need the cause and I need it now." I said.

"Trusting Viktor does not come naturally to me," James said.

"And here I thought we were one big happy family," Viktor said sarcastically.

"Viktor, make the call." I said handing him my phone, "And James, get Julien clearance to get in to see me."

"I'd prefer to get Dr. Wallace's opinion before we bring someone else in on this," James said.

My headache roared its displeasure at my having to speak. I must have made a sound to that effect because Viktor bristled.

"Every time you argue with her you cause her pain. How about you leave now and get that clearance for Julien? I'll stay here and take care of her." Viktor said in a tone that did not allow James to argue.

James stood up and left the room without looking back. My shock must have shown on my face.

"He was being an asshole. Lay back, my dear." Viktor said.

I did what he said and tried to relax.

"I can't believe you told him to leave and he listened to you," I said weakly.

"Stop talking," Viktor said stroking my cheek.

I took a deep breath and tried to relax. I closed my eyes to block out the light and get a grip on the pain. I also realized I was listening to Viktor too. It made me smile.

Viktor spoke to Julien on the phone using a soft voice so as not to disturb me. He made arrangements for Julien to come right away. While he was talking I drifted off to sleep or passed out. I'm not sure which.

I woke sometime later to Dr. Wallace and Julien discussing my condition. It didn't sound like an argument so I assumed all was going well. I tried to listen in to what they were saying but couldn't pick up much. Their voices were pitched low so it was hard to hear.

Before I let them know I was awake I scanned the room to see who was there. Viktor was next to the bed debating whether or not to hold my hand. I could hear him whispering arguments to himself.

“Just take my hand already, Viktor,” I said opening my eyes.

Everyone stopped what they were doing and turned to me. Viktor took my hand and smiled.

“How are you feeling, my dear?” Viktor asked.

“My head still hurts although I do feel a little better,” I said.

He brought my hand to his lips and placed a soft kiss across my knuckles. It was sweet and so unlike him.

“Madame, if you don’t mind, Master Le Veneur would like to speak with you.” Dr. Wallace said.

Viktor stood, draping my hand over my stomach. He stroked it gently before walking away. Julien took his place at my bedside.

“Madame Summers, I am honored to attend you,” Julien said with his lovely light French accent.

“Julien, please call me Ember,” I said reminding him we are friends.

“As you wish, ma Cherie,” Julien said. “Viktor said you are struggling with headaches when you use your powers. Is that an accurate statement?”

“Only when I use my clairvoyance. My other powers do not cause me pain.” I said.

“May I lay my hands on you?” He asked. “I assure you I will not take advantage.”

I nodded my consent. Julien began by taking my hand then ran his fingers up my arm to the shoulder. Goosebumps formed across my body and a tingling sensation formed in my arms and legs.

“Julien,” I gasped.

“Just a moment longer,” Julien said, eyes closed concentrating.

The feeling wasn’t unpleasant and that was sort of the problem. My stomach fluttered like he was leaning in for a kiss. Maybe I was just hypersensitive to a handsome man running his hands over me.

Julien’s hands glided over my shoulders then up my neck moving along the curve of my neck and into my hair. His fingers slid through my hair massaging my scalp and eliciting a moan from me. I would have been embarrassed if it didn’t feel so good.

Julien didn’t stop until his thumbs pressed into my temples. He began to circle over the sensitive flesh until every last hint of pain melted away on a wave of bliss. Whatever his gift was, it had to be magic.

“How do you feel, Ember?” Julien asked, continuing to cradle my head in his hands.

“Perfectly at ease,” I replied.

“*Bon*,” Julien said. “I had hoped that was so.”

I opened my eyes and peered into his face. His eyes were a lovely shade of blue-green and combined with the rest of his features made for a lovely sight.

It must be a pre-requisite of becoming a vampire to be handsome.

"Did you find the cause of her headaches?" Viktor asked.

"That is complicated. I believe I know the cause but the magic is not currently active so I cannot trace it." Julien said.

"What magic?" I asked.

Julien released me gently then sat back in the chair. He looked upon me kindly before answering the question.

"Your blood sings to me, Ember. I would like to explore that further some time but that isn't why I'm here."

"What I found was remnants of a spell that is causing interference with your clairvoyance. Think of it like static feedback when a radio station isn't properly tuned. When you use your Seer ability that feedback builds up and blocks the transmission from getting through. That is what is causing your headaches."

"What I cannot do at this time is trace the origin. The spell appears to be inactive right now. If I could trace it while it is active, I could tell you who placed the spell and when." He said.

"You are certain it's a spell?" Dr. Wallace asked.

"Yes, most definitely," Julien said.

The doctor looked shocked. She clearly thought nothing would be found by this examination.

"How do I activate the spell so you can trace it?" I asked.

"I don't recommend you do so at this time," Dr. Wallace said.

"What do you think, Julien?" I asked ignoring the scowl on Dr. Wallace's face.

He leaned forward and took my hand. The tingling from before returned and I sighed. Whatever it was he was doing made me feel wonderful. He seemed to catch himself and released me.

"Pardon," Julien said bowing his head slightly. "As the Master of my Sire, I should show you more respect."

I sat up and grabbed his hand, "We are friends, Julien. Please speak your mind."

He smiled at our joined hands and said, "I will do anything you desire. If you want to activate the spell, I will trace it. I believe all you need to do is use your clairvoyant power."

"I think you are developing an affinity for the hospital wing, my dear. Think before you leap as they say," Viktor warned.

"You don't think we should trace it?" I asked looking back at him.

"I think we can easily guess who did this to you. What we need is to remove the spell so it cannot hurt you any longer." Viktor said.

"Per the Council's Grandmaster, the highest priority is to get Ember out of harm's way," Marek said walking into the room.

Everyone froze with the exception of Viktor, who walked over and sat down beside me. It felt like he was protecting me.

15

Marek commanded all eyes in the room with the exception of Viktor. It was clear to me that Viktor thought Marek wasn't worth his attention. The two of them were going to come to blows one day and I knew inevitably I would be caught in the middle.

My attention shifted to Julien who looked like he was trying to decide if he should address Marek or me. I decided to let him off easy.

"Julien, how do we remove the spell?" I asked, taking his hand back in mine.

He looked at our entwined fingers and a small smile crossed his lips. When he looked back into my eyes, there was a sparkle there that wasn't present before.

"We need a strong magic user combined with my power," Julien said.

I looked at Marek. The only strong magic user I knew was not someone I could trust. Marek's face was its usual stoic blankness.

"I'm assuming you have someone in mind?" I asked Julien.

"I do," He said.

"Only a Council approved practitioner will be acceptable." Marek chimed in.

I fought not to roll my eyes at him.

"I believe Rowan is on the list," Julien said looking smug.

Marek stiffened. Whoever this Rowan character was, they must not be someone Marek wanted to engage. That made me extremely curious.

"It will take some time to get her here. She's on a contract in France," Viktor added.

"I'll pull in someone else who can do this today," Marek said.

"I'll only work with Rowan. I won't trust this procedure with anyone less skilled," Julien said.

"As the one who will have the spell removed, I'd prefer we go with the most qualified candidate. If that's Rowan, I'll wait for her." I said.

Marek gave me a withering look. I could tell my faith in Julien was bothering him.

Julien looked pleased and said, "My team will make arrangements to have Rowan here by the end of the week. In the meantime, if you have any symptoms call me night or day. Viktor will know where I am in case of an emergency. You have clearance to enter all my properties without notice."

"Thank you, Julien. That is extremely kind of you." I said feeling overwhelmed by his generosity.

"It's the least I can do," He said.

He kissed my hand then looked into my eyes and smiled. I barely knew this man yet I felt like I could trust him. The sparkle in his eyes was likely a vampire trick but I didn't think it was meant to influence me beyond his romantic interests.

Marek cleared his throat then said, "The Council appreciates your service, Master Le Veneur. Madame Summer's assistant will be in touch to firm up arrangements for Rowan's arrival."

Julien took Marek's words as a dismissal and exited the room with Dr. Wallace. He said something about Dr. Wallace helping him to prepare. It was weird to think my life depended on these two strangers. People I liked yet knew next to nothing about.

Julien's eyes lingered on me before he walked down the hall and out of view. It reminded me of the way James used to look at me like he wasn't sure if he liked me or hated me. I hoped for the former.

Viktor was attuned to my thoughts and said, "He values you and is intrigued in a way that confuses him."

"How so?" I asked.

"Your power rivals his which excites him yet he isn't in the habit of bowing down to anyone. His attraction to you is clear but he is uncertain what to do with it," Viktor said.

"I've told him I am unavailable," I said glancing at Marek to see his reaction.

"That is no deterrent to a master vampire," Viktor said.

"Of which I have daily proof," I said rolling my eyes at Viktor.

Marek shifted uncomfortably. He wanted to speak but hesitated in Viktor's company. I didn't blame him.

"I am happy with my fate," Viktor declared sounding sullen.

It bothered me that he sounded weak. Viktor was a master vampire and he should look like one.

"Meekness doesn't become you, Viktor," I said.

"Perhaps you will think of something to perk me up," He said, eyes darting to my neck.

I made a noncommittal sound then looked at Marek. He and I needed to talk. It was clear that wouldn't happen with Viktor hanging around. An idea popped into my head.

"Where is James?" I asked Marek.

"Just outside the door," Marek smiled.

"Good. I'm ready to get out of this room," I said. "Viktor, I won't be able to rest until someone checks on Natalie. If this is a spell causing my pain I want to be sure my sister isn't affected. Will you please check in on her for me? James can show you the way."

"It would be my pleasure," Viktor said standing then bowing to me.

James walked in with an eyebrow raised.

"James, will you please escort Viktor to Natalie's room? I want to make sure she is okay and as her sire, Viktor could ease her if she needs it." I said.

"Indeed. I will take him to her right away," He said and motioned for Viktor to follow him.

James gave Marek a look to which he replied, "I will not leave her side until you return, James."

Satisfied, James nodded then led Viktor down the hall. Marek turned to me as soon as the others were out of sight.

"How about we get you home and more comfortable?" He suggested.

"That sounds wonderful," I replied.

I threw my legs over the side of the bed and stood up. Marek stepped in front of me, pulling me into his arms.

"I am glad that you are okay," He whispered kissing the top of my head.

I leaned into him soaking in his comfort. It felt good to have his arms around me and to be alone. Having James and Viktor constantly at my side was starting to wear on me. I was used to being alone most of the time.

Marek took my hand as we walked out of the hospital wing. He kept hold of it until we were in the elevator. He hit the button for the penthouse then turned to me.

"Alone at last," Marek said.

He pulled me into his chest and kissed me. It was urgent and almost bruising. I pulled back, stopping him.

"What's wrong?" I asked, holding his face in my hands.

He pulled my hands down and held them.

"Within a few weeks' time, you have gone from my charge to a powerful master in your own right. I am unsettled by the many demands for your attention and affection from others." He said.

"Are you jealous?" I asked smiling.

"A jealous master vampire is no laughing matter," He said seriously.

I sighed and said, "Tell me what I can do to make it better."

"I would not have you change." He said looking sad.

"Marek, I..." I started but he interrupted.

"I have only myself to blame. Had I managed to find your sister before she was turned, I could have prevented Viktor from inserting himself into your life." Marek said.

The elevator dinged at the top floor. The doors slid open and we walked to Marek's penthouse. I held my tongue until we were inside his apartment.

"You are not to blame for Natalie and you know it," I said fiercely.

"You were right that night. I should have let you come with me. I was wrong to ignore your feelings. You knew she was in danger that evening and I brushed you aside. That is why I blame myself for Viktor turning your sister into a vampire." He said.

Viktor had been my enemy for the majority of the time I had known him. He pretended to love my sister in order to get closer to me. It was despicable and deceitful but worse was that he made her a vampire against her will.

"You know very well that wasn't something either of us could have prevented. Why are you beating yourself up about it now?" I asked curious to hear why.

"I have disappointed you and I wish to own it." He said.

"I wish I didn't feel any affection for Viktor but our bond makes that impossible. If I can stand to have him around, I think I can put up with a great deal from you." I said.

"You should not tolerate any deceit from those around you. I should not be exempt," he said.

"The last time I hinted about you being deceitful, you went off and tried to get yourself killed," I said.

"My intention was to right wrongs not get myself killed," He said plopping down on the sofa.

I sat next to him curling up against him.

"What does Magdalena use against you? I know she was the one that beat you and cut you up." I said.

He stilled at my words.

"She all but cut out my heart with her words," He said looking stricken.

"What did she say, Marek?" I insisted.

"She threatened you if I resisted her. So I let her take her anger out on me. I did not believe she would kill me. She claims to love me." He said.

"You tricked her into believing you loved her in France. That's how you got close enough for a killing blow even if it didn't actually kill her." I guessed.

I had pieced it all together from several visions.

"And you doubt my intensions with you because of it," He said softly.

It was like he didn't want me to acknowledge it.

"I think it's more accurate to say that Viktor enjoys sowing the seeds of doubt. I do my best to ignore him." I said.

"He is positioning himself as your advisor. You may have named James as your second but Viktor will always try for that position," Marek said.

"Seeing Natalie will calm him down for a while," I said hoping it was true.

"I know Natalie needs him to master her hunger but I hope you will keep him from poisoning her mind. I am learning from Caden that she is very impressionable." He said.

"That I know. My sister has always been easily swayed especially by handsome men. Viktor is more capable than most in that regard. Although I do think he cares for her now that he made her a vampire." I said.

Marek was quiet long enough for me to worry about his thoughts. I could feel there was something he was itching to say.

"I have never seen Viktor in love before. It is strange to see." Marek said.

"I didn't say he loved Nat," I said disagreeing.

"I was not referring to Natalie," Marek said.

I looked at him incredulously.

"Viktor doesn't love me. He loves power." I said.

"Power is attractive but you, *Milaya moya,* are irresistible," He said leaning in to kiss me.

This time it was soft and seductive. He tugged on my bottom lip with his teeth and a zing of pleasure shot through my body. Before I knew what I was doing I had straddled his lap and flung my arms around his neck. His hands found the edge of my t-shirt and slipped under the fabric.

His body was warm and his vanilla scent teased my nose. I wanted to lose myself in his affection. It would erase the vision of him bleeding to death while Magdalena gutted him. I didn't think I could stand to see that again.

"I want you to promise me something," I said leaning back.

"What is it?" He asked.

"Don't ever let someone weaken you by threatening me," I insisted.

I let the fire of my anger and fear show in my eyes.

"I did not believe she would kill me," He countered.

"I saw what happened, Marek. You can't possibly believe she meant anything else," I said.

"She was angry," He said.

I got off his lap and stood up.

"Where are you going?" He asked reaching for me.

"Stepping away before I smack some sense back into you!" I said.

"Ember, I will not die," He said standing up to come after me.

"Says the man who was on the verge of death less than 24 hours ago," I said, throwing my hands into the air.

"I cannot make that promise. I would stand in a fire and burn if it meant sparing your life." He said.

I was startled by his vehement admission. A vampire willing to die by fire is the greatest sacrifice.

"And how do you think I'd feel when you're dead?" I asked.

"The key to that statement Ember is that you would feel." He said softly leaning into my body.

His presence filled my vision and the steely look in his eyes showed he didn't want to argue the point further. Being with a master vampire could be challenging but the rewards so far were well worth the effort.

"We can agree to disagree. I don't wish to quarrel with you tonight." I said.

"Then what is it you wish?" Marek asked.

"To be alone with you uninterrupted," I said.

My phone chose that moment to ring.

"We must steal all the moments we can," Marek said pulling my phone from my pocket and throwing it across the room.

He pulled me into his body and kissed me. I forgot all about the phone when he bit my bottom lip. It was a tiny pinprick of pain but the resulting feeling of him sucking the few drops of blood that welled up off my skin drove me wild. Heat rushed to my core and my breathing became ragged.

"I like where this is going," I said breathlessly.

Marek turned me toward his bedroom and walked me backward while kissing me. His hands roamed my body stroking every patch of exposed skin. My body was flushed and I suddenly felt lightheaded.

I stumbled but Marek was there to keep me upright. We entered his bedroom which was technically our bedroom since I agreed to move in with him. The back of my legs hit the bed. Marek pushed me down then followed me hovering above me.

I entwined my legs with his and welcomed the weight of him against my body. The feeling of being trapped beneath him made my heart race. Technically I could throw him across the room using my power but I let myself feel like a normal human girl. It wasn't a big stretch.

Marek kissed my neck sucking and nipping the sensitive skin. A moan of approval escaped my lips. His answering growl kicked my breathing up a notch. This man, this vampire could drive me wild with the slightest touch.

He dragged his fingers along my rib cage while he pulled my shirt off creating goosebumps all over my body. A flash of heat infused my body with a surge of lust. I pulled at Marek's clothing until I felt his warm skin against my own.

Unlike what the storybooks say about vampires, Marek could warm his body making him feel like any human. I suppose that is part of what makes them so dangerous. Combine their warm skin with their natural charisma and soothing pheromones and humans have no way to know they are dealing with a vampire.

For me, everything that makes them dangerous excites and fascinates me. It used to bother me more about how attracted I was to vampires. I've embraced this life with more enthusiasm lately.

Marek pulled off my jeans and was just about to remove my bra when there was a loud pounding at the front door. A heavy sigh came out of my mouth and Marek stilled.

"We need to start putting a sock on the door or something," I said.

"Ignore it. It might go away," He said.

"You know that doesn't work," I said.

The knocking got louder and I could hear shouting. It sounded like James and Viktor yelling at each other which was impressive considering I shouldn't have been able to hear them. The penthouse is huge with the bedroom on the opposite end of the apartment from the front door.

"I can get rid of them," Marek said not moving.

"We could make them wait," I said pulling him closer.

Marek kissed me and I took that as agreement. I unbuttoned his jeans and he made them disappear along with his underwear and mine. His vampire speed made it look like magic.

The sudden feel of his naked body against mine made me smile. I wrapped my arms around him and took a deep breath of his warm vanilla scent. The aroma was a mixture of his power with the essence of man that all men have. It spoke to me.

Wasting no time, Marek thrust into me. I ignored the faint sound of pounding coming from the front door and focused solely on Marek. He rocked his hips and I locked eyes with him. He opened our bond letting every part of him mingle with every part of me. The brush of his power inside me felt amazing combined with the movement of our bodies.

I met him thrust for thrust while pulling his power around me. Marek did the same resulting in an exquisite push and pull of power that matched the rhythm of our bodies. Within moments I was on the edge of release.

Marek plunged his tongue into my mouth in time with his hard length hitting my core. It drove me over the edge. I came hard and called out my pleasure just as Marek found his own release. We collapsed together on the bed breathing hard clinging to each other.

It was quiet for a few minutes then a soft knock sounded at the front door. It made me laugh.

"Why is that funny?" Marek whispered in my ear before kissing my temple.

I shivered, wanting to roll on top of him and go for round two. I really needed more alone time with Marek.

"Because they think it's okay to knock again," I said.

"I will take care of it," He said then slipped out of my arms to walk naked to the front door.

That was a man confident in his manhood. I watched him walk away paying close attention to how the muscles of his backside moved under his flesh. The view was fantastic from where I was sitting. His broad shoulders and narrow waist combined with his tight ass had me drooling.

I hoped my guys didn't have anything too urgent to share because I planned to spend the night in bed with Marek. I tucked myself under the covers and got comfortable.

The sound of hushed voices drifted into the bedroom. I closed my eyes and tried to will them away. It must have worked because after a while I felt Marek slide into bed with me. He spooned me from behind and pulled me tight into his chest.

Marek didn't say anything so I took that as good news. I relaxed into him and let myself drift off. I didn't realize how tired I was until I was still enough to feel it. Within minutes I was asleep.

The heavenly scent of freshly brewed coffee woke me in the morning. Marek was next to me in bed so I assumed someone else was in the apartment. A quick sweep with my power told me it was James in the kitchen. I wondered if he spent the night or if he was told not to come back until the morning.

I turned over to face Marek and found him awake.

"Good morning," I said.

"It is a very good morning," He said leaning in to kiss me.

I snuggled into him perfectly content to stay there for as long as possible. Sounds of rustling around came from the kitchen distracting me from Marek.

"James is making breakfast," Marek said.

"I'm sensing a full house," I said.

"Viktor was the one making all the commotion last night. He wanted your permission to keep Natalie with him but he said he couldn't get through to you. Long story short, I told them all they could stay if they did not make a sound until the morning." Marek said.

"Why do we have extra people here?" I asked confused.

"I assigned Murphy to your security detail and Natalie is here because Caden had to guard Sebastian last night. It helped to calm Viktor down too which was a bonus." He said.

"I suppose I should go check in with everyone," I said.

"Or we could shower together instead," Marek suggested with a smirk on his face.

I liked his idea much better than mine so I pushed him off the bed toward the bathroom. Marek had the shower going before I made it into the room. We took our time under the hot spray of water.

I pulled Marek toward me so I could access his neck. Not for the first time, I wished I had fangs so that I could bite his neck at will. My cravings for him built while I kissed his neck and nipped at his flesh.

"Hold that thought," Marek said then zipped away.

Seconds later he returned with blood dripping down his neck. I latched on sucking down the caramel bliss. The power contained in his blood exploded on my tongue then flowed through my body. Every nerve ending lit up, bringing a flush to my skin.

When the flow slowed, I bit into Marek's neck to encourage it to continue. He groaned his approval pulling me tightly into his chest. I sucked harder on his neck until there was nothing left of the flow.

Marek pushed me harder into the wall of the shower capturing my mouth with his own. Sex was good but what I really wanted was to be bitten. There was nothing like the bite of a vampire. I was learning that Marek had a more potent bite than others and I was well and truly addicted to it.

Finally, when I couldn't take it anymore, he bit me. My power flared although I fought to real it in as best I could.

With each swallow of my blood Marek took, I felt an answering pulse within me that was as good as any orgasm.

He took one last swallow then healed the punctures. Marek leaned back and smiled.

"Too much for you?" He asked.

"Just enough," I smiled up at him.

"I love you," Marek said stroking my face.

"And I love you," I replied.

16

Marek and I emerged from the bedroom to find my sister and Viktor seated on the sofa and Guardian Murphy at the dining table with James. There was a large breakfast spread out over the surface of the table. I spotted a platter full of bacon and made a beeline for the empty seat near it.

"Good morning, Master," Viktor said bowing his head.

"Morning Viktor. Hello Nat," I said distracted by the food.

When my sister realized Viktor had been speaking to me, she looked at Viktor like he had lost his mind.

"My darling, your sister is my master. I know it is confusing but you must acknowledge her rank as the Master of your Sire." Viktor told her.

"But that isn't possible," Natalie proclaimed.

"Dearest, are you doubting my word as your Sire?" Viktor asked with a steely voice.

My sister stiffened and professed she was sorry. Viktor forgave her then put his arm around her as if they were cuddling. He sat stiffly as if he didn't want to comfort her but it appeared to calm my sister. She was never good at reading body language but it had the effect Viktor wanted because he smiled up at me.

I rolled my eyes and plopped down at the dining table next to James. With Viktor back to normal I could concentrate on filling my belly with food. I helped myself to a little of everything on the table. It felt like I was at a five-star hotel with a personal chef.

Marek strolled over to me looking every bit the polished businessman in his black suit. It reminded me of my ex, Nikko Manetti who wore handmade Italian suits daily. It was a toss-up as to who wore it better.

Marek moved next to me and touched my shoulder.

"I asked our assistant to join you up here this morning." He said. "Sebastian has a few requests for you and there are the arrangements for Rowan to complete. I thought it would be easiest for you to work out of the office here versus going downstairs."

"For today, I agree," I said.

Thinking of having to keep an eye on Viktor and Natalie for longer than a few days made my head hurt. I was responsible for Viktor until we settled his complaint and he stood trial yet there had to be a better arrangement.

Marek leaned over to kiss me goodbye. His lips were warm. He pulled back and licked a spot of syrup off his bottom lip then smiled. I wiped my mouth and gave him an apologetic look.

"My pancakes are better than his," Marek said softly then turned to walk away.

I darted a glance at James who looked annoyed then back at Marek. Marek smirked over his shoulder as he walked toward the door. The view of him was just as good from the back as it was from the front. I was a lucky woman.

"Big talk until you deliver," I yelled at him referring to the pancakes.

I found it particularly endearing that Marek liked to cook for me. He had done so on several occasions since he came into my life. James told me it was unusual for a vampire and it was one of the things that made it clear that Marek cared for me.

Marek waived then left the apartment with a smile on his face. I felt my own stupid grin before catching the eyes of everyone in the room.

"What?" I asked wondering why they were all staring.

"I've never seen Master Volkov grin or talk about cooking *food*. I didn't think it was possible." Murphy said.

"Trust me. You haven't seen anything yet," James said in mock warning.

Her eyes got big before her face split into a smile.

"He's happy," She said as if she didn't quite believe it.

My sister came to the table and plopped down opposite me.

"You're clearly sleeping with him, but what's the deal? Is he your boyfriend?" She asked.

I hadn't talked to my sister about my personal life since she was turned into a vampire. There wasn't time. I guess now was as good a time as ever.

"You could say that," I answered.

"Holy shit!" Murphy said.

"Ciara!" James said pronouncing her name (Kee-rah).

"What? Master Volkov doesn't date. At least he hasn't since he's been with the Council." She said.

"How long has that been?" I asked.

"He's been with this chapter for forty years," Ciara Murphy said.

"So does that mean he isn't your boyfriend and you are just having sex like friends with benefits?" Natalie asked.

"No, we're in a relationship," I said but it sounded a little defensive.

James backed me up, "I don't think anyone that has seen them together could doubt that he cares for her deeply and is committed to her."

It was Murphy's turn to widen her eyes again, "Congratulations Madame, you've landed the most eligible bachelor of the last century."

I choked on my orange juice. It was one thing to know Marek was old. It was something else entirely to hear it laid out in terms of actual years. James slapped my back and made sure I was okay.

"How can you be in a relationship with a master vampire if you aren't a vampire? That can't work. He will outlive you." Natalie pointed out.

"I..." I started to respond but Viktor jumped in before I could.

"What you are missing dear child, is that your sister is a master too. It doesn't matter that he is a vampire, her power is greater and thus puts her standing above his. She has the right to take him as a lover or as a mate, whatever she sees fit." Viktor said crossing his arms and leaning against the windows in the breakfast room.

"But he will live longer than her," Natalie protested.

"Not necessarily," Viktor said.

"Whoa, what? Explain." I said to Viktor.

"Power has a way of extending life, my dear. You met Asher Sands who is human. He's at least a thousand years old." He said simply.

"I didn't realize he was that old," I said marveling at the possibility.

I wasn't sure I believed I could live an extended amount of time (or wanted to if I could) but the concept was intriguing. Asher Sands, also known as the Egyptian, is a magician known throughout the supernatural and paranormal communities as a powerful force. I wouldn't delude myself into thinking I had anything resembling his power.

A knock sounded at the front door. I expected James to get up but it was Murphy who answered the knock. She let the man in and walked with him back to the breakfast table.

"Madame Summers, good morning. It's good to finally meet you. I'm your assistant Benjamin Pierce," He said bowing.

Benjamin Pierce was a short slender man, maybe five foot five with dark brown hair that matched his eyes. He wore thick black-framed Coke bottle glasses that he clearly needed to see anything at all. He had something past a five o'clock shadow on the verge of becoming a beard that made him look older yet he still appeared no more than twenty years of age. He was as cute as a button.

"Good morning. Are you hungry? We are just finishing breakfast." I said offering him a seat at the table.

"Thank you madame but no. If you don't mind, I'll get set up in the office so we can get started. Your first appointment will be here in an hour and I'd like to get you up to speed before then." He said.

"Of course. Go ahead. I'll be right in." I replied.

"May I speak with you privately before you go into the office?" Viktor asked.

"What do you want?" I asked through our bond instead.

He scowled but answered me, *"I wish to accompany you during your day. Guardians are capable security personnel but nothing compares with a master vampire."*

"I don't need your protection Viktor," I said and watched his face fall. I

quickly added, *"but I'll keep it under advisement."*

"Thank you, master," Viktor said out loud bowing deeply.

He grabbed Natalie on his way to the living room and they settled into the couch. Natalie turned on the television and began searching for a movie to watch.

"What was that about?" James asked in a whisper.

Viktor would be able to hear but probably no one else.

"He is worried about my security," I said.

"We all are," James said standing up from the table.

He motioned for me to walk ahead of him, which I needed to remember to do, and I did after grabbing another piece of bacon. James followed me to the office but stayed outside the door as I went in.

Benjamin had stacks of folders and papers spread across the glass and steel desk. He stood patiently until I sat down in the office chair.

"I appreciate you taking time away from your new family to go over a few business items with me," Benjamin said.

"Of course, we have important work to discuss," I said.

"I thought we would begin with a few necessary legal documents and oaths which will allow us to move on to the confidential matters." He said placing a folder before me.

The folder was filled with the usual non-disclosure agreements and standards of conduct. The last document however was new to me.

"What is this?" I asked.

The document was on vellum, most likely made of cowhide, and handwritten in calligraphy. The bottom of the document included a box too large to be a checkbox.

"This one is magical in nature," He said pulling a knife from his pocket. "It requires a blood seal versus a signature."

I read every detail in that document not finding anything concerning. It was an oath of fealty to the Council that not only protected them but also protected me. They were naming me an Associate Counselor to the board. From what I knew of the inner workings, that was a high position of honor and one that Marek also held.

Satisfied, I motioned to Benjamin to proceed. He took my hand and sliced a gash across my thumb. Blood instantly welled up. Before it could drip, he pressed my thumb into the box on the document. A blue flash of light illuminated the document and a buzzing sensation filled my body before dissipating.

Viktor appeared at the door. James held him back with effort.

"It's fine Viktor," I assured him.

He narrowed his eyes at Benjamin when he saw him produce a bandage for my thumb. To Ben's credit, he didn't even flinch. He gathered all the papers back into their folder then he dropped the folder into a black envelope. He sealed it then put it into his messenger bag.

"It would be best to discuss business without an audience, madame,"

Benjamin said.

I made eye contact with James. Without a word, he pushed Viktor back then closed the office door behind them. Instant privacy. Benjamin didn't skip a beat. He pulled the next pile of folders in front of me and set a laptop on the desk.

My team, who I hadn't even met yet, had been working on a few leads. They watched for any clue that may show a new supernatural or paranormal has emerged. Then we deployed an investigator to confirm their identity and power. If confirmed, a Guardian was assigned and Marek's team took over.

It made me think about how I had been found. One of my investigators had to have confirmed my powers or I wouldn't have been assigned James as my Guardian. A feeling of violation overcame me.

"How aware of the investigator will they be?" I asked.

"Your team is the best, madame. They only need seconds to make confirmations. It can happen in a crowd or walking past them in a grocery store. The asset never knows about it." He said.

"Good," I said reading the rest of the report.

We reviewed all the potential assets and associated research compiled by the team. The research was solid on most of the files but I noticed some gaps.

"These three are well researched and can move forward," I said setting those files next to Benjamin. "The rest have gaps."

Benjamin looked surprised. He composed himself quickly then accepted my feedback readily. His reaction confirmed my suspicion that my team thought I was only in this role because I was sleeping with Marek. His rapt attention and frantic note-taking showed me his respect had just been earned.

A knock at the office door interrupted our progress.

"Come in," I said.

James poked his head inside the door and said, "Mr. Manetti is here for his nine o'clock."

"Let him know we are almost ready for him," Benjamin said.

James looked at me.

"Thank you, James," I said.

James nodded then closed the door.

"My apologies madame, I did not realize Guardian Leigh was sworn to you." Benjamin said bowing.

"I'm still learning what that means myself. Why is Nikko here?" I asked changing the subject.

"He needs to meet with you to finalize your response to Master Ivanov's neglect allegation, and discuss Viktor's further legal troubles," Benjamin said.

"I would prefer to have this meeting alone. Your assistance is appreciated but Nikko and I have history." I said.

"I will fetch him then leave," He bowed then left the room to get Nikko.

I smoothed my black shift dress down my front to ensure no wrinkles were present. Then I checked my hair and makeup quickly in a wall mirror. I stepped back behind the desk just as the door opened.

Nikko walked into the room wearing one of his fine Italian suits tailored specifically for him. His brown curls hung longer than usual but still somehow perfectly styled. His soulful brown eyes took me in as if he needed me to breathe. A pang in my heart told me how easy it would be to fall back into old habits with him.

"Ember, it's good to see you," Nikko said smiling.

"It's nice to see you too Nikko," I said motioning to the chair opposite the desk.

He sat down and then pulled a folder out of his briefcase.

"I met Master Ivanov on my way in. He's not what I expected." Nikko said.

"He is different since I bound him. Spending the past twenty-four hours with him has been educational. I'm learning it will be more permanent than I first thought." I said.

"What does Viktor have to say about the situation?" Nikko asked.

"We haven't spoken much about it," I said.

"Ember, either he withdraws the complaint or we go to court. It's that simple." Nikko said.

I got up and paced the room. Sitting made me feel trapped.

"Ember, what's wrong?" He asked.

"I'm confused by Viktor. I feel compassion for a man who kidnapped, tortured, then turn my sister into a vampire. Am I going crazy?" I asked.

Nikko stood from his chair and stopped me from pacing.

"Em, his actions are not yours and what you did to bind him saved your own life. That you have compassion for him is more chemical than conscious. What you will do as Viktor's master is to keep an otherwise unstable man focused on healthier pursuits such as protecting you." Nikko said.

"He is protective," I agreed.

"He grilled me regarding my intentions toward you," Nikko said smiling.

"Why does that amuse you?" I asked.

"Because he so clearly loves you. I can relate. You inspire devotion, Em. You always have." He said.

The regret in his eyes was clear and I tried to ignore it.

"Viktor doesn't love me, Nikko. He wants to own me. Which is something else entirely." I said.

"Answer me this," He said grabbing my hands. "Does James trust Viktor with your safety?"

I had to think about it but realized he had.

"Sometimes, yes," I said.

"Why?" He asked.

"Shit," I said knowing where he was going with that. Viktor wouldn't protect me unless there was a good reason for it and James wouldn't trust him unless he knew Viktor cared about me.

"James knows vampires. That's answer enough." Nikko said.

"Then why is he still going forward with the neglect allegation?" I asked.

"Have you asked him to drop it?" Nikko said.

"No," I said.

"Then ask him. If he is willing, Julien will need to agree. The Council appointed him guardian of Viktor's affairs while he is in your custody." He said.

"I'll ask him. I think he would agree if Viktor does." I said.

"He may be holding out until you drop the formal allegations you brought against him for what happened with Natalie. Sebastian would like you to consider the consequences of Viktor being tried while he is in your thrall."

"The consequences?" I asked.

"Making him your thrall changes everything, Em. The Council is concerned about what a trial will do to your reputation. They value you and don't want you caught up in a scandal." Nikko said.

"I hadn't considered that at all," I said.

"Think it through then talk to Viktor. If you can make this all go away without a trial, the Council would be very happy." Nikko said.

"I'll see what I can do," I assured him.

"Good, now I just need you to sign some paperwork, and then our business will be done." He said smiling down at me.

"Thank you Nikko," I said.

He knew I wasn't talking about the paperwork.

"We've been friends forever. I'll always be here when you need me." He said pulling me into a hug.

It felt good to have his arms around me. I missed him more than I realized. He and I used to be the best of friends before we ruined it by getting involved romantically. It made me think about the relationship I have with James. If we ever took it to a romantic level, we would be risking our friendship crumbling the way mine and Nikko's had.

"I'll grab Benjamin. I think he actually enjoys paperwork." I said.

Nikko smiled at me and it was the sort of smile he used to give me when we were dating. The "I love you for who you are" kind of smile. It made my heart squeeze with emotion. I ducked out of his arms and opened the door to ask Benjamin to come back into the room.

We finished up the paperwork in a professional manner that I missed from working with Nikko before. He was efficient but kind. He was the smartest person in the room but he didn't make you feel bad about it. Instead, you felt good to be in that room with him sharing in his wisdom.

By the time we completed our business I was at ease and comfortable being in the same room with Nikko. I marveled at how easy it was but in reality, it was because he made it that way. He didn't push to reignite a romantic relationship. He stuck to the reason for the meeting injecting his typical friendliness into the conversation. It was something I could handle.

Nikko left Benjamin with a packet of papers to have Viktor and Julien sign releasing the claim of neglect. It seemed too easy but I did still have to persuade Viktor and Julien to sign.

I called Viktor into the office after Nikko left. He and I needed to get some things straight.

Viktor sauntered in looking smug. He probably heard everything discussed in this room. His subservient act was getting old so seeing him looking more himself was encouraging. I needed him to be forthcoming and honest which would be a stretch for him but I was hopeful.

He sat in one of the guest chairs and I positioned myself in front of him leaning on the desk. I didn't need the desk to separate us. I had a duty to do a blood exchange with him and I thought that might brighten his mood before I asked him to withdraw his neglect claim.

We were alone in the office while James guarded the door. Viktor eyed me with amusement and I rolled my eyes. His antics never ceased to annoy. Lately, his quirks had become endearing and it was making my head hurt thinking that an enemy could become someone I cared about.

I held my hand out to Viktor and he took it, coming to his feet before me. The sparkle in his eyes told me he knew he was going to get my blood again. I stifled a shiver. I couldn't tell if it was pleasure or disgust.

Viktor stepped closer and kissed my hand. I couldn't hide the goosebumps that lifted on my flesh. He tried to hide his smirk with a bowed head but it was easy enough to spot.

I turned my hand over to present my wrist to him and he hesitated.

"Master, may I?" He said touching my neck.

The heat that ran through my body at his touch had me hesitating. I'd let him bite my neck before and I didn't like myself afterward. Although if I let him, he might be more agreeable afterward.

"You may," I said in a whisper.

In one fluid motion, Viktor lifted me onto the desk and sunk his fangs into the tender flesh of my neck. He pulled me tighter into his body as our minds linked. I could feel his pleasure as if it were my own. It wasn't the same as a bite from Marek but there was no denying the bliss that overcame me.

I fought off the feeling and pressed my hands into Viktor's chest to keep him a safer distance from me. Viktor twined his fingers in my hair and tugged my head back exposing more of my neck. It made my breath catch. Viktor tensed then pulled me closer taking another deep swallow of my blood.

"That's enough, Viktor," I said.

He released my neck but didn't pull away, "You don't want me to stop."

"I want you to not make this more difficult than it has to be," I said in response.

"Of course my dear but where would be the fun in that?" Viktor said.

"Damn it, Viktor!" I exclaimed.

Viktor smiled down at me and said, "I love it when you curse at me."

"Just shut up and give me your wrist," I said.

Viktor healed the wound on my neck then presented his wrist to me. I grabbed a letter opener from the desk and jabbed it into his wrist. I ignored his shout of pain and brought his wrist to my mouth. He quieted down the second his blood crossed my lips.

He could feel the thrill vampire blood gave me through our bond and it gave him the satisfaction he desired. It also gave him a semblance of control over me that he craved. I wasn't about to disabuse him of that notion.

After a few more swallows, I pushed Viktor's wrist away. He lifted his hand to my cheek and leaned in.

"You don't need to think of this as a transaction. It should be a pleasurable exchange of power." Viktor said.

"You and I have a checkered history. Trusting you and letting my guard down is not in the cards." I said.

"I've never lied to you. Why can't you trust me?" He asked.

"You've attacked me, kidnapped my sister, and turned her into a vampire. How can you not understand that?" I asked confused.

"You are thinking like a human," Viktor said.

"Because I *am* a human, Viktor," I said.

"You are no more human than I am. Your blood makes you Fae, not human." He argued.

"How long have you known about that?" I asked.

It didn't escape my notice that he wasn't shocked to hear the doctor tell me I had Fae blood yesterday either. Marek wasn't the only one that knew.

"Any vampire who has tasted your blood would know it. I've known since I first tasted your sister but she doesn't take after your mother as you do. Your mother tries to hide it but she is clearly Fae." He said.

"My mother?" I asked in disbelief.

"I suspect she is a descendent of the Tuatha Dé Danann. The terrible yet beautiful Fae who think they rule us all." Viktor said.

I tried not to fall over in shock. Although I'd like to deny it, it made sense that my mother would be the one with Fae blood. She wasn't the most caring person and often criticized instead of comforted me and my sister.

From what I knew of their character, the Fae were stoic hiding most of their emotions and then channeling them into wielding their power. My power responded best when I tapped into my emotions which lent credence to what Viktor proclaimed.

"What do you want from me, Viktor?" I asked.

"Why my dear, I want you by my side." He said pressing his lips to my hand.

"That is rather vague, Viktor. We are beyond subterfuge." I said.

He walked away and ran his hands through his hair before turning back to me.

"I am a master vampire, Ember. I do not bow to anyone yet I bow to you." He said.

"Viktor," I started but he interrupted me.

"No Ember! I have been humiliated by enthrallment and yet I find myself utterly devoted to you. It pains me to be out of your presence. To not touch you all day causes me physical pain. You are a neglectful master yet I cannot blame you for it. You don't know what you are doing." Viktor said dropping into one of the office chairs.

"Why haven't you told me?" I asked going to him.

I sat on the arm of the chair and pulled him into me. He leaned his head into my stomach and wrapped an arm around my hip. The way he nuzzled into my middle let me know just how badly he was craving my attention.

"With your ever-present dhampir by your side and your vampire boyfriend, there isn't a moment I can speak freely with you," Viktor responded.

"And I haven't made time for you," I said.

"My intention is not to shame you," Viktor said.

I looked at Viktor and remembered that I needed to ask him to drop the neglect claim. With what he just said I wasn't sure now was the best time.

17

Viktor looked upset but in more of a sad way than an angry one. I tried to think of how I would feel in his place and I drew a blank. There was no way for me to empathize with him. It was a scenario I had never been part of before.

"I will make it a priority to spend more time with you," I promised.

"I would appreciate that," He said.

"There is also the matter of the formal neglect claim you filed. My lawyer wants me to ask you to drop it. Given what you just said, I'll understand if you wish to move forward with it." I said.

"I filed it only to get your attention. I will withdraw it." He said waving his hand through the air as if that would make it go away.

"Julien has to agree. He has been appointed guardian of your affairs while you are in my custody." I said.

"He will. He'll do anything for you." Viktor said.

"Viktor," I said tilting his head to look at me. "Are you sure? I can't stand to see you this way. My power works differently, maybe we can find a way to break this?"

"No. Stop thinking of me as a burden or a weak link. I am anything but weak and my connections in the vampire community are second to none. You have gained a great deal through our bond. Julien is just one example of a vampire who will now back you without question." He assured me.

"If you can agree to stop keeping things from me, I will promise to give you what you need," I said wondering what I was getting myself into.

Viktor pulled me down to his lap so I was seated sideways with my torso turned to him. He moved my arms so that I clasped my hands behind his neck.

"This is what I need," He said softly.

My stomach turned over a few times before I could think of what to say. I didn't have romantic feelings for Viktor. I was certain I never would but he needed me to show affection to him in a way that felt romantic.

"I wouldn't sit in the lap of a friend Viktor. I can hold your hand and lean into you while sitting next to you but sitting in your lap is foreplay." I said.

"You seem to be doing just fine with it now," He countered moving my long hair over one shoulder.

"We are alone," I said defensively.

"Ah, so appearance means more to you than my comfort." He said pushing me away.

I held on and kept him from pushing me off his lap. This dominance game needed to end here and now. Viktor was still trying to be the master in this relationship.

"No. I will do what I want when I want to. You will not push me beyond my comfort zone in public or anywhere else. Had I not wanted to sit in your lap now, I wouldn't be here." I said with steel in my voice.

Viktor smiled. His eyes danced with delight and I could imagine what he was thinking. He has always liked it when I've been assertive in the past.

"And that is why I have no problem standing behind you. You command every room you walk into." He said stroking my hair.

I ignored him and asked, "Can you arrange a meeting with Julien for us today? My assistant has the paperwork needed to withdraw your claim. He can file it with the Council once we have you and Julien sign."

"Yes," He said.

"Good," I said then kissed his cheek and stood up.

I moved back to the desk and when I looked up Viktor was holding his hand over the spot I had kissed. His look was unreadable but the emotions coming through our bond said he was pleased.

Viktor shook himself then asked for my phone. I handed it over and listened while he made arrangements with Julien. He transformed before my eyes back into the master vampire that I knew. This was the version of Viktor I knew how to handle. The vulnerable man I saw earlier was something I made when I made him my thrall. I vowed to never make that mistake again.

Viktor informed me that Julien could see us right away. He was working in his downtown office today which was only a few blocks away.

I called James into the room and brought him up to speed. James pulled out his phone and started making arrangements.

Benjamin got looped into the plans and I asked him to fill Marek in. We all met in the living room before heading down to review the security plan.

My phone buzzed and I saw it was Marek. I answered knowing what he was going to say before a word came out of his mouth.

"Hey," I answered.

"Please do not leave the building. Julien can come to you." He said.

"He cleared some time on his schedule for me. I'm not going to insult him by making him come here. His office is just a few blocks over." I assured him.

"I rather you did not leave," He said.

"You've made that clear but I trust James and Viktor to keep me safe," I said.

Viktor looked shocked then very pleased. He wanted to be trusted and in this, I believed he would have my back.

"You have never faced this kind of danger. Ancient vampires are not rational beings." Marek said.

"I'll be fine, Marek," I said feeling annoyed.

"Then come back to me in one piece." He said sounding resigned.

"I love you too," I said with a smile.

We hung up then I motioned for my entourage to move out.

Natalie went back to her secure room after I assured her she could rejoin us when we got back. Caden met us in the hall downstairs to make sure she made it back safely while Murphy went ahead to get a car that could hold all of us comfortably.

James went over the security protocol with me and Viktor while we walked to the parking garage. I appreciated the attention to detail. While I knew what to do if it were just me and James, I was now responsible for a much larger party.

Murphy stood in front of a black Cadillac Escalade when we arrived at the garage. She opened the doors then jumped into the driver's seat. Benjamin climbed into the third-row seat then Viktor and I sat in the second row. James did a sweep around the car before standing beside the front row passenger door.

He waited until a second Cadillac pulled up behind us then he got in the front seat of our car and we all rolled out. An Elite Guardian team was our backup and they were in the duplicate car behind us. A third car was waiting outside the garage. They took the lead effectively sandwiching me and my team between two other SUVs.

I felt like a high-level dignitary then realized I actually was one. At least from a Council perspective, I was a high ranking member. My eyes darted around the car and to the other vehicles. My nerves shot up to unreasonable levels. Three cars felt like overkill or I had seriously underestimated the threat.

Viktor must have sensed it because he pulled my hand into his and laced his fingers through mine. Our eyes met and somehow it calmed me down. He reminded me that I had power. I wasn't a helpless human woman but a Master in the vampire community. At the very least, I could fake it until I felt it for real.

"We will be arriving in a minute. Stay in the car until I open the door for you." James said.

The lead car sped off to clear the disembarkation zone so we could exit the vehicle. It startled me. Viktor squeezed my hand to reassure me. Not for the first time I wished it was James who had my hand instead of Viktor. I was used to him as a near guard. Viktor was a variable that made me nervous.

Murphy pulled up behind the now empty lead car. The team had cleared the area outside the building. The car behind us stopped and several Guardians stepped out heading straight for the building. They were to clear the path and ensure no danger inside the building.

"Hold for my signal," James said jumping out of the car and motioning to the Guardian team.

I watched James searching for any sign of alarm. He nodded to the team then moved to my door. Instead of watching me, he kept his eyes around us. He held out a hand for me and I took it. He pulled me from the vehicle then paused for a second to allow Viktor to slide out behind me.

Murphy moved to let Benjamin out and stayed with him. Another Guardian jumped in the driver's seat of the car. James pulled me behind him then let go of my hand. Viktor fell in place beside me keeping a hand at the small of my back. It allowed him to watch for danger while knowing where I was.

We made it through the lobby without incident then into the elevator. We arrived on the eleventh floor where more Guardians were standing guard. James led us to a glass-walled conference room where Julien was already seated. His people were outside the door and Misty, the human I met the last time I visited Julien at home, was seated to his left.

Julien rose when we entered the room and he said, "Ember, If I'd known you needed this much protection I would have come to you."

"It's okay Julien. Thank you for making time for us." I said finding a seat across the table from him.

Viktor sat next to me then draped an arm across the back of my chair. James remained standing positioning himself so that he could see the room and the hallway at the same time. Benjamin took the chair to my left and Murphy stood directly behind me.

"Viktor said it was urgent," Julien said taking in my Guardians one at a time.

"I hope my security team isn't a distraction. James and Ciara are my personal guard and can be trusted to be discreet." I assured Julien. "Benjamin is my assistant and will take care of any paperwork. I believe Viktor let you know why we are here."

"He mentioned paperwork regarding his complaint against you," Julien said looking at Viktor.

"The Council seems to think I need your approval to drop my complaint against Ember. I wish to do so immediately. Will you support me?" Viktor asked.

His unease wasn't visible but I wondered if the vampire he made would note the agitation. While he was much improved, it was also clear he had not been okay for a while. I had no doubt Julien knew it.

"Why should I support it? Have you been neglected or has this all been one of your dramas to get closer to a powerful woman?" Julien asked.

Julien's eyes found Viktor's and stared hard. He must have seen what I felt.

"Julien my son, you know me too well." Viktor smiled.

I tried really hard not to roll my eyes at Viktor. Instead, I turned my head to give him a look. If Julien didn't sign these papers I wasn't sure I would like the outcome.

"My dear, do not give me that look. You know I would never do anything that would harm you or your reputation. It was my lawyer's idea actually. I wanted out of that damned cell and he thought this would be the best way to get my way." Viktor said smoothly.

"You do look well for having been imprisoned. You even look happy, which is unusual. I don't know what you have done to my Sire Ember but it has had a great effect. He looks more like himself than he has in years. You seem to have made him younger somehow." Julien smiled.

"You do wax philosophical too often. Are you willing to sign the papers or not? I would like to get Ember back to the compound." Viktor said.

Julien glanced at me and smiled, "Of course I will. Misty will help with any of the legal documents."

Benjamin pulled out a large envelope with all the paperwork. He passed them to Misty and she reviewed them at length. She nodded to Julien then handed him the agreement. He looked them over and agreed to the terms.

Benjamin showed him where to sign then had Viktor do the same. Once complete, he took out a small scanner and made a copy of the agreement. He handed Misty a small USB device that contained the copies.

"The paperwork is complete with an electronic copy sent to Mr. Manetti and the Grandmaster," Benjamin told me.

"Thank you, Benjamin," I said.

"Mr. Pierce, if you would please come with me. I'd like to discuss a few matters with you before you leave." Misty said rising from her seat and moving toward the door.

I nodded to Benjamin that he was dismissed. He followed Misty out of the room. James gave a signal for one of the security team to keep an eye on Benjamin. He was holding important documents that needed to make it back to the Council whole but I also suspected that James wanted him safe as well.

"Ember I would like you to consider using my home for the ceremony on Friday. I'd like to get to know you better and since Rowan prefers to conduct business privately, my home would suit her needs well. We have full medical on-site and your security team would of course be welcome." Julien said.

Julien had a vast estate in an affluent area of Denver known as Belcaro. The house and grounds were gorgeous and I suspected there was an entire underground complex below the main house that held his coven. It would be nice to get a look at that and to form a closer friendship with him.

"That is a generous offer, Julien. I will consider it and let you know my decision." I said.

Viktor sat silently not giving away his thoughts on the proposal. He appeared relaxed but I know he wasn't entirely pleased by Julien's offer.

We all rose from the table and Julien came over to say goodbye.

Julien took my hand and placed a soft kiss on it before saying, "A pleasure as always, Ember."

"Thank you again, Julien. I'll be in touch." I said then turned to find James standing by the door ready to escort me out.

Protocol said for us to reverse the process we used to enter the building but when we walked up to the elevators I had a feeling of dread overcome me.

"What is it?" Viktor asked.

"Something's wrong," I said trying to figure out where the feeling was coming from.

James came closer and asked, "Did you have a vision?"

"No, just a feeling something bad is about to happen," I said looking into James' eyes.

"Murphy, emergency protocol. One asset per car." James ordered then turned to me and Viktor. "Ember, you're with me. Viktor, stay close behind us and make sure no one gets between you and Ember. You'll go with Murphy when we get to the lobby."

Viktor nodded as one of the security team escorted Benjamin to the elevator. Ben looked relaxed as if this sort of thing happened every day for him. The kid wasn't easily ruffled. They disappeared behind the doors then we waited for our turn.

While we rode down in the elevator James got a call saying Benjamin was in the car on his way back to the Council complex. That left the rest of us to get out of here without incident.

We emerged from the elevator with James walking next to me and Viktor glued to my back. Ciara brought up the rear watching both me and Viktor. The Elite Guardians fanned out to secure the lobby. Just as they got in place two men with guns jumped out from an office.

"Gun!" I yelled as I reached out with my power and froze them.

Their guns went off as James knocked me to the ground and Viktor jumped on top of me to shield me. My breath was knocked out but otherwise, I was fine. I lost hold of the gunmen then heard the team take them out.

James pulled me from the floor and searched for injuries.

"I'm fine but that was just the opening act," I said as I felt a group of vampires that were unfamiliar move into position outside.

James hesitated before moving to the door, "No matter what happens, you get to that car. Understood?"

"Dammit James, I can't leave if you aren't safe. I've left you behind before, I won't do it again." I said.

"I'm your Guardian, it's my risk to take." He responded.

"She won't go anywhere without you. Get her in that car. I'll do what I can to draw them away." Viktor said sounding resolved.

"Viktor," I said starting to protest but he held up his hand.

"He's right," Murphy jumped in to say. "You are the priority Madame and we need to move."

A phalanx of Guardians surrounded me when we got outside. Viktor was shuffled to the back with Murphy. I didn't like it one bit but it was too late to go with another plan. We didn't have the luxury of time.

Before I could think we were at the car and James was shoving me inside. As he stepped in an explosion went off blowing up the car behind us. My eyes met Viktor's and he yelled for me to go.

"Viktor, get back inside to Julien!" I yelled.

Viktor nodded as if he heard me then my car was driving away. He was immediately attacked while fighting his way back to the building. We turned a corner before I could see what else happened.

James was already on the phone ordering a team for back up. My phone rang at the same time and I answered.

"Tell me you are okay," Julien said concerned.

"I am but Viktor is still out there. You have to get to him." I said.

"My team is already on their way. What happened?" He asked.

"We were ambushed and Viktor sacrificed himself to ensure I got away. Julien, he is considerably outnumbered." I said worriedly.

"I'll call you as soon as I have an update," He said then hung up.

"We need to go back," I said to James.

"No Ember, we need to get you home. Murphy and the team have Viktor covered. He will be fine." James assured me.

"A car blew up," I said feeling angry. "I should have seen this coming sooner."

"Hey," James said turning my chin so I would look at him. "We were prepared for it. That doesn't make it any less messy but we knew something like this could happen."

James took my hand in his and I closed my eyes. I opened the bond between me and Viktor a crack to see if he was okay. I got the impression he was still fighting but otherwise he appeared to be okay. That helped me relax a fraction as the car pulled into the parking garage of the Council building.

I jumped out of the car, determined to find my own vehicle so I could go back for Viktor. James realized what I was doing and stopped me.

"He is a master vampire who is hard to kill. Let my team handle it." James said.

"I need him back, James," I said with an overwhelming sense of need.

"Have you considered that he may have used the ambush as a distraction to get away?" James asked.

"What? No!" I said stomping off toward the offices.

"It is a possibility," James insisted.

"I am going to ignore you now," I said turning a corner.

James kept up with me until a feeling of fire exploded in my gut. I doubled over grabbing at my stomach.

"Viktor!" I screamed through our bond.

"Where are you?" Viktor asked me.

"I'm back in the Council building. Are you okay?" I asked.

"I'm better now knowing you are safe." He replied.

"Viktor," I said sternly.

"It's but a small wound, my dear. It will heal." He said.

"Are you safe?" I asked.

He paused before replying. I got the sense he was still fighting but it was more or less finished.

"Ember, what's wrong?" James asked.

James was holding me where I had fallen to the floor. I could feel Marek rushing toward us.

"It's Viktor," I said to James. "He's been hurt."

"I am well my dear. I'm with Julien now. He will bring me to you." Viktor said.

"I'll believe you're okay when I see you myself," I replied through our bond.

"Ember," James said as I stood up and started walking back out of the offices.

"He's okay but will need medical attention. Where would Julien come if he is dropping Viktor off?" I asked.

"Main reception but he should take the clinic entrance instead. I'll call him and tell him where." James said pulling out his phone.

I changed course and headed toward the hospital wing where I found Marek. He must have assumed I would need medical attention. Given my history over the past week, I didn't blame him.

"What is going on?" He asked when I rushed past him.

James filled him in between making calls to determine the state of his team. Given the explosion and gunfire, I could only imagine what we would have to smooth over with the human police.

I paced back and forth near the entrance waiting for any sign of Viktor. As I did, it occurred to me why I was so upset. Until this point, I had denied the possibility of having any affection for Viktor. After all, he was supposed to be my enemy.

My supposed enemy walked through the door. I rushed forward to greet him. His stomach was covered in blood and he held a hand to it to staunch the bleeding. Murphy walked in behind him along with a few other Guardians.

Viktor met my eyes and a sort of electricity flowed between us. I came forward and he met me halfway.

"I'm fine," Viktor said.

He pulled me toward him but I pushed him back.

"Don't you ever do that to me again! Do you hear me?" I said on the verge of tears.

"Yes, my love," Viktor said then leaned down to kiss my cheek.

I put my arm around his back and led him into the first available exam room. He laid back on the bed and I helped him remove his shirt. A nurse came in to assess his injury. She asked his preference for blood then left the room.

"Does it hurt?" I asked running my hand below his wound.

Viktor stilled my hand and met my eyes. The look on his face said volumes.

"There are two things sure to arouse a vampire and we have both of them present right now. What are your intentions, Ember?" Viktor said.

Before I could say anything the nurse returned with a pint of blood. I moved away so she had room to start the IV. She started to clean the wound but Viktor wouldn't let her finish and told her to leave.

I sat down on the edge of the bed and used the cloth the nurse left behind to clean up the blood from Viktor's stomach. He didn't say a word. He just watched me do it.

"I should let you rest," I said as I finished.

"Talk to me first," Viktor said.

I looked at the open door and felt Marek and James standing in the hallway. They would hear everything said in this room.

"Later," I said stroking his cheek. "I need to check on some things while you heal."

"I will hold you to that talk," He said.

"I know," I said then leaned down to kiss his cheek.

Instead of touching his cheek as I had intended, Viktor turned his head and met my lips with his own. He pulled me toward him putting some effort into it and causing me to kiss him back. As kisses went it was nice but there was no spark between us. He must have felt the same thing because he let me go without protest.

"That didn't go how I thought it would," Viktor said with a look of confusion on his face.

"You can't force chemistry Viktor," I said softly then walked out of the room.

18

Marek and James were waiting for me down the hall. Both avoided my gaze as I approached them which instantly made me suspicious. I knew my behavior toward Viktor would bother them but I didn't think they would react with embarrassment.

"How is the team?" I asked when I got within a few feet of them.

"The driver of the car suffered major injuries but his prognosis is good. The rest were minor to medium severity like what Viktor sustained." James said.

"Okay," I said taking a deep breath. "I have a phone call to make and some business to discuss with Benjamin. Is Murphy still on my detail?"

Marek confirmed that she was so I asked to have Murphy stay with Viktor until he was healed up enough to leave the hospital. She could escort him to me when he was ready.

"What are you up to, *Milaya moya*?" Marek asked narrowing his eyes at me.

I turned to him and smiled, "Whatever do you mean?"

I kissed him then turned and walked at speed toward my office.

"You know exactly what I mean," Marek grumbled.

I made a noncommittal sound in acknowledgment. I'd fill him in later but for now, the hallways of the Council offices were not the place.

We passed by Benjamin's office on the way to my own. I poked my head in and asked him to join me in my office. The guys followed me in but only one was invited.

"I assume it's your responsibility to find out how Magdalena knew where I was and how she carried out the attack?" I asked Marek.

His jaw ticked as he ground his teeth together, "It is."

"I have some business to discuss with Benjamin. Will you let me know what you find out about the attack? If I'm not available directly, you can tell James." I said.

"Gentlemen, would you give us a moment please?" Marek said.

James stepped out of the room and took Ben with him. They closed the door behind them.

"We need to figure out how to be professional without making people leave the room every time you want to speak with me," I said frustrated.

Marek stepped up to me and pulled me into his arms. Then he kissed me so thoroughly that I didn't remember where we were. I was about to push the suit jacket from his shoulders. Instead, I looked up into his ice-blue eyes.

"Feel better?" I asked breathlessly.

"Much," Marek said smirking.

He leaned into me until I had to grab onto him for balance. He ran his nose up my neck and into my hairline. He must have liked what he found because he pulled back and straightened his suit. I ran my hands down my dress to smooth it out and he watched with heat in his eyes.

"Marek," I started but he cut me off.

"I have meetings most of the afternoon but I look forward to seeing you at home tonight," Marek said softly.

"We have plenty to talk about," I said.

"I'll have dinner waiting for you in the penthouse at six. Do not be late," He said then turned and left my office.

I shook off his behavior then gathered myself up for what I had to do next. Moving behind my desk I opened my laptop as James and Benjamin walked into the room. James closed the door.

"I'm glad to see you safe and sound Benjamin," I commented.

"Thank you, madame. It wasn't my first time to see action." He said and stood in front of my desk.

"Well, I'd like to get right to it if you don't mind?" I said.

He nodded and motioned for me to proceed.

"What is the timeline on Viktor's complaint being cleared?" I asked.

"The paperwork has been filed. The Council just needs to ratify it when they meet this evening." He said.

"Good, I have another matter I'd like them to review. I want to drop the complaint of kidnapping and assault I brought against Viktor. What do we need to do to make that happen?" I asked.

"Are you sure you want to do that?" James asked.

"I am. I want to speak with Natalie first but I'm quite sure she doesn't want Viktor to go to trial. Now that he is bound to me, the responsibility is mine to either punish him or redirect his behavior to more acceptable pursuits." I said.

"Mr. Manetti can draw up the documents you need. Given their reluctance to bring the charges in the first place, I don't think you will receive any opposition." Benjamin said.

"Good, then I need you to do a few things for Viktor as well," I said.

Benjamin left to arrange for Viktor to have a cell phone and his wardrobe brought to the sub-penthouse. He had a business to run and needed to get back to it now that he was no longer incarcerated. His coven also needed to see their Master back in charge.

I asked James to invite Natalie up for a visit. It was time for us to talk about her future. She was a grown woman who didn't need me to make decisions for her. I was in a position to help her and getting her the best possible deal was what I was after.

I picked up my phone to call Nikko. He answered on the first ring.

"Ember, hi," Nikko said.

"Hey, Nikko. I need to speak with you as a client. Are you somewhere you can talk?" I asked.

"Yes, I'm in the office. How can I help?" He said.

I filled him in on the plan to drop the charges against Viktor. He sounded pleased.

"That is what Sebastian wanted but are you sure? He caused you a great deal of pain," he said.

"I think it's what is best for all of us to be able to move on," I said.

"Very well, I'll draw up the documents. It will take a day or two to finalize everything. In the meantime, I can petition the court to delay his trial letting them know a motion is forthcoming." Nikko said.

"Thank you, Nikko. You're the best," I said feeling relieved.

"I...It's nothing really, Em." Nikko said.

I didn't want to know what he was going to say before he changed his mind. I thanked him again and we hung up.

James had been on the phone in the hall within view of me. He walked back into the office.

"Natalie is on her way up and Murphy says Viktor is well enough to leave the hospital," James said.

"Good. They should both be here for the discussion. It affects them both." I said.

"Viktor isn't known for being cooperative at the best of times. You are about to take away a huge amount of leverage you have over him." James said sitting down across from me.

"I think he and I have come to an understanding. As soon as he confirms his intentions with my sister, I'll know what I need to do." I said.

"He and Julien have been up to something from the beginning. Julien isn't the innocent man he makes himself out to be no matter how charming he appears." James warned me.

"I'm not naive enough to think a vampire is anything but a vampire, James. I don't trust Julien as much as you think but he is an ally." I said.

A knock sounded at the door. James moved to stand just behind my chair where he would be in reach of me and able to fight off anyone if needed. I called for the person at the door to come in.

Viktor opened the door, saw us then grinned like the cat that ate the canary. He probably guessed something was up. I lifted an eyebrow in annoyance and sat down without comment.

"How are you feeling?" I asked noticing that he moved as if he wasn't hurt at all.

"Good as new. A little blood and I'm all healed up." Viktor said.

"That's good. Now that you're here, there is something I want to talk with you about. Natalie is on her way up but before she gets here I need to know what your intentions are with her. Before you turned her, you asked her to marry you. She is still under the impression that she is your fiance." I said.

"Natalie is special to me as you know. She is my progeny so I will always care for her but marriages in the vampire community are reserved for the merging of power and wealth. Natalie does not have either." Viktor said matter of factly.

"You need to tell her and explain what your relationship actually is. If after she hears your explanation she is satisfied, then I will drop the charges against you restoring you back to independent status and no longer subject to my custody." I said.

Viktor looked confused at first then became concerned, "I will still be part of your retinue. You will not cut me off?"

"Yes, of course," I answered.

"Very well, I will explain to Natalie." He said looking uneasy.

"With truth and compassion or as much compassion as you are capable of Viktor," I said.

"I have compassion, Ember." He said with contempt.

A knock at the door announced Natalie's arrival. She came in and took the seat next to Viktor.

"Thanks for coming up Nat. Viktor has something to talk with you about then I want to chat with you myself. If you need us, just yell. We'll be right outside the door." I said.

James and I left them alone so they could talk. I hoped everything went well between them. I didn't want my sister hurt but I also didn't want her lied to.

We moved to a seating area just outside my office that functioned as a waiting room. I sat down next to James but instead of feeling comfortable, I was uneasy.

"You'll hear it if she starts yelling right?" I asked.

"I will." He said.

"Good," I said.

"What's wrong, Ember? It's more than your sister making you tense." James asked.

I hesitated, not sure if I wanted to tell him.

"Everything I know about vampires is that they are territorial and when they believe something is theirs, they defend it with impunity. While Marek hasn't shown that side very often I do wonder what might set him off," I said.

"Are you worried we'll get too close to the line? Or maybe Viktor?" James asked.

"That's the thing, the other night I could swear he encouraged me to go to bed with both you and Viktor." I said.

"What?" James asked confused.

"After his run-in with Magdalena, he's been different. It's like he is encouraging me to take on another lover. He's tried several times to step back and 'let me explore my bond' with you and Viktor." I said.

"That isn't what I would expect from him either. Why would he do that?" He wondered.

"You've known him longer than me, James. You tell me." I said.

"The only way to know for sure is to ask him. I'm not volunteering by the way," James said smiling.

"He invited me to dinner tonight. It felt like he was asking me on a date. I swear I could get whiplash from his changing moods," I said frowning.

"Isn't it a good thing that he wants to court you?" James said.

"Court me...wait, what are the vampire courting rituals? I haven't researched the specifics because I didn't think I needed to." I said.

"That might be it, Em. He is treating you like another master vampire. They all are really. He has serious competition and is following the rules even though you don't know them." James said.

"Like what? Give me a summary." I asked.

"You told him the other day that Julien was interested in courting you. Then he went off on his own to prove to himself or to you that he is a badass. Only to fail and look weak in front of you. He knows both Julien and Viktor have declared their interest in you, they only wait for your permission to make the move. If he requests your permission to court you tonight, that would open the flood gates on proposals for you but it would also give him the chance to win you permanently."

"It's old-fashioned but it follows the general principle that the woman chooses the most worthy mate based on her assessment of his skill in bed, his wealth, and his power. If you had a sire, they would act as the one to grant permission to any eligible vampire but since you don't have one, you are the one to grant permission." He said.

"So, he encourages me to play the field so I know what I've got in my own bed. Then what?" I asked.

"Then you select your mate," He said looking defeated.

"And there's the rub...I don't want a mate bond, at least not right now. He knows that." I said.

"I don't think rational thought is possible when a man or vampire thinks they could lose the one they love," James said.

He looked pained.

"Are you speaking from experience?" I asked softly.

"Yes," He said.

"James," I said putting my hand on his cheek and looking into his eyes.

He put his hand on mine and said, "Don't pity me."

"And dhampirs cannot court a master," Viktor said.

I turned, startled. "Dammit Viktor, how long were you listening?"

"Long enough to know you shouldn't be speaking about this in public. If you will please return to the office, your sister would like to have a word with you." He said then bowed before turning around to walk back to my office.

I took a deep breath then went in to see what my sister had to say. I wasn't prepared for the sight of her. She had been crying yet was holding it together.

"Hey Nat, how are you doing?" I asked sitting next to her.

"You knew this whole time and didn't tell me." She accused.

"What I knew was that the man my sister had chosen to marry didn't treat her very well. When you invited me to spend time with you both at the cabin, it became clear to me he was a vampire. By the time I knew enough to tell you, he had taken you away. I left my job and everyone I knew to follow you there and get you back. I was too late." I said.

"You could have told me since I got back," She said.

"Told you what exactly? You already knew he was a vampire. He turned you into one." I said.

"That he had no intention of marrying me!" She said crying again.

"Nat, I suspected it but didn't know for sure until I asked him about it today. Then I told him he had to tell you. It was his decision to make and his responsibility to tell you. I don't know how long he would have let it linger but I couldn't stand to know when you didn't." I said.

"So you are blameless in all of this? If you hadn't gotten involved, we would be married by now." She said.

"No my darling, we would not," Viktor interrupted.

Natalie turned to Viktor with fresh tears.

"What are you saying?" She asked.

"A master vampire does not marry a human. It was a way of getting closer to your sister." He said.

"Then why did you turn me? If you don't care about me, why save me?" She asked.

"Because I knew if I let you die, your sister would not stop until I was dead. She is more powerful than me. I could not risk it." He said looking away.

"You're a monster!" She yelled and covered her face as more tears spilled.

"Natalie, he cares for you. As your sire, he is bonded to you and he will always be in your life to care for you and guide you." I said trying to find something good from all of this.

"How could he care for me? He only wants you!" She said with venom in her voice.

"That isn't true and you know it. Look within him and tell me what you feel." I said.

She closed her eyes and I assumed she searched her bond with Viktor for his feelings. I could tell he was upset and each word from her drove a spike through his heart. While he didn't show affection to her outwardly, he did care for her.

Viktor moved closer to Natalie and stroked her hair. She looked up at him, tears falling down her cheeks. Then she leaned into his hand, taking the comfort that he offered.

"You are mine and nothing will change that," he said.

It wasn't the romantic speech that I was sure she was hoping for but after a few sniffles, she seemed to calm down.

"Natalie, I've been asked to drop the charges I filed against Viktor. It would be best for all of us to move on without a trial and the risk of incarceration. Are you okay with me doing that?" I asked.

"He wouldn't be punished?" She asked.

"He is my thrall, Natalie. I think he has been sufficiently punished." I said.

"Then I guess I'm okay with it. But there is one more thing I need to do," Natalie said.

"What is it?" I asked.

She stood up and turned to Viktor then slapped him so hard he fell backward. He didn't fall all the way to the floor, his vampire reflexes kept him mostly upright.

"Okay, I feel better now." She said grinning.

"I bet you do," I said smiling back at her.

Viktor had the perfect imprint of my sister's hand on his face. I sort of wanted to take a picture to have as a keepsake.

"I want to go back to the bunker now," Natalie said looking less amused.

"Of course. We'll call someone to escort you back." I said standing up to give her a hug.

James stepped out of the office while I said goodbye to my sister. She was a wreck but she would feel better. I know she had a crush on Caden Thorn, her sometimes Guardian. He was helping her deal with being a new vampire but I also thought he had a crush on her too. Maybe knowing that the engagement was over would allow her to open herself up to the possibilities of other suiters.

The office door opened and James stepped back in and said, "Caden will be here in a moment. He was already nearby anticipating you would need him."

Natalie smiled and winked at me confirming she was interested in Caden. Great, now I had to worry about her dating a Guardian, although he wasn't a bad choice. He accompanied me to a vampire event and I found him a little boring but nice.

Viktor stood away from Natalie and looked to be trying not to touch his face. It was still red but the imprint of Natalie's hand had already disappeared. I caught his eye and he looked away immediately. I hoped he didn't brood all day.

Caden arrived to whisk Natalie away and saw that she had been crying. He hugged her and led her away. Her night in shining armor had arrived. She looked happy to leave.

I texted Nikko that Natalie agreed and we were okay to move forward to drop the charges. He sent me a thumbs up and smiley face emoji.

I turned to Viktor.

"Are you okay?" I asked him.

"I'm fine," He said still not meeting my eyes.

"Viktor," I said walking over to him. "I know that was hard but she'll get over it. She never holds a grudge."

"She will never think of me the same way again. I'll always be a monster to her now," He said.

"Then I guess you'll have to prove to her that she's wrong," I said resting my hand on his arm.

"I would like to be alone for a while if that can be arranged." He said.

"Of course. You can go back to my apartment. I asked Benjamin to arrange a few things for you so you may hear from him later. Let me know if you need anything." I said.

Viktor nodded his head then stepped out of the office with James. James would call Murphy to escort Viktor upstairs. In the meantime, I had a few moments to myself. That was something of a rarity these days. I decided to enjoy it before it ended.

19

Work had been piling up in my inbox while I was taking care of personal things today. I took some time to reply to the messages and even set up a meeting with my team so we could all actually see each other face to face next week and get to know one another.

By the time I had finished, it was time to get ready for my date with Marek. As usual, James escorted me upstairs to my apartment. I hadn't heard from Viktor the rest of the day and was a little eager to see how he was doing.

When we arrived at the sub-penthouse, Murphy was standing guard at the door.

"He's been quiet since we came up. Ben dropped off a cell phone and some clothes for him which perked him up a bit." She said.

"Thanks, Ciara," I said then entered the apartment.

I asked James to stay outside. Viktor didn't need an audience if he wanted to talk.

I found him lounging on the couch in a robe with apparently nothing on underneath based on the flashes of skin I could see peeking through. He was watching a movie.

I leaned over the back of the couch and said, "Hey, how are you doing?"

"The bathtub in this apartment is the only good thing here," He said.

"Okay." I drew out the word before continuing, " I'm going to change then head out for a while. Murphy said your phone was delivered."

"Yes, it was." He said snidely.

"Viktor?" I said wondering where the attitude was coming from.

He turned to look at me but instead of the self-loathing I expected, I found him angry.

"What do you want?" He asked with clipped words.

"You're angry with me," I said confused.

"It will pass," He said turning back to his movie.

"Viktor, talk to me," I insisted.

"I do not talk about my feelings Ember of this you should know. Instead I act but my instincts to punish you run contrary to my other emotions." He said.

I walked around the couch and sat in front of him on the coffee table then said, "What do you mean you want to punish me?"

He sat up so fast I didn't see it. He pulled the hair at the back of my head to bare my neck to him.

"I want to throw you to the floor and drain you," He said through clenched teeth.

His lips were inches from my face. I wouldn't be able to stop him at this close range. As a thrall he has to obey me but that didn't mean he couldn't make a move before I could react.

My heart pounded in my chest and I willed it to slow down. Panic and fear were vampire appetizers.

"How would you feel after you did that?" I asked in a whisper.

He looked away from the pulse throbbing in my neck to my eyes.

"I should feel powerful but instead I feel weak! You have turned me into a soft blubbering thing." He yelled.

I blinked away the bluster of his words and searched our bond. His anger was evident but beneath it was something else. It was a tentative thread I decided to pull.

I touched his cheek and at first he flinched but then he leaned into it. He released my hair and I relaxed slightly. I could imagine a master vampire like Viktor wasn't accustomed to compassion.

"We will figure this out together," I promised stroking his cheek with my thumb.

He closed his eyes and let out a breath.

"Natalie hates me," He said sounding like a child.

"She doesn't hate you. She's just upset with you. It won't take her long to forgive you." I assured him.

He pulled my hand from his cheek then relaxed back into the couch, the anger from moments ago gone.

"You said you had somewhere to be. Where are you going? You shouldn't leave the building especially after what happened today." He said.

"I'm having dinner upstairs with Marek. I'm not leaving the building." I said.

"Good," he said.

"Are you going to be okay by yourself?" I asked.

"Will you be back tonight?" He asked.

"I don't know," I said.

He nodded and seemed resigned.

"You should wear your hair up. It shows off your neck and he won't be able to resist you." Viktor said.

His attention was back on the television.

"Thanks for the tip," I said then left him to his movie.

I was tempted to cancel the dinner with Marek so I could stay with Viktor.

His outburst had me worried about his mental state. Although spending time alone might be good for him considering he has been watched and guarded non-stop.

I went to my bedroom and dug around in my closet until I found a green spaghetti strap dress that would do nicely for this evening. It was a little dressy but I wanted something feminine and pretty. I paired it with low heels that would allow me to maneuver better than high heels. These days I never knew if I was going to be fighting or running for my life.

With Viktor's suggestion about my hair on my mind, I clipped my hair up off my neck in a messy chignon. It did show off my neck and I hoped Marek liked the look. Thinking about him made my stomach flutter with anticipation.

I made my way to the door. Viktor was still on the couch but he perked up when I walked by.

"You look ravishing," He said looking me up and down.

"Thanks. I'll see you later," I said smiling.

I met James in the hall. He remained silent until the elevator doors closed.

"You are gorgeous." He said smiling.

"Thanks," I smiled back.

"I'm assuming you'll be staying the night?" He asked.

The question was innocent except for the look on his face.

"James, regardless of what Marek is up to or has said, a polyamorous group is not my thing." I said.

"I may not be able to keep myself from being attracted to you but I can control myself. Although, that dress makes it much harder." He said smiling.

I kissed his cheek then rubbed away the smear of lipstick I left behind. James was some kind of saint. There didn't seem to be anything I could do to anger him.

The elevator opened at the penthouse level. I turned to the apartment door and walked inside.

Marek's penthouse was full of modern finishes that felt a bit cold most of the time but right now, the atmosphere was romantic. All the shiny surfaces reflected light from candles set up around the room in groupings of three or five which added a soft glow. The dining area was set for two with a candelabra and dozens of votive candles spread around.

"Right on time," Marek said turning toward me.

He was dressed in a fitted charcoal suit with a white shirt unbuttoned at the neck. His black hair was brushed back and he was clean-shaven. His stunning blue eyes stood out in the monochrome palette.

"Hi," I said as he stepped up to me.

"*Milaya moya,* you are beautiful," Marek said.

He leaned in and kissed me gently on the lips. A zing of electricity shot through my body at his touch. I ran my hands up his chest over the silky fabric of his shirt. The muscles underneath bunched up and my breath hitched. Did we need to eat?

Marek was absolutely edible in his suit and he smelled so good I leaned in for a good sniff.

"Is this a date?" I whispered into his ear.

"In human terms, yes. Come to the table. Dinner is ready." He said pulling me to the dining room.

Marek pulled a chair out for me and helped me scoot in. The food was already on the table and I could smell something divine.

Marek removed the cloche covering my plate revealing a lobster tail and steak with asparagus. The smirk on Marek's face told me he knew I would love it.

"Who told you my favorite meal?" I asked eyeing him suspiciously.

"I have my sources," He smirked.

He offered me a choice of wine or hard cider and I opted for cider. He poured me one and poured himself a glass of wine then sat on the opposite side of the table.

"It was Sam wasn't it?" I asked knowing she was the most likely to have tipped him off.

"Eat, there is dessert too." He said refusing to divulge his source.

Marek leaned back in his chair and watched me eat. It was sort of weird to be the only one eating but it also wasn't the first time for us. Vampires can eat if they want to but they prefer to only ingest blood.

I took a bite of the lobster and let it melt on my tongue. The buttery goodness delighted my tastebuds and made me feel like I was in a five-star restaurant. I relaxed into the atmosphere and enjoyed every morsel.

Marek smiled at me when I came up for air after polishing off half the meal.

"I forgot to eat today. There was too much going on," I said feeling self-conscious.

"When your day is full of fighting for your life something like that is bound to happen," Marek said.

His mouth drew tight as he spoke and I could see how he was restraining himself from speaking further.

"I suppose that's true," I said taking another bite and ignoring his unease.

I watched him, waiting for any more signs of anger.

"Sebastian told me you are dropping your complaint against Viktor," He said.

And there it was. I would have expected the statement to drip with disdain but it came out conversational instead. Something was off.

"Sebastian asked me to consider it and after speaking with my sister she agreed. I think it's for the best," I said.

"That means Viktor will be a permanent fixture in your life," He said shifting in his seat.

"He was going to be regardless. You've told me yourself there isn't a way to reverse a thrall. Victor will need my blood for as long as he lives." I said.

"There is something else that we are not seeing," He said.

"Marek..." I started but he interrupted me.

“I apologize. I do not wish to fight with you.” He said.

Marek’s emotions were like a tornado inside him. It was impossible to tell what he was thinking but something told me he was jealous of Viktor. Marek was the center of my universe until Viktor became a priority.

“I’ve missed us. It seems that everyone around me has pulled me away from you. Thank you for inviting me to dinner.” I said with a smile.

Marek smiled back and it made my heart thump. This man, this vampire could excite me with nothing but the curve of his lips.

“I have something for you,” He said pulling something from his pocket.

He lifted a small box and presented it to me.

“I wanted something tangible to show you how much I care for you. I have been thinking of a way to show you how much I care for you. It is a human gesture but relevant in this case.” He said.

I opened the box and was nearly blinded by a giant diamond ring. It was a princess cut surrounded by a halo of diamonds set in a rose gold band. Marek lifted the ring out of the box and slid it onto my ring finger.

The stone was bigger than the digit it sat on. I don’t know anything about karat weight but it was big, as in most men couldn’t afford it big. In the candlelight, it sparkled like stars in the sky. It was breathtaking.

“Marek, it’s gorgeous but it’s too much,” I said shaking my head.

I couldn’t stop looking at it. I held my hand in front of me and turned it to watch the glitter of the jewel. It really was breathtaking.

“It is not enough but it will do as a token of my affection,” He said lifting my hand to place a kiss on my palm.

The heat that travelled directly to my core told me dinner was over. I stood up and met Marek at the side of the table. He surrounded me with his arms and I tipped my head up to kiss him. His lips felt like velvet as they glided along my own.

Marek pulled me tighter into his body and I melted at his touch. He knew exactly where to squeeze or caress as if he had known me my entire life.

“I hope there wasn’t dessert,” I said between kisses.

“You are the dessert,” he growled.

Marek lifted me so that my legs wrapped around his waist. I let my shoes fall off my feet as he walked us toward the bedroom. It reminded me of the first time we made love in this apartment. He had carried me to the bedroom that time too.

He set me down on my feet in front of the bed. He broke away from the kiss and licked a trail down my neck.

“I like this dress,” He said as he pulled one strap down from my shoulder.

His mouth was there a second later and I gasped at the feel of his fangs dragging against the tender flesh. I could come from his bite alone but wanted all of him tonight.

I pushed the suit jacket from his shoulders then started unbuttoning his shirt. He tossed the jacket toward a chair where it landed perfectly. His shirt followed next and I reveled in the feel of his bare flesh under my fingers.

Marek pushed me backward until my knees hit the bed. Then he leaned down running his hands from my bare thighs over my backside. He didn't stop until he had pulled my dress over my head and tossed it over where his clothing fell. I was already working on the waist of his pants when he unhooked my bra.

His pants fell to the floor as he pulled my bra away. My breasts escaped the fabric only to be caught by Marek's mouth. He sucked one tight bud between his lips then bit down. The zing of pleasure that shot through my body had me crying out his name.

The satisfied noise he made next was followed by the removal of my undies and a sudden change in my position. I found myself on my back with a hot vampire pressed against me. I grabbed his tight ass and felt his length pressed hard into my thigh. After stroking his member a few times I lined him up with my core then pulled him closer with my legs. He got the not so subtle hint and pushed him self inside me.

We both sighed in pleasure as our bodies connected. He rocked into me with a rhythm that built in intensity with each thrust. I became less aware of my body and more aware of the shear pleasure overtaking every one of my senses.

The silky feel of his skin against mine had my hands drifting all over him to touch as much as possible. The scent of vanilla filling my nostrils each time he leaned in to kiss me. The sound of his husky grunts as he moved in and out of me. The look of love in his eyes each time our eyes met. The only thing missing was the taste of his blood on my lips.

As the thought crossed my mind, Marek dipped his head toward my neck and flicked his tongue over the pulsing vein.

"Yes," I said breathlessly.

He chuckled then sucked the skin over the vein into his mouth. All thought left me as his teeth sunk in. The sharp sting of the bite was quickly followed by a wave of warmth that had me orgasming loudly within seconds. Marek drank down my blood while still pumping into my body in a hard rhythm drawing out my orgasm for as long as he could. His climax came right after mine, ending with one hard thrust that felt so good I thought I might pass out from the pleasure.

Before I could pass out, Marek pulled a knife out from under the pillow and rolled to his side bringing me with him. He cut himself near his jugular. I latch onto the wound and lapped up the caramel nectar of his blood without hesitation.

As I drank, Marek rocked himself inside me gently using the rush I got from his blood to rekindle the fire between my legs. As his blood healed the soreness from our first round, he had me panting in no time for round two.

When his blood stopped flowing, Marek captured my lips in a searing kiss. I pushed him onto his back to straddle him. He grabbed my breasts pinching and caressing as I rode him like a cowgirl on a stallion. I didn't last long. Seeing him staring loving into my eyes was all it took to reach the edge of my control.

Marek pulled me down into his arms. He held onto my hips and pressed into me from below until he too lost himself in the motion of our bodies. We both cried out as we came together. I collapsed on top of him.

He brushed the sweaty strands of hair that escaped my chignon out of my face and kissed my forehead.

"I love you with all that I am," He whispered.

"I love you too, Marek," I said feeling tears spring up in my eyes from the intensity of his words.

He pulled me into him so tight I thought I might not be able to breathe.

"What's wrong?" I asked him.

"I know you need to return to Viktor but I wish you would stay with me tonight," He said.

"I don't have to go back downstairs. He's fine on his own." I said.

Marek kissed me gently then said, "I have work to do. New surveillance data from Magdalena's compound came in and Caden wants to run an idea by me."

"Shouldn't James be in that conversation?" I asked.

"His place is with you right now. Besides, Caden already sent his ideas to James. I'm sure he's reading the report right now while he stands guard." Marek said.

I snuggled into Marek while he spoke. The rumble of his voice through his chest made me smile. It felt good to be this close to him.

"I don't want to move," I said.

Marek pulled my hand up to kiss my knuckles and admire the ring he put there earlier. Even in the dark that damn thing sparkled.

"I'm in no hurry for you to leave, *Milaya moya*," he said softly.

"If I don't move, I'm going to fall asleep here," I said.

Marek sighed then moved to sit up. I groaned right along with him then followed him looking for my underwear as I stood. He handed me a soft bundle of lace then leaned in to kiss me.

"Get cleaned up. I'll let James know you are returning downstairs." Marek said pulling his pants on.

He left the room while putting his arms back into his shirt sleeves.

I used the bathroom then put myself back together as best I could. I couldn't do anything about the flush in my cheeks.

Marek was waiting for me by the door. He kissed me goodnight and I went with James back to my apartment a floor down.

The first thing I did when I got back was knock on Viktor's door. To my surprise, he answered right away.

"How was your alone time?" I asked him.

He wore pajama pants but no shirt. He looked a bit sleepy until he took a deep breath seeing the ring on my finger.

"Is that what I think it is?" Viktor said lifting my hand to look at the ring.

"No, it isn't an engagement ring," I said.

"Ember darling, you are smarter than that," He said.

I took my hand back from him and turned to leave.

"I'm too tired to argue with you. Good night, Viktor." I said.

"Good night, master," He said with a slight bow.

I rolled my eyes as I walked back into my bedroom and closed the door. James was sitting on the edge of the bed.

"I feel like I'm going to hit myself in the face with this ring in my sleep and knock myself out. Why is it so big?" I asked while pulling out some pajamas.

"Only you would complain about a ring being too big. I don't think you'll knock yourself out. Many women survive large karat weights with no ill effects." James said laughing.

"You laugh now but wait until I wack you in the eye with this thing in the middle of the night. On second thought, it could be a good self-defense weapon if used correctly." I said watching the thing sparkle.

"I'm sure Marek intended to make a statement that he has the wealth and means to compliment you," He said.

"Oh well, I guess that's a good reason," I said furrowing my eyebrows in thought.

Viktor's words had me thinking and I didn't like the conclusions I was drawing. I shook the thoughts off and grabbed my clothes.

"I'm going to take a shower. Are you staying?" I asked.

"I will," he smiled.

When I didn't smile back he asked what was wrong.

"I know we talked about having better boundaries than this but I have a feeling I can't shake and I don't want you to be in the other room." I said.

"I'll stay here with you," He assured me.

I nodded then went to take my shower.

20

The ringing of my cell phone stirred me from the warm cocoon of my comfy bed and the man in it. I rolled over to grab the infernal device then answered it.

"Hello?" I said drowsily.

"I apologize for waking you, madame. It's Benjamin. Master Volkov needs you to meet him immediately. He would have called you himself but he had to meet Healer Rowan at the airport." He said.

"Where should I meet him and why?" I asked trying to shake the sleep from my brain.

James was awake now and motioning for me to put the phone on speaker so I did.

"It turns out Rowan is only available for the next twelve hours. Therefore we need to move up the timetable for your spell removal. Marek wants you to meet him at Master Le Veneur's mansion as soon as possible. I've arranged for an extra security team to escort you there." Benjamin said.

I thanked him then hung up. It was still dark outside so I fell back on the bed and stared up at the ceiling. Doing anything this early in the morning was not on my most wanted list.

"We should get moving," James said rolling over to look down at me.

"Should I be worried that Marek didn't call me himself?" I said looking at James.

"Where Rowan is concerned, yes. They have history." He said.

"Great, another ex popping up to say hi," I said dripping with sarcasm.

"She isn't his ex," He said kissing me on the cheek.

James rolled off the bed and said, "We should get moving. I don't recommend keeping Rowan waiting."

"Ugh," I said and got up.

James disappeared out the door to shower in the guest room. I could feel where he was in the apartment without expending too much energy. The more time we spent together the easier it was to find him with my power which was both weird and cool at the same time.

I pinged Viktor via our link to update him then got dressed in jeans and a slightly dressy sweater. I wanted to be comfortable but not too casual. Visiting an ally's home was just as much business as it was personal. This one had the added complication of wanting to court me and seeing the ring Marek gave me was going to cause a stir.

Before we left, I texted Marek. If he was driving I didn't want to use our link.

"What's the deal with you and Rowan? I need to know what I'm walking into." I wrote.

Marek didn't reply until I was downstairs in the parking garage.

"Nothing. What did you do last night?" He responded.

I wrote, *"Fell asleep next to James. You didn't answer my question."*

To my surprise, my favorite car pulled up to the curb, and James was handed the keys. I fully expected a caravan of SUVs again. Instead of commenting, I sat in the front seat where James motioned for me to go. Viktor sat in the backseat while James moved to the driver's side.

I took a deep breath and stroked the sumptuous softness of the leather seat. I could live in this car.

Marek's text came in after I sat down, *"I will not let Rowan be distracted by the past."*

"Details," I typed.

I was not going to let him off easy.

Marek pushed at our bond and I opened up to hear him.

"There is too much to tell by text. The short version is that she and I used to work together. She wanted a more personal relationship but I was not interested. It was recent but I do not believe she holds a grudge. She has been friendly since I met her airplane." He said.

"I bet she's friendly. She's probably hoping to rekindle the spark." I said sarcastically.

"She is a professional first. I would not have agreed to have her do this if she were not trustworthy." He said.

"Okay then, we're in the car. Be there soon." I said.

"I will see you shortly," He said.

I looked around and realized we were already on the road to Denver's Belcaro neighborhood. I had missed a bit while discussing things with Marek.

"Is everything okay?" James asked.

He looked good driving the Maserati. It suited him in a way his Mustang did not.

"We're good. Marek picked up Rowan. They're waiting for us at Julien's." I said.

"How are you doing?" James asked.

"I'm too tired to be nervous," I said yawning.

The sun still hadn't come up and my body was telling me I should be sleeping.

"You've been uncharacteristically quiet Viktor," I noted looking back at the vampire in question.

"I am not myself," Viktor said with gritted teeth.

I immediately became concerned and threw open our bond. His anger was sizzling on the surface. It felt like he was going to explode at any moment. I couldn't help but reach back for him. He shied away from my touch but I could tell it was exactly what he needed.

I unbuckled my seatbelt and turned to climb in the backseat.

"Ember!" James exclaimed trying to grab me so I wouldn't move.

"I wouldn't do this if it wasn't important," I said kissing his cheek.

James calmed a fraction and I took the opportunity to slide in the back next to Viktor. Viktor sat stiffly trying not to touch me but the moment I pulled him toward me he stopped resisting.

"At least put on a seatbelt while you're back there," James said.

I indulged James by engaging the middle seat lap belt then turned to Viktor. Our eyes met and I knew what he needed. His hunger for my blood was pulsing so hard that he felt out of control. It wasn't just the usual thrall/master blood call.

Viktor pulled me closer and ran his nose from my collar bone to my ear taking in the scent. He shuddered slightly but remained tense. From our bond, I could tell he was smelling James and Marek on me and he didn't like it.

Viktor whispered in my ear, "Did you have to sleep with the dhampir too? You could have just shared blood."

"I didn't have sex with James and it isn't for you to decide who I bed or share blood with," I said.

Viktor flinched then leaned into me.

"Master, may I?" Viktor asked moving to drag his lips along the sensitive flesh of my neck.

I couldn't help the goosebumps that erupted over my skin at the thought of him biting me but unlike when I was with Marek, I could use my brain.

"Not my neck," I said.

Viktor snapped out of seduction mode and back into his wounded vampire look. It didn't fool me. I knew he was playing it up trying to get what he wanted.

"You may drink from my wrist but that is all. Take it or leave it." I said holding my wrist up for him to take.

He didn't hesitate long before taking my wrist gently and pulling it to his mouth. He placed a soft kiss on the inside of my wrist before he bit down. It was sensual and damn it if it didn't work. I felt a rush of desire run through my body as he began to drink. It ignited further with each swallow.

I shut our bond down to the barest of openings and reminded myself that Viktor was an asshole. It helped…a little.

Viktor released me after a few swallows just as I had instructed him to do. He took his time healing the wound on my wrist. The second he let go of me I unbuckled my seatbelt and climbed back into the front seat.

James raised an eyebrow at me but didn't say a word. I was certain he could guess what was going on. I decided to deflect the tension I was feeling.

"Where is our backup? I didn't see them in the garage before we left." I said.

"They are on stealth mode. The full dignitary treatment backfired last time so Marek and I thought this was best." James said.

"Good," I said then addressed Viktor, "Are you going to behave at Julien's, or do I have to put a guard on you?"

"I am not a child," Viktor huffed.

It sounded childish to me but instead of arguing I said, "Good. I need you to watch my back while I'm out of it. You know his coven better than all of us and I anticipate I will be vulnerable there."

"There is no safer place for the ritual. They are more than your allies, they are family." Viktor said.

I looked at James and he seemed to be convinced.

"Between the team, Marek, Viktor, and myself you will be safe. I suspect Julien would protect you at great cost." James said.

"Bringing the dhampir in with you will raise questions," Viktor added.

"Viktor, he has a name and a title. Pick one and use it." I said feeling angry at how he was belittling James.

"Very well. Having James as your lieutenant will be seen by some as a weakness. I advise you to station him somewhere less visible." Viktor said.

"Your concern is noted, Viktor but there are only two men I trust completely with my safety and James is one of them. He stays by my side," I said.

James drove us onto Julien's street. Then through the gated entrance. He pressed the intercom and told security who we were. They opened the gate and we drove in.

Marek's blue Chevelle was parked in front of the house. James pulled the Maserati in next to it but I didn't get out right away. Something was tugging on my consciousness. It was like an itch I had to scratch before I could move. It was the prelude to a vision.

James must have sensed it because I felt him grab me. It was too late. I fell into the vision a moment later.

A dimly lit room flickered into view. A woman sat on the floor inside a circle drawn from what appeared to be soot or ash of some kind. Candles were burning at regular intervals with herbs strung in lines between them. The woman was mumbling something over and over. It was causing a buzzing in my head.

The closer I came to her the less I could see of her. It was like my eyes lost focus and clouded over leaving me with just the impression of her. She was swaying within the circle but the reason for it was unknown.

I tried to pull back out of the vision to redirect it elsewhere. There was a definite pull leading me somewhere else but I couldn't extract myself from the image of the woman. The more I pushed, the more the buzzing increased until my head began to pound. The pain hit me swiftly and took my breath away.

The worst pain I had ever felt in my life was now splitting my head open with its claws. A blinding light speared my vision leaving me unable to see anything. I felt my stomach give way to severe nausea that had me emptying my guts onto the floor. Somehow I knew I was actually sick in my physical body, this was more than a vision.

Again, I tried to pull myself out of the vision only to be hit with another intense wave of pain in my head. If this continued, I didn't think I would survive. Pressure grew in my head in time with the pain and all I could think of was cracking my head open to let the pressure out. I needed someone to drill a hole in my head. I knew it would help.

A faint sound began to loop together within the misery. It was similar to the woman's chanting only this new sound was a male voice. The sound was familiar and when I was able to hear it clearly, it was soothing.

I reached for the lifeline that voice represented and was met with another voice urging me to grab on. As I listened harder, the noise of the woman's chanting softened replaced by several voices coaxing me back to myself and away from the pain.

Getting away from the pain became my only goal. I reached out not just with my awareness but also within my blood bonds to find Marek and Viktor. As soon as I did, I found the line connecting me to Viktor and Marek burning brightly. I winced at the light as I reached for it.

When I touched it another line appeared. It was so similar to the other one that I latched on to that one as well. The moment I did, the pain in my head began to fade and my brain was able to make sense of what was happening.

The vision dropped away to the sound of screaming and worried voices. I realized it was me that was screaming so I worked at taking deep breathes until the pain eased enough for me to open my eyes.

James and Marek were on one side of me with Julien on the other side. A woman I had never seen before was holding my head and Viktor was at my feet. It was clear I was no longer in the car and was being held down by everyone.

"Make it stop," I said gasping at the pain speaking caused me.

"This will get worse before it gets better." The woman said.

She had dark skin with brown eyes that flickered violet as she spoke. Her hair was pulled back in dreads dyed a deep purple color. I assumed she was Rowan.

"Ember, we have a faint connection right now. Can you feel it?" Julien asked.

"I can't," I shook my head.

"It will feel similar to me but faint. Try to find it." James urged.

I closed my eyes and pushed the pain as far back as I could. Marek's bond was present pulsing with strength. Viktor was there too but his was weaker. I brushed it aside to find Julien.

I thought of how James had felt to me when I scanned his power and used that to seek the link with Julien. The golden glow of it was just like James.

"Got it," I said.

"Good. Rowan, do it now," Julien ordered.

Everyone let go of me at once except for Rowan. Lightning must have erupted where her fingers gripped my temples because the pain intensified so sharply I couldn't make a sound. It was like being electrocuted and drowned at the same time. All thought emptied from my head and my vision went black.

Some time passed then I came to inside an unfamiliar bedroom. The room was dark but I didn't need my eyes to know the guys were there with me. Their presence was pulsing against my consciousness.

"Dial it back a touch guys, I've had a rough morning," I said.

They all jumped to attention but Marek must have won the lottery because he sat on the bed next to me. He pulled my hand to his chest then brought my palm to his lips and kissed it. An involuntary hitch in my breath had him pausing as if he hurt me.

"How do you feel?" Marek asked.

"Better, but my head still hurts a bit," I said trying to sit up.

"Here," Marek said pushing an extra pillow behind me.

"Is my vision still messed up or are the lights just off?" I asked unable to tell the difference.

"We darkened the room to help you relax," James said moving to stand near me.

His presence was noticeably more comforting than the others.

"Julien said the pain would last for a few more hours then it should dissipate," Viktor said.

"What happened? I only got glimpses between the vision and the pain." I said grabbing my head.

They filled me in on what I had missed. James realized what was happening in the car and dispatched Viktor to get Julien and Rowan. He administered healing treatments until Marek arrived. Marek carried me inside while James kept up the healing powers.

Viktor had them take me to the room Julien had prepared for the ritual. While Rowan prepared for the ritual, Julien traced the spell. With the attack active and nothing to do but wait for Rowan, he took it upon himself to find out who was cursing me. James sent the info from Julien to my team so they could work out the remaining details.

As soon as Rowan had been ready, Julien started the ritual to remove the spell. While Rowan pulled the spell out of me, Julien healed the damage. They ran into trouble during the process and if I hadn't woken up when I did, they may not have been able to remove it at all.

"But they got it right? Tell me there's nothing left." I said searching for any sign of the spell within me.

"They got it all. Besides the lingering effects of the psychic attack, you are back to yourself." Marek assured me.

"That wasn't a coincidence that I was attacked right before we were going to perform the spell removal," I said.

"Either the ones watching you reported your movements and assumed or someone tipped them off," James said glancing at Viktor.

Now that my eyes were adjusted to the darkness, I saw it clearly. In fact, I was seeing really well in the dark now that I thought about it. I kept that tidbit to myself and focused on the topic at hand.

"The vision I had may help put some of the clues together," I said.

"Let your team handle that for now. You have a visitor. Now that you are awake she will want to talk to you." Marek said.

Marek kissed my forehead. James and Viktor did the same then the guys filed out of the room.

A familiar silhouette filled the doorway and I had to blink several times to be sure what I was seeing was real. She walked in and stopped to turn on a lamp before turning to me.

"Mom, what are you doing here?" I asked dumbfounded as to how she knew to come or how she was allowed to be here.

She walked over to my bedside and sat down before answering.

"Rowan is an old friend. She knew I would want to be here when you woke up." My mother said.

"I don't know how to explain," I said feeling bad about lying to her.

"You've gotten yourself into quite the mess, pumpkin. Vampires are the lowest of lifeforms yet you seem to be besotted with them and they with you. I noticed Viktor isn't traveling through Europe with Natalie as you said." She said.

My mother hadn't called me pumpkin since I was five years old. It was unnerving and yet comforting at the same time. The fact she caught me in a lie killed the warm and fuzzy feeling it gave me.

"It's Nat's story to tell," I insisted defending myself.

"And she will tell. Until then, what have you gotten yourself into?" She asked lifting my hand to inspect the ring Marek had given me.

"I don't know where to start," I said.

"How about telling me why you accepted this ring from a vampire." She said.

Her tone of voice made it clear that she didn't like it one bit. When she said vampire, it sounded like she was referring to a dead rat.

"He's my boyfriend." I said.

"Ember Lynn Summers, I did not raise you to be so willfully ignorant. This isn't just a ring it's a token a potential mate gives his intended. It's not so different from human custom. The vampire courting ritual is vital for vampires and vampires alone. If you are to follow any traditions, you will follow Fae customs. Given your power has manifested, if anyone in the supernatural world wishes to have your hand in marriage, they must seek my permission. I am a Fae princess and hold a higher rank than any of these vampires. That means you outrank them too. While you cannot rule in Faerie due to your mixed bloodlines, you are royalty and should be treated as such." She said.

I had to pick my jaw up off the floor to say anything after hearing her words. I couldn't reconcile this woman with the woman I had grown up with.

"Hold on, what does that mean exactly?" I asked.

"No vampire is worthy of my daughter. You should be matched with someone who is equal to you in power and in rank, preferably Fae." She said.

"You act like I'm engaged. It's just a ring. Beside I don't need you to approve of a match for me. I can choose my own boyfriends." I said.

"Boyfriend? Yes. They are temporary at best and while amusing, they don't have to meet my standards. If however, you choose to enter into a bond that lasts for eternity, I will be involved in the decision. I won't see my daughter's name diminished by someone unworthy of your station." She said.

I knew my mom and she was perfectly serious. Thinking back, she hadn't liked Viktor when Natalie brought him home to meet her. When Natalie announced her engagement, my mother had practically choked on her food.

"I barely know him, we haven't entered into anything that would last for eternity," I insisted.

"You accepted a ring from a master vampire, you are courting whether you know it or not. And that ring has an enchantment upon it. You need to give it back to him." She said.

"Enchanted to do what?" I asked.

"A harmless spell common on vampire tokens. It allows him to track your whereabouts." She said.

The shock must have shown on my face.

"Rest now. I'll be back later after I have a few words with our host and your vampire boyfriend. Seriously Ember, of all of them I preferred the werewolf but the dhampir has potential. At least his mother is Fae and his father quarter Fae." She said.

"How do you know they're Fae?" I asked confused.

"It is easy to recognize a fellow Fae besides healing is a Fae gift. Both he and his father wield it. Surely you knew that." She said.

"I didn't put the two together. How do you know his father? From what I understand he was a vampire, not Fae." I said.

"Who else do you know that wields healing powers and looks an awful lot like the dhampir?" She said raising an eyebrow.

"Wait, are you saying Julien is James' father? How can that be?" I asked marveling at the possibility.

It explained why I had instantly been drawn to Julien. His better qualities echoed those of James.

"Of course he is, they are nearly identical in looks even if Julien is more mature looking." She said.

"Clearly I don't have whatever Fae juju you used to see Julien was Fae. I suspected James might have some Fae blood but from what I understand most humans have some quantity of Fae blood. That isn't uncommon." I said.

"Daughter mine, you are in need of a Fae education now. You cannot expect to live in the supernatural world and not know these things." She said with exasperation.

"Maybe if you had told me I was Fae all along, this wouldn't be so difficult now. I would have known all about this and wouldn't have needed to figure any of it out on my own or had to rely on the Council to teach me." I said.

"The Council serves its purpose. Had you never manifested powers, you would never have needed to know. Living in the human world is a risk for all of us, but do you want to leave the humans you love behind, or do you want to keep them in your life? Can you imagine Marek fitting into your friend group? Choosing him means leaving all your friends behind and stepping away from human life. I don't want that for you but if you insist on doing it, I will have a say in how you do it." She said.

"I love him," I said meekly.

"Do you? Or are you addicted to his bite and think yourself in love? Can you honestly tell me that if he had never bitten you, you would feel the same way about him?" She asked.

"I..." I couldn't be sure so I didn't try.

"Vampires are master manipulators, Ember. Are there any signs that he could be with you for reasons other than love? He slipped that ring on your finger and you didn't even suspect an ulterior motive." She said in a more gentle tone.

I didn't want to admit it but what she said brought back all the doubts I had about Marek.

"Yes, there are. I don't want to believe it though. We've been through a lot together. I trust him with my life." I said defeated.

"Marek is a Council loyalist and they need you protected. I think that is the only aspect of him you can trust. What about James? You care for him too. I saw it when you came to dinner." She said.

"I trust him completely. He is the only person I can trust without hesitation." I said.

"And Viktor, he has wronged our family yet he is now your companion." She said.

"That is complicated," I said.

"I've got time," She said.

I explained everything that happened with Viktor from start to finish including the parts that Natalie should have told her. I asked her to keep those parts to herself until Nat could find a way to talk to her about it.

"He is faking this, of that I am sure." She said.

"Faking what exactly? Being a thrall?" I asked.

"Of course he is. While it's possible to enthrall someone with your Fae powers, it is not based on blood. Therefore, he does not require regular blood donations from you. He is simply addicted to your blood. Similar to a heroin addict, he cannot go longer than a day without it. I've seen it enough times to know what I'm talking about." She said.

Her statement blew my mind. If Viktor wasn't a thrall and he was indeed an addict, which made a ton of sense, then my entire situation changed.

"Could Marek be addicted too?" I asked.

"It's possible he is on some level but I did not sense the same level of need in him as I did with Viktor. Marek is a higher power vampire than Viktor, he may be able to resist the pull of your magic better." She said.

"But Ember, you need to guard your blood. It is a potent drug to vampires and other creatures alike. You have given it freely to too many to date. That needs to end here and now." She said.

"Had I known, I could have been more careful," I said implying she was responsible.

"Many Fae children live happy, human lives without the need to know where they come from. I wanted the same for you and Natalie. I still do." She said defensively.

"Knowing that doesn't help me," I said.

"Listen, Ember. You are mostly Sidhe with a little human blood mixed in which makes you able to pass for a human but you have to remember that you are Fae first. Vampires are drawn to you because they cannot resist Fae blood. It is highly addictive to them. I'm actually surprised Marek doesn't show more signs of addiction given what I can sense of how often you have shared blood with him. You need to end this now." She said.

"I don't think I could step back even if I wanted to. I have obligations now and you make it sound like I've allowed at least one vampire to become addicted to my blood. How do I possibly fix that?" I asked.

"I will guide you in how to disengage Viktor and the courting with Marek will end at my say so. What I need from you is a pledge that you will stop giving your blood to vampires. It's too dangerous." She said.

It was a statement that brooked no argument. Logically I understood and knew she was right but I enjoyed a vampire's bite too much to give it up completely.

"I will agree to a temporary stop until I know more and can decide for myself," I said.

My mother nodded in agreement then left me to rest.

21

After a few hours of rest, I was feeling well enough to get out of bed. James was waiting at the door and offered me his arm. I took it and leaned into him taking comfort in his presence. There were uncomfortable conversations to come but having James with me made it bearable.

My mother's visit had left me unable to think clearly and put me in a state of confusion and denial. If the vampires were all clamoring to be near me solely because of my blood, I had a lot to guard against. My relationship with Marek was called into question as well.

The one constant was James. He was my rock. I could count on him to have my back just as I could Sam or Todd. In this jungle of predators, he was my sword and I was going to use it.

James led me downstairs to a sitting room I was familiar with from the last time I had been here. It was a living area near what I guessed was Julien's office. Raised voices came from that room.

"What's happening?" I asked.

"From the sound of it, your mother isn't happy with what Marek has to say," James said.

I sat down on the couch and tried to relax but I couldn't help feeling anxious. My mother is a strong woman who isn't afraid to speak her mind and Marek isn't known to change his mind easily. The two of them together was akin to sparks during a gas leak. I hoped we all didn't get burned in the resulting explosion.

Just when I thought I couldn't take the suspense anymore, my mother walked out of the office. She saw me and made a beeline to where I was sitting.

"Ember, your father and I have an appointment this afternoon with the Council's Grandmaster. While I'm gone, don't agree to anything beyond the scope of your job responsibilities with the Council. I will update you after my meeting with Sebastian. Remember what we talked about before." She said waiting for my acknowledgment.

"I remember," I said.

"Good." She said then turned to James. "You swore an oath to Ember and she trusts you. Prove to me she's right about you. You have my number. I expect you to use it."

"I will," James said.

My mother nodded sharply then left.

When my mother was well out of earshot, James said. "Your mother scares me. I don't know why I didn't see it before but she is every bit a Sidhe princess."

"She is also sharp as a tack. She told me about your parents and how your healing magic is a Fae gift shared with your father." I said raising an eyebrow.

James looked hurt then almost relieved. "I wanted to tell you but dhampirs don't make a habit of naming their fathers."

I pulled at his hand to get him to sit with me. He reluctantly sat then relaxed when I kept hold of his hand to entwine my fingers in his.

"I won't say another word about it but you and I shouldn't have secrets between us," I said.

"I agree," He said.

"My mother likes you. It's a rare occurrence. What's even rarer is that she trusts you." I said.

"We spoke when you were sleeping. She had a lot of questions that she was reluctant to ask you directly. For as much as you say she doesn't care, I think she is just used to hiding her true feelings. Because from my point of view she cares deeply and passionately about you. She has been hidden for your entire life only to announce herself when you needed her most. It comes at great cost to her." He said.

"I think I can guess what it is costing her," I said feeling the pain that I was sure my mother was having now.

"I'm here for you, Em. I know what your mother said to you raises a lot of questions. I don't know for sure if what she believes is true but I'll be here to help you figure it out." James said.

"Thanks, James," I said then stilled when I saw Marek walk into the room.

It was the first time I'd seen him since my mother made accusations of his using me. He looked good in a black t-shirt and jeans although his hair was a bit disheveled as if he had been running his hands through it. It made my heart ache.

"How are you feeling?" Marek asked hovering near the edge of the room.

"Physically much better but my mom dropped some bombs on me that has me confused and angry," I said watching him for a reaction.

"Yes, we spoke at length and she made it clear that she doesn't want me anywhere near you beyond what is necessary for us to work together." He said moving closer.

"And you agreed to that?" I asked searching for his feelings through our bond.

"I was ordered to adhere to her wishes for now." He said but the jumping muscle in his jaw said otherwise.

"Sebastian stepped in? If my mother is who she says then he wouldn't have much of a choice I guess." I said.

"You don't believe her?" Marek asked confused.

"Oh, I believe her. I'm just angry. But angry is a normal state with my mother so I can handle that. What I can't handle is if what she said about Viktor and about you is true. That makes me the biggest idiot this side of the Rockies." I said.

"You are no idiot, Ember. I have not deceived you." Marek said.

"Maybe but you could have deceived yourself. According to my mother, I only have a splash of human blood in me, not the other way around. You could be addicted like Viktor. Either way, my mother is right. We need space apart to figure it out" I said.

"We live together," Marek said.

"Do we? I still haven't moved out of my townhouse. I only brought clothes to the penthouse. I think it would be best for me to go back home. The Council's residence wouldn't give us any space." I said.

"You do not need to be the one that leaves. I can stay somewhere else until we figure everything out. It is safer for you at the Council residence." He said.

"No, I want to go back to my townhouse. It will be good for me to be back among my things in a familiar space." I said.

The muscles in his jaw ticked again.

"Your mother informed me she will be supplementing your security team with a few Fae she trusts. She gave me the details to share with you and James. I think with her enhancements to your security you should be safe there." He said.

Marek was all business but I could sense his inner turmoil. Regardless of what my mother thought I knew Marek believed himself to be in love. I felt it every time I was with him.

"This isn't goodbye," I said.

"Are you sure about that?" He asked.

I didn't know and hesitated to answer long enough that he turned to leave. I jumped up and caught him by the arm.

"I'm not sure of much of anything right now. It's been a rough morning, to say the least. But I know I love you and I'm not giving up on us." I said.

Marek pulled me into his arms and kissed me. It was the kind of kiss that melted your knees. I was breathing hard when he pulled away and the smile on his face was genuine.

"I do love you." He said then released me and walked away.

"I think he's mastered the dramatic exit," James said rolling his eyes.

"We all have our moments. Speaking of dramatic…have you seen Viktor?" I asked.

We found Viktor a short time later. He was entertaining Misty but was quick to shuffle her away when I arrived. She didn't look happy about it.

"Sorry to interrupt," I said stepping into a sitting room that served several rooms at the back of the house.

Viktor stood up and bowed as I walked in. He must not have heard the news yet.

"Won't you sit with me?" He gestured to the sofa he was near.

I sat next to him and tried to think of a way to break the news to him and failed.

"You haven't heard?" I asked.

"You must be more specific my dear. So much has happened today that I hardly know what you are referring to." He said.

"My mother has cleared up some confusion about my heritage and told me you aren't my thrall," I said.

Viktor looked confused but there was also a spark of hope in his eyes.

"If that is true, what is the actual reason for my reliance on you?" He asked.

"I'm almost full Fae which means you are most likely addicted to my blood. She believes that is the real reason for your symptoms." I said.

Viktor straightened then turned his head toward me.

"I have heard of it happening but so few Fae share their blood I did not realize it was possible from someone with mixed heritage," He said looking confused.

"According to my mother, I have only a small amount of human blood. The daily doses I've given you have made it worse, not better. She said she knows what to do to fix it." I said.

"And what if she is wrong?" He asked looking me in the eyes.

"I don't think she is," I said confidently knowing she was right.

Viktor started to panic and I sensed he was on the edge of making a rash decision. He jumped up and started pacing the room. James moved to my side in case he was needed.

"If this is true, I will have no connection to you," Viktor said stopping and staring at me.

"Other than being my sister's Sire, yes," I said.

"Yes, yes dear Natalie." He said and I could see the wheels turning in his head.

"Being Natalie's Sire is enough of a connection to me, Viktor," I said willing it to be true.

He seemed startled out of his thoughts, "Of course it is, my dear."

I stood up to leave but Viktor zipped in front of me before I could move past the couch. I froze him in place. His fangs were out and dripping with venom.

"Viktor, you will control yourself or I will have you returned to your cell at the Council's detention center. Do I make myself clear?" I said.

"Perfectly," He said pulling himself back together as best he could while frozen.

James stepped between us and held onto Viktor while I walked out of the room. He said a few words to Viktor then joined me in the hall.

"Your mother was right," James said staying behind me as a shield between me and Viktor.

"I think so too," I said.

Viktor's behavior was that of an addict, not a subservient thrall.

We made our way back to Julien's office hoping to find him there. I didn't want to leave without thanking him or making sure he had control of Viktor.

I knocked on the closed door and heard Julien say to enter. I found him seated at a large mahogany desk with Rowan seated opposite him in one of the guest chairs. They both turned to me and smiled. It was slightly unnerving.

"Am I interrupting?" I asked hesitating at the door.

"No, not at all please come in," Julien said motioning for me to sit in the chair next to Rowan.

James was going to stay outside but I told him to come in with me. He followed me and stood behind my chair. Julien glanced at him then focused on me.

"I wanted to thank you both for what you did today. I know you agreed to it but it turned into a bigger issue than anticipated." I said to both of them.

"Your mother would have my hide if I did anything less. I owe her for much more than I repaid today." Rowan said smiling.

"And I was happy to help and to learn that Viktor's circumstance is not as dire as he thought. That makes me very happy in more ways than I can say." Julien said smiling.

"Good, because I was hoping you could watch over him until he is better. My mother knows of a treatment for him and I'd like to get that started right away. I let Viktor know but I'm afraid he isn't as happy as you and I are about it." I said watching Julien for any hint of anger.

"I am sure he will see reason once he has time to process the information. I will make sure he is well cared for while the treatment is administered," Julien assured me.

"I will contact your mother and discuss the treatment. I believe I know what she intends to do." Rowan said.

"Thank you, Rowan. And Julien, you have been a good friend to me." I said smiling.

He really was pleasant if I set aside that he completely ignored his own son standing behind me.

"You say that like we will not speak again. I assure you Ember that I intend to maintain our friendship for a very long time. You may call on me or my coven to help you in any way whenever you may need us. I will hear no argument from you in that regard." He said insistently.

"Very well, Julien. I will do that. For now, though, I need to get back to work and take care of some personal business. I will be in touch regarding Viktor." I said.

We exchanged goodbyes then James and I left the mansion. I relaxed on the drive back to the Council compound. It was the last time I would ride in the Maserati for a while since I would be living in my townhome and likely driving myself again.

The thought of driving myself and going back to my home gave me a surge of relief. I've been managed by the Guardians for so long now that I could hardly remember when I could go where I wanted when I pleased. With the threat still looming over me from Magdalena, I wasn't clear to resume life as usual but at least I could recapture some privacy.

When I got back to the office my assistant offered to have my personal items packed for me and brought home. I agreed and spent the rest of the afternoon engrossed in research and then a meeting where I was introduced to my team. We discussed our active cases and reprioritized a few of the more pressing matters. I fell into a groove that was similar to my previous role at the law firm except for this time I was running the entire operation.

A knock at the door took my attention away from my inbox long enough for me to realize it was the end of the day. I went to the door to let James in then gathered my things for the drive home.

"You can drive yourself home and I can follow you or I can drive you in my car. The security team your mother assigned will meet us there. A Guardian team is already on-site to secure the area for your arrival." James said.

"If you don't mind, I'd like to drive myself," I said.

"I'll have your car brought up to the doors in the garage. Are you ready now?" He asked.

"Yes, let's go," I said pulling my bag over my shoulder.

James texted what I assumed were orders into his phone.

I walked with James to the garage and saw my Honda parked at the curb with his Mustang behind it. Without a word, I got in the driver's seat of my car and started for home. A strong feeling of normalcy settled around me as I drove. It was both comforting and foreign.

Twenty minutes later I parked in my carport and James pulled in next to me. A Guardian was waiting by the door for us. He updated James and me on status then allowed us to go inside.

"I'm going to do a quick check of the inside then step out to meet the new team," James said.

My townhouse is super small so it only took James two minutes to sweep the interior. I went to my bedroom when he was done and fell back into the mattress.

My bed is the best part of my home. I spared no expense to get the best mattress and the right bed frame. It was a four-poster dark mahogany stained bed that I loved. I missed it more than I realized.

I must have dozed off because I woke to James shaking me.

"I'm sorry to wake you but the Fae team is here and I thought you should meet them before I go." He said.

"Where are you going?" I asked confused.

"I am off shift for the night. Caden will be in charge until I return in the morning. Marek usually takes the evening shift but he is no longer on your rotation." James said.

"Right, of course, you must want to go home," I said trying to tamp down my panic.

"Em, I can stay if you want me to," He said gently.

"No, it's fine. Go home. Sleep in your own bed for once. I'll be fine." I said.

"So you'll be fine?" He said smiling.

"Are you making fun of me?" I said.

"Just a little bit," he said pulling me in for a big hug.

He walked me to the living room where three people I had never seen before were seated. I assumed they were the Fae group my mom sent but frankly, they all looked mostly human to me. James introduced them one at a time.

Scout was a wiry looking woman with stringy blonde hair and a pronounced jaw with a slight underbite. Her eyes darted side to side like she was unable to look directly ahead. It was unnerving.

The next was Seedrik, who was a man of average height with the most beautiful ebony skin. It appeared to dance in the lamplight as if his skin were drinking in the light.

And finally, Hector was a tall muscular Latino man with long black hair and looks that could take the prize of any sexiest man competition. I had a hard time not staring at him.

Hector spoke next by saying, "If you need us, just say my name three times quickly and we will hear you. Know that we may not be visible but we are always there."

"I appreciate your help," I said.

"Your mother is a dear friend. We are happy to be of assistance." Seedrik said.

"Time to go," Scout said and she visibly blurred.

I blinked and there were three of her walking out the door. My shock must have been obvious because the other two looked at me with pity.

"You will get used to us," Seedrik assured me before he melted out the door.

He literally disappeared as he stepped into the night.

"Get used to us may be a stretch," Hector said smiling.

He winked then stepped outside too.

I looked at James and he just shrugged his shoulders. The Fae were unpredictable and I was glad these three were here to protect me instead of coming after me.

Caden arrived just as the Fae team went outside. I waved hello, told James goodbye, then ordered myself some dinner. Caden stayed outside to give me privacy.

My fridge had a new pint of milk, a carton of eggs, and some butter. A loaf of bread was on the counter along with a box of cereal. The food must have been brought over with my clothes and toiletries. I would need to do a grocery trip but this would get me through the morning.

I sent a quick text to Benjamin thanking him then jumped in the shower to wash the day away. I finished up just in time to get my delivery. I curled up on the couch with my pork fried rice, egg rolls, and fried wontons. It occurred to me that I was eating my pain away but it didn't slow me down.

I debated calling my mom but decided against it for tonight. We could talk tomorrow and hopefully, discover if I needed to worry about my boyfriend becoming my enemy.

22

Fridays at the law firm I worked at before I started my new job at the Council had been slow enough to catch up on work before the weekend. At the Council, Friday was just like any other day because the work didn't end on Fridays. We were a 24/7 operation. There were no weekends off for the Guardians unless they were off rotation for a few days to rest.

My role was technically a Monday through Friday position but that was only office hours. I was on call all the time. The unpredictable nature of our work meant that I had to be ready to go at a moment's notice. It was part of the draw frankly.

One of my favorite things about this new job was the perks of getting to work out and train as part of my day. I met James in the sparing gym before the sun came up so we could work out before going into the office. We also had a new sparring partner for me to try out.

"If you don't hit me with all you have, how will I learn to block it?" Nikko complained.

"Nikko, I don't want to hurt you. This is supposed to be instructive, not deadly." I replied.

"It needs to be realistic but with guardrails. I agree with Nikko. You need to stop holding back and attack him like you do me or Marek. You go all out with me. Nikko won't break. He's a werewolf not a human." James said.

The problem was I had seen Nikko break fighting a magic-user. It wasn't pretty. He needed to learn and I had to allow him to do that but it wasn't easy.

I glared at them both before taking a deep breath and agreeing to do it. Nikko needed this and so did I. He was the only werewolf I knew so this should be good for us both.

"Fine," I said then attacked Nikko.

Using my kinetic power, I pushed him back then stepped into him while throwing a punch at his midsection. He blocked the punch by grabbing my wrist and yanking my arm to the side. I countered his attack with a knee to his thigh and an elbow to his chin. Unable to block both, he took the hit on his chin hard and stumbled back.

James saw me hesitate and yelled, “Don’t back off Ember. Take advantage of his stumble!”

Keeping Nikko within reach was as easy as taking a few steps into him. He didn’t move but he did watch me closely. His eyes narrowed like he thought I was up to something. That’s when I spun to the side and aimed a kick at his knee.

He moved so fast he was more of a blur than I had anticipated. He blocked my foot with his forearm and knocked me off balance by grabbing the heel of my foot. I fell on my ass but had enough presence of mind to roll over so I could get up. Before I did, Nikko jumped on me and pinned me to the ground pressing my face into the wooden floor.

My arms were under me even if my legs were now useless with his bodyweight holding them still. He leaned in like he was going to say something in my ear. I let him put his lips to my ear before I let my power loose pushing him off me easily.

Nikko went flying but his reflexes were so good he was back for more within seconds. I had enough time to get my feet under me and turn toward him before he attacked. He leapt toward me like he was going to knock me down again but I knocked him off course with my power. He fell but rolled to his feet instantly.

That’s when it got interesting. Nikko’s hands blurred then suddenly he had claws. It was an impressive show of strength that he could do it. Clearly, he had been training to use his wolf. I did not want to know how sharp the claws were.

Keeping a safe distance between us, I thought of how to take him down without getting hurt. The only way involved getting him on his stomach or breaking something.

“Are you sure you want me to go all out?” I asked.

Nikko smiled and said, “Give me your best shot, Em.”

I shook my head but James glared at me like I was an idiot.

“Fine,” I said and attacked.

I approached Nikko head on to draw his arms out. He swiped at me as soon as I was within reach. I avoided his claws then grabbed his arm at the elbow. Grabbing his wrist with my other hand I twisted with all my strength until his elbow popped.

Nikko cried out in pain but it only stunned him. He reached toward me with his other arm and dug his claws into my back. I still had hold of his hurt arm which I yanked until his shoulder popped. He raked his claws across my back as he moved away from me. I could feel the blood dripping down my back but I didn’t take my eyes off Nikko.

He was angry now and I used it to my advantage. I faked going for his lower body and he moved to block it. Using his own momentum against him, I pushed him down face-first into the floor. He fell on his injured arm and cried out again. I pinned his body below mine and pulled his unhurt arm up behind him. I twisted it until he yelled then held on.

"I'd call that a win," James said.

"Please don't break my other arm," Nikko panted.

I eased off him then helped him up trying to avoid doing more damage to his arm. In a blink of an eye, his claws were gone. He stumbled once then seemed to be okay.

"Sorry," I said as he winced.

"At least she didn't break the bones," James said.

"I almost wish she had. Then I wouldn't have risked having both arms hurt," Nikko said.

His grimace made me defensive.

"I didn't want to," I said.

They both gave a look like that was the point of the whole exercise.

"How is your back?" James asked turning me around so he could take a look.

"At least I got one shot in on you," Nikko said breathlessly.

James pulled my tank top up to my middle and my workout pants down about an inch to expose all the gashes. They hurt worse now that he was poking at them.

"Yeah, good for you Nikko," I said sarcastically.

"I appreciate you sparing with me. As you can tell, I need a lot of help." Nikko said still breathing hard.

His chest rose and fell as I watched. I caught myself staring and quickly looked away.

"James, help Nikko with his arm," I said pushing him away from me.

"Ember, you are dripping blood in a facility packed with vampires. You are the priority." James said stepping back toward me.

"Fine," I said turning so he could stop the bleeding.

James has healing abilities but he also had a small first aid kit handy when we sparred. You never know who is going to end up bleeding or in need of other medical attention. When there were dozens of vampires around at any given moment, it was also a good idea to clean up any blood immediately.

He did a quick healing treatment but the gashes needed more than his ability could cover. As he cleaned the wounds I hissed and moaned each time something hurt or stung. I may be getting tougher with training but it still hurt to get patched up. It would have been easier to drink some vampire blood but we weren't discussing a certain vampire while we were at the Council facilities.

Nikko needed a trip to the clinic and so did I. James put Nikko's arm in a temporary sling so he could walk without more pain. I felt bad about his arm. He whimpered a few times and it made my heart hurt.

After a quick check-in with medical, I had an IV full of vampire blood and Nikko was relaxing while his reset arm did some initial healing. James was out of earshot talking to one of the nurses.

"It doesn't hurt anymore," Nikko said.

I turned to look at him, "Good."

"You still held back, why?" He asked.

I took a moment to answer. I've known Nikko for a long time and we've been friends forever. Our recent romantic troubles aside, I cared about him.

"I thought I killed you once. I couldn't take you being hurt again. It would break me," I said.

When Nikko had first been dealing with becoming a werewolf, he had attacked me. I hadn't realized at the time that the thing coming after me was Nikko. So I put a few bullets in his chest nearly killing him. Since he was a werewolf his enhanced healing kicked in and he didn't die but it was touch and go for a while.

"I hadn't thought about it that way," Nikko said wrinkling up his eyebrows.

It was sort of adorable. I tried to ignore it.

We were both laying back in recliner chairs so when I turned to look at him I had to move more than my head which hurt.

"Dammit, Nikko. Did you have to use claws?" I asked through the pain.

"I was told to use all the weapons at my disposal." He said with an uneasy smile.

"Yeah well, for future reference they hurt," I said.

James chose that moment to walk over to us.

"Then you will remember that the next time the two of you spar," James said.

"Next time I will kick your ass," Nikko said smiling.

"Oh really?" I laughed. "You have a long way to go, buddy."

A presence filled the room then and my head turned to find the source. He caught my eye, hesitated then walked over.

"Why are you in the infirmary?" Marek asked looking down at me.

I took in his field attire of dark jeans, a t-shirt, and a leather jacket. He must have just come back from visiting all the compromised safe houses. He looked good, but also a little tired.

"It's a minor sparring injury," I said downplaying the gashes.

Marek's nostrils flared and a surge of anger rose from him. He looked at Nikko like he was going to tear his limbs off. James stepped into his line of sight and broke the tension.

"I smell blood," Marek said looking back at me.

"That's because we are in the hospital wing," I said.

"I smell *your* blood," He said and it was clear he wouldn't be pushed off this time.

"You can differentiate between my blood and someone else's blood solely by scent?" I asked curiously.

"Yes," He said as if that was perfectly normal.

"I told them I didn't want to go all out but here we are anyway. I got clawed in the back and Nikko got a dislocated shoulder and elbow." I said.

Marek looked at the IV with distaste, "You will heal better with my blood."

Before I could say no, he took a knife from his pocket and slashed a line in his wrist. The blood domed on the surface and I couldn't help but grab for it.

"Ember, no!" James said but it was too late.

I was already swallowing the caramel perfection that was Marek's blood before the words registered in my brain. Marek sat on the arm of the chair stroking my hair as I drank. The gashes on my back went from stinging to nothing within moments.

After a last sip of blood, I released Marek's wrist. He stayed where he was so I looked up into his eyes. They kept landing on the pulse in my neck as if he was fighting the urge to bite me. I realized then that it was more than desire. He really was addicted to my blood.

"Marek, did you have business to discuss with Madame Summers?" James asked in the most professional voice I had ever heard from him.

It drew my attention to him. He was ready to pull Marek away from me but was holding back until he tried the diplomatic option.

Marek slowly stood then just as slowly turned his attention to James. It was a bad sign that he wasn't in complete control. Seeing him on edge like that hurt to watch.

"I need a moment alone with Ember," Marek said.

It wasn't a request.

"Your current behavior suggests leaving you alone with Ember is a risk to her safety. I will not allow it." James said.

Nikko moved very slowly out of the recliner to stand next to me. It was a clear threat to Marek but he didn't seem to notice. His attention was fully on James.

"I am not asking," Marek said.

"Your orders do not supersede my duty to protect Ember. Step away now or be removed." James said in a tone that demanded no argument.

The tension was so thick in the room that it felt like I was breathing through a thick fog. I realized that Marek had drawn a line and knowing him, he would never back down from it.

I reached out and touched Marek's hand. His attention snapped to me and he looked like he was going to strike a moment before he softened. He didn't realize it had been me at first.

"How about we talk later? I need to get cleaned up before my first meeting." I said hoping he would back down.

He visibly relaxed. It was like I had flipped a switch.

"Yes, I do not want to make you late for a meeting. I will have Benjamin make time on your calendar for later today." He said.

Marek looked disoriented but no longer dangerous.

"Hey," I said pulling Marek toward me. "Thanks for checking on me."

James flinched at the motion then relaxed as Marek became himself again. Marek smiled one of his genuine smiles then moved toward the door.

As Marek left, James pulled out his phone and called in backup. To my surprise, it wasn't Ciara Murphy who he was talking to but Hector, the Fae security guy.

"We have a problem. How close are you?" James asked. "Good, she needs one of you on her at all times even in the Council building. I'll meet you in the lobby to approve access."

He hung up the phone then ran his hand through his hair in distress. I realized then that he saw Marek as a very serious threat and I hadn't seen more than a little anger from him.

"What am I missing?" I asked.

"Not here," James said.

"Then where?" I asked, impatient to know.

"Your office," He said and motioned for us to go.

"I need to change," I said.

"Not until your personal security team is here," he said.

I pulled the IV out of my arm and staunched the bleeding with a tissue. Nikko came with us bringing up the rear as if he was also my Guardian. James didn't have to ask him to do it. He just fell in step with us as if it was obvious he was needed.

James sent a text while we walked. He led us to the lobby at the main entrance to the building. It was where visitors checked in and the public could move freely. To get into the main building you had to have a security pass and an escort.

Hector, Seedrik, and Scout were waiting for us when we entered the lobby. Hector noted my torn outfit and flared his nostrils scenting my blood. His eyes landed on Nikko with his arm in a sling then raised an eyebrow at James.

"Let me get your passes then we can move to a more appropriate meeting space," James said.

He stepped behind the security desk telling the Guardian to pull three all-access security passes. To the Guardian's credit, he didn't blink an eye. He did as James told him without question.

James gave the passes to the three Fae then asked them to follow us to my office. Thankfully it was a short walk. I'm not normally self-conscious but walking through the halls with blood on me isn't the most comfortable thing when your co-workers are mostly vampires.

Ciara Murphy was standing outside my office when we arrived. She nodded at James then moved aside so we could all file in. Murphy asked Nikko to remain in the hall with her. He looked at me for confirmation just like James would. I nodded and he agreed to remain outside.

The rest of us sat at the small round table I had in my office for meetings like these. James started by updating the team on what happened in the clinic earlier.

"Understood, protecting VIP's is what we do best. It's why Mrs. Summers called in the favor," Hector assured him.

"You are acting like Marek is the enemy here. He wouldn't hurt me." I insisted.

"Normally I would agree with you but let me show you something," James said.

He moved to my desk and brought up a program on the computer. He pulled up a few case files and told me to read. The files included all the information the Council had on vampire Fae blood addiction and the circumstances surrounding the myriad of cases they had seen over the years.

According to the data collected, Vampires weren't just more susceptible to influence from the Fae whose blood they ingested but also to others. I read a case where a vampire circumvented the security of his employer in order to let a rival faction in. He was said to be incorruptible by his employer yet the only person who could have given the rivals the security codes was the influenced vampire. He had no memory of doing it, but it had been him.

My thoughts drifted to my vision of Marek being tortured by Magdalena. Did she influence him in any way before he escaped? Or was his escape part of the plan?

I shared my concerns with James.

"In a few of these cases, the addicted vampire was influenced by someone who directly threatened the Fae the vampire was addicted to. Marek admitted to you that he let Magdalena beat him up because she threatened you. She could have used you as leverage to get him to lower his guard enough to be compromised." James said.

"That is insane, James. Marek leads the Guardians for a reason. He is too powerful to be taken advantage of like that." I said.

"Tell me you haven't noticed changes in him since the first time he took your blood," He said.

I thought about how Marek's behavior had changed from an uncaring asshole when I first met him to a softer and more caring boyfriend today. People don't make drastic character improvements in that short a time, so what happened?

"He has changed more than is likely for most people," I said afraid of what that meant for him.

"You used to call him an asshole and were afraid of him. Then something changed. What was it?" James asked.

I looked around the room unsure if it was prudent to speak in front of the Fae. James didn't seem to think it was a problem.

"Everything changed when we were in Arizona," I said.

"The first time you exchanged blood with him was in the hotel room there," James said.

I nodded and sat back in the chair. My eyes filled with tears but I refused to let them fall. Marek loved me, I knew he did. Blood couldn't change feelings like that.

"You said it when we were there, James. I rolled him. Marek's behavior changed toward me almost immediately. I do believe he cares about me but it's possible my blood influenced the speed at which our relationship has developed." I said.

"Stay here. I'll be right back." James said.

"Where are you going?" I asked.

"To see Sebastian. Don't leave this room." He said then hurried out.

A knock sounded at the door a few moments later. Murphy opened the door to say my assistant wanted a moment of my time.

"Let him in," I said.

My Fae security team stood up from the table and positioned themselves around the room. Hector stood beside my chair taking James' usual place.

"Sorry to interrupt, Marek wanted me to make time on your calendar for him. Are you okay with me blocking some time for him this afternoon?" Benjamin asked.

"Yes, of course," I said.

He smiled back then glanced at Hector.

"Your mother called while you were training. She would like you to return her call as soon as possible. She also asked for time on your calendar." He said.

"Okay, I'll call her before you schedule anything with her. It may be something we can discuss by phone." I said.

"Very well. Is there anything else I can help you with?" He said.

"Actually yes, I need to check up on Viktor today. Will you contact Julien's assistant to confirm a time?" I asked.

"I will text you the details once confirmed," He said then left.

I sat in silence for about 30 seconds before looking over at Hector. He must be thinking I'm a crazy person.

"You don't need to worry about us repeating anything we hear. It is our job to be discreet." He assured me.

"I appreciate that," I said.

"Do you usually bleed at work?" Scout asked from across the room.

"No, James insisted we speak with you before I got cleaned up after sparring. When he gets back, I'll head upstairs to shower and change clothes." I said annoyed.

"We will accompany you wherever you go but you may only see me. Scout and Seedrik work best in the shadows. Your mother wanted you to be aware that we are your primary security team going forward. While the Guardian is helpful, he isn't required." Hector said.

"I'm sure you're good since my mother chose you, but I don't know you like I know James. We need to build some trust between us before I would rely on you to have my back like I do James." I said.

"That is fair. We will endeavor to prove ourselves to you." Hector promised.

He looked sincere and the power jumping from his body to mine told me I didn't need to worry about his capabilities. I rubbed my arms to shake the feeling.

James walked through the door. He looked a bit wrung out.

"What did Sebastian say?" I asked.

"He spoke with your mother and wants to keep everything business as usual with the exception of you and Marek not interacting directly unless supervised. Your security team will be staffed by me and at your discretion. The Elite Guardian team assigned to you will now report to you so there isn't a conflict of interest for them." James said.

"How is Marek going to react to this?" I asked.

"Sebastian looped him in while I was in his office. Marek agreed it is what is best for your safety." James said.

"Well, then, if you don't mind, I need to go get cleaned up," I said tugging at my bloody shirt.

James walked next to me and Hector brought up the rear. As expected, Scout and Seedrik drifted off or disappeared, I'm not sure which. They were gone before we made it to the elevators. I wondered if they were going to use the stairs.

We rode the elevator in silence up to my sub-penthouse apartment. Scout was already there when we stepped off the lift. She stood with one hip cocked to the side and an impatient look on her gaunt face.

"All is clear," She said stepping back to allow me into the apartment.

Remembering not to thank her, I nodded my head in acknowledgment instead.

23

James entered the apartment first and did his usual sweep while I made my way back to the bedroom. He sat on the bed while I picked out some clothes. Knowing I would need to change from time to time at work, I made sure an assortment of clothing was left here for my use.

"It must be burdensome to have your belongings and wardrobe strung between multiple residences," James said.

I sighed then sat down next to him.

"It is. This apartment is convenient but it felt really good to be home last night." I said.

James put his arm around me and pulled me in close.

"You can change your mind, Em. Your life has changed significantly in the past few months. Having a familiar place to end your night would ground you in a way this place can't. Don't let Marek's persuasive arguments take that from you." He said.

I wrapped my arms around his waist.

"Are you psychic now?" I asked.

"I know you and care about you. No psychic powers needed." James said kissing me on top of my head.

"Perhaps you're right about needing the familiar." I said.

I got up and grabbed my clothes. My mind was racing from anxiety. Marek was losing it, I knew it. What I couldn't figure out was how to fix it without alerting everyone else to how unstable he really was.

James stayed in the bedroom while I showered and dressed. I wondered if he stayed close because he thought I was in that much danger or if it was because he didn't want to bump into my Fae guards.

I put some effort into my look to compensate for the unease in my chest. If I didn't feel good, at least I could look good and hope for the best.

James was standing by the bedroom window with his back to me when I came out of the bathroom. I had a sudden sense of deja vu. I wondered what he was thinking like I had when I found Viktor standing at that same window.

Instead of tempting fate and engaging James, I called my mother. She answered on the first ring.

"Hey, mom. Benjamin said you called." I said.

James turned around but stayed by the window.

"Are you somewhere private?" She asked.

"Yes, but I'm not alone," I said.

"Then go somewhere private, preferably a bathroom with water running." She said and there was no room for argument in her voice.

"Okaaaaaay," I drawled the word out.

James narrowed his eyes but nodded that he wouldn't try to listen. I went back into the steamy bathroom and turned on the exhaust fan and the sink. I gave my mother the go-ahead.

"Rowan tells me Viktor is in late-stage blood addiction. She needs your participation to create a potion that will end the addiction verses have him go cold turkey. How long has he been drinking your blood?" She asked.

There was no censure in her voice. It felt more clinical which made it easier to answer her.

"He had a taste in February but didn't start drinking regularly until the past week," I said.

"That can't be right. He shows signs of years of addiction." She said sounding distracted.

"Years? How is that possible?" I asked shocked.

"It could be partly due to Natalie donating to him but her blood lacks the power yours has. What of Marek? I understand the two of you exchange blood on a regular basis. I would expect him to be worse off than Viktor." She said.

"He isn't himself but that could be any number of factors. He has never acted addicted as Viktor has." I said.

"Any change in him could be a sign of it. To fix this, you need to meet with Rowan. She will make a potion for them to drink. They need to take it immediately or their hunger for you will override rational thought leaving them only with the need to drink from you." She said.

"And it will cure them?" I asked hopefully.

"As long as the addiction hasn't settled in too far, it will. We won't know until they go through the treatment. And Ember, it is vital that you not let either one drink from you again." She said.

"What happens if they do?" I said confused.

"They die. The treatment was created to end the addiction. Don't get any ideas about what that means for you and Marek. I don't approve of your relationship and won't have you taking unnecessary risks just because you enjoy being bitten." She said.

"Ouch mom, you're talking about my boyfriend," I said.

"Vampires aren't boyfriend material. You own them or you enjoy them for sex. They aren't capable of the level of commitment you require. In your heart of hearts, you must see that." She said.

"We can agree to disagree." I said.

"Rowan will call you to set up a meeting place. When you go, you need to leave your Guardians behind and take only your personal Fae guard. No one but the Fae can know how to make this potion. Promise me you will leave James behind." She said.

"He won't like that," I said.

"Put him on the phone," She said.

I rolled my eyes then turned off the water and fan and went into the bedroom. James was still standing at the window.

"My mother wants to speak with you," I said trying to paste a smile on my face.

He gave me a look but came over and took the phone. He listened for a while then answered some questions. He recited what sounded like a promise then handed the phone back to me.

"Um, what did you say to him?" I asked watching James return to the window.

"He understands that you and you alone are in charge of your security team and that he cannot counterman your orders. He promised to do exactly as you say." She said.

"Thanks?" I said unsure if I was really thankful.

One of the best things about James was his undying devotion to my safety. What if I ordered him to do something that ended up getting us killed?

"Don't overthink it, Ember. Meet with Rowan then make sure Viktor and Marek take their medicine. We can talk about your love life at dinner this Sunday." She said then hung up.

I just stared at the phone. My mother has always made comments about my choice in men but never outright wanted to discuss it. Her preference was sarcasm or direct judgmental hits at the right moment. I shuddered at the thought of what she had to say.

Thankfully, I didn't have time to ponder it for too long. I was needed back in the office to review the daily reports from my team. New assets didn't stop appearing just because my life was a mess.

Marek and I needed to catch up on work-related topics in addition to discussing the potion he would have to take to cure him. I was glad Benjamin was setting up a meeting with him today. We could tackle both topics at the same time.

James and I walked toward the front door in relative silence. He was worried about something but didn't try to tell me what it was. I could guess it had to do with being left behind when I went to see Rowan.

Hector was standing in the living room as if ready to leave. I told him the plan for the day and he nodded his understanding. I glanced at the balcony and saw Scout standing outside. Seedrik was nowhere to be seen but that was normal as I was figuring out.

We left the apartment and found Scout standing outside the door just as we had left her earlier. Given she could split herself into multiples of herself, I wondered if the version of her out on the balcony would be stuck or if she could go through doors. I put the thought out of my head before I hurt myself trying to figure it out. Somethings are just magic.

James and Hector rode down in the elevator with me. Scout met us on the ground floor and I wondered if it was one of her doubles or if it was the real her. James ran point leading the way to my office while Hector brought up the rear. I could feel his eyes on me now and again as he watched out for threats.

Instead of going straight to my office, I veered left and headed to Marek's office. In the process, James was left following me instead of leading. I was growing tired of being led around in my own office but that was only part of it.

I could have called Marek, texted, or linked to his mind but that wasn't my style. I liked to be face to face with him.

"He's probably in a meeting," James said sounding on edge.

"Then I'll wait," I said coming to a stop outside his door.

I used my power to sense if anyone was in the room with him. He was alone so I knocked. He called for me to come in but before I did I gave an order.

"James with me. Hector, stealth mode as backup." I whispered.

Hector nodded then blinked out of focus and finally out of sight. James didn't so much startle as go on guard. I ignored him and walked into Marek's office.

Marek was sitting behind his desk battling a large stack of papers. It looked like the papers were winning.

"Am I interrupting anything?" I asked.

"No, I could use the break." He said smiling.

I relaxed a bit seeing his genuine smile. It lit up his face and made him more handsome. My heart warmed and I felt a similar smile form on my face.

This was us, the real us, not some blood addicted version of a vampire and a Fae. It reaffirmed my knowledge that our feelings were real.

"Good, because I talked to my mother and she has Rowan working on a remedy for Viktor's blood addiction. She wants you to take it as well as a precaution. Then we can stop having a chaperone when we meet." I said glancing at James.

Marek stood up from the desk and walked over to me. He reached out to put his hands on my shoulders then thought better of it. They dropped to his side instead.

"Marek," I said grabbing a hand and squeezing it.

He took a deep breath.

"I was trying to keep this professional," He said looking down at our hands.

The powerful squeeze he gave my hand told me he was struggling. I tried to keep the look of pity off my face but I must have failed. He pulled away and went back to the desk. Having a large piece of furniture between us changed the atmosphere from discomfort to coldness.

Looking into his eyes I knew then and there that he was addicted to my blood and having me close to him was hurting him. I stepped back behind the guest chairs in front of his desk to give a little more space.

"I will obtain the treatment today, all you need to do is take it as directed," I said.

"I can do that," Marek agreed.

"There is one other thing," I said fidgeting with the ring he gave me. "Did you know about the tracking spell on this ring when you gave it to me?"

He met my eyes, "I wanted you to be safe."

"By tracking me?" I said outraged.

I sounded angry even to my own ears. I pulled the ring off and a sense of rage filled me. If the person I trusted with my heart could trick me into wearing a tracking device, I wasn't paying enough attention to my surroundings.

"Ember," James said trying to calm me.

"Did you know about this too?" I turned to James.

"No," James said shocked at my accusation.

I turned back to Marek and threw the ring at him.

He flinched yet caught the ring in midair. His eyes flashed with anger.

"Put it back on!" He yelled standing up behind the desk.

"I won't be tricked or tracked Marek. Of all the people who could do this to me, it hurts the most that it was you." I said.

Marek moved with vampire speed around the desk. James moved between me and Marek but it was Hector who appeared first to grab Marek by the throat before he could get too close. Marek snarled at Hector straining to get away from him. In the commotion I fell backward into the wall jamming my shoulder.

"Continue to fight me and I will separate your head from your neck," Hector said.

"Hector!" I said in warning.

He looked at me like I was the one being unreasonable.

"Ember, please leave the room. It will help him calm down," James said.

"Do not hurt him," I said looking directly at Hector.

He nodded but didn't relax his hold on Marek at all. James didn't need the warning, he knew I wouldn't forgive him if he hurt Marek. James helped Hector hold Marek while I moved toward the door.

I turned and walked out of the room reluctantly. The moment the door closed behind me a clatter erupted from the office. I moved to go back in but was blocked by Scout.

"Let Hector handle it. He won't permanently harm your vampire. You ordered him not to." She said.

I relaxed and stepped back. She was right but it didn't stop me from worrying. Granted I started the fight but Marek was behaving like an uncontrolled new vampire. Through our bond, I could tell his emotions were raw within him and he couldn't differentiate between them and rational thought. It made him more dangerous.

My phone rang. It was Rowan.

"Ember, I'm glad I caught you. I need you to meet me right now. I was able to delay my flight by a few hours but I can't do more than that. I have the potion you need for your vampires but it requires something from you to finish it." Rowan said.

"Tell me where to meet you. I'll be there as quickly as I can." I said.

She made me promise not to bring any Council Guardians then gave me the address. It was a warehouse off Sante Fe Drive near downtown. It would take me maybe fifteen minutes to get there.

The crashing noises continued in Marek's office. I was torn between leaving or going back in. I decided to leave them to it and walked away.

"We should wait for Hector," Scout said following after me.

"He can join us when he's done. My errand can't wait and I'm tired of having an entourage." I said.

I called up Benjamin as I walked to find out how to get my car ready. He protested but ultimately gave in and had my car brought around for me. When I got to the garage, Murphy was waiting.

"No, you can't come," I said brushing past her to get in on the driver's side.

"At least let me drive you, I will stay in the car if you like." She pleaded.

"Benjamin is a little traitor. This is personal Fae only business. You can't be there." I said.

She looked at Scout then glanced around like she expected the rest of my team to come around the corner at any moment. When she didn't see them, she dug in.

"I can't do that. I was ordered to go with you." She said.

"I am ordering you to stay behind," I said and she backed away.

Apparently, the order hadn't come from Sebastian or she wouldn't have backed down. I got into the car with Scout in the passenger seat.

"One moment please," Scout said.

Seedrik popped into view and opened the back door of the Honda. He slid in and nodded to me that we were good to go.

"Hector will join us when he can," Seedrik said.

"Were you in the office with them?" I asked as I pulled out into traffic.

"Yes, your vampire is strong but he is no match for Hector. The dhampir is good in a fight. I like him." He said.

I smiled. It seemed that James made a new friend or at least earned the respect of a new colleague.

"I'm sure James will be pissed when he realizes I left without him," I said.

"Yes, he was but he understands," Seedrik said.

We drove the rest of the way in silence. I was unsure what Rowan would need from me. Fae rituals were not in my wheelhouse of knowledge.

The warehouse had a brick facade with parking in the rear. I pulled in next to a black Cadillac XTS. I assumed it was Rowan's rental car.

My team checked the door but before I could knock, Hector popped into existence next to us. I about had a heart attack.

"I will knock," Hector said pushing in front of me.

Scout and Seedrik melted into the background. In Seedrik's case, he literally melted into the shadows. Scout just sort of diminished.

"How is Marek?" I asked while Hector knocked.

"He is cooling off in restraints. James is supervising," Hector said.

I felt uneasy about the restraints but at least James was with him. He knew Marek better than anyone and could tell when he was safe again.

The door to the warehouse opened and Rowan stood just inside. She beckoned us in with her. I expected an industrial space with metal walls and a concrete floor but was instead greeted by an interior much more refined.

"I thought all these old warehouses were metal monstrosities," I said.

"This is one of Denver's historic 1890s timber frame structures that have recently been rehabbed. A friend of mine owns a few of them and lets me use them when I'm in town. The lack of iron is ideal for Fae spell crafting." Rowan said.

"It's beautiful," I said following her into a large room.

The flooring was wood so rich it gave the feeling of standing in a dark forest. The wood ran from the floor up the far end of the room as if following it could take you into faraway places. The exterior wall was brick and the rest was drywall painted a soft gray tone. A heavy wooden workbench sat in the middle of the room.

Rowan walked over to the table and began pulling various glass beakers and tubes from a leather case. A dozen amber glass bottles sat neatly in a row waiting for her attention. I assumed those were various ingredients for her spells.

She motioned to a navy velvet couch for me to sit on while I waited for her to be ready for me. I sat and watched as she prepared the ingredients. Watching her work was fascinating.

Hector, Scout, and Seedrik positioned themselves around the room into strategic locations. Hector stayed close to me while the others cycled through various nooks or corners eventually disappearing entirely.

Rowan pulled a wooden stool over to her workbench and looked at me.

"Now for your part. Please come sit in this chair," She said.

I did as she asked. I expected the next steps to be magical but instead, she pulled out a syringe and rubber tourniquet just like any medical professional would use to draw blood.

"I only need a small amount of your blood for the ritual. If any is left, I will turn it over to you to dispose of or use as you see fit." Rowan said.

"Why not dispose of it yourself?" I asked curiously.

"Never let your blood out of your sight. It is a direct conduit to you and can be used for nasty spells like the one I removed from you yesterday." She said raising an eyebrow like she was scolding me.

"Noted," I said.

It made me wonder about all the times I had been bleeding in the Council clinic and what may have happened to my blood.

Rowan moved two vials in front of her next to a flat black stone. It resembled a coaster you might set a beverage on but it turned out to be a heating element. At a touch of her finger, the stone glowed. She set the two vials on the stone and waited until the liquid inside started to bubble.

Using wooden tongs, she moved the vials from the stone back to the table. She then used the syringe to squirt some of my blood into each vial. As the contents mixed, it turned an ugly shade of brown.

"When the potion turns blue it is ready," Rowan said. "Administer the potion immediately. It will take a full week for the benefits to take root but the effect will be immediate. Do not allow either vampire to drink your blood before then."

"What happens if they do?" I asked wondering if her answer would differ from my mother's.

It was best to know worst-case scenarios just in case.

"The vampire will either die or be permanently addicted to you unable to control himself resulting in a death sentence. Vampires who cannot control themselves are put down judiciously by the Council." Rowan said.

Rowan packed the vials into a case that looked to be designed to carry them along with what was left of my blood in the syringe. I accepted them from her and stood up to leave.

"Are there any permanent effects I should be aware of?" I asked.

Rowan hesitated then said, "You will lose your bond with them both. The potion severs all blood ties between you. It may be painful for you as well as for them."

"I understand," I said looking at the case as if it were a weapon instead of a cure.

"Your mother does not want me to tell you this, but after the potion takes effect it is possible to restart blood exchanges with your vampires if you wish. The feelings evoked will be muted but it is possible to enjoy their bite again. A bond will not form though, the potion prevents that from happening." Rowan said.

"Can they become addicted again?" I asked.

"There is a small chance of that happening although this potion was created to make it possible for a Fae to share blood with a vampire. Therefore in most cases it is a permanent cure. Time will tell but I must warn you that if either vampire becomes addicted again, the potion may not work for them a second time." Rowan said looking at me with pity in her eyes.

"I appreciate you telling me," I said.

"You have much to catch up on regarding your Fae side. I suggest you make some Fae friends instead of relying on the vampires for information." She said gently.

"I agree," I said smiling at her.

I hoped to consider Rowan a friend. I liked her.

"Goodbye, for now, Ember. You know how to reach me if you have questions regarding the potion or anything else." Rowan said.

"I appreciate your time and your counsel," I said.

Hector led the way out and I assumed Scout and Seedrik followed. It was starting to grow on me to have an invisible security team. They reappeared at the car and we all got in. Hector got in the front seat and left the driving to me.

I handed Hector the potion case then started up the car.

I sent a text to Julien saying I was going to stop by. A text message came back saying I was welcome at the Le Veneur mansion anytime and didn't need to give him a heads up. I smiled at the repeated invitation. I kept forgetting Julien gave me free reign of his properties.

Viktor wasn't a guinea pig but I would feel better if he took the potion before I tried it on Marek. Then I would know any potential negative side effects ahead of time.

We arrived at Julien's home a short time later. His staff let me in without even asking my name. Hector came inside with me while the others remained outside, or at least it appeared that way. Julien's staff gave Hector a wide birth which elevated my assessment of his skill.

24

Julien was waiting for us in the main living room which had a lovely view of the mature trees that lined his property. He sat with a book in his hand but wasn't looking at it. Instead, he was staring out the window at what looked like a brown patch of grass.

I walked into the room and realized what the brown spot could be.

"Is that what I think it is?" I asked.

Julien looked at me as if startled. I knew better. He would have heard us come into the house and approach him.

"The gardener says he can't get grass to grow in that spot. He's replaced the sod twice but each time it dies. He suggests a rock garden or other hardscape as a replacement." Julien said.

That part of Julien's back yard had been the site of a battle I had with Asher Sands. The brown spot was where I had burned him alive and almost killed him.

"A rock garden could be nice," I said unhelpfully.

Julien turned to look at me. I couldn't read his emotions by the look on his face. It's possible he had been reliving the memory. I wasn't sure that was a good thing.

"It reminds me how glad I am that we are friends," He said falling into a smile. "Are you here for Viktor or to see me?"

"Both. I have the remedy for Viktor's condition but I wanted to speak with you before giving it to him. It's possible this will have serious side effects. I want to be sure you were aware of them." I said.

"Nothing permanent I hope," Julien said.

"No, but he may not want to do this if he knows what will happen," I said then filled Julien in on what Rowan told me.

He considered my words for a while before speaking.

"If this will give him back what he has lost, we will proceed. I can keep him comfortable and distracted while the potion takes effect. I do have one condition." He said.

"What is it?" I asked.

He lifted my hand looking at where the ring used to sit.

"Tell me why your finger is now bare," He said.

"It's complicated," I said.

Julien raised a perfectly formed eyebrow at me. He shot a look at Hector then said, "It's rare that I see you without your Guardian. I wonder if we may speak in private?"

"I don't see why not. Hector?" I asked.

I looked at Hector and he nodded his agreement.

"Call when you need me." He said then walked out of the room.

Julien waited until Hector was out of sight before speaking.

"Please sit with me," Julien said motioning to the open seat on the couch next to him.

I moved toward him and sat as he asked. He took my hand and smiled. It was warm and filled with affection.

"We have spoken in the past about my affection for you. As you may know, I am part Fae and would, therefore, be immune to the effects of your blood. I want the chance to get to know you better and see if we have more than mutual attraction in common." He said.

"Julien, I appreciate the offer. I really do, but I have a boyfriend," I said.

"Your boyfriend whose ring you recently removed and who is currently addicted to your blood. Can you say with certainty that his feelings for you are not tainted by addiction?" He asked.

"That isn't fair," I said pulling my hand back.

"I do not mean to be harsh but it is the truth. I know you demand truth above all else. His deceptions have you doubting him and rightly so. What will happen when he realizes he can no longer share blood with you? A vampire who cannot share blood with his beloved is a vampire who isn't whole." He said.

"I don't know," I said truthfully.

"Consider me as an alternative to Marek. You wouldn't be with a vampire if you didn't enjoy some of our more unique aspects and I can assure you that if you shared my bed, it would be extremely satisfying for us both." He said leaning closer.

His lips were so near to mine that all I had to do was bend forward slightly and we would kiss. I wondered what it would be like to kiss him. His lips looked inviting and he smelled so good it was tempting.

I put my hand on his chest and he immediately put his hand on top of mine. I exhaled and he inhaled the same air as if savoring it. It was weirdly intimate.

"I am attracted to you. That's clear. But I am not exactly free to act on that attraction." I said truthfully.

Julien moved his hand to my cheek then slid his fingers into my hair until he grasped the back of my head. My entire body felt tingly as if the blood had either stopped flowing or was pumping so hard it made my nerves vibrate. I looked into his eyes and got lost in their depths.

While I was distracted, he pressed his lips to mine for a kiss. It was soft at first with his smooth lips caressing mine until I found myself kissing him back. His tongue darted between my lips and I moaned sucking it deeper into my mouth until he moaned back. He pulled me in closer and the rush of lust was overwhelming.

My skin felt hot and my clothes felt too tight. I wanted him like I needed him to breathe and that was when I realized what I was doing. I pushed back from Julien breathing hard.

"What is wrong?" He asked.

He looked like sex and blood and everything I wanted from a partner. It freaked me out.

"I'm not thinking clearly," I said.

"It's the blood call," He said leaning his forehead into mine.

"The what now?" I asked unsure what he was talking about.

"Our blood calls to each other. It's a Fae thing. It means our blood is compatible making for ideal mates." He said.

"That sounds conveniently ominous. You've said something like that before." I said trying to catch my breath.

"I've suspected it since I first met you," Julien said closing the distance I had just put between us.

"Julien, this was a mistake. I'm not in the habit of cheating on boyfriends." I said pushing away from him to get some air.

I walked over to the window as if that would somehow relieve the itch under my skin to go back and kiss him some more. The pull was so strong that if he followed me I would give in to the lust. The certainty of it made me rethink what I felt with Marek. It was the first time I truly doubted the strength of my connection with him.

Julien walked up behind me careful not to touch me.

"I have distracted you from why you came here. I will go get Viktor." He said then left the room.

After a few deep breaths, I called for Hector and felt a modicum of relief when he was back in the room. I could also pump him for information. He was Fae.

"Hector, what is the blood call?" I asked softly.

His eyebrows raised just as he took a deep inhale. "What happened?"

"Tell me," I insisted.

"It is the Fae term for finding the one most likely to be your mate. Although more accurately it is someone who will please you sexually," He said.

"So it isn't some kind of kismet?" I asked.

"It is not destiny, it is biological compatibility. You can reproduce with one who calls to your blood better than someone who doesn't. The lust is stronger and the sex is better." He said.

I asked him for the symptoms and what I had felt when Julien kissed me fit. At least I could take comfort in the fact Julien wasn't lying to me. What I couldn't brush aside was my uninhibited response to him. That was all on me.

Had James been here, Julien would never have asked to be alone with me, and that kiss wouldn't have happened. Julien knew that or he wouldn't have mentioned James' absence before asking to be alone with me. James was going to be livid once he found out. He didn't like his father and here I was sucking on his dad's tongue.

The thought should have disgusted me but instead, a shiver of need flowed through me. I could not be alone with Julien again. He was everything I loved about Marek and James put together in one gorgeous package. Damn his good looks and vampire fangs!

My head was so caught up on Julien that I didn't even notice when he and Viktor walked into the room.

"Ember darling, so good of you to visit." Viktor said walking toward the sofa.

He sat on the couch where I had been with Julien. His nostrils flared then he looked at Julien like he was going to tear his head off.

"Sire, Ember brought the remedy she mentioned. She would like you to take it in her presence." Julien said.

Viktor didn't take his eyes off Julien and it unnerved me. He needed more of a distraction.

"Viktor, how have you been?" I asked.

He slowly turned his head to me. When his eyes met mine they showed hurt and betrayal. It wasn't something I had seen from him before. He was usually arrogant and happy to be nearby.

"It would be better if you came and sat with me," He said patting the sofa next to him.

"Not today, Viktor," I said then motioned for Hector to hand me the vial.

The liquid had turned blue indicating it was ready to be used. I removed the stopper and walked over to him. Then I explained to Viktor what might happen.

"Our connection will sever, never to be replaced?" Viktor asked.

"Yes, you don't have a choice here. Not taking it would have worse effects." I said.

Viktor nodded his agreement. I handed him the vial. He brushed his fingers against mine as he took hold of it. When he had control of it, I stepped backward out of his reach.

Viktor brought the liquid to his lips and drank it.

"All that effort only to end up without a connection to you again," Viktor said.

"We are connected through Natalie," I said.

He nodded then doubled over in pain crying out. I felt it with him. The pain was so intense that I ended up on the ground, face-first on the carpet. The bond with Viktor went numb a moment later and I was able to take a deep breath.

Hector pulled me to my feet then over to a plush chair. I sat down feeling dizzy.

Julien was holding Viktor back against the couch but he was looking at me. His concern clear on his face.

"Are you alright?" Julien asked me.

"I'm fine now, but damn that hurt," I said trying to shake off the pain.

"I am fine as well if you care to know," Viktor said dramatically.

I couldn't help my smile. His hysterics have grown on me.

"You say that now but wait a week and you'll be back to yourself and scheming in no time." I said.

"You bring out the best in me," He said managing a smile.

"Maybe we could be friends, Viktor," I said.

"That sounds...mundane," He said.

I laughed. Julien raised an eyebrow at me.

"Take care, Viktor," I said standing up to leave.

"I will walk you out," Julien said.

I hesitated and Viktor narrowed his eyes at Julien. Then Viktor fell back against the sofa as if he was too exhausted to protest more. I moved forward as if I wasn't nervous to touch Julien again.

Hector fell in step behind me when Julien held out his arm for me. I slid my hand into the crook of his elbow and let him lead me out of the room. Touching him felt different, almost electric. It was unnerving and intriguing at the same time.

We reached the front entryway. Hector moved in front of me toward the door. Julien stopped and turned me to face him.

"Will you permit me to call on you sometime? I am serious about getting to know you even if you insist on it being platonic." He said with a sly smile.

"Turn the dial down on the charm, Julien. I don't need it to say yes. Just promise me you'll keep your lips to yourself and we have a deal." I said giving him a small smile back.

"I promise to keep my lips to myself until you ask me to do otherwise," He said.

"Goodbye, Julien," I said rolling my eyes.

"Au Revoir, mon Cheri," Julien said in French.

Julien clearly turned the charm dial the wrong way. He did, however, keep his lips to himself and didn't kiss my hand or cheek. I gave him credit for that.

Hector opened the front door and we exited the house. I followed him to the car then got into the driver's seat.

"Hold a moment, Scout and Seedrik will ride back with us." He said.

I let my head fall back against the seat while we waited. It was quiet in the car for a bit before Hector spoke.

"I am confused. Are you upset about finding a male you are sexually compatible with?" Hector asked.

I looked at him wondering if he was actually curious or if he was spying for my mother. I decided it didn't matter.

"No, I'm upset because I just cheated on my boyfriend by kissing someone else," I said.

"Marek is a vampire. I'm sure he's done worse." He said.

I turned toward Hector with tired eyes.

"Given his age, you're probably right but that doesn't excuse my behavior," I said.

"You need to meet more Fae males. The blood call is more common than you think. You get used to the feelings it creates the more you experience them." He said.

"Are you speaking from experience?" I asked.

"I am. But if I may offer an opinion, you didn't need his blood calling you to kiss that vampire. It may have been a catalyst but you liked him long before today." He said.

I raised my eyebrows at his remark.

"Now you're an expert on my love life?" I said sarcastically.

"Not you specifically but I am an expert on reading body language and expressions. His intentions were romantic and you met with him alone without hesitation." He said.

Hector looked at me like he was challenging me to contradict him. Admitting to myself that I harbored romantic feelings for Julien would be more difficult if I hadn't just made out with him on his couch. His charm wasn't the whole of the story either. The vampire was an enticing package. One that, as Hector pointed out, I had noticed from the first moment I met him.

"You may be right but I don't have to like it. I shouldn't have come here without James," I said.

"Is James your crutch for keeping your other suiters at bay?" Hector asked.

"I don't use James as a crutch," I insisted.

Hector raised his eyebrows at me like he knew I was lying. Maybe I do use James but it's not intentional. He is just so good at being my Guardian and my friend that I don't think about the other stuff when he's around.

Scout and Seedrik appeared and got into the backseat. I took off driving before I thought any deeper into what Hector said. My libido was in the driver's seat and I needed to let my head take over for a while.

James met us in the hallway outside the garage when we got back. He must have been told that I returned by the Guardian who took my car for me.

"How's Marek?" I asked.

"He's confined to the penthouse. How did Viktor react to the potion?" He asked.

"He did fine, nothing but his usual dramatics." I said.

Hector jumped into the conversation by saying, "The effect wasn't isolated to Viktor. It knocked Ember to the floor."

"Are you okay?" James asked then stopped to turn and look at me.

"I'm fine. It was a little painful but it passed quickly." I said brushing past him.

"Maybe you should wait before you give it to Marek. Your connection is stronger with him." James said.

"The sooner I give him the treatment the sooner we can get back to normal or for what passes as normal for us," I said.

The residential elevators were close to the garage so I headed that way. I wanted to see Marek for myself before giving him the treatment. His stubborn streak would probably cause him to refuse the potion but I needed him free from influence. He and James were my steady support in this crazy world I now lived in.

Two Guardians were standing guard outside the penthouse when I arrived. They stopped me until they saw James and received the okay to let me pass. I gave James a hard look. The Guardians were supposed to listen to me as if I was Marek, not look to James for confirmation.

"Next time gentlemen, I expect you to do as I say the first time. Am I understood?" I asked sternly.

"Yes, ma'am," They replied in unison bowing.

I pushed open the front door and walked inside. My security team fanned out and James stuck to my side like glue.

Marek's presence pulsed through our bond. He was in the bedroom but was moving in my direction having felt me in the apartment. It occurred to me that this would be the last time I felt him in this way.

Sadness overtook me and when Marek saw me he knew.

"What is wrong?" He asked carefully.

Words would not come out of my mouth. No matter how many times I tried, I couldn't tell him.

Marek stepped in front of me then he pulled me into his arms. I breathed him in opening our bond as wide as it would go. The vanilla aroma of his skin was tantalizing and the feel of his arms around me was comforting.

Using our bond I said to Marek, *"I have the potion but it will destroy our bond when you take it."*

"We broke the bond once before," He said.

"It's different this time," I said.

"Then we do not do it," He said in a soft voice.

"Not doing it would be just as bad," I insisted.

"Not doing what?" James asked.

"We are doing it. We just need some time alone to discuss a few things," I said.

"Not possible. I'm not leaving you two alone," James said.

"At least I know you will always protect her, no matter what happens." Marek said.

We were about to break us and Marek knew it. He looked sad then suddenly appeared resigned. I realized too late that he not only made a decision but that it was going to cause a commotion.

Marek zipped past James toward the front door. James yelled for him to stop but I knew only one way to stop him.

I froze him in place before he made it to the door. Marek snarled like a caged tiger when Hector appeared before him.

Hector took hold of Marek then nodded at me to let him go. I released my power slowly to be sure Marek wasn't going to hurt Hector. Not that the big guy couldn't handle Marek but I didn't want a repeat of the office incident today.

When Hector pushed Marek back toward the couch I was shocked at the anger in Marek's eyes. It wasn't directed solely at me but that he was so hurt punched me in the gut.

He moved to break free again. I used my power to push him back.

"We have to do this," I said to Marek as Hector pushed him down against the couch.

Marek snarled again and it pushed me to react. I grabbed the vial and moved in front of him. He fought me but after I pushed more energy into my power he became still.

Marek's breathing picked up but I didn't waste any time. After unstoppering the vial, I lifted it to his lips.

"We will find a way through this, together," I said then poured the liquid into his mouth.

25

Hector stepped forward to close Marek's mouth and keep him from spitting out the potion. I kept hold of Marek until the first hint of pain caused me to gasp and lose my grip on him.

It was the anticipation of the pain that had me pulling away from Marek. As soon as the potion kicked in though, neither one of us could do anything but ride the pain.

The pain I felt when Viktor took the cure was a walk in the park compared to what I felt now. My entire body was on fire as if my nervous system was being burned from the inside out. My vision swam as the pain intensified.

Marek cried out in pain and I could feel it as if it was my own. Then a wave of agony hit me that had me screaming and grabbing my chest as if pushing on it would ease the hurt. It was like my body was splitting in two from my heart to my head.

I lost consciousness for a while. When I woke, the bond that I loved and treasured was numb. My heart broke into pieces leaving me with a feeling of despair so deep I wasn't sure I would ever escape it.

Warm hands pulled me into an equally warm body. The pain lifted enough for me to look up. James held me with tears in his eyes. I turned to see Marek and found him curled into a ball alone at the other end of the sofa. He was shaking but otherwise appeared to be okay.

I pushed away from James to go to Marek.

"Don't touch him. We don't know what will happen." James said.

I turned back to James and all the anger I felt came out of me, "Do not tell me what to do."

The words were harsh and he didn't deserve them. James flinched at my angry tone but I didn't try to fix it.

"Marek, are you okay?" I asked touching his back.

He jerked away from me then lifted his face from under his arms. His cheeks were streaked with pink-tinted tears. He seemed to realize that and wiped them away quickly.

"I will live," He said.

His voice was unsteady and he continued to shake even after he sat up. Viktor had looked exhausted after taking the potion but Marek looked completely wrecked. I moved forward to take his hand but he stopped me.

"Please stay back," Marek said.

The tears I had been holding back broke free then. They fell silently but with as much pain as if I was sobbing loudly.

"I'm sorry," I said pushing backward.

James put his hands on my shoulders to comfort me. I sunk into him like it was the only thing I could do to survive.

"We can leave if that would be better for you," James said to Marek.

Marek nodded. I realized he needed time to process this new state of being. Having me there was making it worse.

"I'll check in on you later," I said to him.

He nodded but quickly looked away. I saw the tear fall down his cheek but pretended it didn't happen. My master vampire didn't cry but this Marek did.

James had to help me off the couch and probably shouldn't have let me walk. But I needed Marek to see me walk out under my own power. When we got to the elevator James lifted me into his arms then hit the button for one floor down.

"Where are we going?" I mumbled.

"To the sub-penthouse. You need to rest and it's the closest place we have." James said.

"Fine," I said letting my head fall into his chest.

"You must be doing poorly if you gave up that quickly," James said concern lacing his voice.

"It was a real ass-kicking among other things," I said.

"Watching you go through it was...," James said with his eyebrows scrunched up.

"Torture?" I guessed for him.

"Worse actually," He said.

The elevator opened and James carried me into the apartment. I insisted on the couch instead of the bedroom. I didn't need to sleep so much as recharge.

Hector slipped in behind us but Scout stayed outside to watch the door.

James helped me get comfortable by removing my shoes then asked if I wanted to change into something more comfortable.

"I don't think I can move and I'm starving," I said.

"Did you skip lunch?" He asked going into the kitchen.

"I was too busy to eat but after two big magical hits, I need to refuel," I said.

James didn't find anything in the kitchen so he called down to have something brought up. He knew what to get me without having to ask.

My phone rang while James was on the phone.

"Rowan, hi. I thought you were getting on a plane." I said.

"I will be in a few minutes. I felt you use the potions and wanted to make sure you were okay." She said.

"I'm tired and weak after the second one but that could be more from hunger than any lasting effects from the treatment," I said.

"If you don't feel better after eating, text me. I'll be on the airplane but I have an app that lets me answer my text messages." She said.

"I'll take you up on the offer if I need it," I said.

She told me not to hesitate to reach out to her then hung up so she could board her plane.

"The food will be here in a few minutes. Who was on the phone?" James asked sitting next to me.

I filled him in on my brief conversation with Rowan.

"I'm glad she is looking out for you. This treatment has me worried," He said pulling my hand into his.

"Now that both Viktor and Marek have taken it I feel a little lost. I've grown used to having them buzzing in my head and feeling them tug at me all the time. Now it's a chasm of emptiness." I said.

"I'm sorry you had to go through that," James said looking truly concerned.

"It seems I'm destined to hurt people today. Since I'm on a roll, I might as well confess something to you," I said.

"What is it?" He asked.

I could have softened the blow or danced around the subject but as tired as I was, I couldn't think clear enough to craft the message.

"I kissed Julien today," I said.

He looked confused then laughed. It was a full belly laugh. I couldn't understand why.

"Why is that funny?" I asked wondering if James had lost his mind.

"Because you have looked at Julien like you wanted to kiss him from the first time you met him. And the irony of my biological father becoming intimate with you is not lost on me either," he said.

"I didn't know I liked him until today. How could you?" I asked.

It sounded defensive even to me.

"You look at Julien the same way you look at Marek. It's beyond attraction, I can't explain it really. It's almost like you want to devour them." He said shaking his head.

"Julien calls it the blood call. It's a Fae thing apparently." I said.

"He has enough Fae blood for that to happen?" James asked perplexed.

"He registers as Fae and vampire to me," Hector chimed in.

"Hector thinks I need to meet more Fae and get used to the feeling. I rather lock myself in a room and never leave. After what I just did to Marek, I can't tell him I was kissing Julien earlier this afternoon." I said.

"He will understand," James said.

"I don't want him to understand, James. Kissing is cheating...I definitely cheated," I said.

"How about you beat yourself up over it *after* you get some rest and eat something?" He said pulling me in for a hug.

"Always looking out for me," I said smiling weakly.

"It's what I do best," He said kissing me on the forehead.

James' phone rang and he stood up to answer it. I listened to his side of the conversation and realized what was going on fairly quickly.

When he hung up the phone I asked, "Was that Sebastian?"

"Yes, it was," James said grabbing the back of his neck as if that would stop whatever he had to say. "Marek has temporarily been relieved of his duties and I have been asked to step in as acting Director."

"Did Marek really step back or was he forced?" I asked wondering if Marek was hurt worse than I anticipated.

"From what I understand it was a mutual decision," James said.

"Why does this upset you? You're the most capable person for the job," I said.

"It's an honor to be trusted with the job but having to step aside from guarding you in order to do it bothers me. Sebastian said you were covered by your private security team so you don't need me with you. He's right. Hector by himself is more capable than me. I don't have any doubt you are better protected by them." James said.

Hector raised his eyebrows in the corner but didn't say anything.

"But you rather not leave my side," I said realizing his unease.

He nodded.

"I'm sure you'll find a balance you can live with until Marek is back," I said.

"You're probably right," He said.

"Of course I am. Now go do your job. I'll be fine." I assured him.

James looked at me like he was seconds away from arguing. I stood up and pushed him to get him going. Before he left, he made me promise to call him if I needed anything. It was an easy promise to make.

My food arrived shortly after James left and I dug into the cheesesteak and fries with gusto. My friend Todd says watching an attractive woman eat a large meal is often a turn on for men. I was fairly certain that wasn't the case for Hector. He looked at me with the sort of curiosity that leaned toward disgust.

I leaned back into the couch happy to have a full stomach while I contemplated today's events. My bonds were severed and the people I relied on most would not be around for at least the next week if not longer. It was a bleak outlook that threatened to pull me down into an abyss of sorrow.

Even positive people could crumple at what I experienced today but I decided not to let it flatten me. We still had a crazy vampire on the loose to contend with so I didn't have the luxury of falling apart. I had to power through.

The exhaustion I felt before eating diminished significantly enough after eating for me to head back to the office. Hector and Scout flanked me while Seedrik stayed in stealth mode. Now that I didn't have my bond with Marek overwhelming my senses, I could actually feel where Seedrik was lurking. It was a bittersweet realization.

As I walked down the hall toward my office, I felt every member of the team buzzing on the edge of my senses. If I concentrated, I could tell who or what they were. It was a nifty trick that used to take a great deal more effort.

I picked up on a familiar person near my assistant's office so took a detour there before heading on to my office. James stood by Ben's desk. The poor guy looked frazzled which was concerning because Benjamin didn't seem the type to get rattled easily.

"What's going on?" I asked walking in uninvited.

"Ember," James said looking surprised, "should you be in the office?"

"Yes I'm fine. What's happening?" I asked walking in further so I could see the computer screen they were both fretting over.

Benjamin turned the screen for me to see and my jaw dropped to the floor.

"When was this?" I asked.

The screen showed a video of Marek entering the house where Magdalena was last seen. We had teams surveilling all locations she was associated with, in the hope of figuring out her patterns and uncovering any allies.

"This was taken twenty minutes ago. The Guardians thought it was unusual for Marek not to check in with them before going in by himself. He knows the property is being watched so I'm unsure what he is doing." James said.

"He may not know," I said.

Benjamin gave me a look like I was accusing his favorite boss of turning to the dark side. Which was exactly what I was doing but it didn't mean he had a choice. Technically, Marek shouldn't still be under the influence of Fae blood but Rowan had said it would take a week for the potion to take full effect which made him vulnerable.

"We suspect Marek may have been compromised by Magdalena. That is why he was relieved of his duties today. She may be commanding him against his will." James told Benjamin.

"But we don't know that for sure?" Benjamin said.

"No, he isn't aware of any coercion and we have no proof to state otherwise. It is only a possibility but seeing this has me concerned." I said.

"The Guardians outside his penthouse say he didn't leave by the door. When they searched inside, he wasn't there so he left by an alternate route." James said.

"Which implies he didn't want to be seen leaving," I said feeling my stomach sink.

With our bond shut down, I had no way of reaching him besides a phone. Benjamin mentioned they had tried him several times but he hasn't responded.

"He might answer if you called him," James suggested.

He looked me in the eye and I got the feeling if Marek didn't answer my call there would be dire consequences for him. I pulled out my phone and hit the button in my favorites with Marek's name. I put the phone on speaker so we could all hear then held my breath listening.

He picked up on the second ring.

"Ember, are you alright?" Marek asked.

His voice sounded different from usual like he was reading the words instead of thinking them.

"I'm doing better. How are you doing?" I asked.

My heart raced as I waited for his answer.

"I am well." He said.

Again, his voice sounded different. It was almost robotic.

"James said you left the penthouse. I was worried." I said.

"I desired a walk," He said.

I looked at James and his expression mirrored my own. This wasn't Marek.

"Do you always start your walks by leaving from the balcony instead of the front door?" I asked.

Silence. Breathing. More Silence.

"I am keeping you safe," Marek said softly then hung up.

"That's what he said the last time he went off on his own and we both know how that turned out," I said to James.

I dialed him back but he didn't answer. I tried five times but he wouldn't or couldn't pick up the phone.

James put his hand on my phone to stop me from dialing again.

"He's hard to kill," James said.

"He isn't himself. I don't know what this Marek is capable of allowing to happen. What if she tries to kill him again? I can't sit here and do nothing, James." I said.

"I won't leave him to his fate, Ember. I have a team ready to go in but we have to wait for nightfall. An operation this large needs the cover of darkness." He said.

"I'm going in with them," I said.

"No, absolutely not. That's what Magdalena wants." James said protesting.

"James, you don't have the authority to stop me," I said.

"Ember, please!" James begged.

James could take it to Sebastian and get an order stopping me from going. He also knew that if he did that, I wouldn't listen. I've disobeyed what I was told to do before and I will do it again if it makes a difference between Marek walking out of this alive or ending up dead.

Hector spoke up after James and I had a staring match.

"She is a capable fighter and where she goes, we go. She will come to no harm," Hector said.

"She is capable but she has been nearly killed several times in the past few months. She doesn't know how to retreat or regroup." James argued.

"I don't have a death wish, James. I've been training with you long enough to know how to recognize when I need to step back." I said.

"Except if Marek's life is on the line. Then you'll throw all caution to the wind." He said.

"I would do the same for you and you would do the same for me. Instead of fighting about it, James, bring me up to speed on the plan and introduce me to the team. They need to know I will be going in with them." I said.

He ran his hands through his hair and had a look of frustration.

"Fine, we meet the team downstairs in twenty minutes. The plan has to change now that Marek is MIA. I don't know what he may have shared with the enemy." James said.

I walked with James down to the Guardian meeting rooms and barracks. It was the first time I had been down there and I was more than a little curious to know what it was like. James slept down here when he didn't have time to go home before his next shift and it was where the team met to discuss operations.

We had a few minutes before we needed to meet the team so James offered to give me a tour. Hector stayed at the end of the hall while James showed me the kitchen and dining area. It was small yet efficient. A few Guardians were milling about grabbing food or thermoses which I assumed held warmed blood for the vampires.

The recreation area was larger than the eating space with chess boards, cribbage, and cards along with more modern video games. Couches and comfy looking chairs were dotted throughout. The space was empty now but I could imagine what it was like when filled with Guardians.

Our next stop was the sleeping quarters. James led me down a hallway to the room he shared with Caden Thorn. The room had two twin beds set up like a college dorm but with less storage. The Guardians didn't live here so much as crash here. They had an attached bath and a mini-fridge to cover necessities.

It struck me suddenly that I had seen the room before. I recalled a vision of James walking naked out of the bathroom and my cheeks warmed at the thought. My eyes flicked to him then I turned around to hide my face.

"It's cozy," I said stepping out of the room.

"Caden and I are rarely in the room at the same time so I usually have it to myself," James said following me out.

"It's probably nice to have a quiet place to be alone after spending so much time stuck with an asset," I said.

"I wouldn't call it stuck. I enjoy the work I do and I've found that spending time with the right person is better than being alone." He said.

His words had me turning to look at him. I watched the small smile form on his lips and my cheeks warmed again. This was the handsome, flirty man I met a few months ago. I liked this version of James more than I liked to admit.

"Stop it, James. I've already made a questionable choice once today," I said.

James stepped up closer, pushing my back into the wall.

"Something happened when we stepped into the room a moment ago. What was it?" He asked leaning into me.

"Um," I said squirming.

"Why are you blushing?" He asked.

"Being in this room reminds me of a vision I had the other day. You may or may not have been clothed in it," I said attempting to skirt around it.

The wicked smile that crossed his face made my cheeks burn hotter.

"Were you with me in this vision?" He asked smiling.

"No, and don't ask me anything else. The good part only lasted for the first few minutes of the vision," I said.

"The good part?" He asked laughing softly.

"Stop teasing me, James," I said slipping out from between the rock and the very inviting muscled hard place.

I started walking down the hall only to be told by James that I was headed the wrong way.

"I'm sorry to have flustered you," he said as we walked toward the meeting room.

"No you're not," I said smiling up at him. "You enjoyed every moment of it."

"Yep, I really did. Still am actually." He said smiling.

I bumped into him to knock him sideways a bit and he let out a hearty belly laugh. It was a wonderful sound. I hadn't heard him laugh like that before. It made my heart flutter and I longed to make him do it again.

James threw his arm across my shoulders and pulled me in for a sideways hug. I let my head rest against his side and wrapped my arm around his waist. We walked arm in arm down the hall. Several Guardians stepped into the hall and gave us curious glances. They didn't say a word but I knew we were causing a mild stir.

I started to pull away but James tugged me right back into his side. I looked up at him and realized he didn't care what anyone thought. He was happy and didn't want to pretend otherwise. I smiled and gave him a little squeeze back.

26

We entered the meeting room and James proceeded to take charge. James was dazzling in a military commander meets sexy CEO sort of way standing in front of all the Guardians informing them of the mission strategy. The sexy part may have been my overactive libido but the Guardians in attendance were responding positively to him as well.

The Guardians looked concerned when James explained that their original plan had to be scrapped due to possible compromise but they rallied with ideas when asked to contribute. An hour later they had a good plan together and broke into groups to discuss the finer details.

My team was on the front line of the assault much to James' chagrin. My personal security team sat in on the discussion with us. Hector was arguing with Guardian Johnson on the merit of putting the team's strategy solely in my hands by having me freeze everyone.

"While she is a powerful magic wielder, if she were to become injured, your entire team will be left in a vulnerable position. You need a plan B that doesn't involve her. She can easily be taken away from your team given she is the target of the mad vampire's machinations." Hector said.

"Then why go in with us if she is that susceptible to injury?" Johnson asked.

"I am not weak but I am only one person. Hector's right. You can't base our entire strategy on one person and have a single point of failure. This is a team effort or it doesn't work." I said.

"Then what do you suggest?" Johnson asked.

I looked at James and he shook his head slightly.

"Use me as bate instead. I'm who she wants so give me to her. While my guards and I distract her, you take out her other vampires. Then we take her down as a team and get Marek out." I said.

"It's not the plan I would have suggested but it could work," James said reluctantly. "Hector, Scout, and Seedrik can work in the shadows and I'll stand as your Guardian. Magdalena won't suspect Fae involvement and by the time she realizes they are there, we will have control of the room."

"That just leaves the matter of getting into wherever she is in the compound," I said.

"Team two has that covered," James said. "Caden is leading that team. They will get us in."

"We have plenty of intel on the compound gathered from surveillance and from what Marek has told us of the house and grounds," Johnson said.

"I want to see it all before we go in," I said.

"To be clear, this isn't a rescue mission. Our purpose is to eliminate the threat that Magdalena represents. If we get Marek out of there that is a bonus but he isn't the priority." James said to the team.

Then he looked at me as if to challenge me to say otherwise. He could say it all he wanted. I was going in for Marek. I was angry Marek left and if he wasn't healthy enough for an ass-kicking when I found him, I would wait until he was.

I wouldn't have been as upset had he not circumvented the plan the minute Magdalena crooked her finger. For all the times he insisted she didn't mean anything to him, he sure did jump to attention the second she called for him. That was the act of someone who was deeply invested only I wasn't sure the investment was in me.

Without the blood bond pulsing between us, I was able to look at things more objectively and my once unwavering belief in his love for me was the first to go. It wasn't like I thought he didn't love me at all, but the love of my life scenario I had been building in my head rapidly evaporated.

"I agree with James, the priority for this team is taking down Magdalena," I said.

James gave me a look that said he noticed my choice of words but he didn't comment. The team thought I was on board with the objective and went on their way to finish preparing for transport.

Our team was made up of vampires and one magic-user who called himself a mage. He had the ability to cloak us from view for short periods of time. He could also create projectiles out of energy that could knock down a master vampire. It sounded like a nifty trick.

James went to speak with a few Guardians and I turned to Hector.

"Are you okay with this plan?" I asked him.

"We protect you while you do your thing. It isn't important what we think of the plan," He said.

"Alright then. Let's head back to my office. We can go over the intel the Guardians gathered so we are prepared for the operation tonight." I said.

When I stood up to leave, James saw me and held up a finger for me to wait for him. He finished what he was saying then came over.

"I'll walk with you," He said putting his hand on my lower back.

James kept his hand on me until we left the barracks and got into the elevator. He pushed the button for the main floor and leaned back against the wall. We rode in silence holding each other's gazes. A few times, I thought he was going to say something but ultimately he remained silent.

We arrived on our floor and I followed James out.

When we got to my office, James showed me all the data the Guardians had been able to find out about Magdalena and her compound. It was tedious work but we had to do it to be prepared. Marek's life could be on the line and ancient vampires such as Magdalena are often unpredictable.

I paid close attention to the floor plan of the home she was living in and the security assessment from the Guardian team. Two hours later the twists and turns of the house had become somewhat familiar. We had enough video from tapping into her in-house security that we knew what route to take in and how best to get out. We just needed to know where to find her and Marek right before we went in.

That's where I came in. I had to use my Seer powers to try to figure that out as best I could. It caused me a great deal of anxiety to know that the entire operation hinged on my ability to see what we needed so the team could execute.

"You can do this," James said squeezing my hand.

"Right, here goes," I said then thought about Marek.

Without the bond between us to link us together, I found it more difficult but eventually I found the thread that was Marek and pulled on it. My consciousness was tugged in his direction until I could see him fully. I regretted it instantly.

He was laying naked on a bed. Usually, that would be a welcome sight but from the bruising on his face and body, it was evident he had recently been beaten. He was either asleep or unconscious. I couldn't tell which.

I looked around the room trying to see if there was any indication of where he was but it looked like any bedroom in any house. The walls were beige, as were the carpet and drapes. So instead of looking, I listened. Marek was breathing softly like he was asleep. My heart clenched but I moved on to listen for anything else.

I almost gave up before I heard soft singing coming from nearby. I heard a splash of water and I realized that someone was in the attached bathroom. The singing grew louder before the door opened revealing Magdalena in a silk robe. She hadn't bothered drying off before putting it on so it stuck to her body showing an outline of a voluptuous woman.

She called out to Marek but he didn't stir.

"Lover, you need to wake up. I did not hit you that hard, darling." She said in her thick Spanish accent.

She climbed onto the bed.

My blood started to boil as my imagination conjured up all the ways she could have hurt him. Then Marek moved his head and reached for her. I tried to ignore the stab of pain that hit my heart. I told myself that he was just playing along so he could discover her plans.

He pulled her to him for a kiss. She melted into him as he pulled her into his arms.

"Why are you wet? I explained how the towels work." He said gently.

"They are bothersome to use by myself. I would have my servants do that job but I sent them away for you. So you get my wet body instead." She said pouting.

He tilted her head up by putting a finger on her chin. She looked at him with adoration.

"Next time, I shall dry you. All you need do is call for me." He said.

"Are you saying you will be more agreeable?" She asked.

Her voice sounded uncertain and maybe a little vulnerable. It surprised me.

"I told you. For as long as you stick to our agreement I am yours completely." He said.

"I want you to love me completely, Marco," Magdalena said using the Spanish version of his name. "That woman does not love you. How could she when her tongue is in the mouth of another?"

"What are you talking about?" Marek asked sitting and pushing her back so he could look at her fully.

"My spies tell me many things. They follow her, which you know, and watch what she does and who she does it with. She went to Julien Le Venuer today and ended up in his lap kissing him and grinding against him like they have been fucking for months. Like this." Magdalena said, then proceeded to demonstrate for him.

She moved on top of him until she was straddled over his lap and pulled him into a deep kiss. Marek remained stiff and when Magdalena pulled back his face looked murderous. Magdalena just smiled.

"Your angel is no angel, my love. Does she know how to keep her legs closed?" She purred.

Marek grabbed her by the throat and flipped her over on the bed until he had her pressed on her back. He squeezed her neck so hard she couldn't speak. She just smiled up at him and writhed as if she loved it. She used her legs to pull him closer then wrapped herself around him until he released her neck.

"I hate you," He said through gritted teeth.

"Your hate feels surprisingly akin to love," She said teased.

"You do not know love," Marek said looking disgusted.

"I know your love and I want it now." She said grabbing his ass and pulling his body into hers.

He growled then showed her his fangs. She turned her head to expose her neck to him. He took it as the invitation it was and bit her savagely. She cried out in pleasure then moaned deeply when he moved his body between her legs.

A wave of nausea hit me so hard I dropped the vision and ran for the trash can. Nothing came up but the sick feeling stuck with me.

"What happened?" James asked cradling me into his chest.

"I saw them. Marek is keeping Magdalena busy. She is so sick and twisted." I said shaking.

"Tell me why you're shaking," James said.

"We were right about her having someone follow me. They followed me to Julien's and must have been looking in the window." I said then looked at James like he would tell me it didn't really happen.

"She must have a Seer on staff or we have a security breech. She told Marek what was seen?" He said guessing correctly.

"He was so angry, James," I said.

"I'm certain the anger wasn't directed at you," He said pulling me in for a hug.

"Either she is forcing him to have sex with her or he is playing the lover to keep her pacified. Whichever it is, she has him naked in her bed." I said.

"So the nausea was because you saw them together?" He asked gently.

I nodded.

"Apparently she likes it rough. It made me sick to see him like that, James. That isn't the Marek I know." I said.

"When vampires are together they don't behave the same way they would if they were with a human. Marek is no exception." James said.

"It wasn't the man I know," I said insisting in my mind that his actions were a blind attempt to keep me safe.

"We'll get him back. He isn't the priority for the team but I really don't want to leave him behind for both our sakes. I care about him too." James said.

I looked into his stunning blue eyes.

"I'm quite certain he loves you, James. He respects you more than anyone else I've ever seen him with including Sebastian." I said.

"I'm the only one he'll go into the field with that's for sure. The only thing he and I have ever really disagreed on is you. I suppose when love is involved it ends up complicating everything." He said.

He pushed a lock of hair back from my face. The love in his eyes told me he would do anything for me and I knew I had to make things clear with him. He and I were not romantic even if we courted the edge of going there regularly.

"When we go in tonight I need you to promise me you won't fall on a sword to protect me. Marek is already doing that and it pisses me off that he doesn't trust me to take care of myself. I have my personal guards. Let them worry about protecting me and you worry about fighting beside me as my partner." I said.

"All of my training screams for me to protect you. I'm a Guardian, it's what I live and breathe." He said looking pained.

"Do you protect Marek when you go into a fight together?" I asked.

"No, but..." He started.

"Exactly, we are equals like you and Marek. I kick your ass as often as you kick mine when we train together. So treat me like it." I demanded.

James' eyes softened.

"Ember, you are not my equal. You are far superior to me. It's why I protect you." He said.

"That doesn't make any sense, James," I said confused.

"Why are you going in to get Marek? He can take care of himself. Our mission is Magdalena. You know he doesn't want you to put yourself at risk but you're going to do it anyway. You are protecting him just like he is protecting you." He said.

"Stop rationalizing the irrational!" I said getting upset.

"Then stop asking me to behave as if I don't love you." He said right back.

"James..." I wasn't sure what I was going to say but he stopped me.

"I promise that the three of us will get out of there alive. If I have to carry you both out of there by myself, I will make it happen." James said pulling me in for a hug.

He held me tight and all the pieces of me that were scattered and worried melted into the background. James had us covered. I could trust him at his word and that alone was so comforting that I sighed in relief.

"We do however need to find out how Magdalena learned about you and Julien. We have to assume that even though we changed our plans a bit for tonight, she will know what we are up to." James said.

"Then we need to do something she would never expect," I said.

"What do you have in mind?" He asked warily.

I dragged James out of the office and into the elevator. I didn't speak until we were upstairs in my Council apartment and had turned on the water in the master bathroom. When it was sufficiently loud, I told him my idea. He swore a few times then reluctantly agreed.

"I'll make the call while you put the team on figuring out how she found out about me," I said.

"I hate this plan more than the first one," He said.

"She won't see it coming," I argued.

"I trust your instincts," He said cupping my cheek with his hand.

"I hear a but coming," I said narrowing my eyes.

"But this trick could backfire. I just want you to know that no matter what, we walk out of there together." He said.

"I know. I'll make the arrangements. You've got a security review to launch. I'll meet you downstairs in an hour." I said.

"One hour," He said then turned to leave.

Hector walked in, stopping just inside the bedroom door.

"Why are you wasting precious water resources?" He asked looking angry.

"This is the only way to be sure no one can hear us," I said.

"There aren't any cameras or listening devices in this room. You can turn off the water." Hector said.

"How do you know that?" I asked turning off the taps.

"Scout swept the room before you came in," He said.

"That's a handy skill," I said. "Speaking of skills, I know you can pop in and out of places. Can you take passengers?"

"I can transport one along with me but I don't make a habit of doing it." He said narrowing his eyes at me.

"Can you take me somewhere so that no one knows I left?" I asked.

"It would mean leaving Scout and Seedrik behind which I don't like." He said.

"But will you do it?" I asked.

"Where are we going?" He asked.

I smiled and told him to take us to Julien's house. A moment later I was doubled over trying not to puke.

"Take deep breathes. It will pass." Hector said.

The front door of the house opened and Julien's security team rushed out. I froze them reflexively then heard a familiar voice.

"Ember, will you please release my security team? They weren't going to hurt you." Julien said.

"Sorry," I said pulling my magic back.

Julien motioned for his team to go back inside. They gave me a look before they left.

"To what do I owe the pleasure of your unexpected visit?" Julien asked me.

"May we come in?" I asked.

"Yes, of course," He said.

Julien led us into the house and into the sitting room next to his office.

"Can we go somewhere more private?" I asked.

He raised an eyebrow then motioned for us to go with him into his office.

"I am more than a little curious, Ember," Julien said.

"I'm hoping you will be intrigued by my proposal," I said.

"Well, do tell me, my dear," Julien said smiling.

27

I asked for Viktor before starting in on my request. He alone knew what I was thinking about.

When he came into the room, he appeared hesitant as if we were meeting to plot his end. When he saw only me and Hector in the room with Julien he looked confused.

"Viktor, how are you doing?" I asked walking toward him.

"Why are you here?" He asked holding his hand up to stop me from coming closer.

"I needed your help with a Council matter," I explained watching his facial expressions.

Viktor visibly relaxed.

"What can I help with?" Viktor asked walking further into the room yet avoiding me physically.

"Months ago I believe you contracted with someone to transport me to you using a portal of some kind. Can you tell me how you did it and who it was that assisted you?" I asked.

"Are you renewing accusations against me?" He asked becoming upset.

"No, not at all. I was hoping to hire whoever it was for a very important task." I said.

"Oh, well you know the man. Asher is hard to find but he always comes through in a pinch when needed." He said.

"It was Asher Sanz? Of course." I marveled.

"What do you want with him?" Victor asked.

I explained everything to him and just as I thought, he and Julien were on board. Viktor reached out on my behalf to request a conversation with The Egyptian.

Asher Sands didn't carry a cell phone and didn't use email outside of a broker's correspondence who handled his business. Finding him could be problematic but we didn't have to wait long.

Asher called Viktor quickly and after confirming Asher was available and willing to take on the contract, I responded with all the necessary details. In response, I was given the details of a spell I would need to tether me to Asher and call him at the right moment. Asher gave me the details and I practiced it once to make sure it worked.

The Egyptian made sure I knew it was going to cost me a favor even though the Council was covering the fee. It would be worth it if we accomplish our goal with Magdalena. Our call ended and I finally felt hopeful about our mission this evening.

Viktor puzzled it out while I talked with Asher. He knew I was going after Magdalena.

"What has Magdalena done now?" Viktor asked concerned.

"She has Marek and I want him back," I said.

"If you are going to fight her, I'm coming with you. I know her almost as well as Volkov and I'm good in a fight." He said.

I tried to step back but he grabbed my shoulders to stop me. His eyes were burning with an intensity I hadn't seen in him for a long time. He was ready for this fight.

"You could be compromised. She may know what you know." I said.

"She's never been in my mind and we've never shared blood. She can't connect with me if there is no tie between us." He said.

I was both relieved and upset by what he said. That meant he was safe but it also meant that Marek had shared blood with her recently enough that he was influenced by it.

"You are a formidable fighter," I conceded.

"Ember darling, was that a compliment?" Viktor asked smiling his wicked smile.

It made me laugh.

"Fine, Viktor, you can be part of the surprise party. No one outside this room can know though." I warned him.

"You can count on me." He said satisfied.

"You'll have to arrange your travel with Asher directly. I can't speak for him." I said.

"He owes me a favor," Viktor stated.

I nodded to acknowledge he could handle himself.

"Don't ruin the surprise. I'll see you tonight." I said.

I walked over to Hector giving him a nod toward the door.

"Ember, dear," Viktor called out.

"Yes, Viktor?" I asked turning back around.

"It is a pleasure to be conspiring with you," He said.

The look on his face made my cheeks feel hot. He was turned on by the scheming and plotting. I made a mental note to be careful with him. He was easily pushed into extreme behavior.

Hector and I walked into the next room, closing the office door behind us when we left. Hector pulled me into his arms to get ready to transport us back to my apartment.

"Ready?" He asked in my ear.

"Let's go," I said.

The world shifted sideways and my stomach turned inside out. Just when I thought I couldn't take it anymore, we popped into my Council apartment. My legs gave out but Hector kept his arms around me so I didn't crumble to the floor.

I tried to take a step away from him but he said, "Wait a moment. You will recover faster if you keep touching me."

I was acutely aware of the muscles under his shirt and the strength of his body. He was insanely handsome and I was trying hard not to think of that while he held me. I let my forehead rest against his chest and concentrated on taking deep breaths.

"Am I interrupting something?" James asked walking into the bedroom.

I jumped and almost fell down. Hector kept hold of me but that didn't help. I needed to step away from him.

"We just got back," I said trying to turn my head so I could see James.

"She is almost recovered from the trip but needs another minute. Teleporting can be shocking when your body is not used to it," Hector said.

"How did it go?" James asked leaning against the door frame.

He was eyeing how close I was to Hector.

"Hector, you can let me go now," I said pushing him back.

He let go but guided me to the bed so I could sit down. Sitting felt good.

"It went well. He accepted the contract and we got a bonus with the deal." I said.

"What bonus?" James asked.

"A friend of ours will join in on the surprise," I said.

James raised his eyebrows, "Is this friend trustworthy?"

"Of course he is. I wouldn't have agreed to it otherwise," I said.

"Tell me it isn't Viktor," James said.

I didn't say a word. I just looked at him mashing my lips together.

"I'm not even going to ask why." He said rubbing his forehead.

"He has epic fighting skills and he knows Magdalena better than any of us They've never shared blood so he can't be compromised. He'll be an asset." I said.

He took a deep breath then let it out.

"I trust you. Just give me a minute to let it sink in," He said looking worried.

While James was processing the news, I got ready to go by changing into clothing that was more fight appropriate. A pair of black stretch jeans went on first followed by a sports bra and a long sleeve stretchy shirt. My black thick-soled lace-up boots paired perfectly with the rest of the outfit.

I put my long dark auburn hair up in a ponytail then tucked my three-knife holsters into position. The medium-sized knife went at the small of my back. My largest blade sat hidden on my ankle. That was the emergency blade. I wouldn't use it unless I was down to no other options. And the smallest knife went into a wrist sheath.

When I looked up I realized that James was still standing in the doorway but Hector had left. James was smiling.

"You might want to be more spatially aware. Hector literally had to pop out of the room to avoid the show." James said smiling.

"The show? Why didn't you say something?" I asked walking toward him.

"I didn't want to interrupt," He smiled.

I swatted at his arm and he laughed. The sound brightened my mood.

We left the apartment and met our ride downstairs. It looked like a delivery truck from the outside but the inside was decked out like a troop transport the military might use. I climbed in with my security team and James by my side. The rest of our team joined us a few minutes later then we were on the road.

A staging area had been set up in a warehouse closer to Magdalena's compound so that we could gather and not be seen convening in the open. When we arrived, we were shown to the back of the structure. We could see Magdalena's property. It was approximately a twenty-minute walk from the warehouse.

If all went well, we would hike over after full dark and surprise her. A perimeter of Guardians was already in place to ensure none of Magdalena's vampires made it out into the surrounding farms and homes. The second team would move into position at sunset leaving our group to head in at full dark.

Once we met up with the second team, they would breach the defenses and clear a path for my team to engage with Magdalena. If all went well, we would get in, find Marek, then take out Magdalena with the help of my surprise guests. The Guardians didn't know about the last part of the plan so it was important for my crew to be the only ones in the room when I summoned them.

Asher gave me an incantation to set an anchor point for his portal and alert him. When he received the alert, he would portal in, bringing Viktor with him. Asher was known for delivering on all his contracts. The only one anyone could recall him failing on was kidnapping me.

I hadn't been sure Asher would agree to work for me given the last time I saw him I had burned him to a crisp but he was eager to take on the task. He told me it would be more fun than his usual work. His reputation spoke volumes toward his trustworthiness. If he took a contract, he fulfilled it with one hundred percent commitment.

Having the team assembled within striking distance of our target made my anxiety about what we were taking on come front and center. The planning of the operation and prepping to leave hadn't jumbled my nerves at all. Sitting here looking out at the distant building we were about to invade had another effect.

The last two operations I was involved in didn't have such high stakes and I hadn't planned them. The outcome of those also hadn't depended on me pulling out a miraculous move to take down the bad guy. I was good in a fight and could fight with a team but taking a leadership role was nerve-racking.

Involuntarily I reached for my connection with Marek only to be unable to find the soothing link that once bound us together. The pain in my chest of remembering I would never again feel that kind of connection stopped my breath. I closed my eyes and tried to push the discomfort away.

"Why are you rubbing your chest?" James asked softly while taking a seat next to me.

I looked down and saw that I had my hand pressed into my chest rubbing in circles. My hand stilled and I let it drop into my lap.

"I'm trying to reconcile the fact that I can't connect with Marek anymore. It's a torment I anticipated but hadn't truly felt until now." I said.

James put his arm around me and squeezed. I wasn't sure James knew first hand what it was like to have a bond but he did know the last time Marek was with Magdalena it was our bond that saved his life.

"We'll take down Magdalena and get Marek out safely. I promise." He said.

I leaned into him resting my head on his shoulder. I let myself take comfort from him. We only had a short time before the biggest battle of my life would take place.

Team two prepped to leave and I couldn't sit any longer. The apprehension of confronting Magdalena was too much. I started to pace and practice drawing my knives. It was a training exercise James taught me to improve my knife skills and remind my body what to do before a fight.

Marek was the one that insisted I learn how to use knives. He said relying solely on my innate abilities was setting me up to fail when injured. With as often as I ended up in the hospital wing, he wanted me to have other options if it came down to it. I never would have imagined myself as a knife-wielding fighter but here I am.

"Your back draw is catching at the start," James said.

He turned me around to adjust the holster in the back of my pants. He tilted it so I drew the knife out straight instead of up then out. It improved the speed and felt better too.

"Thanks," I said.

"The sun's about to set. We should go." He said.

I nodded and followed him to where the rest of our team was waiting. We watched as the last inches of the sun dipped behind the mountains then we left. There wasn't much cover out here other than cornfields so we made use of the tall plants to hide our numbers. If anyone saw us, it would be obvious we were not friendly.

James took the lead with me directly behind him. The rest of the team followed closely behind me. We made good time as we half jogged, half walked a mile or so to Magdalena's property. The nervousness I felt before we left melted away as I focused on our destination. The closer we came, the more I was ready to do this.

We ended up crawling on our stomachs the final distance to the house. The second team was already in place around the perimeter of the home. When we got close enough, they breached the doors and windows. The noise was minimal but with a nest of vampires inside they might as well have set off a bomb.

I watched as two Guardians broke through a side door reducing it to nothing but splinters. Several others jumped through windows as the rest of the team followed. It only took them thirty-seconds or less to breach the exterior.

We waited a few seconds before approaching the structure ourselves to give the second team time to do their thing. The lights went out on the property as we approached. James headed to one of the side windows on the house that intelligence said led to an unused bedroom. We ducked below it and listened to the sound of fighting. It was hard to listen to it without jumping in and helping.

The rest of our team positioned themselves at other doors and windows. Each had eyes on James so they could see the go signal. We couldn't go in until the second team told us we had a hole to go through.

Hector settled in on my left while Scout and Seedrik went to other nearby entry points. They would go on stealth mode and meet us inside. James, Hector, and I would enter through the bedroom then go where team two told us to go to find Marek and Magdalena.

Entering half blind was frustrating but it was the best plan we had to get in and out quickly. The sounds inside grew quieter and I looked at James to see what he heard. As a dhampir, his hearing was much better than my own. He nodded sharply which told me it was time to go.

James breached the window followed by Hector. Then I jumped through the window after them. I crouched on the floor with my hand on Hector's back. He didn't need it to know I was there but it helped me keep him close enough so I wouldn't lose him in the dark. I realized my night vision had diminished but not as much as I had expected when my bond broke with Marek.

I hoped my other vampire gifts were still online for this fight. If not, I was more of a sitting duck than I anticipated. I put the thought out of my head quickly.

James touched me lightly on my left shoulder to indicate he was going to move ahead. I tapped Hector's back to alert him. He turned to see James moving and executed a smooth transition to put me between them. When Hector fell in behind me, we were on our feet moving to the hallway.

I pressed my back against the wall as I strained to see if anyone was in front of us and whether or not they were friend or foe. Using my power to detect entities around me, I swept the area and found the path the second team created for us. I motioned to James that we were clear to move.

He moved quickly through the hall toward one of our team members who motioned for us to take a left. I nodded my thanks and stayed behind James until we came to the entrance of a large room I immediately recognized. I'd seen it in a vision when Marek was being beaten and stabbed.

Two master vampires came at us as soon as we stepped into the doorway. James engaged one while I froze the other. James fought his way further into the room while I pushed my vampire to the floor.

I lit his head on fire and pushed more power into it until his face turned to ash. I stomped on his neck crushing the scorched vertebrae until they broke. Before I had a chance to reflect on it, another vampire grabbed my arm. Without thinking, I pulled the knife from my back and stabbed him in the heart.

It slowed him down long enough for me to push him backward and light him up like his friend on the floor. I got a little too enthusiastic with the flames and had to back down or risk burning more than this one vampire.

That was the problem with pyro-kenetic powers. I had to be careful not to burn the good guys right along with the bad ones.

I concentrated the heat of my fire on his neck, turning it to ash. Then I kicked him hard enough to separate his head from his shoulders. It surprised me how well that worked.

Hector stopped another vampire from taking me out from behind. He ripped her head off so easily it looked like popping the head off of a doll. He grinned at me when our eyes met. I shook my head at his mirth. Some people enjoyed the fight more than they should.

I took the moment he gave me to orient myself in the room. I found Marek fighting our Guardians back to back with Magdalena at the opposite end of the room. Seeing him fight against us made me stumble.

Hector grabbed my arm to keep me from falling over another body on the floor. It woke me up enough to remind me why I was there. I couldn't afford to be distracted here, it could literally get me killed.

The pulse of power emanating from Magdalena was stronger than anything I had ever felt. It was almost gravitational in its pull. I could feel myself sway toward her. I righted myself and shut down that part of me that sensed her power.

It helped a little but it scared me that I couldn't shake the feeling. I suddenly understood how Marek could be influenced by her. He told me ancient vampires were infinitely more powerful but until then I hadn't understood it. Feeling it made me a believer.

"Ember!" James yelled while tackling a vampire who had been heading directly for me.

I felt Marek look at me before I turned my head and met his eyes. Without looking away I walked toward him. Hector stepped in to take out a vampire or two as I walked and I burned any others that got close enough to me to be a threat.

James stepped to my side when I was halfway across the room. Marek frowned then looked at Magdalena. When his eyes returned to me they were full of pain. That's when Magdalena locked eyes with me. She smiled and it was the most evil smile I had ever seen.

"Well, if it isn't the Council's darling. I did not expect you to make an appearance." She said cocking a hip to the side.

A few of her guards stood near her. The rest were in bad shape after fighting my team. I felt my Guardians gather behind me. There were four remaining of the ten we started with which was humbling.

James stood to my right and Hector to my left. I approached Magdalena to draw her attention and gage Marek's state of mind. He looked worn down and beaten as he had in my vision.

"You have something of mine," I said to her.

"You are mistaken, child," Magdalena said with a sneer.

Her power flared enough to raise the hairs on my arms. She wasn't happy with me but that was only going to get worse given the circumstance.

"I don't think so," I said pushing power back at her.

My kinetic power knocked her back a step. She snarled at me when she realized what happened. She stepped toward me with a sense of purpose that made my stomach flip. I wasn't going to like her next move.

"Lena, please," Marek begged voice cracking.

His nickname for Magdalena hurt to hear but it got through to her. She turned to him and smiled.

"Marcos my love, she has to be dealt with. I cannot allow the Council to invade my home and do as they please." Magdalena said.

I hated that they had names for each other like longtime lovers. I suppose they were together for a long time compared to what Marek and I have spent together. I shook it off though. I couldn't afford to be distracted.

Magdalena reached a hand toward me and with it came another wave of power that knocked down my Guardian team. I braced against it and Hector and James were the only ones left standing beside me. I decided to try diplomacy in the face of her power.

"Let Marek go and I'll persuade the Council to leave you alone," I said.

"What?" James said turning to look at me.

At the same time, Magdalena laughed and said in her thick Spanish accent, "Marek is not a prisoner."

She was looking smug as if she just revealed the most interesting thing on the planet.

"I'm a Seer. I'm fully aware of what he's been up to." I said.

Marek visibly flinched. He had to know I would see what he was doing with her. I assumed he was a prisoner but he was also actively participating in her bedroom activities. I hadn't expected it but that didn't make it any less true.

"He has always been fun. You, however, are not." She said flicking her wrist toward Marek.

It was a command. Marek struggled to ignore it but it seemed her power was too much for him. He took a step forward then launched himself at me. Hector pushed me to the side and took the brunt of the attack. It kept me from grabbing hold of Marek with my kinetic power.

28

James lifted me off the floor and as he did I grabbed Marek with my power. He pushed back but couldn't break free. He and I had tested wills before and I had won. I hoped this time would have the same result.

While I held him, James pulled Marek off Hector while keeping an eye on Magdalena's people. He shook his head at me and looked back toward team two who were waiting just out of site.

We needed reinforcements but it wasn't time to call up anyone yet. They would be our last resort. I still had a few tricks up my sleeve to try.

I felt a pulse of power from Marek and realized it was Magdalena helping him to push against me. With her help, he broke free. He plowed into me and we fell to the ground. He was stronger than me physically but we were evenly matched in power.

As we rolled, I dropped my knife so I didn't accidentally stab myself with the blade. I used my legs to push Marek away from me and tumbled to the side. He was back within seconds but this time I had the advantage.

I pinned Marek under me and he snarled like a stereotypical vampire with fangs bared. I resisted the urge to pull back and instead, I pulled the knife from my boot. I held him down with my power and put the sharp blade to his throat.

"Kill me before she makes me kill you," Marek whispered.

"Do what?" I asked.

I couldn't believe what he said nor was it something I could do. I could threaten him to make Magdalena react but I wouldn't hurt him.

While I was distracted, Marek pushed me hard enough to throw me against the wall. Hector appeared in time to catch me but then Marek turned on James. He launched himself at my Guardian. It happened so fast all I could do was watch.

James misjudged Marek's attack which allowed Marek to get in too close. Marek wrapped his fingers around James' throat and my heart stopped. I struggled out of Hector's arms just as Marek clawed James' throat.

James met my eyes and then he fell to the ground.

“NO!” I screamed so long and hard that my voice gave out.

I used my power to pushed Marek across the room then ran to James. I pressed my hands into his ruined throat trying to staunch the blood but it just kept pumping out between my fingers.

Tears were streaming down my face so fast I had a hard time seeing. What I could see was serious and if we didn’t get him medical attention immediately, James was going to die.

“Hector! Get him to the med unit.” I yelled.

“I can’t leave you,” He said shaking his head no.

“I order you to take him. Do not let him die,” I told him.

Hector grabbed James and they both popped out of sight, teleported off to the Council medical ward. I sagged forward staring into the pool of blood where James had been laying.

I turned to Magdalena when she started to laugh.

“Do you react that way for any of your men or only the ones you’ve been intimate with?” Magdalena asked.

“You will regret that,” I said glaring in her direction.

I wiped the tears from my eyes effectively smearing blood onto my face. I looked back at Marek but I couldn’t meet his eyes. All I could see was James’ blood dripping from his fingertips. Then I looked down at my own hands and saw his blood there too.

Magdalena walked over on her stiletto heels that gave her enough height to meet my eyes without looking up. She pulled Marek to her side and lifted one of his hands to examine it. She admired the blood then licked it as if it were honey.

“Oh, he was delicious, too bad.” She said smirking.

“He isn’t dead,” I snapped.

“Ember,” Marek admonished.

I looked at him and all I could see was the image of his fingers tearing through the flesh of James’ neck. Marek’s eyes softened a fraction as he looked at me. I had to harden my heart or get myself killed. He wasn’t the Marek I loved. How could he hurt James?

I glared at Marek then turned my attention back to Magdalena. She was responsible for all the turmoil in my life. She was even responsible for my sister being made into a vampire. And she just had Marek try to kill James.

“Wasn’t Marek the one who killed you the last time you died?” I asked.

Marek raised an eyebrow at me but didn’t say a word.

“Had he wanted me dead, I would be,” Magdalena said angrily.

“I suppose he did come running back to you the minute you crooked your little finger,” I said sounding more upset than I had intended.

“That’s because he was never yours,“ She insisted.

There was too much truth in that statement for me to handle. I took a few steps away from her and looked around the room. Besides my hidden security team, I was all alone. Every Guardian left was dead or dying on the floor.

"What do you want? My team is beaten, so clearly, this has come down to you and me." I said.

I felt the flicker of flames on my fingertips. My temper was getting the better of me.

"You do not seem to be suffering too badly over your blonde Guardian. I thought for sure you would fly into a hot rage." She said looking confused.

"James isn't dead," I insisted extinguishing the flames on my fingers.

"It is too bad your other handsome friend had to leave. I would have liked to taste him. Fae males are so delicious. Maybe one of your other friends will come out to play instead." She said looking around the room.

Before I knew what was happening, Magdalena picked up a knife from the floor and threw it behind her. A flicker of light danced on the blade as it flew before it hit its mark. Seedrik came into view as he dropped to his knees. The knife sticking out of his stomach.

"Oh look!" Magdalena exclaimed. "One of your other friends is here to play."

She laughed and clapped with delight. Then she walked over to Seedrik.

While she was distracted I used the knife in my hand to slice a line down my palm. My blood dripped out of the wound as I knelt on the floor. I dipped a finger into the blood and drew a sigil on the floor.

"Ember," Marek warned but I ignored him.

I pooled power into my hand and chanted using the words Asher gave me. At the last sound, I pressed my palm over the sigil and released the power. A blinding flash of light appeared and a wave of power knocked me onto my butt.

Marek was thrown across the room and Magdalena was pushed into the wall face first. That was really going to piss her off.

A portal appeared above the sigil and grew in size until it was big enough for a person to walk through.

"What did you do?" Marek yelled as he ran toward the portal.

I pushed him back with my power while the first person walked out. Magdalena saw what was happening and came after me directly for the first time. I had to let go of Marek to focus on her.

Viktor stepped out of the portal and turned toward Magdalena.

"No, Marek is behind you," I called out to him.

Viktor turned just in time to be jumped by Marek. The two of them fought while Magdalena reached for me. Before she could get a hand on me, Sasha and Kaleb stepped out of the portal and jumped in front of me.

Sasha pushed me backward into Asher, who had just stepped out of the portal. He grabbed me around the waist and I panicked. The last time he held me, he was trying to kidnap me and take me to Magdalena.

"Relax, we are allies today," He said.

"Let me go," I snarled.

He released me then moved away from the fighting to get his spells ready. He needed some of my blood to set a circle of power to contain Magdalena.

We only had seconds to get it completed before she broke away from Sasha and Kaleb. I didn't know why they were there but I wasn't going to look this gift horse in the mouth.

"Follow this line with your blood. Make sure there are no gaps in the line," Asher ordered.

That was easier said than done. Blood drips, it doesn't pour in a nice neat line.

Asher invoked a rune on his chest and chanted while he made the circle. I followed behind him drizzling my blood where he wanted it. I had to keep slicing the wound with my knife to keep the blood flowing.

"Hurry that up!" Sasha yelled.

From the sound of it, they were in the midst of quite a fight. I didn't dare look up or risk missing a spot with my blood. Asher stepped out of the circle and I completed my part a moment later.

"You know the rest," Asher said.

I nodded and surveyed the room. I had to get Magdalena in the circle and keep Marek from interfering. Piece of cake...

As I watched, Marek punched Viktor hard enough to knock him out. Viktor hit the floor and looked like he was going to stay there for a bit.

"Sanz?" Marek said coming toward us.

I moved to intercept him but Asher blocked me.

"I've got this," He said.

"No permanent damage," I warned him.

Asher just smiled and moved toward Marek. If I was lucky, he would still be alive when this was done. We needed to have words about this whole thing. So far he'd made more questionable decisions than I could handle.

"Ember!" Sasha yelled.

She and Kaleb were in trouble. Magdalena had Kaleb by the neck with one hand and Sasha with the other. I froze Magdalena as best I could then helped Sasha pry her off Kaleb. As soon as he was free, Magdalena broke away and grabbed me.

"What trick is this?" She seethed.

"I thought the party needed a few more guests," I said as she punched me in the gut.

My breath whooshed out of my lungs and I doubled over in pain. I tried to push her back with my power but she barely moved. If that continued we were going to have a problem.

Asher stepped up behind her and doused her with a potion. She screamed and turned around to put Asher in her sights. He took a step back but it wasn't out of fear, he was drawing her in.

Magdalena moved sluggishly as if she could only move at human speed. I used my power on her again and this time succeeded in slowing her down. She didn't freeze like most vampires did but she also couldn't shake me off the way she had before.

I motioned for Sasha to take her left side while I took her right. We moved into place then I launch a physical attack. She couldn't block while I held her still but I could move her toward our circle.

Sasha got in a good hit and Magdalena's face turned red with anger. I jumped in to grab her throat and used my pyromancy to burn it. It started to heat but she seemed to have too much resistance to my power for it to do more than mar the surface of her skin.

A shout from behind me had me turning to see Marek being thrown through a wall. Viktor was conscious again and clearly in control. My heart skipped a beat when Marek didn't move.

"Viktor, don't kill him!" I yelled.

Viktor frowned back at me.

"Ember darling, you take all the fun out of a fight," Viktor said.

I didn't have time to roll my eyes at him but I would have if I wasn't already struggling with Magdalena.

"Kaleb, watch Marek. I need Viktor's help." I said.

Kaleb jogged over to Marek's still body. Viktor reacted quickly and was next to me in seconds.

"Is Maggie giving you some trouble?" He asked while putting himself in front of the ancient vampire.

"Viktor, I should have expected to see you here. What is it with this girl that has you so enamored?" Magdalena asked.

"I don't actually know besides that her blood is the ambrosia of the gods." He said honestly.

"Viktor!" I said shocked that he gave her an incentive to want to taste me.

"That is very interesting," She said smiling.

Then she made a move that I couldn't track and before I knew what was happening she had her fangs in my neck. Just as quickly she was pulled away from me by Viktor and a knife was sticking out of her neck.

"Try that again and you'll get more than a knife to the neck," Viktor warned.

I cupped my hand over the bite but it was a clean puncture nothing more. If Viktor hadn't moved quickly she could have drained me.

"Ember, we need to move her," Asher said.

"Help me get her in the circle," I said to both Sasha and Viktor.

Viktor already had hold of Magdalena so he pushed her toward the circle. She must have known what would happen because she pushed back at Viktor so hard, he flew twenty feet. I grabbed her with my power again and this time I also stepped into her to force her physically to move.

She pulled the knife from her throat and thrust it toward my stomach. I pushed it away causing it to slice my side instead of burying in my gut. My arm didn't escape unscathed but it wasn't serious.

"Lena, no!" Marek yelled from across the room as the blade cut.

Magdalena glared in his direction then came at me with the knife a second time. By then, Viktor was back at my side and he grabbed the knife right out of her hand. While she was distracted by him, Sasha kicked her knee. A satisfying crack followed by her scream told me it was broken.

"Marek!" She screamed.

Marek roared from the opposite side of the room. The sound of pounding flesh commenced and I figured Kaleb was taking care of him or distracting him at the very least.

Viktor waved the knife in Magdalena's face and she grabbed it from him. I heard his wrist crack then the knife fell to the floor. Viktor didn't cry out, he just smiled at her. It was unnerving.

I used the distraction to pull my last knife from my wrist sheath. When Magdalena turned back toward me I shoved the knife, point first, under her chin sinking it in deep. She froze and it was what I needed to pushed her back into the circle.

Asher was waiting for her. He pulled her down to the ground and laid a string of beads across her throat. They flashed golden light the moment they touched her skin. Her face contorted into a mask of pain and I believed if she didn't have a knife stopping her tongue, she would have screamed.

"Ember, hurry up. I think she ordered Marek to kill you." Kaleb yelled.

A glance in his direction showed me he was right. Marek was trying not to move but it was taking all his strength.

"Help him!" I replied.

"Ember, I need your full attention here," Asher said.

"Cover our backs," I said to both Sasha and Viktor.

They nodded and stood between us and Marek. Then I turned to Asher.

"Stay out of the circle," He said pushing me back before I stepped on the line. "She is as vulnerable as she will get. We need to burn her together."

I nodded and almost jumped out of my skin when he grabbed my hand.

"It's easier to combine power if we touch," He said smiling.

His smile was handsome but it still unnerved me.

"Follow my lead," He said squeezing my hand.

That's when his power touched mine and a golden warmth spread through me. I pulled on his power and he groaned in response. A quick glance at him said the sound was one of pleasure, not pain. That creeped me out…a lot.

I channeled my unease into lighting Magdalena up with flames. To my surprise, she started to smolder and then caught fire. With Asher's help, I was able to push more power into the flames and her skin began to char.

"Lena, no! You cannot make me do it." Marek screamed from the far side of the room.

Sasha sped away to help Kaleb with Marek. He was fighting in earnest now that Magdalena was burning. From the sound of it, she had given him another order.

I met her eyes and the hatred burning in them took my breath away. I pushed more power into the fire and felt Asher give me more as well. Our combined effort had her skin turning to ashes within the yellow and red flames.

Seeing the results had me pushing harder. Suddenly the flames turned a bright yellow and I knew we had to go hotter or she wouldn't die. I took another hit of power from Asher causing him to fall to his knees but it gave me what I needed. The flames flashed white then her body exploded into dust.

Thankfully, the circle Asher made contained the dust so we weren't covered in vampire ashes. I collapsed next to Asher feeling like I used up all my power to kill Magdalena. If she wasn't dead this time, she wasn't capable of being killed.

Viktor sat beside me and pulled me into his body. He hugged me close and checked me for any injuries. He ripped a few strips of fabric from his shirt and tied them over the wound in my arm. There was nothing he could do for my side wound. He smiled with pride.

"You are everything I imagined you would be, You have done the impossible," He said.

"I had help," I said looking over at Asher.

Asher was laying down now but looked like he was recovering.

"Ember, we have a problem," Sasha said from across the room.

She and Kaleb struggled to hold Marek back. He was still trying to get away from them but I wasn't sure why.

"I'm not done here," I said to Viktor.

Viktor nodded and helped me stand. He stayed beside me while I walked over to Marek.

Marek calmed down when I approached but it was clear he still wasn't himself.

"She's gone. Her compulsions should fade." I told Marek.

"Ember," He said and the anguish in his voice said everything.

"I know," I said.

He was responsible for hurting James and the other Guardians. His life would never be the same. I wanted to comfort him but I was too angry.

"Restrain him however you can. I'll call in the rest of my team to wrap things up here." I said to Sasha pulling out my cell phone from my back pocket.

Scout appeared out of nowhere and looked at Seedrik before turning to me.

"Hector is on his way," She said then turned to help Seedrik.

Hector missed the whole fight but he had been on a more important task.

Getting medical attention for James was more important than helping me kill Magdalena. It turned out I had more help than I arranged. Come to think of it, I didn't know why Sasha and Kaleb were there. I had only agreed to Viktor and Asher.

I made the call to Murphy who was leading the backup team giving her the go-ahead to move in. The conversation was quick and to the point.

Hector walked into the room a moment later looking tired and bloody. I rushed toward him and he held up his hand to stop me.

"He lives," He said.

I sagged to the ground but Viktor caught me before I fell. The relief I felt brought tears to my eyes. James was alive.

"How badly is he hurt?" I asked.

"He's unconscious but the doctors are with him and so is Master Le Veneur." He said.

"Julien is with him? Why?" I asked.

"I brought him there to help." He said as if that explained everything.

"Thank you," I said not caring that I was thanking the Fae.

He gave me an admonishing look before noticing Scout and Seedrik.

"You can repay me by allowing me to tend to my team," He said.

"Go," I said releasing him to care for Seedrik.

Murphy entered the room shortly after and began checking the Guardians for signs of life. I hoped they weren't all dead.

Asher was working to gather the ashes Magdalena's body had become. I approached him asking how I could help.

"Fill this jar with ashes and seal it with the wax," He said pointing to a candle burning just outside the circle.

He had three jars, one of them already filled with ash. I did as he said and filled one with ashes. He filled another and we set the three together outside the circle. I started sealing the jars with wax while he performed a spell that cleansed the ground of any remaining ash and the remnants of the blood circle.

When I sealed the last jar, Marek sighed and slumped between Sasha and Kaleb. I looked at Asher and his confident facade slipped to show worry.

"The compulsions on him should have broken when she turned to ash," He said.

"Does that mean she isn't dead?" I asked looking at the jars.

"That is a possibility," He said eyeing the jars.

"How the hell do we kill her? She is ash. If that didn't kill her what would?" I asked.

"I need to consult a few texts on the subject. In the meantime, you need to keep these jars in a secure location preferably behind a strong ward to block her energy from getting out." He said.

"I will," I said.

I gathered the jars up and shook hands with Asher. He was vital to defeating Magdalena today. Looking back on everything that happened, he was very professional. His reputation was well deserved.

"Call me anytime," He said then walked away.

Viktor took the jars from me and held them. I kept him close to me so I could keep an eye on them. I didn't want them out of my sight.

"Ember, where's James?" Ciara Murphy said walking up to me.

"He was hurt. Hector got him to help in time but it's bad." I said.

"Given the level of injuries the team sustained, I expected worse." She said looking upset.

I ignored the despair she was radiating. If I gave into it, I wouldn't get through this.

"Sasha and Kaleb have Marek in custody. He needs to remain so until

Sebastian determines what to do with him." I said to her.

Marek watched me with weary eyes. He looked like a victim but I couldn't forget what he did. Whether he was under compulsion or not, he had actively participated in attacking us.

I was thankful he was alive but I didn't let myself feel anything else. I would break down in front of the Guardians if I did and this was my job. I couldn't afford to be thought of as weak.

Murphy arranged transportation for me and my team. Seedrik was hurt but he was conscious and able to walk. According to Hector, he was very hard to kill.

We rode together in an SUV back to the Council compound. Viktor held the jars in one arm and me in the other. Seedrik reclined in the rear row back seat with Hector and Scout. A Guardian I didn't know drove us but it didn't really matter.

I wanted to see James and get those jars put in a safe place as soon as possible. I would deal with Marek later. Right now thinking about him was too painful.

Viktor kissed the top of my head and said, "Julien will heal him. James will be good as new."

"You don't even like James," I pointed out.

"I don't have to like him. You care about him. That makes him important to me." Viktor said.

"Viktor, are you still feeling the effects of my blood?" I asked looking up at him.

Viktor is not a caring man so his words were out of character for him.

"Maybe a little but I don't think that is why it pleases me to please you," He said.

"Why then?" I asked.

"I don't like sentimental attachments, but I have formed a pleasing one with you." He said.

I let the statement hang in the air. I knew enough of Viktor to know that admitting he cared about me was difficult for him. He also defended me with extreme fervor and enthusiasm. I wouldn't take his feelings for granted.

29

We arrived at the Council compound and I made a beeline to find James. Viktor said something to the Guardian who drove us to get someone to meet us. I ignored the exchange. The only thing on my mind was James.

I found him in the ICU. He was hooked up to a bunch of machines including a respirator. Bandages covered his neck and his skin looked pale. Splashes of blood covered his bare chest but someone had cleaned his face.

Julien was sitting beside the bed. He rose as soon as he saw me.

"How is he?" I asked coming to James' bedside.

I pulled his hand into mine and hugged it close to my chest.

"The doctor sedated him until his throat heals. He kept trying to talk and ruining the healing treatments." Julien said moving next to me.

"What was he trying to say?" I asked.

"Your name," Julien said. "I think he wanted to return to the fight and make sure you were okay."

Julien's face showed signs of having expended a lot of energy in order to heal James. I was extremely grateful.

"Shit...thank you for taking care of him. Hector said you were here but I don't think I believed it until I saw you." I said.

Julien stepped closer and put an arm around my shoulders.

"You are fond of him. It was the least I could do. Besides, my blood was the best option for him to heal." He said.

"Because he's your son," I said and Julien flinched.

"Ember darling, take the gift, and don't punish the giver," Viktor said.

I turned to Julien and apologized. He very likely saved James' life.

"Regardless of what Viktor says, I am not unaffected by the fact I fathered the boy," Julien said.

"Julien," Viktor said like he was reprimanding him.

"If you're going to start a fight, take it outside." I snapped at both of them.

Viktor looked apologetic. Julien reassured him by patting him on the back.

"He's going to be fine, Ember. I promise." Julien said turning to me.

"You know it means the world to me that you took care of him," I said.

"I do," Julien said.

He leaned over and kissed my cheek. Then he excused himself so I could be alone with James. He tried to get Viktor to come with him but he refused to leave. Viktor set the jars of ash on a counter then came over to me.

"You are still bleeding," He said softly.

I looked down at my shirt where a slice had been taken out of the fabric. My side was seeping blood but I didn't feel the pain. There was too much going on to be worried about.

"I hadn't noticed," I said frowning.

"I can get a nurse or you can drink my blood to heal," He offered.

I chose the nurse. I didn't need to complicate my life by drinking from Viktor.

After I got bandaged up, I sat down next to James with his hand in mine while Viktor pulled up a chair beside us. I watched as James' chest rose and fell. Two hours ago I didn't think I would ever see him alive again. I still had his blood on my hands not to mention ash and other things from the fight.

Overcome with emotion, I let the tears fall silently down my face. Viktor put his arm across my shoulders and pulled me in close. He didn't let go until my tears dried up. Then he found a cloth and wiped my face, hands, and arms clean of all the blood.

James moved and I jumped to my feet. His eyes opened and those gorgeous blue orbs found me instantly. I gently brushed my hand over his forehead and his eyes closed again.

"Hey," I said softly.

James opened his eyes again and they went wide with recognition. He tried to talk but with all the machines and tubes he wasn't able to do more than grunt. He became agitated and tried to pull the tube out of his mouth. I yelled for a nurse and Viktor ran out to grab one.

Viktor returned pushing a visibly angry nurse into the room. She saw what was happening and ran to help James. He coughed violently as she pulled out the tube. She told him not to speak while she checked his neck and throat.

After what felt like twenty minutes but was only about thirty-seconds, she told James he could try to speak.

"Ember," He said with a scratchy voice.

"Don't try to talk too much. I'm here," I said smiling.

James looked at Viktor then back to me. He was searching for injuries.

"The blood isn't all mine." I assured him.

"What happened?" He asked.

I filled him in on everything that occurred from the time he was whisked away to when he woke up. He was still for a minute then reached for some water. I helped him take a few sips.

"Where's Marek?" He asked.

"I assume he's in a cell. I told Murphy to keep him in custody until we knew what to do with him." I said.

"He killed your Guardians and almost killed you," Viktor said.

"Phone," James said grabbing his throat.

"I'll call. Who am I calling?" I asked.

He told me to check in with Murphy and tell her he wants her to lock Marek down in his penthouse. Putting him in the bunker could cause more problems than it would solve. Viktor protested but James insisted he was kept separate.

James then had me call Sebastian to give him an update. Sebastian was understandably upset but was glad I was taking charge. I reminded him that James was in charge and that I was just doing the talking for him until his throat was back to normal.

"Regardless, you are taking charge and that's why I hired you. I'll stop in to see Marek tonight and let you know what I think. In the meantime, get those jars to the vault. James will direct you." Sebastian said.

I hung up and relayed what was said to James. He nodded and started pulling the rest of the wires and tubes out of his arms.

"At least let the nurse do that," I said stopping him.

"This is faster," He said.

"You've been hanging out with me for too long. You're starting to act like me." I said smiling.

James sat up and swung his legs over the side of the bed. He swayed a bit but quickly gained his balance. I stepped into him and pulled him into a hug.

"Don't ever scare me like that again," I whispered.

James responded by squeezing me so hard it felt like my ribs would crack. He let go quickly but I found it hard to move away from him. I glanced at the jars full of ash and knew we had to get them behind wards and locked away.

"That's really her?" He asked looking at the jars.

"It is," I said walking over to pick them up.

"Too bad I can't kill her a second time," James said.

"We're not sure she's dead," Viktor said.

James' eyes went wide.

"Asher is looking into it," I said quickly at the look of surprise on James' face.

"I'll take you to the vault. No offense Viktor, but you're not invited." James said.

"I'm not letting her out of my sight," Viktor said.

"Viktor, I have a security team. I don't need you to protect me," I said.

"Are you referring to the team who did nothing to protect you against Magdalena tonight? One left immediately, another fell too quickly from a minor wound, and the other never stepped up to fight. I don't trust them." He said.

I didn't have a response to that. He was right although I saw it differently until this moment. I suppose I thought they were giving me more space to do my job and not get in the way.

"They didn't help?" James asked softly.

"Before I ordered Hector to leave, he fought beside me. You know that. You were there." I said.

"I'm inclined to agree with Viktor. I trust him to have your back." James said.

I raised my eyebrows at him. This wasn't the first time I'd heard James say he trusted Viktor but it still caught me in the gut. It wasn't that long ago I thought Viktor was the one trying to kill me.

Before we left, I stopped in to see Seedrik and ask Hector and Scout to stay behind. Hector wasn't happy about it but I noticed Scout didn't protest. She only had concern for Seedrik. I ended up having to order Hector to stay behind until I deposited the jars.

Viktor stayed beside me like he had when our bond was active. He kept touch with me whether it was by resting a hand on my back or brushing his arm against mine. Having Viktor act as a caretaker was disconcerting. He was starting to feel a little like that weird uncle you have that you can't help but love.

We walked out of the hospital wing to surprised looks from the doctors and nurses. James said with all the vampire blood coursing through his veins, his senses were heightened and he felt stronger. I was glad he was alive and didn't protest his early departure from medical care.

James led us to an area of the compound I hadn't been in before. Viktor had to wait for us in the hall because he didn't have clearance to go any further. There were a series of hallways and doors that took us into what looked like a bank vault. Only this vault had armed guards and two Belgium Malinois dogs flanking the door.

James introduced me and issued an order to give me access to the vault. It took us thirty minutes to get my DNA coded to the lock on the door and to give me all the codes needed to access this room. Each guard had to touch my hand and I realized as they did that they were glamoured to look human but they were Fae.

Even the dogs weren't really dogs but some kind of dog-like creature. Once the rituals and processes were completed, James had me access the vault. Apparently, the items placed in the vault were coded to the person accessing the vault. Which meant I was the only one who could retrieve the jars.

Knowing that gave me a peace of mind that I didn't realize I needed. I wanted to trust Marek and all the other Guardians but I also didn't know how deep Magdalena's compulsions went or who else she had influenced. Better safe than sorry they say right?

We entered the vault. I expected to see a room full of treasures but instead, there was a terminal that looked like an ATM with a small door to the side. James explained how to operate the system and within moments the little door opened for me to put the jars in. I set them in and the door closed.

An all-clear alert appeared on the screen and I breathed a sigh of relief that the jars were now safe. I hoped Asher found out how to dispose of them properly. I did not want Magdalena to rise up from the ashes again.

With my deposit to the vault completed, we made our way out of the maze of hallways until we found Viktor. He was looking agitated from being left behind.

"You okay?" I asked him.

"I will be. Where are you spending the evening?" He asked.

"I'd like to go home," I said.

The thought of laying in my own bed tonight sounded fabulous.

"I would like to invite you to come home with me. I have a penthouse nearby in a secure building. None of Magdalena's operatives would know to look for you there. We could bring Natalie with us. She is suffering in that underground bunker." Viktor said.

I bit my lip trying to think of what I wanted to do. I turned to James. He was scratching at his neck.

"What do you plan to do? I can't imagine you are going to keep working." I said.

"I'd rather go with you but my place is here tonight. I would feel better if you went with Viktor or stayed here in the penthouse tonight. I know you want to go home but the townhouse is harder to protect. Magdalena may have been dealt with but she could still have operatives in the city." He said.

I inhaled a deep breath then let it out. Their arguments were sound.

"It would be nice to spend a little time with Nat," I said.

Viktor smiled and when he smiled, Viktor looked like a man selling cologne in bikini briefs. It really brought out the rugged good looks he has. It's a good thing I wasn't interested in him romantically because that smile could do things to a woman's libido.

"I will have my staff ready the penthouse for our arrival," Viktor said.

He pulled out his phone and started barking orders. While he did that I turned to James. I made him promise he would get some rest. Vampire blood or not, he almost died today.

"I promise," He said looking at me with love in his eyes.

I pulled him into a hug and then found it difficult to let go. James had a dangerous job where he could be killed any time he went into the field. It hadn't bothered me until today but then I realized that without the bond to Marek I was feeling differently about James. It reminded me of when we first met and I couldn't think of anything but him.

James noticed I held on too long.

"I won't break, Ember. I'm a dhampir. That makes me hard to kill." He said.

"Forgive me if I don't believe you after what I saw happen today," I said.

"It's not the first time I've had my throat ripped out by a vampire. No one teleported me to a doctor then and I survived even after losing most of my blood. Marek knew that." He said.

"What are you saying? That he did it knowing it wouldn't kill you?" I asked confused.

"Yes, he did. He could have broken my neck and tore my head off but he didn't." James said.

My mind raced with the possibilities. I'd seen Marek kill before. He preferred to rip off someone's head to ensure they wouldn't get back up. Marek warned me enough times to finish the kill that I knew it was what he would have done had he intended to kill James.

"How are you okay with that? He still could have killed you." I said.

"I've known Marek for a long time. You and I both know he doesn't do anything without a reason. Even when compelled by an ancient vampire, he had choices. He acted as a Guardian should, and protected you at all costs." James said.

"You are more forgiving than me," I admitted.

"I didn't say I forgive him, just that I understand him." He said.

I caressed his cheek seeing the hurt within him. I had the same mix of anger and love for Marek burning within me. We would get through it together but for tonight I needed to tuck myself away and wait for Sebastian to tell us his thoughts.

"I guess I'm going home with Viktor. Shit, that's a statement I never thought I would make." I said looking at the ceiling as if it had a clue for me.

Viktor gave James the address then called someone to pick us up.

James leaned over and kissed my cheek.

"Call me if you need anything. I'll let you know when I hear from Sebastian." James said.

He walked away and I turned to Viktor. He was watching me intently.

"Shall we go?" He asked.

"Yes," I said.

We picked up Natalie, although she was resistant at first, then left for Viktor's loft. My security team came with us despite Viktor's protests. We all pilled into a large SUV driven by one of Viktor's men.

I hoped it would be a quiet night. I was exhausted and bruised from the fight and I needed to sleep for about twenty hours. Looking at Viktor's obvious merriment at having my sister and I with him made me think this evening was going to be more tiring than I hoped.

Viktor's building had an express elevator from the parking garage to the penthouse. We rode it up in two groups my sister, Viktor, and me going up first. The rest of my team and a few of Viktor's staff brought up the rear.

We exited the elevator and walked into a vestibule. The walls were painted a deep navy blue. The door was huge and stained deep ebony black. Viktor turned the shiny silver lock and opened the door.

We walked in and were greeted with the smell of a delicious meal being prepared. My stomach grumbled and both Viktor and Natalie turned their heads toward me.

"What? I'm hungry." I said feeling self-conscious.

"What will *we* eat?" Natalie asked.

Viktor gave her a look of indulgence and annoyance.

"We will have a goblet of warm blood when your sister's meal is ready and not before." He said with a hint of censure that Natalie didn't pick up.

Natalie moved into the living room. Seeing her move around I realized this was a place with which she was familiar. When she dated Viktor, they must have spent time here together.

Viktor stepped up beside me and said, "Do you like it? Your room is over there."

He gestured toward a door on the left of the living room. I looked around the loft. The floor to ceiling windows alone were stunning. I knew that in daylight I would be able to see an expansive view of the mountains. What wasn't there to love?

"It's gorgeous, Viktor but you already know that," I said.

A knock at the door told me Hector had arrived. Viktor said his staff would let him in but I suddenly felt uneasy. Something was wrong.

"No, Viktor. I don't think it's Hector." I said.

Viktor met my eyes then ran for the door. Before he got there, the door flew open and Marek stepped into the room. Viktor stopped him by grabbing Marek by the throat.

"Release me!" Marek snarled in Viktor's face.

"You are trespassing in my home, Volkov. I am within my rights." Viktor yelled.

Marek paused long enough for me to walk over to him.

"Why are you here? You were under guard when we left." I asked.

"I...I do not know," Marek said realizing where he was.

Hector stepped into the loft and grabbed Marek from behind helping Viktor hold him. Hector looked at me and it was clear he thought Magdalena's last order was still riding Marek. It made him come after me.

"Hold him while I make a call," I said.

I dialed James and went to look for a bathroom so I could talk without anyone hearing me. I found one and turned on the water. Then I called James.

"Ember, what's wrong?" He said when he answered.

I could imagine him pacing back and forth as he listened.

"Marek broke through the front door of Viktor's loft. I think he's still under the influence of the last order Magdalena gave him. He clearly got away from whoever was guarding him so I only trust you and Viktor right now." I said.

"Stay there. I'm on my way." He said and he hung up.

It wouldn't take long for James to get here. I expected him within the next ten minutes. James drove fast when he needed to.

I went back into the entryway. Marek was now sitting on the floor holding his head in his hands. Viktor stood between him and me with Hector right in front of Marek.

"How did you get away from the Guardians?" I asked him.

Marek looked up at me and the look on his face was one of complete devastation. It made my chest hurt.

"Who was guarding me?" He looked distressed.

"I'm not sure. Murphy handled the orders." I said.

"I do not remember leaving," He said looking lost.

"Marek, you're going to have to go in the bunker after this. Sebastian didn't want that but if you keep breaking out of the penthouse we'll have no other choice." I said.

"You could hold me offsite." He said.

"Why would I trust anything you say to me right now?" I asked.

"Because if you do not lock me up I am afraid I will kill you," He said.

Viktor growled and lunged toward him.

"No, Viktor. He had more of my blood to work out of his system than you. We won't know for sure if he is able to control himself until next week." I said.

Viktor looked at me confused and then he straightened up.

"How long has he been drinking your blood?" Viktor asked.

"Not relevant. James will be here any minute. We hold Marek until then." I said.

"James?" Marek asked.

"Yes, thanks to Hector and a blood donation from Julien he's alive," I said.

The look of relief on Marek's face told me he thought he was dead. I would have said more but a Guardian team burst from the elevator a moment later. James showed up seconds afterward. His hair was wet as if he just got out of the shower.

My cheeks heated the moment I saw him because my memory flashed back to a vision I had of him naked fresh from the shower. In the vision, he answered a phone call from me and said the same words he spoke to me minutes ago. When I called him he must have been in nothing but a bath towel.

The Guardians put Marek in handcuffs and leg irons. He looked like he was headed to a high-security prison.

"Are you alright?" James asked grabbing my shoulders and looking for injuries.

"I'm fine. I felt him coming before he busted through the door. I had time to warn Viktor." I said.

James looked at Hector and narrowed his eyes.

"What were you doing?" James asked Hector.

"Helping Viktor take him down," He said with a hint of anger in his voice.

"James, Marek clearly knows every way to escape the Council. He can't go back there. We need another option." I said.

"What are you suggesting?" James asked.

"Maybe Julien can help," I said.

"And owe him another favor?" James shook his head, clearly not happy with the thought.

"He's my friend," I insisted.

"And a master vampire who trades in favors. You need to be careful." He warned.

"We need this handled properly and he can do it," I said.

"Fine," He said.

I called Julien and he was more than happy to help. He sounded very pleased to hear from me.

"Ember, I can do as you ask. We have a place we keep master vampires that should please you and keep Master Volkov contained." Julien said.

"Thanks, Julien. I feel like you are doing a lot of favors for me lately. I hope I'm not imposing." I said.

"Nonsense, it is my pleasure. Sasha will meet your Guardians at my estate and show them to the private cell. How long will we be holding him?" He asked.

"For the remainder of the week I think but I'll consult with Sebastian to be sure." I said.

"I will have my team prep for a long term stay just in case. Am I authorized to bill the Council or will this be something you are taking care of personally?" He asked.

The question threw me off long enough that he said my name again to be sure I was still on the line.

"This is a Council matter, please bill that account," I said.

"It is always a pleasure speaking with you, Ember," Julien said and hung up.

That vampire was going to create complications I didn't need in my life but for now, he was a friend.

30

I gave the Council Guardians instructions to take Marek to Julien's estate and ask for Sasha. They acknowledged and started to move him out but Marek asked for a moment.

"What, Marek?" I asked.

His face went blank at my sharp tone. I regretted it the moment it happened.

"James is right about favors adding up with Julien. Be careful." He said.

I let out a long sigh.

"I can handle Julien. What I'm worried I can't handle is you." I said feeling the raw emotion of the moment.

Marek straightened up and replied, "You need not handle me at all. I am not your problem to solve."

Marek turned around leaving me to watch him be led into the elevator by a Guardian. As the doors closed between us, I was left wondering if his words meant more than I thought.

"Are you okay?" James asked coming up behind me.

He laid his hands on my shoulders and I leaned back into him for comfort.

"I'm fine," I said.

"He isn't himself," He said. "I'm not sure he knew what he was saying."

"I doubt that," I said.

James pulled me in for a hug.

"I've got to go with the transport. I'll check in on you later." James said.

"Okay," I said.

James kissed me on the cheek then left as Viktor started barking orders at his people to get the door fixed. I slipped out of the room amid the commotion.

I closed the door of the guest room behind me and leaned against it. It wasn't until this moment that all the events of the past weeks have caught up with me. The weight of it all dragged me down physically. My butt hit the floor and I crumpled inward like a paper bag being wadded into a ball.

The first tear escaped and it allowed the dam to break. All the pain and torment I felt came out in a rush of tears.

The crying turned into a full body shake with wracking sobs that wouldn't stop even when I tried to breathe. Moments later warm arms scooped me off the floor. I choked on my snot a few times before getting control of myself. Several tissues appeared in front of me and I used them to dry my face and blow my nose. When I was finally able to focus I looked up to see the faces of pity surrounding me.

Natalie looked like she had been crying too but Viktor looked angry. He was pacing the room as if he couldn't figure out what to do. I shook my head at him knowing exactly what he was thinking.

"It isn't any one person's fault. The stress of the past weeks just caught up to me." I said.

"I will kill him," Viktor said.

"No you won't," I insisted.

"Em, what can I do? There has to be something." Natalie said.

"Nothing. I'm sorry. I didn't mean for you to hear any of that." I said pushing away from them.

Viktor grabbed me to keep me from walking away. I turned back to look at him. He held my hand tightly.

"There is no shame in grief," He said.

The intensity in his eyes had me sighing.

"Thank you for taking care of me, both of you." I said looking between them. "But I need some time alone."

Viktor pulled me into his arms.

"I would kill anyone that harmed you. If Maggie wasn't already ash, I would rip her head off her shoulders then do the same to Volkov. He is to blame for much of your pain whether you see it or not." He said.

"You can't fix everything with violence Victor but I appreciate the sentiment," I said.

He let me go reluctantly then walked toward the door. My sister took his place pulling me in for a hug. She squeezed a little too hard but I didn't mind. It felt good to be loved.

"I'll check on you later," She promised or maybe it was a threat.

Either way they left me alone. I didn't have any tears left to cry but I wasn't ready to put my wall of confidence back up.

I looked out the floor to ceiling windows that led to a large balcony and discovered the jaw-dropping view. It drew me outside immediately. I slid the enormous glass door aside and walked onto the tiled patio. The city lights combined with a hint of mountains in the distance grounded me.

One of the things I love about Colorado is the expansive mountain views but when you're downtown, you also get the dazzling city lights. The sparkle next to the majestic beauty of nature is my kind of eye candy. I could sit on this balcony all day and night and never get tired of the view.

I sunk into one of the lounge chairs.

My phone beeped with a text message from James telling me he tucked Marek in at Julien's without any trouble. Sasha was babysitting him while he was there. I felt relieved that he was taken care of and not just shoved in a box.

For as much as I worried that Julien was positioning himself in my life, I was grateful for his help and support. People warned me about Marek as they have with Julien and I didn't listen to them. For better or worse I've let myself like Julien enough to bring him into my inner circle.

Julien helping James to heal was the topper on the cake of our friendship. Even if he knew doing it would endear himself to me, vampires do not give their blood away to just anyone. You have to earn it and you better be worthy.

I could sit out on this balcony forever but I needed to get cleaned up. I took two more deep breathes before walking toward the bathroom. I hoped to find a bathtub but instead found a large steam shower. It would have to do.

I stripped down and got the hot water flowing. Once I figured out how to get the steam to work, I was enveloped in a cloud of warmth. I pulled off the bandage on my side and my arm and let the water soothe my tired muscles. It did wonders for my mental state. I finally relaxed.

As much as I loved the excitement of vampire and Fae matters, it was good to have time to decompress. Marek and James have been my outlet for relaxing or working out tensions. Without them to demand I rest, I had to do it for myself.

Just as I turned off the water, a tingling sensation wrapped around my head. A vision hit me hard just seconds later.

Marek screamed and threw himself against a cement wall. Dust and debris rained down over him but it didn't stop him from doing it again. As if that wasn't enough, he started punching the wall. It barely made a dent in the wall but his fists were quickly covered in blood.

Someone was yelling at him to stop but it didn't phase him. Several vampires entered the room, one holding a large syringe. Two held Marek down while the third stabbed the needle into Marek's neck. He slumped over on his side, defeated.

The vampires left the room and the only sound was of Marek whimpering. I could barely make out what he was saying but it didn't make any sense. It shattered my already bruised heart.

I pulled myself out of the vision and grabbed a robe from the bathroom door. I found my phone and called Sasha immediately. She answered on the second ring.

"What's happening?" I demanded.

"I was about to call you. Marek is having some sort of breakdown." Sasha said.

"James said he was doing well earlier," I said.

"He was fine for a while then he grabbed his head suddenly and started yelling. He kept saying "she's gone" and "what have I done," over and over again." Sasha said.

"I'll be there as soon as I can. I need to check on him myself." I said.

"I'll let the guards know to expect you," She said.

"Thanks," I said and hung up.

I threw on some clothes from the small bag I brought along. All I had was jeans and a t-shirt but that would have to do. I towel dried my hair as best I could then headed out the door.

I met Hector outside the bedroom and filled him in on where I was going. Viktor heard me and insisted on coming along.

"No, Viktor. But I could use a car." I said.

"My driver can take you but shouldn't James handle this?" He said.

"He could but this is personal." I said.

His lips formed a thin line but he stopped protesting. He called his driver to tell him to expect me.

Hector and I picked up Seedrik and Scout on the way to the car. Viktor's driver had the SUV running and waiting at the curb. We piled into the vehicle and headed for Julien's estate.

My stomach churned the entire ride. When we pulled up to the estate, we were told to use the side entrance. Sasha met us there and led us to where Marek was being held. Kaleb was outside the cell when we arrived.

"He's calmed down but still mumbling something," He said.

"Thanks, Kaleb. Can I go in?" I asked peering through the small window in the door.

Marek was on the floor bloody and bruised. He wasn't moving but his eyes were open staring into nothingness.

"You can but not alone. He's been sedated but as a Master he is capable of anything. Julien would kill us if you got hurt." He said.

"Fine, but what you hear stays in that room." I insisted.

He agreed then opened the door for me and followed me in. Marek looked up at me. The pain was clear on his face but it wasn't the physical pain that was hurting him. The mental anguish is what was hitting him so hard.

I kneeled on the floor next to him and brushed the hair out of his face. His eyes closed at my touch.

"What have you done to yourself?" I asked softly.

He rolled away from me, landing on his back. He stared up at the ceiling as if it would give him the answers he needed.

"Why are you here?" He asked in response.

"Why do you think? You threw yourself against the wall like you were trying to break yourself." I said.

"They called you?" He asked.

"No, I saw it," I said.

He turned his head toward me sharply and it made Kaleb jump forward. I held up my hand to stop him. He relaxed a bit and I looked back at Marek.

"You must hate me. Why would you come here?" Marek asked confused.

"Because I love you despite the fact you are a pain in the ass," I said.

Marek narrowed his eyes at me and I couldn't help but smile at him. It was the most Marek thing to do after what I said. His disapproval told me he hadn't lost his mind after all.

"You should be ready to kill me after going to Lena and what I did to James. I don't deserve your love." He said.

He said the last part as if he were speaking to himself and he believed what he said.

"Oh I'm angry with you, that's a fact. But it isn't a black and white situation. You were influenced and while I saw you fight it, you couldn't fight everything." I said.

My thoughts flashed back to seeing Marek in bed with Magdalena. The pain was still sharp and it cut me but not as deep as what he did to James.

"James said something similar but I did not believe him either," He said.

"I am not the one with a history of lying. If you are to believe anything it should be what I say." I said with anger.

He winced at my words but he nodded in agreement.

"I am sorry for everything I put you through. My memory is clear regardless of how clouded my mind was at the time. That I am sure is one of my punishments." He said.

I cradled his hand in both of mine. His arm was stiff at first then relaxed as if now that we were touching he could finally exhale.

"Kaleb, I am going to sit up. Please do not kill me for moving." Marek said.

Kaleb raised an eyebrow but didn't move while Marek sat up. I let his hand go so he could use it to push off the floor but as soon as he was up Marek pulled me into his body. Kaleb did move then but stopped when he saw what was happening.

I wrapped my arms around Marek's waist and inhaled his vanilla scent. The aroma of caramel was strong with all the blood covering him but it was a scent I associated with love and sex. It was pleasing.

"Are you going to stop throwing yourself into walls now?" I asked.

"Only if you insist," He responded softly.

"I insist," I said.

Marek squeezed me tight then ran his hands down my back soothing every nerve and sending the tension away. Finding myself in his arms after all that had happened made me want to cry again. I thought for sure he would be dead instead of here with me now. Hell, I thought we would both be dead.

We sat together holding each other until Kaleb started to clear his throat clearly unsure we should be in the cell any longer. He must have forgotten he was doing me a favor.

"I no longer present a danger to Ember," Marek said to Kaleb.

"I'll believe that when I'm ordered to stop protecting her," He said.

"Are you really free of her?" I asked leaning back so I could look into his eyes.

He nodded and I could see within his blue eyes that they were finally clear of Magdalena's influence. I brought my hands to his cheeks and pulled him in for a kiss.

He broke away from the kiss with a troubled look on his face.

"You should go." He said glancing up at Kaleb.

"Are you ordering me around again?" I asked trying to be playful.

"I would prefer to have you in my arms forever but I am afraid that is no longer possible. Go. I am making your friends nervous." He said.

He wasn't dismissing me in that situation. It was more.

"What are you saying, Marek?" I asked not wanting to believe what I was thinking.

"Kaleb was right. I am a danger to you. You came in here with no regard to your own safety and you're sitting here as if nothing has changed. Everything has changed, Ember. Forget me. I have brought nothing but more danger in your life. I have not protected you from anything. I not only failed in my duties as a Guardian but also in loyalty to you as your lover." He said.

"Marek..." I started but he interrupted.

"No! Go, Ember. I do not want you near me." He said turning away from me.

The shock of his words had me stunned. Kaleb grabbed me by the elbow and led me out of the cell. Sasha let out a sigh of relief when the door was secured.

I was still staring at the door when a familiar voice sounded from nearby.

"Madame Summers, are you determined to get yourself killed?" The Grand Master said.

His tone was brusk and hinted at his anger. I turned to catch the look on his face. He was furious.

"I sought only to defuse the situation as best I could," I said.

He gave me a hard look then said, "You will stay within the guardrails of your office. Guardian Leigh should be here diffusing the situation, not you."

"This is personal," I insisted.

"It shouldn't be. Marek promised me his relationship with you would not get in the way of either of your duties but we know that not to be true. You will step away from that relationship or step away from the Council. You cannot have both." He ordered.

"Sebastian, that isn't a choice I want to make," I said shocked.

"You will make it or I will make it for you. Now go before I decide to dismiss you anyway." He said.

There was nothing to say to that, so I turned and walked toward the exit.

Sasha caught up with me before I could exit the building.

"Will you stop in to see Julien before you leave?" Sasha asked.

"I hadn't planned on it," I said confused.

"I think you should. He'll want to see you." She said.

I held back the emotion I wanted to let out. While we were friendly, Sasha and I were not quite friends. Unloading my pain on her was not in the cards.

It was a political thing to say hello to someone doing you a favor. Although Julien was being paid, he only agreed to keep Marek here because of me.

“I’ll stop in to see him. Thanks for the reminder.” I said.

She gave me a hug before I left and I couldn’t help but feel like she was like a little sister. She didn’t act like the other vampires. It was likely because of her lack of years.

As I walked, my Fae guards spread out with the exception of Hector who remained at my side. I wandered the house until I found Julien. He was sitting by himself on the back patio. I sat in the chair beside him.

We sat in silence so long I wasn’t sure if either of us would ever say anything. Then I looked over and saw that Julien was staring at me. The look on his face was unreadable.

“What are you thinking about sitting here all alone in the night?” I asked.

“Vampires live so long that sometimes we forget what it is like to love as a human loves. I am not so old that I can’t remember what it is to be mortal. I still long to feel a love that burns eternal. But I can taste it whenever I am near you.” He said.

“The fact I make you feel alive does not mean eternal love is likely,” I said gently.

Julien turned and took my hand. He looked at me as if he needed me to breathe. It made my heart thump with anxiety.

“Maybe not, but I will enjoy the pursuit.” He said kissing my hand.

“Julien, I enjoyed our kiss but it wouldn’t be fair to you to lead you on. I agreed to see you socially because I enjoy your company and value your friendship.” I said.

“I saw your visit with Marek,” Julien said holding up his phone and showing me the video feed.

Marek was laying on the cot and appeared relaxed and comfortable.

“That’s handy,” I said tightly feeling like my privacy had been violated.

“Given Marek’s transgressions, I hope you don’t fault me for holding out hope. I’m not beyond playing the long game.” Julien said.

I took a deep breath then let it out. He had a point.

“I’m too tired to offer a rebuttal,” I said.

“Is there anything I can do for you? I have plenty of rooms if you would like to stay here.” He said.

“Thank you for the offer but I’m expected back at Viktor’s tonight,” I said.

“Well then, good night, Ember.” He said kissing my hand again.

I was starting to really like it when he did that so a smile popped up on my face before I could stop it. Julien preened from the reaction and smiled back. The mixed signals I was giving him were obviously encouraging him to pursue me. I just couldn’t figure out how to stop doing it.

31

I must have fallen asleep in the car on the drive back to Viktor's loft because when I woke, Viktor was carrying me. It wasn't the first time I had been carried somewhere, but it felt especially humiliating today.

"My legs function. You could have just woken me up, and I would have walked on my own," I said.

"Hector couldn't wake you, so my driver called me to intervene," Viktor said.

"Nonsense, I'm a light sleeper," I said.

Viktor raised an eyebrow giving me a look that said the contrary was true. I huffed out a breath and held on while he walked me into the guest bedroom. He set me on my feet next to the bed and took a respectful step backward.

"I feel I should confiscate your phone so you aren't interrupted until after you've had time to rest." He said.

"My phone wasn't what made me leave," I said, sitting down on the edge of the bed.

I started removing my shoes, and Viktor took that as an invitation to sit with me.

"Your vision was an excuse to go see Volkov. You have staff who can take care of errands for you. If you handle everything yourself, you end up dead on your feet from being spread too thin." He said.

"Are you speaking from experience?" I asked looking over at him.

"I am," He said. "If you can't trust your team to take care of things on your behalf, you need a new team."

"I barely know my team, but they're researchers, not field operatives," I said snapped.

"I'm surprised you are settling only for what you were given. Where is your fire, Ember?" He asked.

"It may be sleeping," I said, stifling a yawn.

"When was the last time you fed?" He asked.

Viktor wasn't talking about food. Vampire blood had been an almost daily staple for me for weeks. It helped me stay sharp and overcome fatigue, among other things.

"I can't rely on vampire blood to sustain me," I said feeling the pain of Marek telling me to go away. "Look what happened when I shared blood with you. It practically enslaved you, and it made Marek vulnerable to Magdalena. I'm not willing to do that again."

Victor tipped my chin up, so I was looking into his eyes. He looked super serious.

"I freely give you my blood with no expectation of receiving your blood in return. I would give my life to protect you." He said.

"Viktor," I whispered but couldn't find the words.

I was overcome with emotion. It had been a hell of a day, and the night was drawing to an end. If I didn't get some sleep soon, I would make a fool of myself.

"Accept the gift for the treasure that it is or stop inviting me into your life." He snapped.

The intensity in Victor's eyes made me swallow hard. He was dead serious.

"Okay," I said.

Viktor narrowed his eyes at me as if I had just done something sneaky.

"I'm tired enough to admit I need it. Are you going to make me beg now that you already offered it?" I asked.

"No," he said, then pulled me onto his lap.

I was distracted enough that I didn't realize what he was doing until I was straddling him. He held me tight and by the look in his eyes he was struggling with whether or not to do more than hold me. I felt the bulge in his pants and couldn't keep myself from shifting against it.

Viktor made a pleasing sort of rumble then grabbed his pocket knife. He brought it up to his neck and I followed the movement with my eyes. I watched the blade pierce his flesh. When the first bead of his blood pooled on the surface, I closed my mouth around the wound. Sucking hard, I swallowed the first mouthful of his blood and it was exquisite. I'd drunk from Viktor before but this time it was better, more intimate somehow.

I felt the edge of our old bond as I drank. It became closer to where I could grab it with each swallow.

"Think before you pull on that thread. There is no going back if you reopen the bond." Viktor warned.

"It's what you want though. Isn't it?" I asked pulling back to look into his eyes.

The conflict within him was clear in the expression he wore on his face. He wanted it, but he didn't want to want it. That summed up the entirety of our relationship.

"It's inevitable. We are drawn together by more than the promise of blood bonds." He said.

"Then perhaps we leave it alone," I said, pulling back so I could stand up.

The moment I moved, he responded by rolling me over so that I was beneath him. He pressed himself between my legs and pulled my left knee up to his hip in one smooth motion. His hand moved down my thigh and cupped my butt.

I responded without thinking by pulling him closer. My body reacted to his out of instinct. A man's weight against my body was a heady thing. He felt good. Victor started to roll off of me.

"Where are you going?" I asked.

"You need your rest," He said as if that explained everything.

"I feel more rejuvenated now," I said licking the last of his blood from my lips.

"I'm sure you do but in a few minutes you are going to crash and no amount of attention from me will keep you awake. Let it happen." He insisted.

"I don't believe you," I said right before a giant yawn overtook my face.

"You just proved my point. Besides, you would regret it in the morning. If we choose to continue this amorous adventure I fully expect you to be awake and in possession of your full faculties. I would rather upset you for leaving you untouched than for taking advantage of you in your weakened state." He said.

He stood up beside the bed and after another large yawn, I agreed with him.

"Understood," I said.

The corners of his lips turned up in a sexy smile that had me questioning why I was letting him go. That reaction alone let me know he was right. I would regret getting intimate with him in the morning. I don't know where my brain was but it wasn't in control of my actions.

"Good. Now sleep. I'll make sure no one disturbs you until you are rested." He said and left the room.

Viktor a gentleman? Who would have thought?

I struggled out of my jeans then fell into the soft bed. My exhaustion was so bad that I pulled the comforter up to my chin and instantly relaxed enough to sleep. My brain wasn't finish with me though and kept replaying the events of the past few weeks.

It pained me to think that my mother was right but her assertion that I am addicted to vampire blood. However the theory gained more evidence every day. The fact I was ready to take Viktor to bed after a few sips of his blood told the most compelling story.

Maybe I was spending too much time with the paranormal and not enough time with the normal. I wasn't sure if proximity was the problem or if it was chemical. What I did know was that I was ready to figure out how to survive in a world where vampires were a constant temptation. All I had to do was figure out how to resist the irresistible.

A note from the author…

Ember Summers will return in the next book in the series. There is no end planned for the series yet. Ember is just getting to know who she is and how she fits into her world. There is plenty to explore there and she keeps attracting the most interesting characters while leaving behind those she cannot trust. Who will catch her eye next and what new trouble will come her way?

In the meantime, look for a spinoff series coming soon featuring Sasha La Veneur. Sasha is a newly turned vampire with a dangerous job tracking down bounties for the La Veneur coven. Her beauty often has her playing the bait to draw out their targets but she is a master level temptress with hundreds of captures already under her belt. It isn't until a strange request comes in that she second guesses what she is doing and why. Somehow this bounty is different and the reaction she has to him gets the attention of her master, Julien. An angry master vampire is often a deadly master vampire. How will she come through alive and protect what she loves?

I hope you love these characters like I do. Thank you for reading!

Follow Nichole M. Bridges on social media to be the first to know about the next book in the series.

Instagram: @author_nmbridges

Facebook: @nmbridgesauthor

Website: www.nmbridges.com

Other books by Nichole M. Bridges

Ember Summers Series

Ember's Fire

Ember's Shadow - Into the Darkness

Ember's Blood

www.ingramcontent.com/pod-product-compliance
Lightning Source LLC
LaVergne TN
LVHW010608100826
845148LV00014B/2893

* 9 7 8 1 7 3 4 3 4 1 6 2 1 *